False Fortune

By the same author

Heir Apparent
Family Claims
Spurred Ambition

False Fortune

A Pinnacle Peak Mystery

Twist Phelan

Poisoned Pen Press

First Edition 2007

10 9 8 7 6 5 4 3 2 1

Library of Congress Catalog Card Number: 2007924780

ISBN: 978-1-59058-363-0 Hardcover

Poisoned Pen Press
6962 E. First Ave., Ste. 103
Scottsdale, AZ 85251
www.poisonedpenpress.com
info@poisonedpenpress.com

Printed in the United States of America

for j

friends first
friends always

Acknowledgments

My sincere thanks to:

Barbara, Rob, and the rest of the team at Poisoned Pen Press. Three makes it a better story than two.

D, for grace under pressure, patience, attention to detail, and an unending supply of carrot sticks.

B, whose "Let me see what I can do" always gets done, and with style.

My Australian outrigger teammates—hut, hut, ho!

The well-meaning lifeguard who helped me tape up my broken ankle after I tripped running away from him. Urine really isn't an antidote for jellyfish stings.

We are not the first
Who, with best meaning, have incurr'd the worst.
For thee, oppressed king, am I cast down;
Myself could else out-frown false Fortune's frown.
Shall we not see these daughters and these sisters?

King Lear, ed. Sylvan Barnet (Signet 1963),
act V, scene III, lines 4-8

Chapter One

Monday, November 2

"I think we're being followed."

Hannah Dain adjusted her rearview mirror, trying to get a better view of the driver in the white SUV. Looking for a license plate would be pointless—Arizona didn't require them in the front.

"Of course we are," Shelby said. "This is the only road around the lake."

"I mean the car behind us. I saw it when we stopped for gas."

Her sister glanced over her shoulder, then rolled her eyes. "At the one station this side of town. Do you know how many SUVs there are in this state, especially white ones? Stop being paranoid." Shelby consulted the map print-out on her lap. "Anyway, we're almost at the fry bread stand."

"If you say so."

They hadn't seen a road sign for at least twenty minutes, not even a mile marker. In this part of the desert, land took a long time to change. If you didn't know where you were going, you didn't belong out here, Hannah thought.

The grill of the white SUV filled the side-view mirror, shining through the words stenciled in the glass: *Caution: objects in this mirror may be closer than they appear.*

No kidding, Hannah said to herself. If the hulking vehicle were any nearer, she'd be able to see the bugs splatted on its chromed front. She pressed down on the Subaru's accelerator, pushing the needle on the speedometer from fifty to fifty-nine. Landscape rushed by in a blur of desert colors—sagebrush green, red rock, yellow sand. The SUV grew smaller in the mirror until it looked like a toy car.

Shelby grabbed the door handle. "Hey! Slow down! These curves are making me sick."

Hannah eased up on the gas. The tortuous road was called *El Espinazo del Diablo*—the Devil's Backbone—and ran along an arête, with canyons nearing a hundred feet deep dropping off to either side. The canyon to the south was filled with volcanic rock dotted with cacti, the one to the north with water. The latter was dubbed Lake Lagunita, one of those bilingually redundant names like Table Mesa and Calle Road that Hannah found so annoying.

They came up on another vehicle. Hannah checked for oncoming cars, then steered around a pickup with a sheep in its bed. Unlike the four-lane parkway that carried casino patrons to the west side of the rez—the Tohono O'odham Indian Community—the road to the south entrance was single lane, and cars came at one another at great speed. Most of the traffic was tribe members, and alcohol-fueled crashes were frequent.

"So tell me more about your case," Hannah said.

All Shelby had said during last night's phone call was that she was co-counsel in a toxic tort case involving radiation contamination, and needed to video the old mines that had been used as dump sites. The mines were on the rez, reachable only by a barely maintained axle-busting dirt track—impassable with Shelby's red sports convertible, but no barrier to Hannah's trusty Subaru wagon. As Shelby had never learned to work a stick shift, Hannah would have to drive, too.

They were heading for the eastern shore of Lake Lagunita, directly opposite the area where Hannah paddled most mornings before work. She had taken up kayaking as physical therapy for her twice-injured shoulder. The manmade lake straddled the boundary between Pinnacle Peak and the rez, and non-tribe members were restricted to the town-owned side, near the casino.

Her hard-plastic boat strapped to the roof, Hannah had met her sister at the boathouse that morning. Now they were on the south side of the lake, halfway to their destination.

"I don't know all that much. Daddy just told me about it," Shelby said.

Richard Dain was on leave from the firm, serving as a special prosecutor in a federal case back East. Dain & Daughters employed only four attorneys. With Olivia Parrish still on sabbatical in Africa and Hannah specializing in business law, Richard's pending cases had become Shelby's responsibility.

"Where did the radiation come from?"

"In the 1950s the tribe let the Department of Defense test some top-secret project on the rez," Shelby said. "Probably an atomic bomb, but no one will say for sure. Whatever it was, leftover uranium ended up being dumped into old mine shafts, and poisoned the groundwater. We represent the tribe members who lived next to the dump sites and drank the water. Lead counsel is Franklin Rowley. He and Daddy went to law school together."

"Toxic waste? Mass tort? Wow. Sounds like one of Elizabeth's trials."

Hannah regretted the words as soon as they were out of her mouth. Their mother wasn't an easy topic between the two sisters, and recent discoveries had made things even more complicated for Hannah. She had yet to tell Shelby about Elizabeth's affair—the one that had produced Hannah—or about her newly discovered half-sister, Anuya.

And Hannah planned to keep the secret for a while. Never close in the past, she and Shelby were finally intersecting, with a wobbly not-quite-friendship the result. In fact, since Hannah had rejoined the firm last month, Shelby had been almost nice to her younger sibling. Hannah didn't want her recent discoveries to jeopardize their fledgling relationship.

Besides, given how rocky things had been with Shelby, Hannah wasn't all that sure how she felt about having another sister. She and Anuya had exchanged several emails, and Hannah was content to leave it at that for now.

Shelby's voice broke into her thoughts. "Do you think she would have been a good mother?"

Hannah blinked. Elizabeth Dain had died within days of giving birth to Hannah, twenty-eight years ago. "I...I don't know," she said.

"Everyone says she loved her work. And Daddy, too."

Hannah winced, then hoped Shelby hadn't noticed.

"But no one ever talks about her as a parent," her sister continued.

Was Shelby trying to tell her she knew about the affair? About Anuya? Hannah fixed her eyes on the line where the pavement disappeared into the horizon. "You were only two when she died, Shelby. She didn't have a lot of time to be a mom."

Hannah steered the Subaru around a pothole and the conversation back to a safer topic.

"Isn't the government going to say the radiation came from uranium that was already in the ground? How are you going to prove the contamination is the DOD's fault?" Hannah knew most of the radioactive ore used during the nuclear era came from mines in the Southwest. The tribe's water supply could have been polluted through natural causes.

"We don't have to. The government admitted liability, supposedly because of national security, though what can be so important fifty years later is beyond me. Franklin thinks it's because private contractors—who are also big political contributors—want to start mining on the rez again."

"For more uranium? I thought we won the arms race," Hannah said.

"This is about fuel for nuclear power plants. China and India are building reactors like crazy, and our government is pushing nuclear energy as an alternative to oil."

"So what will the victims get?"

"Anyone who can prove damages is entitled to reparations. Apparently, the side-effects of radiation poisoning are pretty ghastly—nerve damage, paralysis, blindness. Franklin thinks video of the mines and the plaintiffs' houses will make the jury more sympathetic. He wants to remind them of how things were on the rez before the casino."

Housing, schools, hospitals—Hannah knew they had all been made possible by the *ka-ching!* of slot machines and the clatter of chips on poker tables. Only after her temporary job with the tribe had she seen the dark side of such wealth.

A tote bag decorated with a designer's logo was at Shelby's feet. She took an atomizer from an outside pocket and spritzed both sides of her neck, something French and flowery.

Hannah wrinkled her nose. "Is that perfume?"

"Of course. I would never use eau de toilette. Want some?"

"No!" Hannah lowered the window halfway. "You're stinking up the car."

"And that would be a bad thing?"

With an expression of distaste, Shelby picked up a half-empty Gatorade bottle from the passenger-side footwell and set it in the cup holder. She glanced around the car's interior, taking in the paddling suit draped over the back seat, Post-its bearing scribbled training times stuck to the glove box, the partially eaten PowerBar protruding from the dashboard cubby next to an iPod with its headphone wires in a tangle. "You look ready for your *Modern Squalor* magazine photo shoot."

Hannah grinned. "I like my spaces to have a lived-in feeling."

Shelby snorted. "Don't you mean *homeless*?"

"This car is a temple to athletic endeavor."

"Not a religion I'd belong to." Shelby reached into the tote bag again, this time taking out a camcorder. She touched a button on the silver case and a lens emerged.

"Cool. Is that yours?" Hannah asked.

Shelby squinted through the viewfinder. "Jake's." The corners of her mouth curved upward. "Works indoors, even with the curtains drawn."

Hannah held up a hand in mock disgust. "I *so* didn't want to know that."

Jake Lyman was an EMT and volunteer firefighter whom Shelby had met while she was in rehab. Jake had been inspecting the premises for fire-code compliance. Even in sweats and no makeup, Hannah's sister was a head-turner.

What had surprised Hannah was that Shelby had given Jake a second look. From blue-collar stock, he wasn't her sister's usual date material. And Hannah had been dubious about a relationship that began while her sister was supposed to be climbing the twelve steps. But the romance had taken hold, and was still going strong after two months, a long time in Shelby-years. Hannah was fine with it—she liked Jake. Maybe the new boyfriend, not the stint in rehab, was the reason for her sister's change in attitude toward her?

Romance was not on Hannah's agenda, at least not soon. She had broken up with Cooper Smith—for the second time—at the conclusion of the tumultuous events surrounding her brief career as a contract lawyer for the Tohono O'odham tribe six weeks ago. Too many pending family issues left her no time for someone else, she had told herself.

The road curved along the shoreline, and Hannah glanced at the lake. The water was green, the same shade as Cooper's eyes. She remembered what it felt like to lose herself in their depths and tightened her grip on the steering wheel.

"So are you and Jake going to move in together?"

"Why would you ask that?" Shelby's tone was sharp.

Hannah glanced at her sister, surprised. "Because he spends nearly every night at your place. That is, when you're not at his. Or is the reason you're wearing that gray suit two days in a row just because you like it so much?"

"Not that it's any of your business—" Shelby's eyes widened. "Look out!"

Hannah yanked her attention back to the road. Two mountain bikers pedaled side by side, straddling the shoulder line. She jerked the wheel and the Subaru swung wide, narrowly missing the inside cyclist. In the rearview mirror she saw one of them raise his hand. But instead of the expected finger, he gave her a friendly wave. Eyes still on the mirror, Hannah noticed the white SUV had gained ground again. She watched it swerve around the cyclists, then shifted her attention back to the road ahead.

Shelby pressed a hand against her stomach. "I'm not feeling so great. Do you have any water?"

"No, but you can have the rest of that Gatorade."

Shelby looked at the lime-colored contents of the bottle and shuddered. "Now I am going to be sick." She peered through the bug-dotted windshield. "There's the fry bread stand. Pull in. They'll have something"—she forced a swallow—"not so fluorescent."

Hannah steered the Subaru across the opposite lane and onto a swathe of gravel. The car crunched to a stop, and Shelby threw open the door and dashed for the portable toilet next to the makeshift stall. A quarter mile ahead was the south entrance to the rez, where only tribe members and permit holders were allowed to enter.

Hannah got out of the car more slowly. She pressed her hands into the small of her back and stretched, watching the white SUV approach. Its speed slackened, and for a moment Hannah thought it was going to turn in. But then the car sped up again, and it roared by the turnout. As it passed, Hannah saw that the blond woman behind the wheel was talking on a cell phone.

No wonder she was tailgating. Hannah headed toward the fry bread stand, conceding that Shelby was right about the driver of the SUV. The events of the past summer and fall notwithstanding, there were enough bad people in the world without her having to invent them.

The fry bread stand—a *latillo* roof supported by four posts—leaned to one side, looking as though one more puff of wind would push it over. Two wooden tables with mismatched chairs were arranged in front of a flour-dusted counter. Sitting in one of the chairs was a small woman with skin the color of reddish earth. Broad-shouldered and wide-hipped, she was shaped like the jar of flour next to the griddle. A sign tacked to one of the posts said NEVER TOO HOT, NEVER TOO COLD. In smaller writing were the words *in winter* after HOT and *in summer* after COLD.

The Indian woman stood.

"Fry bread? Very good."

There was a pyramid of juice containers and bottled water in a Styrofoam container on the floor, ice cubes puddling around them.

"Just a water and an orange juice, please." Hannah opened her wallet.

"Can make with saguaro jam. Or like taco. Very good."

"The drinks will be fine."

The woman shrugged as if to say it was Hannah's loss for passing on the fry bread, and took the bills.

"Keep the change," Hannah said.

The woman shrugged again. "No coins."

Carrying the water and juice, Hannah walked over to the portable toilet's door and rapped on it.

"Shelby, you okay?"

"Go away," came the muffled reply, followed by a retching sound.

Shelby was barely a month out of rehab. Hannah knew post-discharge therapy often included a drug that would induce nausea if alcohol was ingested. Had Shelby relapsed? Hannah raised her hand to knock again, then paused.

Not that it's any of your business. Shelby's words echoed in her head. Although things between them were better, they were still far from great. Hannah didn't know her sister's favorite color, what movies made her cry—if any even did. How could she ask Shelby if she were drinking again?

Hannah turned away from the toilet door. She spotted another sign propped against a boulder. WATCH OUT FOR RATTLESNAKES. Doubting this one was a joke, she kept her ear tuned for the telltale buzz as she walked toward the far end of the turnout.

It was one of those perfect November mornings, the kind that could almost make her forget the summer and its sledgehammer heat. Horsetails of clouds trailed across nearby peaks, and the air was laden with the soapy pungence of creosote. A hummingbird cased her orange shirt, rejected it, and retired to a nearby bush.

A low wooden guard rail, more decorative than functional, rimmed the gravel parking area. On its other side, the ground dropped abruptly away. Hannah walked to the rail and looked over. Sixty feet below, Lake Lagunita lapped at the cliff base. A band of white mineral-stained rock separated the green of the lake from the red canyon walls. There was something surreal about the huge quantity of water and a nearly fifty-mile coastline in the middle of the parched landscape. The water was relaxed and clear, and Hannah could see the contours of the canyon that had been drowned when the river collected behind Diablo Dam. The gray boulders strewn across the bottom looked like sleeping turtles.

An engine growl broke the quiet, and Hannah glanced over her shoulder. The white SUV came into view again. It passed her and turned in to the graveled area, stopping on the other side of the fry bread stand next to the Subaru.

The blond driver got out and walked to a mass of brittlebush next to the drop-off. Squinting into the sun, Hannah made out a *descanso* tucked among gray-green leaves. The roadside memorials to accident victims dotted the Southwest's highways, reminders that mass times velocity squared often had a horrible outcome.

Hannah watched the woman take a square of blue from her purse and place it under a rock next to the shrine. She stood for a moment with her head bowed, then got back into the SUV. The heavy vehicle lumbered back onto the pavement toward town.

The door to the portable toilet was still closed. Hannah debated knocking again, but instead walked over to the *descanso*.

A bunch of poppies was propped against the base of the white cross. Heads heavy in the heat, the flowers looked as if they were panting. Next to them was a blue envelope, *Garth* written on the front in the same script as the *Garth Weller* that had been hand-lettered on the wooden crosspiece. Curiosity tugged at Hannah, but she left the envelope where it was.

"Howdy, Hannah!" boomed a male voice.

She turned to see the cyclists they had passed on the road bumping over the gravel toward her. The two men braked to a stop, unclipped their pedals, and took off their helmets.

"Hi, Jerry Dan," Hannah said, recognizing the generous grin and just-woke-up hair.

Jerry Dan's grin widened. "I thought that was your green Subaru."

He laid his bike on the gravel, careful not to scratch the titanium tubing. Hannah's gaze roved over the aerodynamic arcs and top-of-the-line components, then cut to the Port-A-Potty. She was relieved to see that the door was still closed.

Jerry Dan Kovacs was a trial lawyer with another firm in town. Hannah had met him three months ago, when he bought her mountain bike through an online auction—the same bike Shelby had given her a scant two weeks earlier. The gift was a replacement for the bike Hannah had lost as a result of last summer's events. But Hannah was done with mountain biking, the sport too grim a reminder of those terrible days. Unable to bear having the bike around, she had sold it—without telling Shelby.

"What are you doing way out here?" Hannah asked.

"Training for the State Orienteering Championships." Jerry Dan indicated his companion. "Dr. Glouster's a prof at ASU and the course designer. The race is going to be on the rez this year."

The other man nodded a greeting. "Ed Glouster."

"Hi," Hannah said. "So what's orienting?"

"Orienteering," Jerry Dan said, emphasizing the *ee* sound. "You use a compass and a topo map to navigate through a series of control points, usually on bike or foot, sometimes skis. The person with the fastest time wins."

"Sounds like an ordinary race to me," Hannah said.

"Not exactly. The course is kept secret until the day of the race, and has a staggered start, so there's no following other competitors. You choose your route based on the map, and the best way isn't always the shortest distance between two control points. So not only do you have to be fast, you have to be able to navigate, too. Gives a sports klutz like me a chance. Plus now I'm riding a hot bike, thanks to you." He patted the top tube affectionately. "Me and Silver are going for the win."

"Silver? Not Trigger?"

As Hannah had learned the day he picked up the bike, Jerry Dan was a fan of all things cowboy. Roy Rogers was a particular favorite—she recalled something about a petition for an honorary Oscar. The Lone Ranger had merited only a passing mention.

Jerry Dan looked pained. "Trigger was a palomino." At Hannah's puzzled expression, he added, "A gold-colored horse."

Hannah glanced at the bike's titanium frame, gleaming white in the flat light.

"Hi ho," she said, stifling a smile.

A door banged, loud in the still air. Hannah jerked her head to see Shelby standing in front of the blue cubicle.

"Gotta go," she said. "Nice to meet you, Dr. Glouster. Good luck at the race, Jerry Dan."

Hannah hurried over the gravel toward the fry bread stand, wishing she had donated her bike to charity. Shelby stood in the meager shade of the *latillos*. Hannah held up the water bottle and juice carton.

"Orange or not orange?"

Shelby chose the water. Lifting up her pale hair, she pressed the bottle against her neck with an unconscious grace that Hannah no longer envied, then nodded toward Glouster and Jerry Dan. The two men were looking at the *descanso*, their bikes still on the ground beside them.

"Who are they?"

"Those cyclists we passed on the road." Hannah popped the tab on the juice container and gulped down the pulpy liquid. Winter in Arizona was like summer everywhere else—temperatures in the seventies. And being near the lake always seemed to make her thirstier. She finished off the juice, tossed the empty container into a rusty drum next to the counter, then burped. Catching Shelby's frown of disapproval, she made herself burp again.

Her sister sighed. "Can we get going? Some of us have other things to do."

Sweat shone on Shelby's ivory skin, and Hannah noticed that her sister's hand shook slightly as she sipped from the bottle of water. Did Shelby's *other things to do* include getting a drink? Worried, Hannah thumbed the remote.

Shelby opened the door on the passenger side and sat down. "Do you think we're not close because we didn't have a mother?"

Hannah put a hand on the door frame to steady herself. She and Shelby didn't have these types of conversations. In fact, until her sister's stint in rehab, they hadn't talked much at all.

The automatic response—*Of course we're close*—pushed against her teeth. But seeing Shelby's expression, Hannah bit back the denial and opted for the partial truth instead.

"I don't know. Probably didn't help that I wasn't around much."

From fourth grade on, Hannah had attended boarding school back East, going on to the Ivy League and law school. After graduation three years ago, she had come to Arizona and joined the family firm. But until recently, she might as well have stayed away, for all the warmth shown her by Richard and Shelby. Their aloofness had stung. And despite Hannah's newfound understanding of family history, it still did.

"But now you're staying? At the firm, I mean." Shelby dropped her eyes and fiddled with the camcorder.

Something twisted inside Hannah. *Until you find out my secrets and want me to leave.* "I'll be around," she said.

Insects hummed around them, their buzz gradually drowned out by the sound of an approaching vehicle. The now-familiar white SUV hove into view, moving fast.

The big truck veered into the parking lot. Fishtailing on the gravel, it barreled toward the Subaru. The same woman was at the wheel, shoulders hunched, hooded eyes staring straight ahead.

She's going to hit us. Instinctively, Hannah grabbed Shelby's arm and yanked her sister from the car.

"Hey!" Shelby exclaimed as she went sprawling.

The SUV banged into the Subaru's bumper, splintering the plastic taillight cover and denting the metal. Unhindered by a parking brake, Hannah's car began to roll forward. The SUV, now heading for Jerry Dan and Ed, didn't slow.

"Jerry Dan! Look out!" Hannah yelled.

The two men scattered while the SUV stayed its course. Just missing the bicycles, the big vehicle plowed over the *descanso* and into the stand of brittlebush. Branches scraped against its door panels and snagged on its side mirrors as the SUV cleared the chaparral and crashed through the guardrail.

"Oh my God," Shelby whispered.

Hannah watched, slack-jawed, as the SUV ran out of ground. The vehicle plunged over the cliff edge, trailing wisps of brittlebush. Seconds later, a belly-flopping *splash* careened off the canyon walls.

"Hannah! Your car!" Jerry Dan shouted.

The Subaru, helped by momentum from the slight downhill, was still rolling. Hannah broke into a run. If she could just get to the still-open door, jump in, and pull the emergency brake…

The Subaru was twenty feet from the edge of the cliff. Hannah ran faster. She had pulled even with the rear window when her foot slipped on the gravel. The car kept going as she fell to her knees.

"No!" she cried as the front bumper hit the guard rail. The flimsy wood gave way.

The Subaru teetered on the edge for a moment before succumbing to gravity. With a sickening scrape of its undercarriage against the rock, it slid out of sight.

Chapter Two

Jerry Dan sprinted across the gravel, Glouster right behind him.

"Hannah! Are you okay?"

Hannah got to her feet, brushing the dirt from her pants. "Yeah, thanks."

"What about your friend?" Jerry Dan said.

Hannah whirled to see Shelby still sitting on the ground. She rushed toward her.

"Shelby! Are you hurt?"

"I'm fine, jus' a little dizzy."

A patch of gravel rash bloomed on Shelby's arm and her eyes looked out of focus.

"She may have a concussion," Glouster said. He took off his jacket and, after helping a mildly protesting Shelby lie down, covered her with it.

"No, I've got a touch of the flu." Shelby wiped at her mouth with the back of her hand.

Hannah looked around for her purse, then realized it was in the Subaru. "Do either of you guys have a cell phone?"

Jerry Dan fumbled in the rear pocket of his jersey, extracting a small flip model. Hannah took it from him and peered at the tiny screen. No bars. The tribe's new cellular network was only partially constructed. Most of the towers were on the west side of the rez, near the casino.

"No service." She handed the phone back to Jerry Dan.

The woman from the fry bread stand scuttled toward them, her apron strings trailing like streamers from her waist. Hannah spread her index and pinkie fingers and pantomimed holding a handset to her ear.

"Telephone?" she said, even though she knew a land line was unlikely.

The woman shook her head, jangling her silver earrings. "Radio." She held an imaginary microphone to her mouth.

Hannah looked toward the fry bread stand. A tall, slim aerial winked in the sunlight. From her job with the tribe, she knew the Office of Tribal Affairs, known among the O'odham as the OTA, monitored a certain VHS frequency 24/7. The channel was designed for use by tribe members living in the more remote areas of the rez. Messages ranged from calls for help changing a tire to birth announcements.

"Call the OTA," she said to the woman. "Tell them to send an ambulance, firemen. *Ayuda. Medico.*"

The woman nodded vigorously. Her moccasined feet raised small puffs of dust as she scurried back to the fry bread stand.

Hannah looked at her sister. Shelby lay quietly with her eyes closed. Some pink had crept back into her cheeks.

"Dr. Glouster, can you stay with her?" she said.

"Sure. And call me Ed."

Hannah tugged at Jerry Dan's arm. "C'mon!"

"Where are we—"

"The SUV."

They ran to where the cars had disappeared. Standing carefully at the edge of the cliff, they looked down at the lake. Hannah felt as though she were on the roof of a seven-story building.

Just above the water's surface, about forty feet from shore, was the Subaru. Its front wheels rested on top of the partially submerged white SUV. Hannah's kayak floated nearby, jarred loose from the roof-rack straps by the crash.

Using her hand as a visor, Hannah stared at the driver's window of the SUV. At first she couldn't see anything except pumpkin-colored water covering the bottom half of the glass. Then a woman's face appeared above the waterline. Her eyes were wide open and her mouth gaped like a fish's.

"We have to help her!" Hannah said.

She sat on the ground and scooted forward until her feet were dangling over the cliff edge. The slope, covered with sandstone shards, was nearly ninety degrees. The sun reflected off the rocks, searing her face and burning her eyes. Hannah wished for the climbing gear and sunglasses that were in the Subaru.

"I'm going down," she said.

"Shouldn't we—"

With a deep inhale, Hannah pushed off just as she heard a diesel engine upshift from the direction of the road. Someone close by must have overheard the O'odham woman's radio call.

"Wait for help," she shouted over her shoulder at Jerry Dan.

His reply was lost in a rattle of scree as she slid down the rock on the seat of her pants. She tobogganed down the slope, feet in front of her, dodging the granite upthrusts and cholla cacti as best she could. As a rock climber, she had never been comfortable on shale. She knew the easier it was to go down, the harder it would be to come up.

She started to pick up speed as she skidded down the slope on her back. The lake rushed toward her, and Hannah waited for the impact, imagining what a broken bone would feel like.

A thin shelf of limestone rimmed the water's edge. When her feet hit this "beach," Hannah managed to jam a heel into a crack to stop from falling into the water. She leaned against the rock wall.

The water level in the passenger compartment of the white SUV had risen since she started her descent. She waded into the lake, the scattered boulders on the bottom making the going difficult. She heard a yelp behind her, followed by the sound of falling rock, but didn't turn around.

The lake was deep and cold. At first the coolness soothed her abraded back, but soon she was shivering. Her feet no longer touched bottom, and she started to dog-paddle. When she was within a few feet of the cars she treaded water and surveyed the situation.

The Subaru still rested on the SUV. But now the water covered about two-thirds of the bigger vehicle's driver's side window. The SUV was sinking.

Hannah quashed the impulse to paddle forward and yank on the driver's door. There was no way she could open it against the pressure of the water. And the moonscape of boulders on the lake bottom made the arrangement precarious. She could send the SUV farther underwater, even roll it.

Something nudged her raw shoulder. Hannah yelped and turned to see what had hit her.

The bow of her kayak floated within arm's reach. Hannah grasped its plastic nose and frog-kicked closer to the SUV. She could see the blond woman, her head resting against the seat back. Her eyes were closed, but her mouth and nose were above water.

"Hey!" Hannah yelled. The woman didn't respond. Was she unconscious? There was a shout from above, but Hannah ignored it.

Still gripping the kayak, Hannah propelled herself forward. She rapped her knuckles against the top of the window.

"Wake up!"

The woman didn't move. But the Subaru did.

Metal screeched against metal, like a bow rasping across a violin string. Both vehicles canted toward Hannah, raising the water level inside the SUV another half inch.

Another shout, this one closer. Hannah looked over her shoulder. Jerry Dan was waving at her from the spot where she had landed moments earlier. Where were the emergency techs, with their climbing gear and first aid equipment?

Jerry Dan began to wade into the lake. Hannah turned back to the SUV. The water was up to the woman's chin, but her eyes were still closed. A shaft of sun highlighted her face.

Sun? Hannah boosted herself onto the bow of her kayak so she could see over the top of the SUV. The sunroof was open.

Hannah pushed down on the front of the kayak, then let its buoyancy propel her up out of the water. Grabbing the rim of the SUV's sunroof, she boosted her torso through the opening, grateful the vehicle didn't sink further.

Her head nearly collided with the woman's. Hannah grabbed the headrest and their cheeks brushed. The woman's skin was chilled but not cold. Hannah slipped her hands under the woman's armpits and pulled, but the woman didn't move. Nylon webbing scraped against Hannah's arm. *Seatbelt.* The Subaru creaked and the SUV lurched forward. Turbid water gushed through the roof opening.

Hannah took a gulp of air. She dove forward with hands outstretched, feeling for the seat edge. The swirling water blotted out the day, and blanketed her in silence. Her fingers touched metal and she walked them over the buckle until her thumb found the seatbelt release.

The tongue slid free from the catch. Released from its web binding, the woman's body began to float upward. At that same moment, hands grabbed Hannah's waist. Startled, she smacked her head against the edge of the sunroof and inhaled a lungful of muddy lake water.

Chapter Three

Free of the car, Hannah burst out of the water and sucked in a breath. Her flailing hands found plastic, and she clung to the kayak. She gagged and coughed, blew water from her nose, wiped silt from her eyes. Jerry Dan's head came into focus, bobbing a few feet away.

"You okay? I thought the car was going to roll on you," Jerry Dan said as he grabbed the other end of the kayak.

The woman's body had floated halfway through the sunroof opening. Her head rested on one arm. Her mouth and nose were clear of the water, but her eyes were still closed.

Hannah squinted at the cliff. "Where are the EMTs?"

"Not here yet. Some truck showed up. I tried to flag it down but it wouldn't stop."

Hannah looked at the woman. "We have to pull her out the rest of the way."

"Shouldn't we wait? If the cars roll..." Jerry Dan's voice trailed away, but Hannah heard the rest of his thought. *We could be trapped and drown.*

"We can do it. Hold on to my legs with one hand and the kayak with the other," she said.

"If the SUV starts to move, you have to let go."

"Just make sure *you* don't. Now start kicking."

They maneuvered the kayak next to the submerged vehicles. Hannah felt a rush of adrenaline.

"Ready?" she said, letting her legs float out behind her.

Jerry Dan grasped her ankles. "Ready."

Hannah grabbed the edge of the sunroof opening with one hand and the woman's wrist with the other. She felt the SUV start to sink under the added weight.

"Pull, Jerry Dan! Pull!"

Hannah heard frantic splashing, then felt a hard tug on her ankles. She let loose of the sunroof and snatched a handful of the woman's shirt as Jerry Dan yanked her backward. She felt like the rope in a tug-of-war. The familiar ache flared in her shoulder.

The woman's body slithered through the opening. Hannah rolled over onto the water's surface, slung an arm across the woman's chest, and pulled her onto her hip. The woman's feet cleared the sunroof just as the SUV began to slide forward. Hannah sensed more than saw the big car descend into the lake depths. With a metallic shriek, the Subaru followed. Now half-submerged, the back end of Hannah's car stuck up like a diving duck's tail. The medium-brown water turned chocolate with sediment churned up from the bottom.

The kayak's nose cut through the wavelets created by the shifting vehicles. "Grab on!" Jerry Dan said, maneuvering the stern.

Hannah wrapped her fingers around the deck netting. The woman's head lolled in the crook of her neck.

"You're going to be okay," Hannah panted into her ear. She held on to the woman and the kayak while Jerry Dan propelled them toward shore.

When her toes stubbed against bottom, Hannah let go of the boat and started to wade through the rocky maze. Miraculously, her shoes had stayed on during her descent and swim. Even so, her right ankle twisted on a stone, and she fell hard on one knee. Keeping the woman in a lifeguard's grip, Hannah grasped a ridge of rock, hoping that something that had resisted a millennium of monsoonal poundings was good for another thirty seconds. Muscles in agony, she staggered to her feet, her strength decreasing with each step.

Jerry Dan let go of the kayak and slogged through the shallows. He grabbed the woman under the arms, and together he and Hannah half-carried, half-dragged her onto the narrow strip of beach.

Once they were clear of the water, Hannah felt for a pulse. It was thready, but there. She put her hand on the woman's chest, felt the light rise and fall of her ribs.

Shouts came from above, followed by the sound of limestone bits tumbling down the rock face. Hannah looked up. Two men, black against the burnt white sky, were rappelling down the cliff.

"Hold their top lines, Jerry Dan. I'll stay with her."

Hannah knelt next to the woman, trying not to shiver. She was drenched—clothes flattened, hair plastered to her scalp, water pooling at her feet. For once, she wished for July temperatures, when the air cracked with heat like a shattered windshield and the sunlight weighed a thousand pounds.

From close by a bird chirred. The woman moved at the sound. Her eyelids fluttered, then opened.

"Where am I?" she said.

"Next to the lake," Hannah said. "Hang in there—help is on the way."

The woman swiveled her head toward the water. Her eyes were open extra-wide, the irises nearly obscuring the pupil. Hannah recognized the symptom of shock.

"The lake?" the woman said.

"Your car went over the cliff," Hannah said, feeling a stirring of resentment. *And sent mine over, too.*

"It was a mistake," the woman said, making Hannah regret her ire. There would be time later to sort out what had happened, and shock victims were supposed to be kept calm.

"Don't worry. We're going to get you out of here," Hannah said.

"I –ould have died," the woman whispered and closed her eyes again.

Hannah stared at her. Had the woman said *could* or *should*? Was this an accident…or a failed suicide? The arrival of the two EMT climbers cut short her speculation. The snake-wrapped-around-stick logo on their white shirts marked them as emergency medical technicians. They unloaded their gear on the beach and went to work.

"Are you having difficulty breathing, ma'am?" one of the EMTs asked Hannah.

"No."

He inspected her flayed back. "That looks pretty raw. Pain anywhere else?"

My knee hurts from hitting the rock and my shoulder's sore, too. "I'm fine," Hannah said. "Just cold."

The EMT unwrapped a space blanket and draped it around her shoulders.

"Even though this is the desert, you can still get hypothermia. Wait here while we check out your friend."

"She's not my—" Hannah began, but the EMT had already joined his companion.

The two men checked the woman's pulse and airway, then her blood pressure and eyes. One of them started an IV while the other assembled what looked like a human-sized bread basket. Hannah watched the EMTs work, the space blanket clutched at her neck. A slight breeze coursed under the sheet of fabric so that it fluttered like a superhero's cape behind her.

"Did she regain consciousness? Say anything?" one of the EMTs called to Hannah.

Hannah hesitated. What if she hadn't heard correctly? Did she really want to brand the woman as a suicide?

"Just a few words. Then she was out again."

What sounded like a groan came from the lake. Hannah looked over in time to see the rest of the Subaru slip under the water's surface. The loss smarted—the station wagon had been her first car.

Her kayak drifted next to the shoreline, hemmed in by partially submerged rock. Still holding the space blanket around her, Hannah waded into the shallows and grabbed the bowline. With a grunt, she pulled the kayak onto the beach.

The two men strapped the woman, still unconscious, into

the rope basket. Jerry Dan held the IV bag while the two EMTs threaded the top ropes they had used in their descent through the four corners of the apparatus.

"Aren't you going to call a helicopter?" Hannah asked. She had hoped to hitch a ride. The loose limestone was going to be a difficult ascent, even with a harness.

One of the EMTs rubbed climber's chalk on his hands. "The MedEvac crew is on the north side. Climber with a broken leg had a heart attack, or a guy having a heart attack broke his leg. Either way, the chopper wouldn't be able to get here for another hour. So we're going up the old-fashioned way."

Hannah heard an undercurrent of glee in his words, akin to the nervous smiles of firefighters en route to a blaze. *Men's joy at putting work-toys to use.* The basket holding the woman began its trip upward.

The gurney's ascent went faster than Hannah had expected. She could see two people at the top of the cliff on belay. One worked the ropes holding the woman's cradle, while the other assisted the EMTs climbing on parallel lines. In a matter of minutes, the basket was safely over the rim.

"They're coming down for you!" one of the EMTs shouted as an ambulance siren began to whine.

The people who had been on belay clipped onto the top ropes and began to descend. Wrapped in his own space blanket, Jerry Dan stood next to Hannah and watched the two men speed down the cliff face.

"We had to climb a rope in gym class. I hated it," he said.

"You got down the cliff all right."

"That was different. It was an emergency. Besides, what goes down doesn't always come up again."

"This isn't gym. You'll be on belay. If you fall, the rope will catch you after a foot or so."

Jerry Dan looked at her, saucer-eyed. "I thought all I had to worry about was climbing. Now you're telling me *falling* is a possibility, too?"

The two men touched down on the beach.

"You guys ready?" one of them asked. Jerry Dan moaned softly.

"Jake?" Hannah said.

"Hey, Hannah," said the taller of the two men as he walked toward her. Peroxide-tipped hair stuck out from under his Diamondbacks cap. Instead of an EMT uniform, he wore a white shirt with a blue swirl on the pocket.

"Are you on duty?" Hannah asked.

"No. Miguel's on Dispatch, and he called me when Shelby's SOS hit. I came as fast as I could."

Hannah felt a twinge. *Must be nice to have someone care that much about you.* She reminded herself that it had been her choice to leave Cooper.

"Is Shelby okay? I'm worried that she might be—"

"Just a touch of the stomach flu," Jake said. "She's waiting in my truck."

"Let's get out of here, then," Hannah said.

Jake held out a climbing harness and Hannah stepped into it. The other man was adjusting a similar rig on Jerry Dan, who looked miserable.

"He's a newbie," Hannah said under her breath to Jake. "And not too thrilled about climbing."

"Hey, Kyle," Jake called. "Why don't you guys go first?"

"Cool by me," the other EMT said.

"See you at the top, Jerry Dan," Hannah said, and flashed him an encouraging smile. He responded with a weak wave.

"Don't look down," Jake added.

Jerry Dan nodded stiffly. Grasping the top rope, he took a small step up the rock face.

The breeze had gained in enthusiasm, and Hannah pulled the space blanket closer. At the rate he was going, Jerry Dan's ascent would take some time. She walked over to the lake's edge. The sediment had settled and the water was clear. A silver flash of minnows swam just under the surface, casting shadows on the crumpled roof of the SUV. The Subaru lay on its side, its metal underbelly exposed.

Jake joined her. "Shelby told me what happened. Tough about your car."

"Yeah." Hannah turned away from the water and squatted next to her kayak. A cursory examination revealed a few scrapes on the plastic, but no punctures or gashes. She straightened up.

"The kayak comes, too."

Jake frowned. "It's too long to carry on your back—you'd peel right off the wall. Even if each of us took an end, it'd be tough going."

Hannah set her jaw. "I just lost my car, my purse, and my favorite pair of running shoes. That means four hours standing in line at the DMV, an afternoon of phone calls to credit card companies, a month to break in new shoes, and who knows how long dealing with the insurance company. I'm not leaving my boat."

A hoot sounded from above. Jerry Dan stood silhouetted on the cliff's rim, his arms raised in a triumphal *V*.

Jake grinned. "By now I know better than to argue with a Dain sister. Let me see what I can do."

He uncoiled an extra line and rigged a sling to suspend the kayak between them. "This should work. But if it starts to slide, we have to let it go."

Hannah tugged on a knot. "Deal."

They clipped in to the top lines. Hannah reached for her first hold, a short throw up and to the left. The clump of limestone, light and porous, broke off in her hand.

Jake tugged his cap low over his blond-tipped hair, then looked up.

"Ready!"

"Belay!" came the answering shout from the top.

They started up the slope. Hannah's last climb of note had been up the side of a building. This one wasn't any easier. The cliff, eroded by weather rather than rushing flood water, was rough, the jagged rock creating friction against her tattered clothing. That, and hauling the boat, made progress slow.

Halfway up, Hannah made the mistake of looking down. The lake rippled and whorled like tie-dyed silk, and she nearly lost her balance as her eyes shifted from vertical to horizontal. The woman's voice came back to her. *I could have died...I should have died.* Fighting vertigo, Hannah hugged the stone with white-tense hands.

"Everything okay?" Jake asked. "We can send the basket down if you want."

"No, I'm just resting for a sec." Hannah forced her gaze upward and reached for a knob.

Bracing with her bruised knee, she pushed off with her other foot. It slipped on the scree, and she dug into a crack with her elbow to stop herself from sliding. The rope holding the kayak chafed her shoulder and the plastic hull banged against her shin. Perspiration trickled from her forehead down the bridge of her nose, creeping along her dry lips and into her mouth, leaving a briny taste. Hannah paused again. Maybe bringing the boat wasn't such a good idea after all.

She threw a few more holds, then glanced up, cheered to see they were near the top. *Ten more feet.* Hannah took a step, then another, trusting her weight to the rope.

An EMT's face appeared at the cliff's edge. He reached down, grabbed her under the arms, and yanked her over the lip. Someone else unslung the kayak as she lay on the ground. Freed from the boat, Hannah rolled onto her back and looked up at the sky. She was surprised the sun wasn't yet overhead—it felt as if the day should be older. She was wet, drained from fear, and enormously relieved. If she never climbed another thing, it would be fine with her.

The next half hour passed in a blur. Vehicles crowded the parking area, each one with red lights flashing. The strobes were almost hypnotizing. Huddled under another space blanket, Hannah spoke with an EMT, then a deputy, then another deputy, pausing only to sip something hot from a thermos. The questions left her memory almost as soon as they were asked.

At one point Jake had stopped by. "I'll take you and Shelby back to town."

Hannah had nodded wordlessly, then resumed answering questions. She told the police everything that had happened—almost. *I could have died. I should have died.* She kept the woman's words to herself.

After telling her that a crane had been summoned to get the Subaru and the SUV out of the lake, the last person wearing a uniform left. While the O'odham woman counted her profits from feeding hungry EMTs and sheriff's deputies, Hannah joined Shelby and the others, now gathered where the cars had crashed through the railing.

Jerry Dan and Glouster straddled their bikes while Shelby leaned against Jake, who stood behind her with his arms wrapped around her waist. Despite the heat, his jacket was draped over her shoulders.

Hannah sat down on a section of intact guardrail, beside the remnants of the *descanso*. She nodded at Jake.

"Thanks for helping me climb out."

He grinned. "I just wanted to have a good view if you fell."

Jerry Dan fingered a piece of broken brittlebush. "It was an accident, right?"

"Don't know—she never came to so I could ask her," Jake said. "Only person she talked to was Hannah."

"Just a few words. Didn't make much sense," Hannah said quickly.

Shelby yawned. "Jake, can we go now?"

He hugged her. "Sure."

Hannah used the crosspiece from the ruined *descanso* as a crutch to get to her feet.

Shelby gasped and pointed.

"That's our expert witness!"

Hannah examined the name inked on the wood. "Garth Weller?"

"He is—was—going to testify about the radiation contamination. Franklin told me he'd been killed in a car accident. But I didn't know this was where it happened."

Ed spoke up. "A week ago. He was a good man."

"You knew him?" Shelby asked.

"I'm a geology professor at ASU. Garth was the department head. He told me a little about your case—government dumping radiation waste from Cold War projects into old mines, right?"

Jerry Dan looked from Shelby to Hannah. "You guys are doing that case? I heard trial is for damages only." At Shelby's nod, he gave a low whistle. "Should be some big numbers."

"Are the contaminated mines near here?" Glouster asked.

"On the northeast side of the lake," Shelby said. "That's where we were going when that woman smashed into our car." She patted Jake's hand. "I rescued your camcorder, honey. Hope it still works."

"It's a damn shame that part of the rez is closed," Glouster said. "Some of the best rock art in the Southwest is in the caves on that side of the lake. Garth told me about some pictographs he'd seen during his trips to collect samples for your case. But the contamination means the tribe will never open the area to the public."

Jerry Dan scanned the parking turnout. "Wonder why he crashed. This is the widest part of the road."

"There was some talk of suicide," Glouster said.

Shelby pulled Jake's jacket closer around her. "I want to go."

"We have to take off, too. I've got an eleven o'clock class," Glouster said.

"Hannah, how about you and I getting together for a training session some time?" Jerry Dan said. "You did win the Desert Classic two years ago, and seeing as you used to own—"

"Sure," Hannah said, cutting him off.

"Great! I'll talk to you later then." Jerry Dan buckled his helmet. "*Shalom*, y'all," he called as he and Glouster pedaled across the gravel toward the road.

While Jake loaded her kayak into the bed of his pickup, Hannah collected space blankets and water bottles. By the time she had picked up all the trash, Shelby and Jake were deep in conversation. From his intense look and the tear tracks on her sister's cheeks, Hannah could tell it wasn't the time to intrude.

Still thirsty, she swigged from one of the bottles and wandered over to the edge of the turnout. A square of blue caught her eye—the envelope the woman had left at the *descanso*. After a moment's hesitation, Hannah picked it up and opened it.

There was a note card inside, the looped half-cursive writing matching that on the wooden crosspiece. *I'm sorry, Garth. It wasn't worth it.*

The aftermath of a failed romance? *I should have died. I could have died.* The note made the suicide scenario more likely. Hannah slid the card back into the envelope and stuck it in her pocket. She'd give it to the police, let them decide.

"Hannah!" Shelby called, her voice impatient.

"Coming." Hannah took another drink from one of the water bottles, then pitched them and the space blankets into the trash barrel and hurried back to the truck. Jake tilted the front seat, and she climbed into the Lilliputian space that passed for a rear passenger compartment, pushing aside a jacket emblazoned with the same blue swirl that was on Jake's shirt.

"New EMT uniform?" she asked as she folded the jacket into a makeshift pillow, then lay down as best she could in the tight quarters.

"Baseball rec league," Jake said, turning the key in the ignition.

Shelby glanced back at Hannah. "Did I see you drink out of one of those bottles? The germs…"

"Are a lot tastier than the ones in the lake." Hannah was suddenly conscious of how tired she felt. Her body was leaden with weariness. "If it makes you feel better, next time I'll pretend it was Communion."

"We aren't Catholic," Shelby said tartly.

"Doesn't seem fair that they have special protection," Hannah said.

"Home or law firm?" Jake asked.

"Law firm," Shelby said. "I have to get back to work."

Even though she would have voted for *home*, Hannah didn't say anything. The old Shelby would have taken the day, even several days, off. Hannah wasn't about to squelch her sister's new work ethic.

The truck pulled onto the pavement and the MP3 player started up. A country singer's voice crooned from the speakers and Hannah's eyelids closed.

"I told you we were being followed," she mumbled before drifting into sleep.

Chapter Four

"Would you rather I'd let her drown?" Hannah said, fastening the button on her cuff. She had showered in the firm's small locker room and put on the suit she kept at the office for emergencies.

"I don't see why you had to be the one who jumped off the cliff and pulled her out of the car. You don't even know her!" Clementine banged the desk drawer for emphasis.

Hannah's secretary was opinionated, dressed like a slutty teenager, and loved to gossip. She was also a highly skilled multitasker and as protective as a she-wolf when it came to her boss. Hannah couldn't imagine working with anyone else.

"Why should that matter? Just because someone's a stranger I can't help her?"

Hannah jammed her foot into a low-heeled shoe. A part of her had leaped at the chance to rescue someone, anyone. A subconscious attempt to ease the guilt she still felt over the recent deaths of people she had known? *Would they still be alive if I'd done things differently?* The question ran through her mind on sleepless nights.

"Any other advice?" she asked Clementine as she tucked in her shirt.

"Since you asked, it's time for you to get back into the swim."

Hannah finger-combed her wet hair. "I thought you wanted me to stay out of the lake."

"I'm talking about dating. You need to dive in. Look at

Shelby! That girl is halfway human now that she's finally seeing someone who doesn't make a wading pool look deep."

"Enough with the water metaphors. And I told you—I don't want to date."

Despite the demands of attending law school most nights after work, Clementine had made it a personal mission to find Hannah a new boyfriend. Last week she had tricked her into attending a wine tasting for singles by billing the event as a reception for the business bar. And the prior week's continuing legal education seminar had turned out to be speed-dating for lawyers.

"If you don't date, you're going turn into one of those old ladies who lives alone with too many cats and when she dies the cats eat her," Clementine said.

Hannah gave up trying to smooth down her cowlick. "This is what you think about instead of studying for Con Law?"

"I've got that class wired. Professor hasn't called on me since I asked what the cops do about the one phone call when Amish people get arrested."

"Seriously, Clementine—is law school going okay? You've been looking pretty beat. Yesterday you were sleeping at your desk."

"I was not. That was a highly specific yoga exercise designed to relieve work-related stress."

"Funny, my instructor never taught us downward-facing keyboard."

"That's because you're in the beginner's class." Clementine's voice softened. "Law school is going fine. I just got the second-highest score on the Crim Law midterm." She pulled her penciled brows into a mock scowl. "No comments about my family background giving me an advantage."

"Wouldn't dream of it."

Hannah had only recently learned her secretary's father was a crime boss serving time for racketeering, loan sharking, and bookmaking. "White-collar crime, Italian-style," Clementine had said.

"Will you please call my insurance and credit card companies?" Hannah said.

"Already on it."

Hannah picked up a sheaf of papers from her inbox. "What are these?"

"Emails. I signed you up for eMate.com."

Hannah stared at her secretary. "The Internet matchmaker?"

Clementine nodded, her earrings swinging with enthusiasm. "Good—you've seen their ads. It was easy. I got you a throw-away email address, created a profile, and used your credit card to buy a six-month membership. They've got a seventy percent success rate."

"Success at what? Lining up victims for weirdos?"

Clementine gestured at the stack. "Already forty-two men emailed you since yesterday!"

Hannah started flipping through the pages. "If you don't count the ones whose photos show them shirtless, wearing a gold chain, or standing next to their mother, how many does that leave?"

Clementine squinched her face in concentration. "Three? Maybe four?"

Hannah kept reading. "One of them is asking for a photo of my feet, another wants to know how I feel about wearing leather." She dropped the emails onto Clementine's desk. "And you wonder why I choose to be alone?"

"If you're going to be picky, we can tweak your profile. I'll cut the parts about *Halloween* being your favorite classic movie and sleeping in the nude."

"You posted on the Internet that I sleep in the nude?"

"Don't you? This place is so freaking hot, I thought everyone in Arizona—"

"That doesn't matter! It's not the sort of information I want announced to the world!"

Clementine nodded thoughtfully. "Good point." She started typing on her keyboard, reading the words aloud as she went. "Prepare…to…be…surprised…in…bed."

Hannah pressed her fingertips to her temples. "We aren't doing this. Not now, not *ever*."

"A few more weekends by yourself and you'll be begging me

for help. I'll be waiting for your call."

"Don't waste time sitting by the phone," Hannah snapped. Not because what Clementine said was wrong. But because her secretary might be right.

"I won't be changing my number, either." Clementine gathered up the emails. "Anyway, what's so bad about asking for a picture of your feet? I think it's kind of sweet."

Hannah briefly closed her eyes. "I need to go to the car rental place. Would you please call me a cab?"

Her secretary picked up the phone. "Bummer about your Subaru. And right after you got your tires rotated! I guess it's a good thing you didn't buy those spinners I liked."

Clementine drove a muscle car, and had tried to persuade Hannah to accessorize her Subaru in a similar style. So far Hannah had resisted flame door decals, zebra-print seat covers, and spinning wheel rims.

Clementine punched in numbers on the phone. "After the insurance check comes, maybe you can get something hot. How about a Corvette? Men love those cars."

"I can drop you at the rental agency," another voice said. "After I stop to see Franklin."

Shelby's casual pants had been replaced with a cream suit and blouse, and her hair was smooth. Hannah swiped at her cowlick, feeling disheveled. As her sister got closer, Hannah noticed she still looked pale, despite the fresh makeup. Then again, maybe it was the hue of her clothes.

"Meet you outside," Shelby said. Hannah smelled the same perfume she had spritzed on in the car.

"I'm on death-hold," Clementine said. "God, I hate classical music." Holding the receiver away from her ear, she tapped orange-and-rhinestone-tipped fingers on the stack of emails. Then her face lit up.

"You don't want to date anybody else 'cause you're still hot for Cooper!"

Hannah blew out a dismissive breath. "That's ridiculous. We're done."

Her secretary ignored her. "He might not have hooked up with someone new yet. Sure he's hot, and has that cowboy thing going, but you never know. You should call him, say that—"

"I'm leaving," Hannah said. She grabbed her jacket and hurried to catch up with Shelby.

"Why are we going to Franklin's office?" Hannah asked as they crossed the parking lot to Shelby's car, past stuccoed walls dripping with bougainvillea that would turn blood red by December. "What's wrong with calling, or email?"

"His secretary left a message while we were on the rez. Last night he had some sort of heart thing. He's in the hospital."

"That's awful! Will you be able to get a continuance in your case?" Shelby had told her a trial date was about to be set.

"I don't know. When I called, the hospital said he was sleeping and wouldn't put me through. That's why I'm going by in person."

Hannah opened the car door, hearing the edge in Shelby's voice. She didn't blame her. The trial would be her sister's first not directly under Richard's supervision, and a large fee was at stake. What if Shelby had to try the case by herself?

Shelby and Hannah walked through the hospital's front entrance.

"Is this going to be hard for you?" Shelby asked.

Hannah faltered. Did Shelby know about Hannah's midnight B&E of the records room? What Elizabeth's medical records said about Hannah's father?

"Er…"

"I mean because of Adrienne and all that."

Hannah felt a moment of sadness remembering the dead girl even as relief eased the pounding of her heart. "Thanks, but I'm fine. How about you?"

"I'm okay."

Hannah glanced at Shelby, saw her lips tighten. Other than a brief conversation in the immediate aftermath, the sisters had yet to talk about what had happened last summer.

There was a crowd in front of the elevator.

"Stairs?" Hannah said.

Shelby hesitated, then said, "Sure."

They climbed to the second floor. Shelby, who abhorred exercise as much as Hannah reveled in it, had to use the handrail halfway up.

"There's the nurse's station," Hannah said. Shelby, still winded, nodded.

Hannah asked the woman behind the counter where Franklin's room was.

"Mr. Rowley is having some tests done. He should be back in twenty minutes or so," she said.

Hannah and Shelby found some empty chairs in an alcove. Shelby sat straight-backed with her legs crossed while Hannah slouched, trying to get comfortable in the scoop of hard plastic. In the hallway, a man whispered urgently into his mobile under the sign forbidding cell phones.

Shelby opened her purse, took out an atomizer, and sprayed herself.

"Would you stop that?" Hannah said, waving her hand. "People are going to think I'm wearing that stuff. What, does Jake have a perfume fetish?"

"No! This was a gift from..." Shelby let her voice trail off, and Hannah realized who had given her sister the perfume. *Cooper.*

Hannah had started dating Cooper when she was in law school back East. One evening out, he consumed more than his usual glass of wine. Hannah unsuccessfully tried to claim the car keys. On the way home, he swerved to avoid an obstacle in the road and overcorrected. The car hit the gravel shoulder and skidded into a tree.

Hannah was unhurt, but Cooper wasn't so fortunate. Two operations to fuse the shattered ankle left him with a limp and a surly temper caused by omnipresent pain. Hannah endured his moods for a few months before breaking up with him right before graduation. Diploma in hand, she moved back to Arizona to take the bar exam and join the family firm.

Cooper, also an Arizona native, followed a few months later. Wealthy from the sale of his software company, he bought a small ranch north of Pinnacle Peak. He did some computer consulting work, with the Dain law firm among his clients. He and Shelby had dated for several months, parting as friends. Last summer, Cooper and Hannah reconnected again. This time, Hannah had assumed it would be permanent. That was before family issues reclaimed her attention. Six weeks ago, she had asked him for some time apart.

"I saw him the other day," Shelby said. Hannah didn't have to ask who *him* was. "He looked good."

"Mmm," Hannah said. First her secretary, now Shelby. When had her love life become the topic of the day? Hannah blamed the new media—blogs, camera phones, reality television. Privacy didn't stand a chance.

"I mean, he wasn't limping," Shelby said. "Probably started physical therapy again."

Hannah stood. "I'm going to look for a vending machine. Want anything?"

"Some crackers. I like the water kind in the green box."

"We're at the hospital, not a gourmet deli. Any crackers are going to be stale and come with 'cheese' that by law has to be spelled with a *z*." Hannah picked up her purse. "I'll see what I can do."

She wandered down the corridor and turned the corner. In the first nook was a vending machine, paneled in plastic "wood" with *HEALTHY TREATS* emblazoned across the top. Two nurses surveyed the selections through the glass. Hannah took her place behind them.

"She drove into the lake?" said one, pushing coins into the slot.

"Took another car with her, too," said the other as the first nurse yanked on a knob. A candy bar fell into the catch bin.

"How is she?" said the first nurse.

"Still unconscious," said the second nurse. She fed a dollar bill to the machine. "Some detective is waiting around for her to wake up."

Dresden was here? Hannah backed away from the machine, no longer hungry. She and Pinnacle Peak's only detective had become acquainted the past few months under unfortunate circumstances. He was privy to Hannah's darkest secret, the one she would never tell anyone. Even though she hadn't done anything wrong at the lake that morning, Dresden wasn't someone she wanted to see.

Almost nothing wrong, Hannah mentally amended, thinking of the envelope she had picked up at the accident site. Did not telling carry the same penalties as lying?

The two nurses walked past. "I love your perfume," one of them said to Hannah.

"It's not—I mean, thanks." Right now, all Hannah wanted to do was get out of the hospital without Dresden seeing her. *I'll wait for Shelby in the car.*

She started down the hallway at a half-jog. When the man stepped out of one of the rooms, she couldn't stop in time.

"Oof!" Hannah said as they collided. The man's torso was like an extra-firm mattress.

"Excuse me." The man steadied Hannah by the shoulders. But instead of releasing her, he peered into her face with wise-owl's eyes.

"Ms. Dain?"

Of all the hospital rooms... "Hello, Detective," Hannah said, trying to ignore her galloping heart.

"I was planning to stop by your law firm later today to speak with you," Dresden said.

Hannah smiled wanly. "Glad to save you the trip."

Dresden released his grip. As usual, his white-blond hair was cut short enough to stand at attention and he wore clothes that would pass military inspection. His sleeves bore an iron's crease and his shoes were as shiny as Hannah's still-damp hair. He took a notebook out of his pocket and—also as usual—got to the point.

"What happened this morning?" he said, fixing her with a steely gaze, a weapon Hannah didn't doubt had brought hardened criminals to their knees. *Relax.*

"A woman sideswiped my Subaru. Both cars ended up in the lake..." She described the planned trip to the mine site, the stop at the fry bread stand, the collisions, the water rescue.

"Had you ever seen her before?" Dresden asked when she had finished.

Hannah shook her head. "I don't think so. What's her name?"

Dresden paged through his notebook. "Nathalie Soule. She's a lab tech in ASU's geology department."

Hannah thought about the note Nathalie had left at the *descanso. Romance between co-workers?* "How is she doing?"

"Don't know yet. She's unconscious, and on a ventilator."

"Any idea why she did it?"

"We're not sure she *did* anything. It'll be a few days before we know if it was an accident or something else."

Of course it was something else. "She never slowed down, not even after she hit my Subaru."

"And that may have been caused by something mechanical with her car." Dresden paused. "Do you recall seeing any injuries on her? Perhaps cuts on her arms?"

From a prior suicide attempt? "No, but I wasn't looking. And it was rough getting her out of the car and up the cliff. She could have gotten the cuts then." Hannah realized she was defending the woman, and decided to stop talking.

"What you did was very brave. And very dangerous." Dresden's expression softened for a moment. "If you could have met my sister..." He closed his notebook. "I thought you were going to stay out of harm's way from now on."

Hannah spread her hands. "I was just an innocent bystander." She felt a little hurt by the detective's tone. Granted, she had been involved in what most would call police business the past few months. But she thought she'd helped a bit, too.

A doctor emerged from the hospital room that Dresden had just left.

"You can go back in now, Detective," he said. "But she's still on the vent."

"Have the tox screens come back?" Dresden asked.

"Negative for drugs and alcohol," the doctor said.

A second man appeared in the room's doorway. His longish hair was flecked with gray and stood up as though he had been running his hands through it. The number of pleats on his pants proclaimed his suit's age.

"I told you, my wife isn't an addict!" he said. Hannah heard *un peu de français* in his accent. "And she doesn't drink and drive, either. This was an accident. Have you checked her car yet? I know there's something wrong with the brakes or steering. I'm going to sue—"

"Mr. Soule, the vehicles are being removed from the lake as we speak. They'll go straight to the police garage to be examined," Dresden said. He nodded at Hannah. "This is the young woman who pulled your wife out of the car."

Hannah extended a hand. "Um, it's good to meet…I mean, I'm sorry about what…"

The man grasped her hand in both his own. "Thank you so much for saving my wife's life!"

"Other people helped—" Hannah began. He interrupted her.

"What did she say to you? One of the EMTs told me she came to for a few seconds when you pulled her out of her car."

Hannah knew this was the time to disclose what Nathalie had said, to turn over the note she had found at the *descanso*. But seeing Mr. Soule's anguished face, she knew she couldn't. It wasn't for her to tell him his wife was having an affair, and that she had tried to kill herself after her lover died.

"She wanted to know where she was, and I said the lake." Hannah gently extracted her hand from his grasp. "I have to get back. Best wishes to your wife, Mr. Soule."

"I'll be in touch, Hannah," Dresden said.

"Great," she said brightly. *Just great.*

The older lawyer was nestled in a thicket of white pillows. With his pink cheeks and twinkling eyes, Franklin Rowley looked more like Santa Claus than a heart patient.

"Yesterday afternoon I agreed in principle to a settlement with the government lawyers," he said.

"That's wonderful!" Shelby said. "What's the final figure?"

He beamed at her. "Four million dollars to any person who lived within a mile of any mine since 1952, the year the government started dumping."

"Wow," Hannah said.

Franklin tapped his chest. "Apparently my heart felt the same way."

"Did you contact the tribe?" Shelby asked.

"I did, and they're just as pleased. Not because of the money—it's a drop in a bucket compared with gambling revenues. They were concerned a trial over contaminated water might affect casino traffic. Plus, they've been trying for several years to vacate that section of the rez. Now that the claim is resolved and damages awarded, maybe the last residents will finally relocate."

"Wait a minute," Hannah said. "People still live there, even though the water is poisoned?"

Franklin looked rueful. "I'm afraid so. The tribe offered everyone a house, free and clear, in the new subdivision next to the casino, but there were a few holdouts."

"Now what happens?" Shelby asked.

"A pretrial conference has been set for this afternoon at one. The government's lawyers will be there. A representative of the tribe, too." A frown creased Franklin's face. "This blasted place won't release me—something about running more tests. Shelby, you're going to have to appear. Tell Judge Neufeld the case can be taken off calendar because there's a settlement. Let her know we'll get the dismissal order to her by the end of next week."

A nurse appeared, pushing a wheelchair. "Time for x-rays, Mr. Rowley."

"Ah, my lovely chauffeur," Franklin said. "I'll let you two ladies be the ones to tell Richard the good news. His share of the fee should make him very happy."

Hannah knew mass tort cases were usually handled on a contingency-fee basis, with the lawyers getting a percentage of any proceeds. Even sharing the fee with Franklin, Dain & Daughters would make out well.

"I'll call you as soon as the hearing is over," Shelby said.

"Hope you feel better," Hannah said. She could tell from the relieved look on Shelby's face that her sister already did.

"You should have taken a cab. I don't want to be late for court," Shelby said as they sped along the road toward the town airport. Pinnacle Peak's only car rental agency was located in the terminal.

"We're almost there. That truck blocked us in at the hospital for less than five minutes."

"I knew it wouldn't move as soon as I saw that blue logo on the door—same as the one on the truck that wouldn't stop for Jerry Dan this morning. I should call the company."

"You don't really believe those How-Am-I-Driving numbers are legit, do you?" Hannah said. "The calls all go to some place in Iowa or one of those other *I* states. They pretend to take down your complaint, but really just capture your phone number to sell to telemarketers. Anyway, we're here."

Shelby pulled into a parking slot and opened her door. "Where's the ladies' room?"

The rental agreement was waiting, and Hannah had the keys to a Ford SUV in fewer than three minutes. *Good job, Clementine.* She was pleased her secretary had reserved something big enough to carry the kayak.

After stopping at the terminal's snack bar to buy a bagel and an iced tea, she walked outside. Shelby's red BMW was still at the curb.

Hannah's stomach clenched. There was a cocktail lounge in the terminal. Did her sister need some liquid courage before the settlement conference? *Not that it's any of my business...*

All of a sudden, Hannah realized that it was. Otherwise, sisterhood would be no different from friendship—good until it was over. No matter what their differences were, her and Shelby's bond of DNA couldn't be so readily severed.

She turned to go back inside. Food and drink in one hand, Hannah grabbed the door handle with the other and pulled—at the same time someone pushed against the glass on the other side. The door opened with a rush, slingshotting the person into Hannah's extra large iced tea.

Shelby yelped as brown liquid cascaded down the front of her clothes.

"Look what you've done!" Both her suit and blouse were stained, dark gold splotches against ivory.

"Oh God, I'm so sorry! It was an accident." Hannah tried to dab at the wet marks with a napkin.

Shelby batted her away and looked at her watch. "I'm supposed to be in court in fifteen minutes."

"We could switch clothes?" Hannah started to take off her jacket.

Shelby looked with horror at her sister's navy suit. "Are you kidding? That thing is polyester. And *way* too big."

"I hardly think the difference between a size two and a size six—"

"*You* have to go to court for me," Shelby said.

"But I've never—"

Shelby grabbed Hannah's arm and dragged her toward the parking lot. "You heard what Franklin said. All you have to do is tell the judge the case is settled and make nice with the client. Give me the keys to the rental and take my car. It's faster."

She opened the BMW's door and made shooing motions at Hannah. "Go! You can't be late."

Hannah climbed in and started the engine, then lowered the window.

"What if—"

"Don't worry, nothing will go wrong," Shelby said. "Now hurry!"

"Okay, okay. See you back at the firm."

"My dry-cleaning bill will be waiting," Shelby called as Hannah pulled away.

Chapter Five

A small knot of people were gathered at the base of the courthouse steps. Like the rest of the structures in the town's main square, the courthouse had a western-style façade, with tall narrow windows and slat siding. An old wooden rail stood next to the curb, though it had been nearly a century since lawyers had hitched their horses to it instead of parking their cars down the block.

"Excuse me," Hannah said, weaving her way through the throng. By now, she recognized the local press. And because of recent events, some of them knew her, too.

"Ms. Dain! Are you one of the lawyers?" one of men said. He held a small tape recorder.

"I'm not here—"

"Do you represent the tribe?" called the woman from the local cable station.

Hannah hesitated. Why would the media be covering a pre-trial conference? Usually they were pretty boring. "Yes, but—"

The reporters surged toward her.

"You think the tribe's sovereign immunity should be upheld?"

"Why shouldn't employment laws apply to the rez?"

"Does your client dispute the sexual harassment claims?"

Hannah held up her hands like a drowning person. "I have no idea what you are talking about."

"Aren't you here for the motion to dismiss the casino worker's lawsuit?" said the man with the tape recorder.

Hannah now understood the furor. She had read in the

Express about the female blackjack dealers and cocktail waitresses who were suing the casino, claiming gender and age discrimination, sexual harassment, and labor code violations. The casino had responded with a motion to dismiss. Under the Constitution, Indian nations existed like parallel universes, subject to completely different laws and customs. The tribe claimed this immunity from most state and federal laws extended to the casino.

Hannah shook her head. "Different case."

As swiftly as an outgoing tide, the crowd retreated down the steps, murmuring its disappointment. Hannah was left alone, save for a dark-skinned woman in her twenties holding a small boy by the hand.

"Miss? You are the lawyer for the O'odham, yes?" the woman asked.

"I don't have anything to do with—"

"The poisoned water case?"

Hannah blinked. "I'm appearing for plaintiffs," she said cautiously.

"My name is Espera Bustamente. This is Fernando, my son. I call him Nando."

Hannah looked down at the toddler. "Hello, Nando. I'm Hannah."

The little boy gaped up at her. His fingers were stiffened into hooks and he wore a patch over one eye. *Effects of radiation poisoning?*

"You smell good," Nando said. His face crinkled into a smile.

Hannah smiled back. "Thank you. My sister's perfume."

"I am the plaintiff in your lawsuit," Espera said.

The tribal representative. "Of course. Mr. Rowley said you would be coming."

Espera frowned. "I did not talk to Mr. Rowley."

"It was probably someone from his office who called. Mr. Rowley's going to be fine, by the way. I'm here because my sister, Shelby—she's the other lawyer on your case—anyway, she—"

"We are here to find out when the trial will begin," Espera said.

"The trial?" Hannah said. "Mr. Rowley has settled—"

Ignoring Hannah, Espera turned and beckoned to two other young women at the bottom of the stairs to join them. One wore an oversized denim dress and held a baby in her arms. The other cradled a framed photograph.

"This is Constanza and this is Lupe," Espera said.

Hannah introduced herself.

"We live near the mining sites, and drank from the poisoned wells when we were pregnant," Espera said. "Our children drank the water, too. Constanza's daughter was born sick and died the first week. Now her other daughter is ill. Neuropathy, the doctors say. Lupe had a *jelly baby*—born without bones. He died, too."

Lupe held out the photograph to Hannah. The tiny figure in the hospital crib looked like a rag doll. Hannah forced herself not to recoil.

"And there's my son," Espera said. "He has the stinging in his muscles. Soon he will need braces on his legs. In two years he won't be able to walk or see." She stroked the little boy's hair. Nando clutched a plastic car between his clawed hands, unresponsive to her touch. "He is the reason I go to court against the government."

"I don't know how long the paperwork will take, but I would imagine the money will be paid in a few weeks," Hannah said.

"Money? What money?" Constanza said.

"From the settlement. The case is over—the government agreed to pay. Didn't Mr. Rowley explain all this?"

"I told you, I did not talk to Mr. Rowley," Espera said. "The case, it cannot be over."

"The settlement is very generous. I'm not sure you would recover more if you went to trial."

"What do we want with money? It cannot cure our children. The doctors say half will die before they are sixteen," Constanza said.

"Money? Bah!" Esperanza said. "The casino gives us more than we can ever spend. The lawsuit is to expose the lies." Her voice came down hard on the word *lies*, and the two other woman nodded.

"But I thought the tribe—"

"Lied to us, too," Constanza said. "They said what was happening to our children was from a bad gene. The leadership only cares about the casino. They don't want anything to stop the whites from coming to gamble."

"The Department of Energy and the utilities convinced the elders of my father's generation that as keepers of the land, the tribe had an obligation to accept nuclear waste," Espera said.

"The steel containers holding the plutonium will degrade long before the radioactivity. And what about earthquakes? If a container ruptures, the contents will explode," Constanza said.

"We want our day in court." Espera wrapped an arm around Nando's shoulders. "I want the world to see my child, to understand that money isn't going to solve this problem."

"Didn't the tribe declare the rez a nuclear-free zone last year?" Hannah asked.

"That doesn't apply to the poison already in the ground," Constanza said.

Lupe spoke for the first time. "Elder Brother warned us about taking resources from the earth. The Navajos tell the story of being given a choice between yellow powders—the yellow dust from the rocks and corn pollen. They chose the pollen, because they knew if they didn't leave the yellow dust in the ground, it would become evil. They were smarter than the O'odham."

"The danger of nuclear waste has been known for a long time. How come you didn't move?" Hannah asked.

"Until they built the casino, our leaders told us it was safe," Espera said.

"Exile and expropriation has been the Indian's fate for almost two hundred years. We thought the warnings were more lies to let them round us up again," Constanza added.

Hannah felt something stir in her gut. Caught between tradition and a hard place—too often the case when it came to women and children.

"Ms. Dain, those bombs that fell on Japan sixty years ago fell on America, too. *Our* America. Indian Country was Ground Zero." Espera clutched Hannah's arm. "We want a chance to be heard."

A Town Car eased to a stop in front of the courthouse and discharged two men in suits. The group of reporters converged, shouting questions.

"It's not really my case—" Hannah said as the group moved up the steps. She glanced at the clock on the courthouse. The settlement conference was supposed to start in five minutes. "But I'll see what I can do," she said.

In line for the metal detector, Hannah saw a familiar face.

"Zel?"

A man turned, and his face brightened in recognition. He threaded through the crowd toward her. A phone headset was hooked over one ear, and his cargo pants, pockets loaded, sagged dangerously.

"Hannah! Are you here for the employment case against the tribe?"

Zel Kassif freelanced for the *Express*. He and Hannah had met two months ago when he was chasing a story. Initially put off by his dogged persistence, Hannah had allowed her chilliness to thaw now that he was dating Clementine.

"Pretrial conference on another case. Do you know anything about nuclear waste reparations?"

Zel held up a finger. "So get me his home number then!" he said into the headset, then switched off the device.

"No wonder Clementine says you're a workaholic."

Zel mopped the sweat on his shaved head with his shirt sleeve. "Don't call me a workaholic—makes it sound like I'm not having fun. How about a work partier?" He extracted a notebook from one of his bulging pockets and flipped it open. "Are we talking about the Pentagon's roster of death-dealing real estate? Is there a story?"

"There are some people you may want to talk to, but first I need to ask you some questions." Although she had only known him a short time, Hannah was already impressed with Zel's near-encyclopedic memory. Clementine wanted him to try out for *Jeopardy*.

He eyed the crowd filing into the nearest courtroom. "You gotta make it fast. I need to get a good seat in there."

"What do you know about lawsuits against the government caused by health problems from uranium?"

"During W-W-Two, the feds needed uranium to build the bomb. Of course they came to the Southwest, the Saudi Arabia of uranium. Turned out some of the richest deposits were on Indian land, including our local rez. The government appealed to the Indians for help—guardians of the earth, national defense, blah, blah, blah—and the Indians said yes. Remember, this was pre-casino, so the tribes were dirt-poor, excuse the pun, so they were happy to get the storage fees and the jobs. But nobody told the Indians how dangerous the ore was, even though by the end of the Manhattan Project there was pretty good evidence that working with the stuff could cause all sorts of cancers and other health problems, usually of the fatal variety."

"This case I'm working on involves storing nuclear waste," Hannah said.

"When we were well and truly into the nuclear age, the feds needed a place to dispose of the depleted stuff. With plutonium having a half-life of something like 25,000 years, they wanted it kept someplace remote. So they called the Indians again. Again, patriotism and poverty made a compelling case. In return for the modern-day equivalent of a handful of beads, the tribes allowed the government to bury the stuff on the reservations, usually in played-out mines."

"Do you know if other tribes are suing for damages?"

"A few are. Congress established a compensation fund, and I think the payouts have been big—five to seven million dollars. I've heard that the government is making nice because it wants the Indians to allow mining again. Up the supply and the price comes down, which is a good thing when you need to lock in ten years' worth of fuel before you bring a nuclear reactor on line. Right now, uranium trades for about sixty bucks a pound.

Less than ten years ago it was as low as seven dollars."

So why did Franklin think a four-million-per-plaintiff payout was good? Hannah wondered.

Zel backpedaled toward the courtroom. "Gotta go. Mind telling the sexiest secretary in town I might be late to dinner tonight?"

"Will do. Thanks."

After he was gone, Hannah took out her cell and called Clementine.

"Yeth?" Her secretary's voice sounded groggy.

"Clementine, were you sleeping again?"

"Of course not! Wassup?"

"Can you pull up the verdict statistics for uranium contamination cases?" The firm subscribed to a database that kept track of lawsuit judgments and settlements.

"Sure."

Hannah heard the sound of typing. Clementine always forgot to use the *Hold* button.

"The average is a little over six million, more if it's a kid," her secretary said a moment later.

Six mil? Franklin's number was just two-thirds of that, and with nothing extra for children. Did he just want to avoid trial? Or was there another reason he was letting the government off the hook?

"Thanks. By the way, I ran into Zel. He says he might be late tonight."

"Isn't he the sweetest? I'm telling you, buying that nine-ninety-five bottle of Big Sexy Hair was one of the smartest things I ever did. Did you call Cooper yet?"

"Talk to you later." Hannah closed the phone. Someone touched her elbow.

"Shelby Dain?" The speaker was a man in a white shirt and off-the-rack suit in a grim shade of gray. He might as well have *government lawyer* sewn on his lapel.

"You've got the Dain right, but I'm Hannah."

The man looked confused. "I was told—"

"Shelby's my sister. She had a conflict, so I'm covering the settlement conference for her."

The man offered his hand. "Gabriel Burke, attorney for the government. Did she or Rowley have a chance to bring you up to speed?"

"I think so." Hannah noticed he had nice eyes. Green, like… she caught herself. "Four million per plaintiff, payable—"

Burke held up a hand. "Whoa! Our agreement was two million per plaintiff, with the tribe putting up a matching amount." He opened his briefcase, took out a piece of paper, and handed it to Hannah. "Here's Rowley's email."

Hannah scanned the paper. Burke was right—the government was to pay each class member two million dollars, with the tribe to contribute a like sum. The terms of the settlement would be confidential, payment to be made within a week of signing the documents.

"Today should be a quick in and out. All we have to do is tell the judge he doesn't need to set the case for trial because it's been settled." Burke looked pointedly at her ringless left hand. "Maybe we could grab lunch afterward."

"But I won't be handling the settlement," Hannah said.

Burke smiled. "I wasn't planning on talking about it."

Hannah colored. "Ah…"

Burke's smile became wry. "You're seeing someone. Should have known."

"No. Yes." Hannah's face became redder. "More like catching my breath."

"If you ever get your wind back, give me a call." Burke handed her his card. "See you in there." He disappeared through the courtroom doors.

Hannah waited for her flush to subside, her thoughts on the settlement. Why was the tribe kicking in money? Was that why the settlement terms were to be kept secret?

She was debating whether to call Shelby when a dark-skinned woman in a black dress and nice jewelry walked out of the courtroom. At first glance, Hannah estimated her to be in her late thirties, but as the woman got closer, she added ten years.

"Are you Shelby Dain?" the woman asked.

"She's my sister." Hannah thought how annoyed Shelby would be to find out two people had mistaken her for someone who'd wear a suit that didn't need to be dry-cleaned. "I'm covering her court appearance today."

"I hope it wasn't another emergency?" the woman said. "I heard about Franklin."

To Shelby, ruined clothes ranked right up there with a heart attack. "No," Hannah said.

"I'm Phyllis Juan, liaison for tribal litigation."

The woman was tall for a Tohono O'odham. Her carefully penciled eyebrows, shaped like upside-down *V*s, hovered above her eyeglass frames like a pair of distant dark birds.

"I hope you weren't waiting too long. The judge scheduled the tribe's hearings back-to-back. From what I could tell, though, things seem to be going well for us on the first case." Phyllis shook her head. "Not that the tribe did anything wrong. I still don't understand how those people thought they had a case."

The words popped out before Hannah could stop them. "I imagine the women had no idea that by taking a job with the tribe, they were giving up many of the protections other working people in this country take for granted."

"The Indians' right to immunity is granted by the Constitution." Phyllis' tone was chilly. This isn't your client or your case, Hannah reminded herself.

"But of course," she said. "I just meant that the female employees probably didn't realize the implications." *How could they?* Hannah refrained from adding. Given the jobs they had held, it was unlikely that any of the women had attended, let alone graduated from high school. She also didn't add her belief that in writing the laws that granted sovereignty to Indian nations, Congress surely didn't anticipate it would be allowing four hundred casino-owning tribes to operate like imperial principalities, sidestepping lawsuits brought by angry vendors, contractors, and employees, and dodging environmental and other regulations.

"You do know the toxic water case has been settled?" Phyllis had put the syrupy sweetness back into her voice. The dulcet tones set Hannah's teeth on edge.

"Yes. That's why I'm here—to let the judge know."

As Phyllis nodded approvingly, Hannah caught sight of Espera and the other women. They moved down the hallway as a group, close to the wall, as though afraid of being noticed.

Hannah added impulsively, "Assuming the plaintiffs approve."

Phyllis shot her a glance. "What you mean?"

"I spoke with Ms. Bustamente and some of the other residents. They seem to want their day in court."

Phyllis looked annoyed. "What they should want is what's best for their children. They shouldn't be—don't need to be—living in that area of the reservation. For two years we've offered them alternative housing near the casino. The tribe will cover all their costs, even give them a house for free."

"I'm not sure it's just about the money," Hannah said. She could understand the overwhelming pull of home, despite accompanying disadvantages.

"This case needs to be resolved," Phyllis said. "It's bad for the tribe's image."

Hannah couldn't contain herself. "Is that why the settlement is so low and the tribe is paying half?"

Phyllis' eyes hardened. "Casino revenues allow the tribe to take care of its own. We don't need to rely on money from the federal government anymore."

The courtroom doors opened and people started to stream out. The pack was led by a half dozen women, some crying. Reporters thrust microphones in their faces and shouted questions.

The scene reminded Hannah of why she hadn't gone into litigation. Every case was a story with two sides, like a book printed in English on its left-hand pages, Spanish on its right. The Spanish version was always different from the English, with the jury deciding which story was most appealing. Hannah preferred negotiating business deals, where everyone was more or less on the same page.

She spotted Zel on the fringes of the crowd.

"Excuse me," she said to Phyllis and went to the reporter. "What happened?"

"The expected. The judge granted the tribe's motion to dismiss. The plaintiffs can proceed, but against the individual defendants only," Zel said.

No wonder the female employees were upset, Hannah thought. They could sue the men who had harassed them, but the tribe itself was immune.

"Catch you later," Zel said. "I have to file my story before deadline."

Hannah followed Phyllis into the courtroom. It was empty, save for an old man in the second row. He looked at them expectantly, as though waiting for a repeat of the prior hearing's drama.

"Winning that motion saves the tribe a lot of money and legal hassle," Hannah said. "You must be relieved."

"Of course," Phyllis said.

Hannah watched the older woman worry a thread on her cuff, heedless of the damage to the expensive garment, and wondered if Phyllis were telling the truth.

Chapter Six

Phyllis sat in the front row while Hannah took a seat at one of the counsel tables. Not being a trial lawyer, she had never been on this side of the bar before.

She glanced around the room, wrinkling her nose at the faint smell of carpet cleaner. She expected more pomp, more circumstance in a place where such important decisions were made. But the room was plain and small, with only four pews for spectators. Dark paneling made the windowless space feel even more cramped. The Arizona and United States flags flanked the judge's bench, which featured a copper cast of the state seal on its front. Over the vacant jury box hung the sole piece of artwork—a lithograph of the Lady of Justice holding her sword and scales. Behind her an angel hovered, hands outstretched.

"That's the Angel of Mercy."

Hannah started at the sound of Burke's voice.

"Judge Neufeld always mentions it after she instructs a jury." The government lawyer took his seat at the table across from Hannah's. "She tells them it's Mercy's job to keep the sword of justice from being used too swiftly. Then she reminds them that Justice isn't blind, only blindfolded."

"Not exactly what the government would like a jury to hear before they begin deliberations in a criminal case?" Hannah said.

"Got that right," Burke said.

Hannah squinted at the picture. Under the two figures ran the words *Seek wisdom to temper justice with compassion.*

The door behind the judge's bench opened and the bailiff appeared. Taking his place next to the bench, he called the courtroom to order.

"Hear ye, hear ye, the District Court for the State of Arizona is hereby..."

As Hannah listened, she gazed at the Justice lithograph. *Wisdom...justice...compassion.*

"All rise," the bailiff said.

An older woman in black robes appeared and took her place on the bench. Her squarish head on a thick neck and impassive gaze reminded Hannah of a sphinx.

"Be seated," the bailiff said, then called the case and asked the parties to announce their appearances.

Hannah and Burke stood.

"Gabriel Burke, for the defendants."

"Hannah Dain, for the plaintiffs."

Glancing again at the lithograph, Hannah noticed the scales in Lady Justice's hands weren't exactly level. The artist's intent or just a trick of the eye?

She and Burke took their seats while the judge looked at the papers in front of her.

"We're here for a pretrial conference, and to set a trial date. But I now understand the parties have made some progress toward settlement. Is that correct?" the judge said. From the terseness of her tone, Hannah wondered if after the prior hearing, she'd had her fill of lawyers.

Burke stood. Hannah hadn't seen so much up-and-down since an acquaintance's church wedding two years ago.

"The parties have settled the case, Your Honor. We should have the stipulated dismissal filed by the end of the week." Burke sat.

"This seems to be the tribe's lucky morning," the judge said. "You concur in counsel's statement, Ms. Dain?"

Hannah got to her feet. She noticed Espera and the two other women in the back row of the courtroom. Nando sat beside his mother, staring into space. She followed his gaze and realized he was looking at the Justice lithograph.

"Not exactly." Hannah heard Phyllis' intake of breath behind her.

The judge frowned. "Ms. Dain, this court is very busy. Is this case settled or not?"

Now Burke was looking at Hannah, too. She shifted her weight from one foot to another, wishing her pants had pockets to jam her hands into.

"Um, not," Hannah said, then added, "Your Honor."

The judge swiveled her head toward Burke, who had gotten to his feet again. "What's going on, counselor?"

"I don't know, Your Honor. I have an email from Mr. Rowley confirming the terms of the settlement." Burke extracted the piece of paper from his briefcase as he spoke. "He's lead counsel on the case. An unexpected health situation prevented him from attending today."

Hannah felt her face grow hot. Was Burke implying she didn't have authority to speak? She glanced at Espera, and felt a stab of nervousness. *Did* she have authority?

"Ms. Dain?" the judge said. She peered down from the elevated bench, but Hannah thought her tone was less peremptory than before. "Do plaintiffs agree to the settlement?"

"No, Mrs. Judge."

Espera's voice was so soft that at first Hannah thought she had imagined it.

"Your Honor!" Burke said. "Plaintiff's counsel is repudiating—"

Phyllis rose and began speaking. "This is absurd! The tribe..." Lupe and Constanza started to chant, "No settlement! No settlement!"

"Order!" shouted the judge and banged her gavel. At the sound, the courtroom quieted.

"Only counsel is permitted to address this court. Anyone disregarding that rule will be removed." The judge pointed the gavel for emphasis. She picked up a folder and opened it. "According to the case caption, the plaintiffs are represented by the Law Office of Franklin Rowley and the firm of Dain &

Daughters. Is that correct?"

Hannah found her voice. "Yes, Your Honor."

"Ms. Dain, you are a member of Dain & Daughters?"

"Yes, Your Honor."

"Has a settlement agreement been reached in this case?"

"Yes, Your Honor," Hannah said, then corrected herself. "I mean, no." Out of the corner of her eye, she caught Burke's smile.

"Ms. Dain—" the judge began.

"The lawyers reached an agreement, but the plaintiffs didn't," Hannah said in a rush.

The judge sat back in her chair. "I see." She glanced down at the folder. "Are any of the plaintiffs present today?"

Espera rose. "Yes, Mrs. Judge. Espera Bustamente."

"Is what Ms. Dain said correct?" the judge asked.

"Yes, Mrs. Judge. We do not want to settle."

"Then this court will set the matter for trial. Bailiff, how does four weeks from today look?"

"The calendar is clear, Your Honor," the bailiff said.

Hannah's mouth dropped open. Trial was to begin in four weeks? What if Franklin weren't recovered by then?

"Your Honor," she began. "Plaintiffs ask for a continuance until we can be sure of the status of Mr. Rowley's health. He's lead counsel in this case."

"No objection," Burke said quickly.

"Motion for continuance denied," the judge said. "To me, lead counsel doesn't mean much more than whose name goes on top of the pleadings. Plaintiffs are represented by two sets of lawyers. I see no reason why Dain & Daughters can't try this case."

Phyllis rose. "Your Honor, if I may be heard."

"And you are?" the judge said.

"Phyllis Juan, litigation liaison for the Tohono O'odham nation."

"As I explained earlier, Ms. Juan, only counsel may address this court," the judge said.

"Dain & Daughters no longer represents the tribe, Your Honor," Phyllis said.

Hannah slowly shut her eyes, then opened them again. As much as Shelby didn't want to try the case, Hannah was pretty sure getting fired would be even less desirable to her sister.

The judge sat back in her chair and regarded Phyllis with a little smile. "Ms. Juan, I'm afraid neither you nor the tribe is a plaintiff in this matter." She looked at the back of the courtroom. "These ladies are. And I haven't heard anything from them about discharging Dain & Daughters. In any event, I've set a trial date. Under local rules, counsel may not be dismissed absent a showing of cause. And I see no such evidence here. In fact, I know Richard Dain, and am confident his firm will be able to ably represent plaintiffs in Mr. Rowley's absence." The judge looked at Hannah. "In fact, I'm sure of it."

Hannah smiled back weakly.

"I hereby order that trial in this matter be set for November 30th, with Dain & Daughters—specifically, Hannah Dain—as lead counsel for plaintiffs." The judge gathered up the folders in front of her.

"All rise," the bailiff said.

The judge disappeared through the door behind the bench.

"The court is now in recess," the bailiff said.

"Do you know what you've done?" Phyllis demanded.

Pissed off my father. Really pissed off my sister. Hannah remained silent.

"Guess I'll see you in court," Burke said, then nodded at the lithograph over the jury box. "If I'm not mistaken, you just helped Lady Justice wield that sword." He picked up his briefcase. "Nice perfume, by the way."

Chapter Seven

Hannah trailed a furious Phyllis out of the building.

"I don't care if he's in the ICU, I want to speak with him," Phyllis said into her cell phone as she stalked down the courthouse steps. She listened for a moment, then snapped the phone shut. Without another look at Hannah, she left.

Hannah barely noticed. She was still reeling from what had just happened. She wasn't a trial lawyer, and now she was in charge of a case with her equally inexperienced sister? A case with millions of dollars at stake?

"Howdy, Hannah."

The man wore a suit with a bolo tie and cowboy boots. She looked at him without recognition.

"It's me, Jerry Dan. I just got out of law and motion. What are you doing here?"

Hannah roused herself from her daze. "Covering a hearing for Shelby." *And doing a bang-up job of it.*

"Remember that mountain biking session we talked about? How about this week?"

The judge's voice sounded in Hannah's head. *Four weeks to trial.* "My schedule is pretty full. I'm sorry."

The corners of Jerry Dan's mouth drooped. "Sure."

"Wait." Hannah put a hand on his arm. "It's not what you think." She poured out the tale of the morning's events.

"A month? And you've never tried a case before?" Jerry Dan said.

"I've never *seen* a case before," Hannah said.

"Well, if you need any help…"

Hannah's mouth twisted. "How about breaking the news to my sister?"

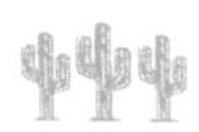

Shelby's reaction was worse than Hannah had expected. She went into the bathroom and threw up.

"Hannah, all you had to do was tell the judge the case was settled!" Shelby said when she finally emerged from the stall. She dampened a paper towel at the sink and dabbed at her mouth.

When her sister dropped her head over the basin, Hannah could see the dark roots of her hair and felt a stab of worry. Shelby would sooner miss the Second Coming than an appointment with her colorist. More proof that she was drinking again? If stress made alcoholics more vulnerable to falling off the wagon, Hannah knew she wasn't making things any easier.

"Bring me the makeup bag from my bottom drawer," Shelby said from behind a curtain of hair. "Then we have to call Franklin."

Hannah and Shelby walked to Clementine's desk.

"Clementine, please call Franklin Rowley's room at the hospital," Hannah said.

"Is that barf on your sleeve?" Clementine asked Shelby. "Or has Chanel come up with a new kind of lace?"

In her secretary's lexicon, *Chanel* became *channel.* Hannah had once heard her secretary turn a reservation for a luncheon buffet into a date with the singer from Margaritaville.

Shelby stripped off her jacket as though it were on fire.

"That's what happens when you go to lunch on the day the doc comes to the firm to give flu shots," Clementine said. "You know, it's not very consid—"

"Clementine…" Hannah said.

Her secretary opened the phone book with an aggrieved air. "All I'm saying is if someone gets sick, she shouldn't be here infectin' the rest of us." Clementine started tapping in numbers.

"Especially the rest of us who have to get ready to try some big case in a month."

Hannah draped the offending jacket on the coat rack next to Clementine's desk, then herded Shelby into her office and shut the door.

"That woman is beyond disrespectful," Shelby said.

Hannah dropped into her desk chair. "Yes. But she's a great secretary."

The intercom buzzed.

"She should be fired," Shelby said.

"You want to tell her?" Hannah flipped the speaker switch.

Shelby bit her lip. "I really needed you to come through on this, Hannah," she said quietly.

Hannah had the feeling her sister was conveying something beyond her words, but before she could pursue it, her secretary's voice boomed into the room.

"He's on line one."

"Thanks, Clementine." Hannah hit the button. "Mr. Rowley? I've got you on the speaker. Shelby's here."

"How did the hearing go?" Franklin's voice was scratchy with static.

"Um, not exactly as planned."

By the time Hannah got to how the case had been set for trial, Franklin was shouting. Hannah wondered if she should call a nurse on the other line. *I'm driving my sister to drink and Franklin to a heart attack.*

"Mr. Rowley, you should probably try to calm—"

"Calm? I'll be calm when you tell me how the hell we're supposed to go to trial in a month when I haven't found a new expert witness yet! Why didn't you tell the judge that Weller died, use that to buy more time?"

"The judge didn't seem like she wanted to hear—"

"Never mind. I'll call Burke, put the settlement back together before he realizes we don't have an expert."

"I don't think we can do that. The plaintiffs told me they don't want to settle."

"Espera was at the hearing?"

"She and a few of her neighbors."

Franklin made a sound of disgust. "That woman is going to queer this case for the rest of the class. I'll sever her claim, settle everyone else out."

Hannah felt a prick of anger. She knew there was strength in numbers when it came to litigation. Lawyers weren't allowed to advance costs, and she doubted Espera could pay for expenses like transcripts and expert witness fees by herself. "You can't do that."

"I can do whatever the hell I want. It's my case," Franklin said.

"Actually, the judge designated Dain & Daughters as lead when she set the trial date."

"What! You conniving—" Franklin broke off, and Hannah heard him gasping for air.

"Hello?" A new voice came on the line, a young woman's. "Mr. Rowley is going to have to get off the line now. You've made him quite upset."

"I'm sorry," Hannah said. "Please tell him I hope he feels better." She had a sudden thought. If Franklin wanted to settle, he wasn't going to find a replacement for Garth Weller. "And tell him I'll look for an expert witness, too." She hung up.

"How do you plan to do that?" Shelby asked. Still looking weak from throwing up, she hadn't said a word during the call to Franklin.

Hannah tried to make her voice light. "Yellow Pages?" She had no idea how to find a qualified geologist, let alone one who would testify.

"I need a drink," Shelby said. Seeing Hannah's look, she added, "Of *water*. Ralphing makes you thirsty." She pushed herself out of the chair. "Let me know how the conversation with Daddy goes. I'm going to Jake's."

Hannah's heart sank at the thought of calling Richard. Her discovery of Elizabeth's secrets had resulted in a sort of détente between them. Conversations, though, were still limited.

She opened the address file on her computer. But instead of looking up the listing for Richard's hotel, she scanned the names under *S*. Finding the number she was looking for, Hannah punched it in and waited for the recording.

"Flying S Ranch, Cooper Smith here. Leave a message."

Hearing the familiar voice, Hannah felt a liquefying in her limbs. She realized she was engaged in a kind of reverse courtship—as soon as she fell in love with Cooper, she started falling out of it. Now that they were apart, she missed him more than ever. It made no sense, but Hannah couldn't help it, no more than she could help the chemistry that was between them. So unbeknownst to Clementine and anyone else, she left messages on his ranch voicemail. She never asked Cooper to call her back, and so far he hadn't.

"Hey, it's me. Sort of a wild day today..."

As she talked, Hannah thought about how Cooper's green eyes harbored a private cool, giving the impression he stood apart from the material world. From being rich or going to Tibet twice? Either way, Hannah envied his composure. Especially now.

"...so it looks like I'm a trial lawyer." Hannah took a breath. The machine beeped and disconnected.

Her hand hovered over the *Redial* button. There were things she wanted to ask him. Was his limp really better? Why had he left his favorite sweater at her condo? She let her hand drop and looked out the window.

Staghorn cholla poked up past the sill, its stems reddened from drought. A snarl of dead brittlebush scudded across the parking lot.

Hannah toyed with the pens in the holder on her desk. Even though it had been a long day, she considered going for another paddle. Usually her evening workouts were at the gym, but this week the air-conditioning was being serviced. Bikram yoga was one thing, Bikram treadmill quite another.

Hannah abandoned the pens and decided to pass. The cars going into the lake would undoubtedly be the talk of the boathouse, and she wasn't up for questions.

The door to her office opened.

"I'm outta here." Clementine patted the mass of black curls

pinned to her head with a pink jaw clip. "You know, you really should take another look at those emails. I'd lend you my bottle of Big Sexy Hair."

"Good night, Clementine," Hannah said and picked up the phone again.

Richard Dain answered after the first ring.

"Um, it's Hannah."

"I understand the hearing didn't go quite as planned."

Franklin must already have rung to complain. *Tattletale.* Hannah explained what had happened.

To her surprise, Richard wasn't critical. "The plaintiff is in charge. You have to do what she wants."

"Mr. Rowley doesn't see it that way."

"Franklin is an old friend. He's also an average lawyer—was passed over for partner by his firm. That's why he had to open his own practice. The judge made you lead counsel, Hannah. You have to do what you think is right."

Hannah was tempted to ask him what she should do to get ready for trial, but she stayed silent. Old habits died hard.

"How's your sister?" Richard asked.

Which one? Hannah wondered if he knew about Anuya. "She's got the flu. And she's pretty mad at me."

"Both will pass. You'll do fine, Hannah." He hung up.

Hannah leaned back in her chair. Her gaze roved over the desert landscape on the other side of the window as she basked in the afterglow of possibly the best telephone conversation she'd ever had with Richard.

A pickup truck drove into the parking lot. Seeing the mountain bike in the bed, Hannah knew who was driving even before he parked and got out of the cab. What did Jerry Dan want?

Chapter Eight

"Howdy!" Jerry Dan tipped his cowboy hat. "I was on my way to the furniture auction at ASU when I saw your law firm's sign and decided to stop and see if you wanted to go, too. Figured you could use some stress relief after court today."

"Retail therapy usually comes in the form of shoes, not tables and chairs," Hannah said. "But then I'm not much of a Manolo person."

"What—or who—is a Manolo?"

"My feeling exactly. Anyway, thanks for the invite, but—"

"Are you still looking for an expert witness? On our ride back to the car this morning, Ed mentioned he might be interested."

Hannah felt a trickle of hope, quickly dammed up by realism. "Trial's in four weeks. Do you think he'd have time to do the work?"

"That's all the man lives for. Ed had a problem with alcohol a while back—lost his wife, nearly lost his professorship. He got into orienteering through his AA sponsor. That and work is what fills his days. If anyone can get the job done, it'd be him."

Hannah studied Jerry Dan's eager face, then glanced at the bike in the pickup bed. She didn't believe for a minute that his visit was spur of the moment. And had Glouster volunteered—or had Jerry Dan suggested he offer his services? Didn't matter—trading cycling training tips for an expert witness was more than fair.

"Thanks," she said.

Jerry Dan took out his cell phone. "Let's give him a call." He tapped in a number, listened, then closed the phone.

"Voicemail. He spends a lot of time at the lab, doesn't always answer his phone. We could stop by on our way to the auction."

"Let's go," Hannah said.

Maybe I'll buy a desk for the condo. Two months ago, planning to take a job with a Boston firm, she had shipped her furniture ahead. After getting back together with Cooper, she made arrangements to get her stuff sent back, only to learn there had been a fire at the warehouse where her furniture was stored. She had put off buying new stuff, not knowing what kind of life she was choosing things for. A single woman's? In Arizona?

Using her laptop on the kitchen counter was making her wrists sore. And having moved past the point of thinking life could be as flawless as a page from an interior design magazine, Hannah liked the idea of owning furniture with some experience.

Jerry Dan made good time to ASU, detailing Glouster's background as he drove—former uranium miner and dynamite expert turned geology professor, amateur archaeologist, and orienteer. Hannah listened, enjoying the raised vantage point offered by the truck. Riding above the other cars' roofs may not have been safer, but it sure felt like it. She wondered if she should consider something bigger as a replacement for the Subaru. The image of the white SUV slipping under the lake's surface came to mind, and Hannah tabled her car-buying thoughts.

The parking lot was full of student cars, Japanese and European models with parking permits on their bumpers. Jerry Dan cruised two aisles before finding a space big enough for his truck.

They found the Geology building and wandered the corridors until they came to an office with "Dr. Edmund Glouster" engraved on the removable fake-wood nameplate. Jerry Dan tried the door. It was unlocked.

The room was small, made even more so by the rocks and fossils filling the bookshelves, and the drawings of petroglyphs and plants papering most of the wall space. Running along the ceiling was a timeline showing the geologic ages. Someone had sketched dinosaurs and a family of *homo sapiens* in their respective periods. Hannah had read somewhere that a third of all people believed dinosaurs and prehistoric man had been on earth at the same time. How many thought the creatures had been kept as pets, too?

The smell of cigarettes hung in the air. There was an empty mug on the desk, a dark ring around its inside rim.

"Looks as though he just left," she said. "Smells like it, too."

"I'll leave him a note, tell him we'll stop by after the auction." Jerry Dan scanned the cluttered desk. "That is, if I can find a blank piece of paper."

While Jerry Dan hunted for paper and pen, Hannah wandered back into the corridor. She thought about calling Shelby to tell her she had a lead on an expert witness, then decided to wait until it was definite. Her sister had enough stress. So much that, like it or not, Hannah knew she would have to be more than a figurehead, and step up to a real role in the case. If her sister started drinking again because of the pressure, Hannah would never forgive herself. If only the first trial she would see weren't also the first case she'd try. She made a mental note to TiVo *Law & Order.*

Jerry Dan emerged from the office. "We better hurry. Don't want to miss the preview."

They found the auditorium where the auction was to be held, and walked up and down the rows of furniture in the preview area. Most was university-bland, the light wood treated with something that made it resistant to pen marks and janitor's mops. Although not one who cared much about adding *decorated* to her interiors, Hannah didn't see anything she would want in her condominium.

Then she spotted the desk. It stood solidly in a corner, a dark-mahogany and curlicued galleon moored in a sea of Scandinavian-style blond.

"This is the one." Hannah kept her voice low so as not to attract the attention of other prospective buyers.

Jerry Dan eyed it dubiously. "It's kinda big."

Hannah was busy testing drawers. All glided open. She ran a hand over the beveled edge.

"I want it."

She liked the solidness, the dings on its legs. This was a desk with a history. Hannah figured if the piece had survived academia, it could handle a career in law, too. She wrote down its lot number.

The auction was already underway when Jerry Dan and Hannah took their seats. Bids were noted by the auctioneer in an incomprehensible blur of words. Hannah sat on her hands, afraid that any movement would result in her owning a steel bookshelf or a collection of fluorescent light fixtures.

The desk's lot number was called.

"Lot fifty-seven, lot fifty-seven. Do I hear one hundred dollars?" said the auctioneer. Hannah's hand shot up.

"I have one hundred. Do I hear one hundred twenty-five?" the auctioneer said. Someone else made a bid. "One twenty-five. How about one hundred fifty?"

"It's better to jump into the bidding later," Jerry Dan said. "Scope out your competition."

"But I want to make sure I get it," Hannah said. After raising her hand intermittently as the bidding climbed to three hundred dollars, Hannah finally thrust her hand toward the ceiling and left it there. Bidders gradually dropped out, until the desk was Hannah's for four hundred and seventy-five dollars. She resisted a squeal of delight.

"This is fun!" she said.

"You must love eBay," Jerry Dan said.

"Never go there." Previously owned furniture was okay, but not used clothes or personal items. Renting bowling shoes made her squeamish.

"You go pay for your new desk. I'll see if I can find something to wheel it out with."

The dolly they borrowed also served as a ramp to push and pull—adding a few new scratches in the process—the desk into the bed of the pickup.

"There's an old lariat in the back seat that we can use as a tie down," Jerry Dan said.

Hannah handed him the rope. Someone called their names.

"Good to see you again!" It was Glouster. He wore baggy corduroys, a green John Deere cap, and a torn leather jacket so stained that it was difficult to tell its original color. From five feet away, Hannah could smell the cigarette smoke.

He held out a calloused hand. Hannah took it, and was pulled into a hug that lasted too long and involved too much back-patting.

"Did you see Jerry Dan's note?" she said, breaking off the embrace.

"That's what I came to talk to you about." He gestured at Jerry Dan. "Come on down here."

"In a minute. Almost finished tying this down."

Hannah heard the sound of drawers opening and shutting. "I bought a desk for my condo," she said.

"Hope you got a bargain. Thanks to some dot.com alum's donation, all the science buildings are being redone. Some of that stuff they're selling has been there since the university was founded." Glouster took off his cap, ran a hand through graying red hair. "I understand you're looking for a new expert witness..."

Hannah described the tests they needed done, and agreed to Glouster's hourly rate.

"Trial starts in a month," she said.

"Testing for uranium contamination can take some time. I'll need to get out to the dump sites right away."

"You won't have to," Hannah said. "Shelby told me Dr. Weller collected samples before he died. I'll get them over to you tomorrow."

Glouster frowned. "I usually collect my own."

"Sorry, but you can't. You need a permit from the tribe to be in that section of the rez. OTA is running about two weeks behind processing applications—not enough time before trial starts."

"No problem, then. I'll use Garth's samples."

Jerry Dan jumped down from the bed of the pickup and joined

them. Glouster hugged him as vigorously as he had Hannah.

"Thanks for setting this up," Glouster told him.

"Thanks for taking the job," Hannah said. "I'll get the samples and the retention letter to you tomorrow." They exchanged contact information, then Hannah and Jerry Dan got into the pickup.

As they drove out of the lot, Hannah thought about her new expert witness. He had looked disappointed, even peeved, at not being able to do his own fieldwork. According to Jerry Dan, Glouster usually worked by himself. Not that Hannah could fault this—she wasn't known for playing well with others. Still, after the confrontations with Franklin and Phyllis, she could do without any more people problems.

Chapter Nine

Hannah and Jerry Dan managed to get the desk up the stairs of her condo without herniating the walls or themselves. Once the massive piece was installed in her second bedroom, Hannah stepped back to admire it. The desk anchored the room, its well-used look imparting an air of experience, even competence. She might not be a trial lawyer, but she had the furniture of one.

"I'll get that set of race wheels from the garage before you leave," Hannah said. "They're really light, and going tubeless will make the ride a lot more comfortable."

"I appreciate the loan," Jerry Dan said. "You know, I never thought the kid who flunked rope in gym class would have a shot at winning something like this."

"A state championship in anything is pretty cool," Hannah agreed. She had more than a few cycling trophies stashed in the back of her closet, but her obsession with the past didn't extend to reliving old glories.

Jerry Dan took out his cell phone and looked at the time on the screen. "Ten o'clock! I didn't realize it was so late. Would you happen to have a bottle of water for the road?"

"Of course."

When Hannah came back from the kitchen with the requested bottle, Jerry Dan was tugging on one of the drawers in the new desk.

"What are you doing?" she said.

"Checking to make sure everything is still in alignment after all that moving around. All the drawers work fine except this one. It's stuck."

Hannah pulled on the knob. Nothing happened. Bracing her hand against the top, she gave it a good yank. The drawer opened about half an inch.

"Hold on," she said, and went back to the kitchen, returning a moment later with a table knife.

"I could come back tomorrow with some of my carpentry tools," Jerry Dan said. "You don't want to wreck your knife or your desk."

"I can buy another knife at Target for two dollars. And this desk looks like it's been through worse."

Hannah slid the knife into the opening and wiggled it around. "Feels like something is jammed in there." She poked around some more, then pulled on the knob again. The drawer opened, revealing a folded piece of paper.

"What's this?" Hannah said.

"Probably some paperwork from the auction people."

Jerry Dan reached for the paper, but Hannah picked it up first. She unfolded it.

Sketches of mountains surrounded a wavy-edged oval where small boats bobbed. Miniature coyotes and javelinas—desert wild pigs—trotted under saguaro cacti next to un-PC teepees. A dotted line wended from one corner to the other, and an arrow pointed to an *N* in the upper corner.

"Looks like a map," Hannah said.

Jerry Dan studied it over her shoulder. "It's the rez, near where we were today. Look—there's the fry bread stand."

A car smaller than her thumbnail was parked next to a hand-drawn rendition of the shack. Stick figures sat at tiny tables.

"Look at the dotted line—maybe it's directions to a gold mine," Jerry Dan said.

Hannah grinned. "Dr. Glouster told me the furniture being auctioned was from the science building. Engineering, mineralogy, geology—if there's gold out there, those are the people who would know how to find it."

Jerry Dan took the map and rotated it ninety degrees.

"I've got it! It's the map to—" He paused dramatically.

"Where?" Hannah said, unconsciously lowering her voice to match his.

"The grad students' next kegger!"

Hannah was annoyed, more at herself than Jerry Dan. For the barest of moments, her mind had entertained the possibility that the piece of paper really was a treasure map.

"I better hit the road. It's been a long day." Jerry Dan crumpled the map into a ball. "Where's your trash?"

"Give me that." Hannah took the piece of paper and smoothed it open on the desktop. "I'm keeping it."

Jerry Dan raised an eyebrow. "Why?"

"Because it's a work of art. Look at the drawings of the animals and the cacti. Besides, it's an omen." She pointed to the upper right quadrant. "This is where the mines are in Shelby's lawsuit."

"It already brought good luck. You found a new expert witness tonight," Jerry Dan said. Carrying his bottle of water, he left.

Hannah suppressed a yawn. She didn't know where Jerry Dan got his energy. Maybe he did have a chance of winning that orienteering race.

Thinking about that morning's events reminded Hannah that she had one more thing to do. Last summer had taught her to respect—fear, actually—the desert more than ever. Hannah had vowed never to go anywhere without a sleeping bag, first-aid supplies, flashlight, energy bars, and water in her car. As her emergency kit had been submerged along with the Subaru, she set about assembling another.

When she stowed the new bin of gear in the rental SUV fifteen minutes later, she noticed the bike wheels that Jerry Dan wanted to borrow leaning against the garage wall. Hannah considered calling him, but a glance at her cell phone showed it was almost eleven o'clock. As zealous as he was, Jerry Dan probably wouldn't be on his bike again until tomorrow. Delivery of the wheels could wait until then.

She hoisted the kayak onto the SUV's roof rack and went upstairs to take her second shower of the day—third, if she counted the lake.

Towel wrapped around her, she padded from the bath to the master bedroom. Her condo was an average-sized two-bedroom, but since Cooper had left, it seemed too big for one person. Solitude no longer held the same satisfaction for Hannah. For the first time she understood why people might not want to live alone.

Looking for sweats and a clean t-shirt to sleep in, Hannah opened the closet. On exactly one-half of the rod were a gaggle of hangers holding her clothes, mostly gym wear and suits for work. There weren't many dresses or skirts, and nothing longer than her knees. The other half, where Cooper's clothes had hung, was bare. Although she would deny it, part of her believed that as long as there was room for his stuff, their time apart was temporary. Reclaiming the space would mean the split was permanent.

Not caring that her hair was still wet, Hannah climbed into bed. She was almost immersed in the liquidness of sleep when the doorbell jarred her awake. Flailing like a drowning person, she sat up, her bad shoulder knotted with pain.

Cooper?

She turned on the light, blinking against its brightness.

Probably Jerry Dan, coming back for the bike wheels.

Nevertheless, she closed the closet door before stumbling down the stairs.

The peephole glass, scarred from dust storms, was impossible to see through.

"Who is it?" she called, pushing her still-damp hair behind her ears.

The response was muffled.

Hannah unbolted the door.

Chapter Ten

A teenaged girl stood before her, palms pressed together in front of her chest.

"Namaste," she said.

Before Hannah could respond, the girl produced a garland of bedraggled marigolds and draped it around Hannah's neck.

Even if she hadn't seen last month's emailed photo, Hannah would have recognized her half-sister.

Dark-eyed, with more gold in her skin than Hannah, Anuya Moore had the same willowy build, slight overbite, and classic nose that Hannah used to think was Italian. And there was no doubt from which side of her family Hannah got curly brown hair.

"A-Anuya, what are you—"

The rest of her question was cut off by a hug, one of the full on, heart-to-heart kind. Anuya's hair smelled like jasmine, but wasn't strong enough to mask the stale odor emanating from the wilted flowers. Hannah had read somewhere that gardeners planted marigolds to keep bugs away. Now her nose told her why.

Anuya released Hannah. "Hi, Sis! Face-to-face, at last."

"I didn't expect—"

"I got an interview at Bioscience! When you said we'd get together for the holidays, I thought it'd be okay."

"Holidays?"

Hannah had planned on making a trip to New York in late December. Never had she dreamed Anuya would come to Arizona, and certainly not in early November.

A crease appeared between Anuya's brows and the beginning of hurt shone in her eyes. They were the color of roasted coffee beans—dark brown flecked with black, just like Hannah's.

"Oh man, I am so stupid. You didn't really mean it, did you?"

"No, I did. It's just that—"

Anuya picked up a large backpack from the porch. A miniature stuffed monkey dangled from one of the zippers.

"Where's your bathroom? I gotta pee." Without waiting for an answer, she walked past Hannah and started up the stairs.

"Um, go right at the top." Hannah shut the front door and followed more slowly. She was sorry for bruising Anuya's feelings. But what worried her more was explaining Anuya to Shelby. *I'd like you to meet my new half-sister, the one I've never told you about.* So much for her newfound closeness with her older sibling.

Would she and Anuya turn out to be as distant? As she listened to the sound of water running in the bathroom, Hannah wondered how much they had in common. Did she like thunderstorms? Did frozen yogurt give her brain freeze? Did she hate old movies? We're not twins, Hannah reminded herself, not even full sisters. She twisted a piece of her hair around her finger.

Five minutes later Anuya emerged with a damp face and freshly glossed lips. She shrugged off her denim jacket to reveal a t-shirt printed with an outline of the Taj Mahal and the words *Got Outsourcing?* One section of the shirt's hem was tucked into the waistband of her cargo pants.

"How did you get here?" Hannah asked.

"Flew."

Hannah heard the unspoken *Duh.* Not even thirty years old, and already she was talking like an addled adult.

Anuya threw herself onto the sofa and looked around the room. "Holy cow! Where's all your stuff? Did your crib get cracked?"

Hannah didn't want to explain how her furniture—rather, the ashes of her furniture—had ended up in Boston. "I'm going through a minimalist stage."

"You don't even have a table and chairs."

"But I have a desk." Hannah perched on the edge of the

coffee table. "Why didn't you call me from the airport? I would have picked you up."

"I did, but your cell went straight to voicemail."

Hannah remembered switching her phone off at the auction, not wanting a call to interrupt bidding.

"I took the shuttle, but the guy dropped me off on the wrong block. All these houses look alike."

Hannah's townhouse was one red-tiled cookie cut from the same mold as hundreds of others, residences master-planned for uniformity, esthetics, and blandness. Composite counters, beige carpet, white walls, "personalized" from a list of add-ons. Nostalgic for the East Coast, Hannah had splurged on the working fireplace, even though it never really got cold enough to justify using it. Landscaping, exterior color, even the number and size of pets (cats, small dogs, and caged birds—no more than two of each or three total—permitted, no snakes or pygmy goats) were all regulated. Stepford housing for the new millennium.

"I got lost a few times when I first moved in," Hannah said.

The last thing Hannah wanted to do was make her half-sister feel unwelcome. She still remembered Shelby's unenthusiastic greeting upon her arrival after law school. Since learning of Anuya's existence two months ago, Hannah had imagined many times how this moment would play out. Past midnight in her condo wasn't one of the scenarios, but she was determined that they get off to a good start.

"It really is wonderful to see you," Hannah said. "And congratulations on Bioscience."

The new science and math-themed high school had garnered national attention. Students worked in labs rivaling those of universities and private research facilities. The curriculum was rigorous, and included internships with local researchers, hospitals, and college professors. The arts weren't neglected—students had to study either Spanish or Mandarin Chinese, and guitar or piano. Hannah thought it sounded like a haven for nerds.

Envisioning Anuya at high school reminded Hannah of her responsibilities. "We should call your mother, let her know—"

"How about some tunes? My iPod died an hour ago."

"Sure." Hannah got up, glad to have something to do.

Her MP3 player had gone into the lake, but Cooper's was still in the portable speaker. She intended to give it back to him… after she listened to the songs on it a few more times. Country, jazz, old school rap, newer pop—she listened to each one, trying to figure out what it was in the melody or lyrics that had made him choose it. Now she scrolled through his playlist and, after a moment's hesitation, dialed up some Ravi Shankar.

As the first strains of the sitar tinkled through the speakers, Anuya made a face. "When you come to my house, do you want me to play the Dixie Chicks?"

She got up from the sofa and prowled the room, examining Hannah's few possessions. A bike helmet was tried on, a jacket draped over the chair was scrutinized for fashion potential, the flat screen TV (Cooper's) was met with a nod of approval. Hannah changed the music, glad all the photos of her and Cooper were digitally stashed in her laptop.

At fourteen years old, Anuya was starting to look like a woman, but the evidence of childhood still lingered—frayed yarn friendship bracelets around thin wrists, the plastic flower on the elastic that held her thick black hair, pen doodles on her rubber clogs. Even so, her sister had an air of street smarts that Hannah doubted she would ever attain. Product of growing up on the urban East Coast or the other side of the DNA helix?

Anuya sat back down on the sofa.

Hannah cleared her throat. "We should get a few things straight."

"You mean like who does the dishes and not hogging the bathroom?" Anuya's accent was New York, with South Asian around the edges.

"Not exactly."

Anuya reached for her backpack and toyed with the little monkey charm. "This is Hanuman, the god who gets rid of people's troubles. He's my good luck charm."

"We need to—"

Anuya fixed Hannah with her dark eyes. "You shouldn't make friends with an elephant keeper unless you have room to entertain an elephant."

Hannah could feel the beginning of a headache knocking at her temples. "What?"

"It's a Hindu saying. You shouldn't have invited me if you didn't want me to come." Anuya thrust her chin upward and looked at Hannah from under lowered lids.

Seeing the pose, Hannah suddenly understood what was going on. She wasn't so far into the adult world to not recognize when she was being played. Picking up her purse, she took out her cell phone.

"Let's call your mom and tell her you got here okay. Then we can talk." Hannah opened the phone. "What's the number?"

Anuya's chin lowered slightly. "She's asleep. I'll call her in the morning."

"I think we should call her now." Hannah reached into her purse again and took out her pocket pc. "Didn't you email me your number? Let's see—K, L, M…here it is."

Hannah started tapping on the screen with the stylus and Anuya capitulated.

"Okay, okay, she doesn't know I'm here." Anuya folded her arms across her chest and dropped her gaze to the carpet.

"Where does she think you are?"

"On break with Christie in California."

"Anuya! You—" Hannah stopped, remembering her own spring-break trip to Paris when she was a junior at boarding school. She had told Richard that she had a head cold, and that the doctor advised against flying to Arizona. Oddly, her schoolmate who had organized the jaunt was named Christie, too, though Anuya's friend probably spelled her name with a lot more *Y*s. She put away the phone.

"It's past midnight. We'll call in the morning."

"Thank Krishna! You're the best, Sis!" Anuya's jangling bracelets sounded like a tiny alarm as she jumped up to envelop Hannah in another hug.

Hannah felt a stinging behind her eyes. She blinked and extracted herself from Anuya's grip.

"There's no guest bedroom, but I've got an extra sleeping bag. You okay on the sofa?" In addition to the emergency kit in the car, her few forced overnights in the desert had made Hannah vow never to be without spare warmth again. When the local camping store went out of business, she had bought a half dozen sleeping bags at discount.

"Yeah, sure. I sleep on my friend's couch at least once a week."

Hannah started to ask why, then reconsidered. She thought it would be best to get to know Anuya by peeling off layers, rather than cutting directly into the heart of the onion. Fewer tears, anyway.

She laid the sleeping bag on the couch, wincing at the pain that stabbed through her shoulder. Anuya noticed.

"What's wrong with your arm?"

"Sports injury." The story of how her shoulder had been injured—and re-injured—wasn't one she wanted Anuya to know. "Are you hungry?"

"Yes! I ate only nuts on the plane. All the other food was gross—nothing vegetarian."

"How about some tomato soup?" Hannah had been surprisingly pleased to learn that she and her half-sister shared the same dietary preference.

Anuya shrugged. "Sounds okay."

"So you were raised Hindu?" Hannah said as she looked for the can opener. Anuya hadn't talked religion in their emails. In fact, they were still in the *What are your favorite movies and food?* phase.

"Mostly, with a little Baptist from Dad thrown in at Christmas and Easter."

Their father had been Baptist? Hannah imagined herself as a little girl dressed in white lace sitting on a hard church pew, a gospel choir singing in the background.

"I don't really believe in all those gods, not like my mom does—I mean, there's like three hundred million of 'em!" Anuya grinned. "She thinks *holy cow* is like swearing." Anuya sobered. "But there are some things that are true. Like burrus."

"What's a burru?"

"A bad spirit. My grandmother told me about them. They look like big dinosaurs and can eat things—even people—in one gulp."

"Really." Hannah wondered how Anuya reconciled attending one of the country's most scientifically oriented high schools with a belief in evil spirits.

"It's true! My grandmother wouldn't lie about something like that!"

Hannah scrutinized the earnest face, thought she saw a faint smile. Still, she had the sense that if Anuya didn't believe, she didn't rule out the possibility. Maybe her sister—with her *Namaste* and marigolds—wasn't all that different from the Hispanic teenager in the hiked-up plaid skirt and white shirt knotted at the waist who hedged her bets by half-genuflecting when passing a church. Irrational belief? Or better safe than sorry?

"I'm sure your grandmother is very wise."

"Some of the things people do are just dumb," Anuya said. "Like my brother. I mean, he went to biz school, but he still got his wedding date okayed by the astrologer."

Hannah felt the blood drain from her face. "A brother? You never said anything about—" Just how many half-siblings—and half-cousins—did she have?

"I didn't want to freak you out. He was away at school when I was growing up, and now he works in New York and India, so I never see him much. That's why it was so cool to find out about you."

The parallels in their sibling situations weren't lost on Hannah. She felt both gratification and guilt as her thoughts went between Shelby and Anuya.

Hannah set two bowls of soup and a plate of food on the counter. Olives, baby carrots, her favorite crackers—cheddar bunnies—and, despite Anuya's admonition, a few squares of dark chocolate. *It's a health food, not candy*. And right now Hannah could use the sugar hit.

"Ready to eat?" she said.

Anuya surveyed the food. "Do you have an extra plate?"

"Sure." Mystified, Hannah got one out of the cabinet and handed it to her.

"What's really weird is that my brother's, like, only a year younger than you are," Anuya said as she transferred three olives, two carrots, and a dozen cheddar bunnies from the platter onto the plate.

Conceived right after Elizabeth died. Mind reeling, Hannah ate a piece of chocolate, then another.

Anuya picked up a cracker, looked at it closely, then dropped it onto the plate as though it were poison.

"It's a bunny! I thought you were vegetarian."

"*Bunny* is just the brand name." Hannah knew Brahmins were strict vegetarians for anti-cruelty reasons, and hoped she had closed her closet door that morning. She really wasn't up for a lecture on leather shoes.

Anuya took a tentative bite, chewed, then popped the rest of the cracker into her mouth. "They're pretty good," she admitted through a mouthful of crumbs.

"Have the rest." Hannah pushed the platter toward her.

Anuya wrinkled her nose. "It's *jhoota*."

"Jay-whatta?" Hannah said.

"Unclean."

"Unclean? The crackers are straight from the box! And the carrots were washed this—"

"That isn't what I mean. You know about castes, right?"

Hannah nodded. She had a vague understanding of the strata of Indian society from art films.

"My mother's family is Brahmin, the upper one. When she was a kid, only other Brahmins could prepare their food. And they didn't just have to, like, wash their hands first, they had to take a *bath* before they went into the kitchen."

"I'm afraid I don't have any Brahmins on staff," Hannah said. "And I prefer showers to the tub."

Anuya looked affronted. "My mother knew things couldn't be the same in America. So she changed the tradition a little bit. One of them is not eating off other people's plates. I know there isn't anything wrong with the food, but I can't help it."

Hannah thought of Richard's childhood warnings against "buying food on the street" that had kept her from ever tasting a New York pretzel. "I understand."

"Mom's not weird," Anuya said. "Just Hindu. And most of what she says is harmless, like eating certain spices to keep your body in balance." She picked up another cheddar bunny. "Although you know, turmeric would make your sore shoulder feel better."

"I'll keep it in mind," Hannah said. She dipped a carrot stick into her soup.

"Oh my Krishna! Dad used to do that!"

Hannah paused, the carrot halfway to her mouth. Dipping vegetables into soup was genetic? What about how she brushed her teeth, curled up in a chair to read, liked music from the seventies? How many of her habits were predetermined by people she had never met?

"Mom made him be vegetarian. Told him it would be good karma for reincarnation."

"Do you believe in that?" Hannah asked. "That how you are in this life determines how it goes in the next?"

"No," Anuya said. After a moment, she added, "Not really. But it doesn't hurt to be careful."

Hannah wondered if intent or results counted more. If the latter, she'd better start being nicer to bugs. With the way things were going, she had a fair chance of joining their ranks if there was a next time around.

Anuya ate a pickle. "Why are you vegetarian?"

To annoy Richard. During her breaks from boarding school, Richard would take Hannah and Shelby to a local fish and steakhouse for dinner. It was an old-fashioned place, with cracked red-leather booths, smoke-stained walls, and ancient waiters. Hannah would stare miserably at the red juice leaking from a cut of meat, trying to ignore the faint smell of fish, while Shelby—who lived at home and went to day school—talked nonstop about the things she and Richard had done or were going to do when Hannah was away. In eighth grade Hannah had declared her conversion to vegetarianism and the restaurant outings had mercifully stopped.

"I don't like meat and fish very much," she said. "Want some tea?"

"Got any chai? Plain tea sucks."

"Sorry, no," Hannah said. She filled two mugs from the tap and put them into the microwave, then opened the cupboard.

She scanned the labels on the canisters. "Regular green… green with jasmine…decaf green."

"Regular."

The microwave dinged. Hannah removed the mugs and dropped a teabag into each. "Sugar?"

Anuya took the offered packets, dumping enough of the white granules into the mug to make her blood sugar drop around her ankles. It made Hannah's teeth ache to watch her. But as she sipped from her mug, Hannah thought Anuya was right about the beverage's wimpiness. Right now she wished the *T* she were drinking had *G &* in front of it.

Anuya set down her mug and yawned. Hannah tightened her jaw to avoid catching it.

"Tired?" she asked.

"Yeah," Anuya said. She got up, stacked the dishes into the sink, then walked over to her backpack and took out a baggie holding a toothbrush and toothpaste.

"I'll get you a pillow," Hannah said.

She returned with the least-lumpy of the collection on her bed and a clean pillowcase. Anuya was lighting a small candle on the coffee table. She then shucked her jeans, giving Hannah a glimpse of *Hello Kitty!* underpants, and slipped into the sleeping bag.

Hannah gave Anuya the pillow and looked at the candle. Was her half-sister afraid of the dark?

"I think I've got a nightlight around here."

"The candle is for Diwali." Seeing Hannah's puzzled expression, Anuya added, "Festival of lights? Big Indian holiday? On the night of the new moon you light candles and leave the front door open so Laxmi can come in and count your money."

"Laxmi?"

"The goddess of wealth. If you've said your prayers, she'll double your money."

"That sounds nice, but I don't know about leaving the front door open. How about if I don't turn the deadbolt all the way?"

"Diwali's also when you're supposed to visit relatives. When you said we'd get together over the holidays, that's why I thought you meant now." Anuya pulled down the corners of her mouth. "Should've known you were on the white people's calendar."

For a moment Hannah felt politically incorrect for assuming *holiday* meant Thanksgiving or Christmas, then caught herself. Her half-sister may profess to be a non-believer, but apparently she wasn't above using Hindu traditions and beliefs to get her way.

She smoothed the pillowcase. "I'm glad you decided to visit."

"It's my dharma." Anuya pulled off her bracelets. "The right thing to do. Keeps things cool in the cosmos."

She removed her oversized hoop earrings and dumped them on the coffee table, then rubbed an earlobe between her fingers.

"Man, those clip-ons hurt." She wriggled around in the sleeping bag, trying to get comfortable.

"Why don't you get your ears pierced?" Hannah asked. "I thought everyone did it these days."

"Everyone white, you mean. Indians and blacks have been into piercing for a thousand years. My mom has been after me since I was twelve to get my nose done. 'Just a little gold stud, Anuya. Will make you so beautiful.'" Anuya smiled impishly. "But I won't do it. Ears, belly, eyebrow—no way." The grin became wider. "Drives her crazy."

Hannah smiled. *So teenage rebellion is cross-cultural.* Find out what a parent wants and do the opposite. She leaned over to turn back the edge of the sleeping bag so the zipper was away from Anuya's face. The teenager looked up at her.

"Is it really okay that I'm here?"

Hannah smoothed a strand of glossy black hair off Anuya's forehead. "Yes. Now go to sleep. We have to get up early to call your mom."

Anuya wobbled her head in a way that simultaneously looked like a nod of *yes* as well as a shaking to signify *no*. Hannah recalled the move. She figured it still meant the same as when she had used it—*okay, I hear you, sure*. Not to be confused with *I agree*.

"I almost forgot." Anuya sat up, dragged her backpack close, and rummaged inside. "Here." She held up a small box wrapped in gold tissue paper and topped with a bedraggled bow.

"You didn't need to bring me anything," Hannah said.

"It's the Hindu way," Anuya said. "Open it."

Hannah untied the ribbon and used her fingernail to loosen the tape without tearing the paper. When the last piece of tape was unstuck, she unfolded the paper to reveal a small carved wooden box.

"It's beautiful." The box was sandalwood, decorated with carved elephants. Their raised trunks showed the marks of the craftsman's knife.

"My brother brought it back from his last trip to India," Anuya said. "I have one just like it on my desk. It's where I keep, you know, special stuff."

Hannah held the box close to her nose and inhaled. The fragrant wood smelled like a pencil sharpener, a scent that she liked. It reminded her of the start of the school year. She had always looked forward to September—a new beginning with teachers and friends, the end of the summer in Arizona with Richard and Shelby.

"Thank you," she said, the words catching in her throat.

Anuya lay down again and pulled the sleeping bag close around her.

"See you in the morning, Sis," she said, her voice muffled by the down.

"See you." Hannah got to her feet.

She wasn't one to cry, but her allergies had been acting up lately, and she didn't want Anuya to get the wrong idea.

Chapter Eleven

Tuesday, November 3

Hannah woke to the buzz of the alarm. She slapped the button on top of the clock, wishing she could sleep in. It had been a full twenty-four hours—the car going into the lake…the pretrial hearing…the furniture auction…the arrival of…

She sat up in bed. Anuya!

Hannah walked into the living room in her pajama bottoms and camisole to find Anuya sitting cross-legged on the floor, eyes closed and her hands resting on her knees. The air smelled sour. *Another candle?*

Hannah stood quietly and studied her sister's features, comparing them with her own. Surely their wavy hair was from their father, along with their broad shoulders and dusky skin. After that? She wasn't sure.

Anuya opened one eye. "I'm meditating. Wanna try it?"

"Not my thing," Hannah said.

Heeding the suggestion of a cycling coach, Hannah had dropped by a meditation center several times. But her overactive brain and underdeveloped sense of patience made fidgeting inevitable, and she had always quit before the session was over. Her route to nirvana would have to be a more active one.

"I was about done anyhow." Anuya rose gracefully from her sitting position, the bells on her ankle bracelet tinkling. Hannah noticed a silver ring adorning a brown toe.

"By the way, you snore," Anuya said.

Hannah was indignant. "I do not."

"Do too. Worse than Dad."

Her birth father snored? Was anything unique to her?

"I don't snore," Hannah said, less forcefully this time.

Anuya propped her hands on her hips. "If you're asleep, how would you know if you snore or not?"

Because Cooper would have told me. Remembering the warmth of his body snugged against hers, Hannah felt heat of a different kind rise in her.

"Because I always sleep on my side," she said. "When's your Bioscience interview?"

"Tomorrow."

What was she going to do with Anuya all day? With the trial set, she couldn't miss work. And how was she going to keep her away from Shelby?

"I'm hungry," Anuya said.

"Let's see what I've got."

The odor was stronger in the kitchen. The garland of marigolds lay on the counter, the edges of the blooms already turning brown.

"Phew! Those things really stink," Anuya said. She scooped up the wreath of flowers. "Where's your trash?"

"Wait! Not yet."

Shelby had never sent her flowers. Hannah filled a salad bowl with water and floated the garland on top, then opened the door to the pantry.

"I've got instant oatmeal and microwave dinners. Or we can go out for something."

"Oatmeal. My hair looks too funny to go anywhere." Anuya gestured to the espresso machine on the counter. "Can I have a latté?"

"Sorry, but I'm out of coffee. We can grab some on the way."

Like the MP3 player, Cooper had left behind the espresso machine when he moved out. Hannah had never reminded him about the stainless contraption, secretly viewing it as an eight-hundred-dollar promise to return.

She set out two bowls and spoons, then took four packets of maple-cinnamon flavored oatmeal from the box in the cupboard. She was about to tear them open and dump them into the bowls, but hesitated, remembering what Anuya had said last night.

"Just pour them in," Anuya said, as though reading Hannah's mind. "I told you—my mom's the religious one, not me."

Hannah added tap water to the cereal and put the bowls into the microwave.

Anuya boosted herself onto the kitchen counter. "Why don't you have a boyfriend?"

Hannah wiped up some spilled oatmeal, cleaning more of the counter than was necessary. "I'm taking a break from dating."

"You need to get married soon. Otherwise you'll be too old. Your family should have…" She sucked in her lower lip. "Sorry," she said. "I forgot."

"It's okay," Hannah said. While there were many reasons she wished she had known her birth parents, arranging her marriage wasn't one of them.

Anuya's face brightened. "I know! I'll find you someone."

First her secretary, now her sister. "Do you let your mother choose your boyfriends?"

"That's totally different from a husband."

Hannah looked at Anuya. "You're kidding, right? You'd let your mom choose who you'd marry?"

Anuya shrugged. "Why not? I'll make up my own mind when it comes to things like college and a job. But a husband is forever. Why wouldn't I want help? Otherwise it might be like when I painted my room purple."

"An arranged marriage is like a purple bedroom?" Hannah said.

Anuya rolled her eyes. "My mother and my aunties told me painting my room purple would be a bad idea. And they were right. I don't want to end up with a purple husband."

Hannah had a vision of Cooper with Violet-Beauregarde-hued skin. "What about—um—romance?"

Anuya's expression became sly. "You mean sex?"

"I mean love."

"If someone's a good match, you fall in love with them. Look at the Taj Mahal—a king built it for his wife, and they were in an arranged marriage. And what about the *Kama Sutra*? That book was written for people in arranged marriages, and it—"

"Okay, time to call your mom," Hannah said as a memory of a particularly intimate moment with Cooper warmed her cheeks. Maybe Anuya was right. Given the mess that was Hannah's love life so far, perhaps a date picked by someone else was the way to go. But she was drawing the line at Clementine's foot guy.

"We can't call her," Anuya said with big-eyed innocence. "She's at work."

Hannah had forgotten about the two-hour time difference. "Okay, we'll ring her there."

"She's not supposed to get personal calls."

Hannah put both hands on her hips, then let them drop as she recognized the pose of the scolding adult. "We have to tell her where you are, Anuya."

"Not right away," Anuya pleaded. "I told her not to expect me to call for a few days. If she finds out I'm not with Christy, she'll make me go home."

Hannah had a flash of insight. "Does she even know about your Bioscience interview?"

Anuya cut her eyes away. "I wanted to see if I got in before I told her."

Another thought occurred to Hannah, this one more terrible. "Does she know about *me*?"

Anuya looked affronted. "Course she does. Even though he wasn't Hindu, Dad always put an extra chair at the table during Diwali. You do that for family members who aren't there. He and Mom didn't say anything, but I knew it was for my sister."

"If they didn't talk about me, how did you know?"

"My name," Anuya said. Her voice went soft. "It's Hindu for *second daughter*."

Something tightened in Hannah's chest, making it tough for her to draw a breath. Anuya clasped her hands under her chin.

"Please, Hannah, don't tell her. It's only for a few days—I gotta be back for school next Wednesday. Don't you want to get to know me better?"

Hannah couldn't suppress the happiness that washed through her. Shelby had never been this nice. But thinking of her other sister reminded Hannah of her problem.

"*If* I let you keep your secret," Hannah said, stressing the first word, "then you have to keep mine."

"Anything!" Anuya said, bouncing on her toes.

"You can't tell anybody we're related. Especially Shelby."

"Shelby?" Anuya stopped bouncing. "You mean your other sister?" Her face darkened. "Is that because you're ashamed of me? You don't want your white family to know you've got a brown—"

"No!" Hannah reached out her hands. "I haven't told her about you because we don't really get along, at least not until recently. And she's been through some—" Hannah hesitated, not wanting to tell Anuya about the events that led to Shelby's rehab stay—"stressful stuff, and I don't think this is the best time to break the news to her."

Anuya reluctantly allowed Hannah to grasp her hands. "So who am I supposed to be?"

Hannah thought briefly. "The daughter of a friend from back East, out here for a Bioscience interview." She squeezed Anuya's hands. "Just for a few days. But before you leave, we'll tell both Shelby and your mom."

"Okay."

The tell-tale smile tugged at the corner of Anuya's mouth again, making Hannah realize that her indignation had been feigned, an act to distract Hannah from calling her mother. Her half-sister was turning out to be a cross between a slightly self-absorbed, sophisticated American teen and a traditional South Asian dutiful daughter. But Hannah didn't care. She wanted

Anuya to stay. She took a last swallow of tea and dumped the rest into the sink.

"I have to get ready for work. Do you want to stay at the condo until I get back? I could call a cab, have it take you to a mall in Scottsdale, or the movies."

"I want to hang with you. Don't worry, I won't be bored."

Anuya's boredom was the least of Hannah's worries. But her sister's pleading expression made her capitulate.

"Shelby and my secretary"—*my nosy, meddling secretary*—"will be there. You remember our agreement?"

"Yeah, yeah. I'm somebody else's kid." Anuya jumped down off the counter. "Can I bring my iPod?"

Hannah cleared her throat, louder this time. Clementine raised her head from her desk and blinked. Seeing Hannah, she picked up a folder and fanned herself.

"Whew! Guess I left the top off the Wite-Out. You probably got here just in time."

"You were sleeping again," Hannah said.

"I was not. You call Cooper yet?"

"For someone who's supposed to be studying civil liberties, you don't have much of a grasp on the idea of privacy, do you?"

"Can I help it if I know you better than you know yourself?" Clementine fluffed her bangs. "Who's this?"

"Clementine, meet Anuya," Hannah said. "She's the daughter of a friend, out here for a Bioscience interview."

"That genius-kid school?" Clementine said.

Anuya scowled. "I'm not a kid."

Clementine eyed the teenager's sequin-trimmed tan sweater over a pink and brown t-shirt that read *JLo Rocks* over a graphic of the singer. Hannah had vetoed the yellow crew that read *I'm a real Indian.* "Cute top. I love Jennifer Lopez."

Anuya thawed a bit. "Me, too! Which song is your favorite?"

Clementine waved dismissively. "I don't care about her music. I just love her because her butt looks big. Pants, dresses, whatever she wears. And it looks super-big in shorts."

Anuya giggled.

"Clementine, would you get this delivered to the frame shop?" Hannah said, taking a large envelope from her briefcase. She didn't want her sister and her secretary getting too chummy. Clementine was a pro at prying secrets loose and even better at broadcasting them.

"What is it?"

"A map Jerry Dan found in the desk I bought last night."

"You went furniture shopping?" Clementine said. "And who's Jerry Dan?"

"I thought you didn't have a boyfriend," Anuya said.

"Does that mean you don't want to see the emails that came today?" Clementine said.

"Whoa!" Hannah held up a hand. "Jerry Dan is a guy I know from cycling. We ran into each other yesterday and I said I'd give him some training tips. He dropped by the firm yesterday, and mentioned the furniture auction at ASU. I decided to go and ended up buying a desk. The map was in one of the drawers."

"Can I see it?" Anuya asked.

Hannah unclasped the envelope. "I want to have it framed as a gift for Shelby. It shows the part of the rez that's involved in her lawsuit." She thought of the judge's order. *Make that our lawsuit.*

"And when was the last time your sister gave *you* a present?" Clementine muttered.

The bike that was now Jerry Dan's. Hannah shot a warning look at her secretary, then glanced at Anuya. But the girl was absorbed in studying the drawing.

"That looks like a trail," Anuya said, pointing to the dotted line on the drawing. Her voice rose with excitement. "Aren't you glad I lit that candle? This has gotta be from Laxmi. I bet it's a treasure map, like to a gold mine or something."

"Lax who?" Clementine said.

First Jerry Dan, now Anuya. "People have been looking for gold in Arizona for a long time," Hannah said. "Without much success, I'm afraid."

"Then it's a map to something else," Anuya said. "Maybe robbers stole something and hid it, and these are the directions to where it is."

Clementine looked thoughtful. "That's a possibility. I remember when my Uncle Sal—"

"Laxmi couldn't have left anything, because I didn't unlock the door," Hannah said. "It's probably just some geology student's sketches from a field trip."

"Who's Laxmi?" Clementine said.

"A Hindu god—" Anuya began.

"We need to get to work." Hannah knew Clementine's curiosity could go from Hinduism to Anuya's ethnicity to her half-sister's parentage in nanoseconds.

"You can say that again."

Hannah tensed at the familiar voice. She turned to see Shelby walking toward them, her loose, flower-printed dress swirling around her knees. White-blond hair swept her shoulders and the pale skin of her bare arms gleamed like pearls.

"Is that your sister?" Anuya whispered.

"The resident cactus," Clementine said under her breath. "Welcomes you with open arms, then sticks you to death."

Hannah's initial shock had been replaced by a weakening that almost made her stagger. The idea of Shelby and Anuya together, each a different half of her, was overwhelming. For a moment, she felt like an aerialist who had lost her nerve in the middle of the tightrope, torn between moving forward and going back. She gathered herself.

"Remember our deal," she whispered to Anuya. Getting the bobblehead waggle in response only ratcheted up her alarm.

A good offense... "Things will be fine, Shelby. The government's conceded liability. All we have to prove is damages."

"Which we can't do without an expert. I just got off the phone with Franklin. He still hasn't found anyone. And—thanks to you—we have a trial date, which means we're running out of time. If—"

"We have an expert," Hannah said. "The guy from the lake—

Dr. Glouster. I met with him last night and he's ready to go. All we need to do is send him the samples Weller collected."

Shelby pressed the tips of her fingers to her temples, closed her eyes, and took a deep breath. She opened her eyes again and looked at Hannah.

"Why do you keep doing this?"

"What do you mean? I thought you'd be happy. We have an expert!"

"An expert we had to find because you wouldn't settle the case! Just once you might think about not taking things to an extreme."

Hannah felt her skin grow warm. "I was doing the right thing."

"There's right, and there's really right, Hannah. That's how you and I are different. If a neighbor pounds at the door at 2 AM screaming that his house is on fire, I'd call 911. You'd run across the street and try to put out the fire with a garden hose, completely unaware that you're not wearing pants!"

"I'd call my girlfriends to let them know some cute firemen were coming over," Clementine said.

Anuya giggled. "In my neighborhood you'd think the guy was drunk and make sure the deadbolt was on."

Shelby looked at Anuya. "I don't think we've met. Are you one of the plaintiffs?"

Anuya bristled. "I'm not that kind of Indi—"

"Anuya's the daughter of a friend from law school," Hannah said. "She's out here for a Bioscience interview."

"Oh," Shelby said. "Well, good luck."

"Thanks," Anuya said tersely. Seeing Hannah's warning look, she added, "Uh, nice perfume."

Same scent as yesterday, Hannah realized. Shelby was known—infamous, even—for her fickleness when it came to men. Hannah wondered if this was a subtle signal that Jake's star was on the wane...and Cooper's on the rise again. The flowery smell suddenly seemed overpowering. Hannah felt queasy.

"How nice of you to say," Shelby said sweetly, then frowned

at Hannah. "Just hurry up and get the samples to this guy."

"I'm taking Anuya on a tour of the firm," Clementine announced. "C'mon, let's grab a soda," she said to Anuya. "Then I'll show you the javelina tracks in the parking lot."

"What's a javelina?" Anuya asked.

"Wild pig. They're like the outlaw bikers of the desert—can really mess you up if you make them mad. That is, if they see you. They're as blind as Mr. Magoo. But don't worry—I have a gun."

"Way cool!" Anuya said. "Can I see—"

"No!" Hannah said. "Clementine, you absolutely cannot—"

Hannah's secretary raised her hands in a placating gesture.

"Just kidding. I don't carry at work. This place is pure white-bread. If any thugs did show up, they'd be looking to off a lawyer, not a lowly secretary."

Anuya giggled.

"No guns," Hannah said. *So much for Anuya and Clementine not getting too chummy.* Knowing her secretary lived by the maxim that everything not specifically prohibited was permitted, Hannah said, "No smoking, no alcohol, no drugs, no—"

"I don't take drugs!" Anuya said.

"And the only thing I'm hooked on is phonics," Clementine said. "I get your drift, Boss. We'll be fine." She frowned. "What kind of name is Anuya, anyway?"

"Hindu," Anuya said.

"From India?"

"Brooklyn."

Clementine beamed. "Get out! I'm from south Jersey! So are you sneaking into clubs yet? If you need a fake ID, I can hook you up—"

"Clementine!" Hannah said.

"Who's Mr. Magoo?" Anuya said.

"Girl, don't you watch the Cartoon Channel? There's a TV in the lunchroom."

"See you later," Anuya said. She followed Clementine's wide hips down the hall.

"*A gun?* Hannah, you have to fire her!" Shelby said when Clementine and Anuya were out of hearing range.

The feud between Hannah's secretary and Shelby was longstanding, continually fueled by Clementine. Usually her sister was able to roll with Clementine's provocation. But today she seemed rattled.

"Is everything okay?" Hannah asked.

"Of course everything's okay."

"You seem a little tense."

"Having an employee who's armed and dangerous doesn't make you nervous?"

"Clementine would be dangerous with or without a gun," Hannah said, making a mental promise to find out just when and where Clementine packed heat. She feared her secretary considered stashing a gun in her glove box outside the definition of *carrying at work*.

"That girl—Anuya?—looks familiar," Shelby said. "Have I met her mother?"

"I doubt it," Hannah said. "Let's go find those ore samples."

An hour later they had gone through all the case materials, but had come up empty-handed.

"Those stupid rocks aren't here!" Shelby said. "I called Franklin's secretary. They don't have them either."

Hannah was reading from the beginning of the correspondence file. "This is interesting. That Phyllis person hired Franklin to litigate the case."

"And he brought Daddy in because he didn't have the resources to handle it by himself. So?"

"Wonder why the tribe didn't choose a better-established law firm to start with?"

"You mean like us—the firm that lost the rocks?" Shelby sat down heavily in one of the conference room chairs. Hannah thought she looked tired.

"Sometimes I wonder if it's a good idea to work with your

family," Shelby said. "On the one hand, you know them too well. But then something happens, and you realize you don't know them at all."

Hannah shut the file, wondering what her sister was getting at. *Elizabeth? Anuya?*

"I could call the lab and ask for a copy of Weller's report," she said. "That would give Glouster something to work with until we find the missing samples."

"Do it," Shelby said.

The intercom buzzed. "Jerry Dan Kovacs to see Ms. Dain," said the disembodied voice.

Hannah depressed the *Talk* button. "Tell him I'll be right there."

"Isn't that the guy who jumped into the lake with you yesterday?" Shelby said.

"He's here to pick up some bike wheels. I'll call the lab as soon as he's gone."

Jerry Dan's bike, Anuya, their mother's indiscretions—Hannah was feeling the weight of keeping so many secrets from Shelby. But she didn't have a choice, at least for the moment.

"Clementine, call Desert Mountain Labs and ask them to email us a copy of Weller's report on the ore samples in Shelby's case," she said as she passed her secretary's desk.

"Sure thing, Boss."

Hannah retrieved the bike wheels from her office, then noticed the room was empty.

"Where's Anuya?"

"In the reception area talking to that Jerry Dan and looking at the map you found in your desk. I photocopied it before I sent it to the framers. Speaking of maps, these topos were just delivered from Rowley's office."

Hannah took the rolled-up sheaf of papers and headed for the reception area.

Anuya and Jerry Dan sat in the lobby looking at the paper open on Anuya's lap.

"The cowboys who kidnapped the Indian princess demanded

a ransom of gold," Jerry Dan said as Hannah approached. "Her dad paid it, but the cowboys wouldn't give her back. So her dad asked for the help of a friendly monster. The monster rescued the princess and took the gold away from the cowboys and hid it. The princess' dad put a curse on the cowboys and any white people who went looking for the gold. No one's ever found it."

"A *monster*? Sounds bogus," Anuya said.

"The Tohono O'odham who told me the story swears it's true."

Anuya looked unconvinced.

"What are you two talking about?" Hannah said.

"Howdy, Hannah! I'm trying to talk Anuya into prospecting for gold with me. I figure she qualifies as an 'Indian' princess, so I'll be protected from the curse."

Anuya held up a small chrome disc. "He showed me how to work his orienteering compass on your map."

"You really need to see the topology to plot a course," Jerry Dan said.

"Like this?" Hannah unrolled the topo Clementine had given her. Jerry Dan and Anuya bent over the drawing.

"What do those numbers mean?" Anuya asked.

"Elevations." Jerry Dan laid the photocopy on top of the larger map. "Let's see if we can match any of the landmarks to those on the map from the desk." He pushed the paper around the topo. "Look at that—they're the same!"

Anuya compared the landmarks on the topo to the ones on the photocopied sketch. "Holy Krishna! You're right."

Hannah looked over her sister's shoulder. The sketch from her desk did match the topo. And it included the area where the government had dumped uranium.

"The map to the princess' gold," Anuya whispered.

"Finding it would score you some points with Bioscience," Jerry Dan said.

Hannah looked at two pairs of eyes gleaming with speculator's hope.

"The answer is *no,*" she said. "Even if there is treasure hidden on the rez, it's going to have to stay there. Non-tribe members aren't allowed in that area."

"You're right." Jerry Dan stood. "Thanks for the loan of the wheels." He pointed at Anuya. "Any time you want an orienteering lesson, let me know." With a "*Shalom*, y'all," he left.

"Ms. Dain?" the receptionist said as Hannah rolled up the topo map. "Your secretary wants me to tell you to stay away from your office because it's infested." The woman frowned. "Should I call pest control?"

"No, thank you. I'll handle it."

She was going to have to talk to Clementine about her latest euphemism for "Shelby is looking for you." At least *bug-infested office* was an improvement over *viper in the house.*

Anuya in tow, Hannah walked down the hallway to find Shelby pacing beside Clementine's cubicle.

"I've been looking for you."

Hannah put on a smile. "I'm in hiding from everyone who's happy. You're with a great guy who thinks you look good in jeans, so that includes you."

Anuya giggled and Shelby flushed. "If that's your idea—" She collected herself. "Ms. Juan is on the line. She refuses to talk to me—says she'll only speak with you." Her sister sounded annoyed.

"Ms. Who?" Hannah said.

"Juan, Phyllis Juan—the tribe's litigation liaison?"

The snarky O'odham woman who had been at the hearing. "Clementine, would you please show Anuya to an empty computer terminal?"

"Sure." Clementine winked at Anuya. "Sorry, but our network is controlled. No porn or online gaming."

The phone on Clementine's desk started to beep, a reminder that a call was on hold.

Shelby shooed Hannah into her office. Hannah hit the *Speaker* button on the phone.

"Ms. Juan?"

"I've just come from the tribal council meeting. On my

recommendation, the council unanimously passed a resolution endorsing settlement of the uranium litigation."

Shelby flashed two thumbs up. Hannah turned in her chair so she wouldn't have to look at her sister.

"As the judge said yesterday, Ms. Juan, only the plaintiffs can decide whether to settle. My instructions are to go to trial."

"Lawyers are supposed to advise their clients, Ms. Dain. Isn't it your responsibility to recommend a settlement?"

"If I think it would be good under the circumstances, yes. Liability has been admitted by the defendants, but the proposed settlement is much less than that offered in similar cases. Also, my clients say they want their day in court."

"Ms. Dain, do you understand that I am the litigation liaison for the tribe?"

"Yes."

"And therefore in the position of deciding which outside law firms will handle tribal legal matters?"

"If by that you mean do I understand that Dain & Daughters won't be considered for other tribe legal work if I don't settle this case, yes, I do," Hannah said.

Shelby made a small strangled sound.

Phyllis Juan's tone, already cool, dropped a few degrees. "I would never make such a threat, Ms. Dain. That would be unprofessional. But I will say that if you take this case to trial, expect a lawsuit for malpractice if the verdict is less than the proposed settlement."

"That again would be the plaintiffs' prerogative, Ms. Juan," Hannah said, her jaw stiff with anger.

"Furthermore, if you do not stop bothering residents on the reservation, your firm's access to the non-public area of the reservation will be revoked."

"That's ridiculous! I haven't bothered any tribe members. And if you bar us from the areas where the uranium was dumped, we won't be able to prepare for trial."

"Then I'd advise you to proceed with care," Phyllis said.

The buzz of a dial tone filled the room. Hannah punched

the *Speaker* button and the sound disappeared.

Why was the tribe so hot to settle this case? Hannah could see it if liability were in question, but the government had conceded the point. Once the reports on the samples came in, the case would be the litigation equivalent of shooting fish in a barrel.

"We need to find those test results," Shelby said.

The intercom buzzed again.

Clementine's voice came through the speaker. "Desert View Labs is on the line."

"Here's the next best thing." Hannah grabbed up the handset. "Do you have the test results from the Weller samples?"

She listened for a moment, then frowned. "Is there another—" Hannah listened some more. "Okay. Thank you." She replaced the phone receiver.

Shelby rocked back and forth on her high heels, arms crossed. "Did they find the test results? What do they say?"

Hannah looked at her sister.

"Desert View Labs has no record of Garth Weller ever sending in any ore samples to be tested."

Chapter Twelve

"Then he must have sent them someplace else!" Shelby said. "Where else—"

Hannah shook her head. "Desert View told me it's the only facility licensed to test uranium in the state."

"So what are we going to do?" Shelby sat down and started to fan herself. Hannah would have poked fun at her caricature of a Victorian lady if her sister didn't look so upset.

"It's no big deal, Shelby. Dr. Glouster will collect his own samples. He wanted to do it in the first place, but I told him we couldn't wait for him to get clearance from the tribe, and that he should use Weller's."

"Or we can talk to the plaintiffs about settling. Do you really think Phyllis Juan is going to issue an access permit to Glouster? She'll drag her feet."

"Ed doesn't need a permit. He'll be with me." Hannah took a small card out of her desk drawer. "This says I have the right to go anywhere on the rez except Council chambers and the sacred sites. It also allows me to be accompanied by an assistant." Hannah put the card away. "Dr. Glouster just became my new litigation aide."

"Phyllis Juan is going to be furious."

"Only if she finds out. We'll be in and out before she knows it."

Hannah called Glouster.

"I'll go by myself," he said after Hannah told him that Weller's samples were missing. "No reason for you to waste your time watching me dig up dirt."

"We can't get you credentialed in time. Technically, you'll be there as my assistant."

"I don't mind taking my chances with the tribal police."

"No!" Hannah said, imagining Shelby's reaction if their newfound expert was arrested. "Besides, I have to show you where the dump sites are."

Glouster chuckled. "I'm an orienteer, and a geologist. Makes me pretty good at reading maps."

"I'm not sure how accurate the ones we have are, even the topos."

"Okay, then. When and where?"

"How about right now?"

Glouster agreed to meet her at the fry bread stand at noon. "I'll bring my field truck with my tools. I have a pretty good idea what type of rock is out there, but it's better to be prepared. Speaking of which, you still may want me to get my own access permit. Never know when you may need me to go back out there."

"This trip will have to do it." Applying for a permit for Glouster would tip off Phyllis, something Hannah didn't want to do, at least until they had new samples.

The light on the side of Hannah's phone started to flash, indicating Clementine needed to speak with her.

"I have another call, Ed. See you in about an hour." Hannah pressed the intercom button.

"Yes?"

"The husband of that woman who drove into the lake yesterday is on the line. He's called twice, says it's really important that he speak to you. Probably wants to talk you out of suing."

"I'll take it." Hannah picked up the phone. "This is Hannah Dain."

"Ms. Dain, this is Philippe Soule. We met yesterday at the hospital."

"I remember. How's your wife?"

"That's why I'm calling. Nathalie regained consciousness early this morning."

"That's good news!"

"Yes. She'd like to thank you for what you did."

"Please give her my best. Unfortunately, my schedule is a little full—"

"Ms. Dain, that isn't the only reason I would like you to stop by. Nathalie can't recall what happened. Last thing she remembers is the car going into the lake."

"I'm sorry, Mr. Soule, but I don't see—"

"The doctor said it might be some sort of short-term amnesia. It's really upsetting her—she goes from crying to staring at the wall. I was hoping that seeing you might jar her memory, help her get past this."

Hannah hesitated. She had a ton of trial prep still to do. On the other hand, it might be her only chance to find out what Nathalie's *ould have died* meant.

"I'm going to a meeting now. How about if I stop by afterward?" Hannah hung up on his third *thank you.*

Her next call was to Shelby.

"I'm meeting Dr. Glouster at the site so he can collect more samples. Want to come?"

"After our last trip to the rez? I don't think so." Shelby was silent for a moment. "Are the rocks he's going to collect really radioactive?"

"A little, I guess." Hannah checked the clock on her computer. "I'll let you know how it goes."

She had just finished changing into jeans and sneakers when Anuya appeared in her doorway.

"Hey, how's it going?" Hannah asked as she laced up a shoe.

Anuya shrugged. "Okay. Clementine is pretty cool." She twisted a piece of hair around her index finger. Hannah recognized her own gesture, usually a prelude to a request.

"I heard you on the phone. Can I come with you to the reservation?"

Hannah was about to say no when she caught herself. Did she really want Anuya at the firm with Shelby when Hannah wasn't there? An idea popped into her head, one that would keep her half-sisters apart and pay back a favor, too.

"Sure. Come in here for a minute."

Anuya settled herself in a guest chair while Hannah made a phone call.

"Jerry Dan? Still interested in looking for treasure?"

Glouster was waiting for them at the fry bread stand, standing next to a dented white van that looked to have been the beast of burden on many field trips. He wore cargo pants with a notebook hanging out of one pocket and a faded t-shirt featuring a dinosaur. A sweat-stained hat with a flap in the back protected his neck from the sun. He glanced at the kayak on top of Hannah's SUV.

"Glad to see you rescued your boat."

"Yeah," Hannah said, hoping Anuya wouldn't ask what he was talking about. She quickly moved on to introductions.

"Stegosaurus," Anuya said, pointing at Glouster's shirt. "Jurassic Period."

"That's right. You like dinosaurs?"

"They're okay."

"You should see the dinosaur museum in Phoenix. This Friday it's unveiling a new exhibit—a dinosaur that was discovered in Arizona." Glouster extended an arm. "All this was underwater two hundred million years ago. Makes for good fossil-hunting."

Anuya shook her head. "I'm looking for the Indian princess' gold. I'm half-Indian, so I don't have to worry about the curse."

"I did some engineering for several gold and oil mining companies in South America. The rez doesn't really have the geology for high grade ore." Glouster smiled indulgently. "On the other hand, you never know. In any event, I wouldn't worry about any curses."

"Curses are real. My grandmother—"

"Aren't there petroglyphs out here, too?" Hannah interrupted.

Glouster nodded. "Because of the dry air, they don't fade or crumble. First time, I was only a few feet away before I saw anything. The designs can be hard to see when the sun is overhead, or when they're done in colors that blend into the rock. Scared me—I thought I was seeing things." He winked at Hannah. "I don't believe in ghosts, but I wouldn't be caught camping out here alone."

Anuya jerked her hair into a ponytail and fastened it with an elastic from around her wrist. "Not all ghosts are bad, you know. Some protect us, or show us the right way. Like my dad. He's watching out for me and—"

"I wonder where Jerry Dan is?" Hannah glanced at her cell phone, but it was only a modern-day pocket watch so far from a tower. She listened for the sound of an engine, but heard only the churr and whine of unseen bugs.

"We should get started if you want samples turned in to the lab today," Glouster said.

Hannah rolled out the topo map. "So which mine should we go to?"

Glouster extracted a pack of Marlboros from his shirt pocket. He shook out a cigarette, put it between his lips, and lit it in a series of well-synchronized movements. He blew out a stream of smoke while he studied the X's that marked dump sites. After a minute, he placed a thick yellowed thumbnail on the map.

"Let's try this one. Looks to be the easiest to access. And some of the other sites aren't too far away if I'm wrong."

Glouster took a GPS from his shirt pocket. Hannah looked with envy at the device. She wanted one for navigating to remote paddling spots. *New car first.*

Glouster entered the coordinates from the map into the device. "All set."

They pulled back onto the road, Glouster leading the way in his van. Anuya made parabolic waves out the window with her hand. They drove until the pavement ended, past the sign that marked the reservation boundary. *No Trespassing—Travel by Permit Only* read large red letters on peeling white paint. Below was a smaller sign: *Danger! Those without a gallon of water each, turn back now.*

The dirt track slashed across the expanse of beige like a thick brush stroke across a blank canvas. Hannah's rental car crunched along in the van's slipstream of dust, following Lake Lagunita's eastern shore. A fence of thin wire strung between skinny wooden posts paralleled the road, too low and flimsy to keep out anything but the most elderly sheep. Below, the edge of the lake lapped at cauliflower-shaped boulders. Far-off mountains glistened in the afternoon sun, never seeming to get any closer.

They forded several dry stream beds, passed shriveled bushes and giant saguaros that reminded Hannah of lonesome cowboys. Now and then they passed structures pieced together from plywood and corrugated metal that obviously were without electricity or water. Hannah wondered if utilities marked the difference between *shack* and *house*, the Third World and the First. Most looked abandoned, per the tribe's edict.

A less-used dirt track branched off the main road, and Glouster turned onto it. Hannah followed, wrenching the steering wheel to avoid a pothole. The surface was really churned up. Axle-deep ruts cut across the yellow dirt for hundreds of yards, evidence of an epic struggle to maintain forward movement.

They bucked over the rough terrain for a few minutes. Then Hannah saw a flash of red lights and the van slithered to a stop in the sand. She parked behind it, and she and Anuya got out. Dust kicked up by their tires powdered her skin.

It was nearly noon, the air clear and still. A glance in any direction took in a hundred miles, the raw landscape empty, lacking even litter. El Piniculo rose in front of them, slightly to the west. Its three-thousand-foot apex was barely visible over El Diablo, the tallest in a line of peaks that poked up from the earth along the lake's shore. The mountains looked like vertebrae of the dinosaur on Glouster's t-shirt.

Hannah started toward the white van, nearly twisting an

ankle on raised tire tracks, more of the same that had made driving in so difficult. She noticed fresh impressions mixed in with the rain-hardened tread marks. Phyllis had said this section of the rez had been closed, even to tribe members. Was the tribe checking on the dump sites? More likely the ruts were from the resident evacuation. Only loaded moving vans could make grooves that deep.

Glouster squatted and shaded his eyes with his hand. His skin was a dark walnut color and his eyes were weathered, with wrinkles at the corners. Slick with sunscreen, his face looked like crinkly wax paper. Years of fieldwork, Hannah guessed, noticing his work boots were worn almost through at the heels.

He pointed at a pile of sand about a hundred yards away.

"See the tailings? There's the mine we're looking for."

Hannah squinted, spotting the opening into the earth behind a screen of glossy-leafed plants topped with dozens of slender seedpods.

"Should get some decent readings," he said. "Those prince's plumes growing around the entrance mean there's uranium in the soil."

Hannah looked at the columns of yellow blossoms, patchworked across the stark ground, two dozen clusters at least. She thought about Shelby's question. Just how much contamination was there?

"I've seen some of the kids. They're in bad shape," she said to Glouster in a quiet voice, not wanting Anuya to hear.

He shook his head. "If their mothers drank contaminated water while pregnant, they didn't have a chance. Neuropathy is an ugly disease—it destroys corneas, muscles, nerves, organs. One study puts the average age of death at ten. For a while they thought it was caused by a genetic mutation among the tribe. But when the number of cases leveled off instead of kept going up, they knew it had to be environmental."

A rumble sounded in the distance, like faraway thunder. Hannah instinctively flinched and looked up. After last summer, rainstorms scared her. But the sky was unsullied by a trace of cloud. The sound became mechanical, and a few minutes later, Jerry Dan pulled up in a blue pickup even dustier than Glouster's van.

"Jerry Dan!" Anuya cried.

"Howdy! Sorry I'm late." Jerry Dan climbed down from the cab.

"Didn't know this was going to be a party," Glouster said, then disappeared into the back of his van. Hannah heard the scrape and thump of things being moved around. *Probably used to working alone.* She hoped the geologist would be less prickly on the witness stand.

"I've got the map!" Anuya held it aloft.

Jerry Dan plucked the photocopy from her hands and folded it. With a wink at Hannah, he said, "You can't go waving it around like that. It's supposed to be secret."

Anuya clapped a hand over her mouth. "Sorry," she said through her fingers.

Glouster reappeared with a tool bag slung over his shoulder. "I'm going to get to it, while it's still full light."

This time of year, darkness came early and fell hard. During several after-work paddling sessions, Hannah had been caught out after sundown, one moment in luminescent twilight, the next engulfed in tar-black.

"Want some help?" she asked.

"Uh, probably a good idea to let him do it on his own," Jerry Dan said. "Don't want the defendants to be able to suggest you influenced the results."

"Of course," Hannah said, feeling embarrassed.

"Let's go, Jerry Dan," Anuya said. She swung her hair over her shoulders, a wavy obsidian waterfall.

"Just a second, you two," Hannah said. "I didn't realize we'd end up so far into the rez. Any prospecting has to be done on the other side of the boundary, back where the sign is."

"But I want to follow the map!" Anuya said.

"Anything you find will be the property of the tribe," Hannah said.

"I don't care. I want to find the princess' treasure."

Jerry Dan produced his orienteering compass. "How about if we poke around just a little? I doubt anybody will notice us."

Hannah sighed. "All right. If you run into anybody, tell them you're part of the litigation team."

"Praise Shiva!" Anuya said, pressing her hands together.

"Don't forget water," Hannah said. "There's a bottle in the back of the car."

"But I'm not thirsty."

Hannah thought of the sign at the rez entrance. "I don't want you to get dehydrated."

Anuya rolled her eyes, then navigated over the ruts to the rental car while Jerry Dan unfolded the map. He looked at it, then at his compass, then at a nearby rock formation, then back at the map again.

"Thanks again for recommending Dr. Glouster," Hannah said.

"No worries. Have you thought about using him as leverage at the bargaining table? Could add ten, even twenty percent to the settlement number."

Hannah gazed across the low, hot plain, gashed by the water-filled canyon and thrust up by rocky peaks and mesas at the fringes. It was some of the starkest, most open-air country she had ever been in. *And tainted with poison.*

"No," she said. "We're going to trial."

"Case like this, the government is going to bring in senior lawyers. Even with Ed's testimony, the verdict could be a lot less than they're offering."

"I know." Hannah's tone was snappish, even though she knew he had a point.

Jerry Dan refolded the map. "I didn't mean to offend." His drawl flattened *I* to *Ah*. "Even if you do win, the feds could appeal, drag the case out for years. That what your clients want?"

Hannah was about to reply when a scream echoed off the rocks. She looked toward the vehicles. Anuya was nowhere to be seen.

Chapter Thirteen

"Hannah! Help!"

The cries came from behind a clump of chaparral. Hannah and Jerry Dan sprinted toward the sound. Pushing through the scratchy bushes, Hannah saw Anuya looking up at them from a narrow hole about twelve feet deep. The teenager reached her thin arms upward.

"Get me out of here!"

Anuya's eyes were ringed with white like a spooked horse's. She clutched a piece of creosote in one hand, and Hannah got a whiff of the plant's greasy odor as she dropped down onto her belly.

"Here, grab on," she said, wrapping her fingers around one of Anuya's wrists. She began to pull, but stopped as pain knifed through her bad shoulder.

"Ahhhh!" Her gasp was involuntary. Tears blinded her, and for a moment Hannah was back in time—prone beside another fissure, holding on to another sister. She blinked, and the memory dissolved.

"Here, let me help," Jerry Dan said. Lying down next to Hannah, he grabbed Anuya's other arm. "Pull!"

"Ow!" the teenager cried as her knee scraped against a protruding rock.

"Hold on—we're almost there," Jerry Dan panted.

With a final heave, they pulled Anuya over the lip of the opening. Jerry Dan helped her to her feet. Using his arm for support, she limped clear of the chaparral. Hannah followed.

"What happened?" she asked, kneading the sore spot on her shoulder.

"I picked up a rock and a snake was under it!" Anuya shuddered. "I started to back up and fell into the hole."

"Probably a red racer," Jerry Dan said. "They're harmless."

"I know," Anuya said crossly. The knee of her jeans was torn, revealing a patch of scraped skin. She inspected her wound. "I'm gonna have a scab."

"There's a first aid kit in my glove box," Jerry Dan said. "Think you can walk over there?"

The look Anuya gave him was more withering than the desert sun. "Of course." She tugged at her shirt, making sure just one corner was tucked into her pants. She bent to retie her shoe, and a tattoo peeped over her waistband.

Something else Anuya's mother didn't know about? Hannah was beginning to wonder just how many secrets there were in her two families.

"We should go into business together, Hannah," Jerry Dan said. He moved his hands over an imaginary storefront sign. "Desert Rescues Unlimited."

She thought about the last few months. Shelby…Tony…"No thanks."

Despite her bravado, Anuya stayed close to Hannah on the way to Jerry Dan's truck, eyes pinned on the ground. Hannah remembered her first foray into the desert after living in a city. Blistering heat, spiny plants, dangerous animals, treacherous rocks—the place forced endurance, mental and physical, of a sort unanticipated by urban living.

"I don't like snakes, either," she said.

"I'm not afraid of snakes," Anuya said stoutly. She lowered her voice. "It's small places I hate."

Hannah wanted to ask why, but the look on her sister's face told her she wouldn't get an answer.

As Jerry Dan helped Anuya into the truck's passenger seat, Glouster reappeared, carrying half a dozen baggies filled with dirt. Hannah saw the date and some other numbers had been written on the baggies with a marker.

"I collected samples from the entrance as well as deeper in the mine. Do you want me to test both?" Glouster said.

"Just the stuff from the top," Hannah said. According to what she had read in the case files, crops grew in and drinking water filtered through the top layer of soil. Contamination of that dirt would be the most relevant to the case.

Glouster opened the back of the van. "I can't believe how hot some of this stuff still is," he said over the clank of tools. "My Geiger meter was screaming." When he had finished stowing the baggies and his gear, he joined them at the truck.

"What happened here?" he asked, seeing Anuya's torn jeans.

"Minor injury," Hannah said. She popped open the pickup's glove box. Orienteering maps, tubes of sunscreen, a rodeo program, an opened pack of cigarettes…"Where'd you say that first aid kit was?"

Jerry Dan looked chagrined. "I just remembered—I lent it out during my last race and forgot to get it back."

"I got one," Glouster said. He picked up the cigarettes. "Thought you gave these up."

The top of Jerry Dan's ears turned red. "Last month—bad for training. Take 'em if you want."

Glouster tucked the pack into his pants pocket. "Abstaining from alcohol is enough deprivation for one lifetime."

He fetched a battered tin box from his van and opened it to reveal bandages, antiseptic cream, and other paraphernalia. With practiced ease, he cleaned Anuya's wound.

Hannah watched, unconsciously rubbing a scar on her finger. Barely six weeks old, it, too, had been an injury dressed by another. She shut her mind to the memories.

After Glouster had applied the last piece of tape, he handed Anuya a clear bag filled with small white crystals in blue liquid.

"Keep this pressed on it for at least twenty minutes. Won't bruise so much."

"What about looking for gold?" Anuya asked.

"We can go treasure hunting another day," Jerry Dan said. Seeing Anuya's glum face, he added. "How about prospecting for pizza instead?"

"Yes!"

Hannah looked at her quizzically. "Isn't pizza jha…jha…"

"Jhoota? Not if I get my own. With extra olives and mushrooms, please."

"Sounds good to me," Jerry Dan said. "Ed, you in?"

"Thanks, but if I leave now, I can get these to the lab before the three-o'clock closing time."

"Ask them to put a rush on it," Hannah said. "We'll pay any extra charges."

With a wave, Glouster climbed into the van. Hannah watched it trundle down the bumpy road, its engine rattle gradually being replaced by the static of cicadas. A lot was riding on some baggies of dirt.

"So, you up for pizza?" Jerry Dan said to Hannah.

She glanced toward Anuya. The teenager leaned against the rental SUV, her shoulders juking to the beat in her headphones. She shifted her gaze to the lake. In the waning sunlight, its surface gleamed like old silver. Hannah wanted to spend time with her younger sister. But after the complications of the last two days, she yearned for things that were simple—a kayak, a ribbon of water, the clarity of desert air.

"Sure," she said, still looking at the lake. She could smell the water.

Jerry Dan pushed his hat back on his head. "If you want to go for a paddle, I can grab a slice with Anuya and drop her at your place."

"Of course not! I'm—"

Jerry Dan shushed her. "Go. You'll be happy that you did."

Anuya was equally happy. "Jerry Dan and I have to plan the treasure hunt."

Fifteen minutes later, the blue pickup was headed back to town with Anuya hanging out of the window shouting "*Shalom*, y'all" as Hannah pushed off the shore in her kayak.

The sun had dipped lower, turning the granite walls a juicy watermelon orange-pink, nearly shocking against the subtle iridescent purple of the talus slopes beyond. An organic smell rose from the vegetation along the water's edge.

A few fireflies appeared, looking for trouble. Hannah ignored them and began paddling slowly, not expecting to have much energy. But a rhythm took hold in her shoulders, and her mood lifted. Sport was both mental and physical therapy for her. The noise, the closeness, the emotion of civilization could become unbearable, and she needed the distance and concentration provided by athletics.

Something chemical released in her cells, and Hannah doubled her stroke rate, thrusting her paddle into the water and pulling as hard as she could. The kayak surged forward. She poured it on, pulling triple time, and the boat cleft the surface. Droplets of moisture flicked onto her forearms like sprinklings of holy water.

Admittedly, there was a certain futility to it—her blade pushing the water aside, only to have it fall back to be pushed again. But Hannah liked the relentlessness of the medium, the way the lake was something to be gotten through. She felt invigorated by every stroke. All that mattered was movement, one arc blending into another.

A mile from shore she abruptly let up, letting the kayak drift while she enjoyed the heaviness of tired muscles. She laid her paddle across her knees and let her feet drop into the water. Her toes brushed against the iciness that marked the end of the sun's reach. Still straddling the kayak, Hannah lay back until her head rested on the deck. She felt the boat move up and down, as though the lake were breathing. Early stars blinked at her like tiny eyes. Out of range of the insects' cacophony, she heard only air.

Hannah hadn't been to very many places where ancient history was so tangible. Settlements on the East Coast generally went back only several centuries. But people had lived in the desert more or less continuously for at least four thousand years.

She felt the presence of those who had gone before—the place in the sun where someone had sat, the tree under which someone had collected firewood. Maybe Anuya was right about reincarnation, and ghosts of others were around after all.

So does that mean Elizabeth and Tel...?

Hannah shivered and sat up. The sun had disappeared behind the mountains, and the cold had started to penetrate her clothes. Sliding her feet under the footwell straps, she dropped her paddle into the water and pulled. The kayak barely moved. She stroked on the other side, with the same result.

A breeze lifted her hair at the roots, cooling the perspiration there. Even heading into a chop, the going should not have been so hard. Then Hannah noticed how low her craft was riding. It was moving through the waves, instead of over them, and the water, now inky black, was only a couple of inches from the deck instead of the customary eight or ten.

She was sinking.

The kayak had a sealed deck, the air inside the hull providing the craft's buoyancy. Hannah had checked for cracks after the accident and found none. In her haste to get into the water that afternoon, she must have scraped the boat's underside against a rock. Unbuffered by wind or water, many of the granite pieces had razor edges, sharp enough to slice plastic and allow the kayak to take on water.

Pushing against one foot pedal, backpaddling on the opposite side, Hannah pivoted the boat until it was pointed at the closest shore. She started to paddle, feeling as if she were pulling through sludge, and tried not to think how far she was from land, or that the lake was nearly a mile deep in places. The only sound was the soft *ker-plup* of her paddle, but Hannah knew it was a deceptive peace, like the eye of a hurricane. Fear metastasized as her muscles started to burn, then cramp, and her hands became raw. Water lipped over the deck—freezing, hypothermia-inducing water.

Chin tucked, she kept paddling, her arms moving almost of their own volition. *Right, left, right, left*—the tattoo beat in her brain. When the edge of her paddle at last nudged sand, she didn't break rhythm until the boat ground to a shuddering stop on the shore. She stepped down, slightly euphoric to feel the coarse sand between her toes.

Hannah staggered onto the narrow beach and lay down on the grainy sand, letting what remained of the sun's warmth in the earth soak into her depleted muscles. Relief ran through her, weighing down her arms and legs. The music of the water lapped metronomically against the rocky beach.

Hannah had always heard that being in Nature was safer than walking a city street or driving a car. She didn't believe it.

A small shape hurdled past overhead. Startled by the flutter of sound, Hannah sat up abruptly. A bat. Another swooped past, just discernable in the lingering shreds of twilight. The furred pair veered to the smooth surface of the lake, banking and rolling an instant before slamming into the water, on the hunt for insects. Hannah strained to hear the whisper of their wings, now and then glimpsing the tiny forms as they darted past the growing brilliance of stars.

She got to her feet. The strip of sand ended at the base of a short, sloped cliff. After making sure the kayak was well-beached, Hannah walked up the wind-polished rock, bent at the waist, using her paddle like a tightrope-walker's pole. Her lower back twinged with pain, the aftermath of paddling the over-heavy boat.

At the top, Hannah was back in the desert proper again. El Piniculo stuck up like a giant monster tooth on the horizon, dark purple against velvety violet. A track of sand split the chaparral, running through the landscape like a strand of bent wire—the dirt road she and Anuya had driven down hours earlier. Using El Piniculo as a compass point, Hannah figured she was about halfway between the mine where her rental SUV was parked and the fry bread stand, a walk of several miles to either destination.

An unseen coyote cut loose with a long, dolorous aria, punctuated with staccato yips. Hannah shivered. Nature divided the world into two shifts—cactus wrens that chased bugs in sunlight gave way to bats seeking a new cast of insects, keen-eyed hawks surrendered the sky to owls with stereo hearing. Hannah preferred the daytime. Eager to get back to modern lights, she started along the road, her paddle now a weapon against the dark.

The engine's rumble was so low-pitched, Hannah at first thought she was imagining it. Only when she turned and saw the approaching headlights was she convinced. The shafts of yellow sliced through the darkness. Dropping the paddle, Hannah started waving like a castaway signaling a plane.

The twin beams came closer, the oversize chrome grill between them catching pinwheels of light. A semi pulling a trailer, Hannah realized. She moved to the left side of the road, still signaling with her arms.

"Stop! I need a ride!" she shouted, even though she knew the driver couldn't hear. The rig came closer, and Hannah could see the company name and blue swirl logo stenciled on the cab door, illuminated by the running lights. The engine's roar subsided for a moment as gears shifted.

He's going to stop. Relieved, Hannah bent down to retrieve her paddle, hoping it would fit in the passenger compartment. Arm still raised, she waited on the shoulder.

Instead of slowing, the truck accelerated.

"Hey!" Hannah yelled. "Stop!" She got the barest of looks at the driver as the truck thundered past—blue baseball cap pulled low over white-blond hair, pale face staring straight ahead.

She ran after the rig, but all she got was a lungful of dust. The truck kept going. Hannah glared at its taillights, their dim red proof of untouched brakes.

"Jerk!" The whinny of the engine receded until all Hannah heard was desert again.

Why didn't he stop? Hannah had to admit she wouldn't pick up a stranger in the middle of nowhere. But then, she wasn't a truck driver. Maybe the paddle had put him off.

She began walking north toward her car again. The air was cool, a reminder that desert nights could dip below freezing.

In the gathering dark the chaparral took on the forms of various animals—jackrabbits, coyotes, javelinas. Hannah walked faster. When she passed a group of boulders, she imagined for a moment that the rocks had come alive, then realized she was just scaring herself. And doing a good job of it.

She had just gotten used to, if not comfortable with, the quiet when a mechanical whir broke the stillness. This sound was higher, less substantial, than the truck's. Two headlights moved toward her, the left slightly askew, like a lazy eye.

A car. Hannah dropped the paddle and moved to the shoulder. She raised an arm and waved, conveying what she hoped was restrained sanity.

The headlights bobbed up and down as the car approached. The beams caught Hannah, and she raised her other arm against the glare, feeling like a bug skewered by a pin. Brakes keened, and the car—an older American sedan—jerked to a stop. Its headlights cast lopsided puddles of faded yellow on the dirt track.

With the creak of a metal spring, the driver's door opened. Suddenly nervous, Hannah grabbed the paddle and squinted through the darkness. A small figure got out.

"Ms. Dain?"

It was Espera Bustamente.

Chapter Fourteen

The old car wallowed toward the mine site, Hannah's kayak lashed to the roof and her paddle poking out a rear side window. Espera was an experienced rez driver—steady gas, loose but controlling hold of the wheel, easy on the brakes. Hannah was impressed as they ploughed through a sand trough with barely a fishtail.

"Thank you so much," she said again. "After that truck didn't stop, I figured I was in for a long walk."

And a scary one. Secure in a metallic, moving product of civilization, Hannah felt her tenseness ease. Night was a different thing in the desert than the city. The profound absence of light—the stars too far away to matter—was disorienting. Hannah couldn't shake the sense that something terrible lurked in the folds of darkness. She preferred to see danger coming.

"Those trucks! I hear them for many months, always late." Espera sliced the air with a slim hand. "Another way the tribe does not care about us. I bet workmen do not drive past the houses next to the casino, at least not when people are sleeping."

"Why are they out here? I thought this part of the rez was closed."

"That is what I say to the OTA, too. They tell me it is dirt from the construction—more houses near the casino." She snorted. "We are used to living with space between us. Now they want us lined up like bean plants."

The rental car was where Hannah had left it, a small mountain in the middle of the flatness. The moon had risen, and slabs of granite shone through the sand like pools of spilled mercury.

"Where's Nando?" Hannah asked as she and Espera boosted the kayak onto the SUV's roof. A handful of fireflies flitted aimlessly about. Hannah felt a breath of wind on her cheek. The next moment a bat swooped out of nowhere and, with a blur of wings, scooped up one of the dancing motes of light.

"With Lupe. She doesn't like town very much, so she watches him when I go to the store."

Hannah put the paddle in the backseat. "Thank you again."

"I'm glad I could help." Espera opened her car door. But instead of getting in, she turned to Hannah. Her eyes were dark wells in the moonlight.

"Don't settle the case."

Hannah touched the other woman's arm. "I won't."

After Espera had driven off, Hannah retrieved the flashlight from her emergency kit. She played the beam along the kayak's underside. The light found a foot-long slit on the bow, just under where the hull curved.

The edges of the slit were smooth, as if made by a knife.

The windows of Hannah's condominium were dark when she pulled into the driveway. Anuya must have gone to bed early. According to the dashboard clock, it was half past eight, which translated into ten-thirty New York time. Hannah rummaged through her purse for her keys, wishing she had remembered to bring the extra garage door opener. When she put the key into the lock, the front door popped open.

She walked into the foyer, planning to talk to Anuya tomorrow. Even through crime in Pinnacle Peak was a fraction of that in a city, no reason to make it easy for would-be burglars.

Hannah took off her shoes and climbed the stairs, trying to be quiet. An acrid smell hung in the air. *Cigarettes?* She and Anuya definitely needed to talk.

The sleeping bag on the couch was empty and the door to Hannah's bedroom was closed. Anuya probably wanted to sleep on a bed after a night on lumpy cushions.

Hannah padded into the laundry room, the cool tile feeling good on her bare feet, and shed her paddling togs. After pulling on a t-shirt and shorts from the pile of clean clothes on the dryer, she walked into the kitchen. She was starving. After checking in the refrigerator to see if Anuya had brought home leftover pizza, she grabbed the box of cheddar bunny crackers from the pantry, bumping her hip on a partially opened drawer.

"Ouch," she said softly and rubbed the sore spot. After grabbing a bottle of water, Hannah sat on the sofa.

Had someone slit the kayak? If so, was it just to scare her? Or had the intention been worse? If Hannah had gone on her usual morning paddle, she would have been swamped miles from shore. And when had it happened? At court? The law firm? In the desert?

In the midst of mulling all this over, Hannah noticed Anuya's backpack. Every pocket had been unzipped, and the contents dumped onto the carpet. She had watched her half-sister carefully pack away her things that morning. The mess seemed out of character. Her eyes slid to the hall closet. Its door yawned open, exposing an athletic bag on the floor—a door that had been closed and an athletic bag that had been on the closet shelf when she and Anuya had left.

Hannah's stomach did a small flip-flop. Getting up, she went to the bedroom. She carefully turned the knob and cracked the door. Moonlight shone through the window onto the empty bed. Hannah flung the door open the rest of the way.

One of the closet doors was off-track, exposing empty hangers and puddles of clothes on the floor. Most of the dresser drawers were half-closed. The condo had been searched. For what? And where was her sister?

"Anuya? Anuya!"

There was no answer. Hannah raced back to the kitchen counter and took her cell phone from her purse. With shaking fingers, she called Jerry Dan's number. His cheery "Howdy" could barely be heard over the background noise.

"Jerry Dan, where are you? Where's Anuya?"

"We're just about to leave Danny's. The kid changed her mind about pizza, decided she wanted to see where real cowboys hang out. Do you want us to bring you something?"

"No, I'm fine. Listen, I know this sounds crazy, but my condo's been searched. When I got here the front door was open, and it looks like the closets and drawers have been gone through."

Jerry Dan gave a low whistle. "You must really have the feds nervous, Hannah."

"The feds?"

"Your lawsuit on the uranium poisoning. Whoever broke in was probably looking for details on your case."

"That doesn't make sense. The government has admitted liability. All we're trying is the damage issue."

"I bet they put in wiretaps," Jerry Dan said.

Hannah wasn't in the mood for conspiracy theories.

"Just bring Anuya home, okay? And don't say anything about this to her."

"On our way."

Hannah hung up. She was considering calling Dresden when her cell phone rang. *Restricted* glowed on the screen, but she answered it.

"Stay away. It's not yours," said a male voice. Before Hannah could answer, the phone went dead.

Hannah set her mobile on the kitchen counter as fear rattled around under her ribs.

Maybe Jerry Dan wasn't so crazy after all.

Chapter Fifteen

Wednesday, November 4

Anuya had insisted on sleeping on the couch, even though Hannah wanted her to share the bed.

"You snore too much!"

Not wanting to scare her, Hannah had kept quiet about the break-in and the phone call. But she made sure the doors and windows were locked, and got up several times during the night to check on Anuya. The teenager had slept the slumber of the young—deep, demon-less, arms flung outward like a rag doll's.

Soft morning sun filtered through the spaces between the window blinds. Hannah lay in bed, her arms wrapped around a pillow, staring at the alarm clock on the nightstand. Its ticking was loud, reminding her of water dipping from a faucet. She used to have an electric one with rotating numbers, but Cooper had replaced it with an old-fashioned dial-and-hands model.

"Need to see a friendly face in the morning," he had joked. The clock was another thing left behind when he moved out.

Hannah watched the minute hand jerk from 4:59 to 5:00. Reflexively, she braced herself for the alarm, even though it was switched off. She knew another clock, one in a ranch house several miles north, was ringing at that moment. Cooper kept cowboy hours—early mornings and early evenings. Every day—Saturdays and Sundays included—he woke at five. After kissing her, he would quietly roll out of bed and go into the kitchen to make coffee.

Hannah thought about the last time Cooper had kissed her. It had been at the truck when they'd said good bye. At the time, she hadn't thought about it being the last time. And now she wished there hadn't been a "last time" at all.

Hannah considered phoning him. But what to say? *Someone slashed my kayak, broke into my apartment, and left me a threatening message.* She imagined Cooper's response. *Back off. Let the police handle it.* She decided not to call. He'd already been through too much drama, thanks to her.

She thrust the pillow aside and went into the living room to wake Anuya. There was a lot to do.

Two hours later, Hannah steered the rental SUV into the law firm's parking lot. Anuya was in the passenger seat, dressed for her Bioscience interview later in the day.

Hannah had decided to tell Dresden about the break-in at the condo. Not so the police could catch whoever had done it, but to get it on record. Her prior dealings with the detective hadn't been the smoothest, and she wanted to bolster her credibility in case something else happened.

Which it won't. The more she thought about it, the more Hannah believed the break-in was simply random. Her television and other electronics had been lost in the Boston fire, and her laptop was at the office. The search was probably the work of a frustrated burglar disappointed at the slim pickings.

Hannah had also re-examined the slit in the bottom of the kayak. Man-made? Now she wasn't so sure. It could have been caused by a really sharp rock, or even damage overlooked from the car crash.

Clementine's head was on her desk. Her eyes were closed and her cheek rested next to her pencil cup.

"Any calls?" Hannah said loudly. Anuya giggled.

Clementine blinked and sat up. "Huh?"

"Are you tired because you're staying up late studying?" Hannah said. "Maybe we need to talk about—"

"I was just listening to a weird sound coming out of my computer." Clementine scowled at a still-giggling Anuya. "What's so funny?"

"There's a Post-it stuck in your hair."

Clementine extracted the square yellow paper with dignity. "I put it there, to remind me that Shelby wanted to know when Hannah arrived."

"Tell her I'm here." Hannah pushed open the door to her office.

She immediately knew something was wrong. To anybody else, the office looked as it had the night before. But Hannah could tell someone had been through it, just like her condo. The inbox angled away from the desk edge. One of the credenza drawers wasn't shut flush. The tower of cardboard cartons in the corner leaned at a new angle.

"Who was in here messing up stuff?" Anuya said.

Hannah shot her a look. "What makes you say that?"

Anuya pointed to Hannah's collection of rocks on the credenza. "When I looked at those yesterday, they were all in a line. Someone's moved them."

Since taking up kayaking, Hannah had kept an eye out for the odd fossil. The creatures who had lived in the shells predated the dinosaurs. And even though she couldn't comprehend in any meaningful way how long ago that had been, Hannah liked the mementos from back when the desert was a giant ocean. She looked at the now-jumbled collection of rocks and decided she couldn't keep Anuya ignorant any longer.

"Maybe this was done by the same person who broke into the condo last night."

Anuya's eyes went wide. "Someone came into your place when we were asleep?"

Hannah put out a reassuring hand. "Before we got there. They looked through our stuff, but I don't think anything was taken."

"What were they looking for?"

Hannah shook her head. "I have no idea."

"No idea about what?" Shelby said.

Today's dress was a soft material, belted in a way that made her look curvier than usual. The now-recognizable flower and citrus scents wafted in with her.

Hannah explained about the break-ins.

"Nothing's missing," Shelby said.

"Right," Hannah said.

"But you think a burglar was here just because some rocks might have been moved?"

"They were!" Anuya said.

Shelby rubbed her forehead, then looked at her sister with a pained expression. "Do you lie in bed at night and think up these things, or do they just pop into your head?"

"Someone went through my office and condo. I know it!"

"Doesn't your cleaning lady come every other Tuesday? And janitors go through the firm five nights a week. Probably one of them moved some stuff, forgot to close a drawer."

"My cleaning lady isn't due until *next* week. And the janitors have strict instructions never to touch papers."

"Are you sure it wasn't"—Shelby glanced at Anuya—"a former roommate looking to collect the rest of his stuff?"

Hannah's face burned. "No."

Her intercom buzzed, and Clementine's voice boomed into the room. "Shelly, your secretary is looking for you. And Hannah, I forgot to tell you—Phyllis Juan stopped by earlier. She wants you to call her."

Shelby moved toward the door. "We've got four weeks until trial. I suggest you focus on proving damages, not chasing phantom burglars. And for the last time, tell your secretary my name is *Shelby*!" She stalked out.

Hannah picked up the phone. "What's Phyllis' number?" she asked Clementine.

"Don't you have to make another call first?"

"To who?"

"Cooper! You need to tell him about the break-in, and—"

"Give it a rest, Clementine," she said quietly into the receiver. "I've had my chance—twice. No going back for thirds."

"Who says? You made a mistake. And you can fix it. See, I've got this theory—"

"Great," Hannah muttered.

"What? Anyway, you and me, we're the poster children for our generation. I don't pay my bills or exercise. You treat people like they're Scandinavian furniture or last season's handbag—you don't get attached."

Hannah was stunned—and hurt. The terrible events of the past few months had all stemmed from trying to fulfill what she saw as her obligation to family.

"I do too get attached," she said with a glance at Anuya, who was sitting in one of the guest chairs, ostensibly reading.

"Only to people who don't care about you," her secretary said.

"We're not talking about this anymore. What's Phyllis Juan's number?"

The litigation liaison picked up Hannah's call immediately.

"Have you reconsidered settling?" Phyllis asked.

"I spoke to Espera last night. She wants to go to trial."

"Well, that isn't why I called. Espera and the others are still refusing to move. Something about not leaving their birthplace." Phyllis cleared her throat. "You seem to have some influence with the group. Perhaps you could raise the matter?"

"I'll try." Hannah thought about the prior evening. "Are the truck runs part of a strategy to drive out the residents?"

"I don't know what you're talking about," Phyllis said.

Hannah described the trucks she had seen on the day of the crash and last night.

"That area has been closed for over a year—no residents, except for the holdouts, no business activity. Perhaps the excavation company is using the road as a shortcut to the landfill. I'll speak to the foreman."

Only after she hung up did Hannah remember the fresh tire tracks beside the mine that Glouster had tested. If traffic was barred from the contaminated area, had they collected samples from the wrong site? She was looking for the topo map to double-check the location with Glouster, when Clementine buzzed her again.

"Philippe Soule is on the line. Says he's Nathalie's husband?"

Hannah winced. With everything else going on, she had completely forgotten about her promise to stop by the hospital. She picked up the phone.

"Mr. Soule, I am so sorry. Things became rather hectic and—"

"Could you possibly come by now?" Soule's voice was tight. "You may be the only one who can help her."

Chapter Sixteen

Hannah dropped Anuya off early for her Bioscience interview, with cab fare to get back to the firm. She offered to stay with her until her appointment, but Anuya had strenuously objected.

Hannah drove along the palm-fringed streets to the hospital. Like most buildings in Pinnacle Peak, it was more horizontal than vertical, with a flat roof and earth-colored walls. Hannah recalled her last entrance through the window of the records room, and was glad to be going in the front door this time.

Nathalie had been moved to the top floor, where there were a half-dozen suites for high-roller patients. Hannah got off the elevator and turned down the corridor, ending up in a small lobby. Thin men and women, many with balding heads and bruised arms, sat in plastic chairs next to a curtained-off area. Some listened to MP3 players, others read, still others dozed. A few looked at her, but no one spoke.

Hannah realized she had blundered into the chemo ward. Its wan occupants reminded her of the consequences of radiation exposure. Conscious of her healthy thighs and muscled arms, she mumbled an apology and retreated. She consulted a map posted next to the elevator and found the correct corridor. A nurse pointed her to Nathalie's room.

The door was open and she looked in. A flower arrangement featuring three lilies and a contorted piece of bamboo sat on the dresser, next to the plastic pitcher that seemed ubiquitous to all hospital bedsides. On the floor were two suitcases of vinyl luggage marked with a designer's logo. A man slumped in a chair next to the bed, like a boxer in the late rounds. The skin on his face was slack, and there were blotches of blue under his eyes. He looked worse than some of the cancer patients.

A woman lay in the bed, a large bandage on one side of her forehead. Hannah saw a gleam under puffy lids.

"Nathalie?"

The woman nodded, then looked at the sleeping man and slowly raised a finger to her lips.

"I can come back—" Hannah whispered.

"No." Nathalie's hand fluttered in a wave, and Hannah moved into the room.

"I know who you are," Nathalie said. "The lake…thanks."

Hannah shifted her weight, unsure what to say. She finally decided on "Glad you're going to be all right."

"Brake problem…meant to have it fixed." Nathalie's voice was weak.

Was Nathalie claiming that her plunge into the lake was an accident? "But I saw you—" Hannah stopped. "At the *descanso,* I mean."

Nathalie shook her head, wincing at the movement. "Mr. Weller…worked with him…paying my respects."

"I read your note," Hannah blurted.

Nathalie sucked in a breath. The man in the chair stirred.

"Sorry, I must have dozed off for a moment, honey." He rubbed his eyes, then noticed Hannah. "Ms. Dain! Thank you for coming. Maybe you can help Nathalie remember the accident." He put a hand lightly on top of the sheet and looked at his wife. "This is the woman who pulled you out of the lake."

Nathalie's dark eyes met Hannah's. "Thank you. And I'm sorry. They told me about your car."

"I'm glad you're going to be okay," Hannah said.

Mr. Soule looked angry. "Chevrolet is going to answer for that brake defect, you can bet on that. Nat could have died."

I could have died—was that what Nathalie had said when

Hannah towed her to shore? Or had she said *should*? And what about the note? *I'm sorry, Garth. It wasn't worth it*—a sentiment from a colleague or a lover? And did Nathalie really not remember? The questions clamored inside Hannah's brain...where they would stay as long as Philippe Soule was within earshot. Hannah wasn't going to be the one to suggest either a suicide attempt or an affair.

She heard a faint buzzing. Philippe slipped a cell phone from his pocket and opened it.

"I must take this, *chérie*." He got up and kissed Nathalie on the forehead.

"He didn't kill himself," Nathalie said as soon as her husband was out of the room.

Hannah was startled. "Are you talking about Garth Weller?"

Nathalie gave the barest of nods.

"Do you have any proof?"

"I know the mindset." Nathalie's gaze wavered. "He didn't have it."

"Look, I know you...cared for him. But—"

Nathalie's eyes snapped back to Hannah's. "I loved him, and someone killed him."

Hannah studied her. "You don't have amnesia at all, do you? You remember everything."

Something flickered across the other woman's face. *Fear?*

"You should go," Nathalie said.

"Is someone threatening you?"

"Please—leave me alone."

At that moment a nurse bustled in, carrying a tray with a small paper cup. "Time for your meds," she said cheerily. She helped Nathalie into a sitting position, then poured her a glass of water from the pitcher. She tipped the pill from the cup into Nathalie's hand. Hannah recognized the tablet's shape and color—an antidepressant, the same one Shelby had taken in rehab.

"Our patient needs to rest now," the nurse said in a syrupy voice.

Hannah hated the coercive *our* as much as the royal *we*.

Ignoring the nurse's look of disapproval, she bent down to whisper into Nathalie's ear. "The samples Mr. Weller collected—where are they?"

"I don't know," Nathalie said, and closed her eyes.

Hannah straightened up. She took out a business card, wrote her cell number on the back, and tucked it under the pitcher.

"There's my number. Call if you remember anything else." She let the nurse shoo her from the room.

Nathalie obviously hadn't told her the whole story. But were her lies to cover up a suicide attempt or an affair—or both? Did she know where the missing samples were? And what about her claim that Weller had been murdered?

Walking out of the hospital, Hannah was certain of only one thing—it was time to call Detective Dresden.

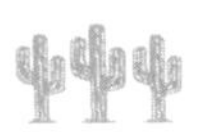

Hannah huddled in a doorway in the hospital corridor. The phone call wasn't going as she had hoped.

"All I'm saying is that you should look into Garth Weller's death. It may not be suicide."

"I thought you were staying out of police work," Dresden said.

"Me, too. But Weller—"

"—is still an open case. The medical examiner's report is weeks away. This isn't like *CSI*. In any event, why exactly does your"—he paused—"*friend* think that Mr. Weller's death wasn't suicide? If there's evidence—"

"There isn't," Hannah said. "She just knew him really well, and doesn't think he's the type to kill himself."

"The FBI has authority over crimes on the reservation. Unlike my department, it doesn't initiate investigations on civilian directive."

Did Dresden just make a joke? "I know, but I have a feeling..."

The detective sighed. "We'll look into it, informally, and only because your *feelings* have turned out to be major problems twice so far this year. And *we* means the sheriff's department. Not you,

Ms. Dain. No more meddling in police business."

The *meddling* reference stung, but Hannah didn't hear real annoyance in his tone. Could he be developing a soft spot for her?

"Thank you, Detective," she said.

As soon as she had hung up, her phone beeped, indicating that a voicemail was waiting.

Clementine's message was brief. "Your sister is going to bust a seam on her designer duds if she doesn't talk to you. Which given the few pounds she's gained, might actually happen."

Hannah rang Shelby. "What's going on?"

"Franklin wanted me to tell you that he and Phyllis have set up another settlement meeting with the government lawyers. A private one—the judge doesn't know about it."

"When did this happen? Why didn't they tell me sooner?"

"Franklin said he tried to call you, but could only get your voicemail."

Hannah regretted heeding the hospital sign that asked for all cell phones to be turned off. "But Espera—"

"Has agreed to the settlement discussions, according to Franklin."

It took Hannah a moment to recognize that the grinding sound in her head was from her teeth. Had Phyllis "gotten to" Espera? How?

"We should at least wait until we get the test results on the samples before we meet with the defendants," she said. "Call Franklin and convince him to postpone. I'm on my way back to the firm now."

As she pulled out of the hospital parking lot, Hannah broke her rule against driving and talking on her cell.

"Dr. Glouster? We need those test results as soon as possible," she said after his voicemail's digital greeting. "Please call me as soon as you get this message."

She snapped shut the phone and tossed it onto the passenger seat. In less than twenty-four hours, she had gone from reluctant bystander to fully committed champion of Espera's right to go to trial. And she was beginning to wonder whether Nathalie might be right about Garth Weller not killing himself.

So much for her promise not to get involved.

Shelby was gone by the time Hannah arrived back at the firm. And no one answered at Franklin's office.

"Dammit!" Hannah said under her breath. Anuya, curled up in the guest chair, looked up from her book.

Clementine appeared at the doorway. She gave an exaggerated sniff. "Didn't know you liked perfume, Boss. A little weak, but not bad."

Hannah yanked on a desk drawer. "I'm not wearing any! It's left over from Shelby."

"Whatever. Just wanted you to know I'm outta here. Gonna sacrifice myself to the black hole of consumer debt to save the jobs of fellow Americans."

"What?" Anuya said.

"I'm going shopping," Clementine said.

"Could you take Anuya down to the lunchroom and see if she wants a drink before you go?" Hannah asked.

"I'm not thirsty," Anuya said.

Hannah looked at the phone. Clementine raised a knowing eyebrow.

"I thought you had cold feet."

"More like chilly toes," Hannah said.

"C'mon," Clementine said to Anuya. "Let's go put salt in Shelby's yogurt."

When she was alone, Hannah dialed Cooper, then hung up when the voicemail came on. She thought about Boston, and breaking up with him after the car accident. Sure, there was the bar exam and the job at her family's firm, but they both knew her exit had been her choice. Then there was six weeks ago, when she had bolted again. How was she going to convince him that she now was ready to go forward without doubts?

I have no idea. Hannah picked up her briefcase.

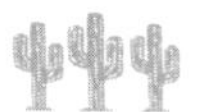

Anuya was quiet on the drive to the condo, intent on her book.

"How'd the interview go?" Hannah asked.

"Fine," Anuya said without looking up from her reading. The book had a dinosaur on its cover.

"Anything in there about Arizona fossils?"

"Yeah."

Their conversation didn't become more syllabic once they were at the condo.

"Hungry?" Hannah said after they were upstairs.

Anuya shook her head.

Teenagers. "I'm going to patch my kayak in the garage. Come or don't come—I don't care."

"I'll come," Anuya said, to Hannah's surprise.

She watched silently as Hannah sanded down the edges of the gash, then cut a sheet of plastic to size and painted waterproof epoxy on it.

"I think it's mean not to tell people I'm your sister!" she said as Hannah pressed the plastic patch against the boat's underside.

"Anuya—" Hannah began, still holding the patch.

Her sister turned and ran upstairs.

"Wait!" Hannah called. She impatiently counted off the number of seconds called for by the glue's directions, then went after her.

The living room and kitchen were empty, and the door to the bedroom was shut.

Deciding to give Anuya time to cool off, Hannah started to sort through the laundry, still unwashed from the dip in the lake. A pocket of her pants crackled, and she pulled out Nathalie's note.

She reread the text. If it wasn't an indirect apology for a lover's suicide attempt, then what did the letter mean? Could it have something to do with the ransacking of her condo and office?

Putting the note aside, she gathered the clothes Anuya had worn yesterday, now in a pile next to her backpack. Under them was a business-sized envelope. The return address read *Bioscience High.*

Was it about today's interview? Despite her reluctance to

snoop, Hannah opened the letter. It was dated six weeks ago.

We are pleased to offer you admission...

Hannah pulled her brows together. If Anuya had been accepted, why the interview charade? The answer was on the second page.

Please provide proof of your family's Arizona residence and...

According to the letter, Anuya had told the school she was living in Arizona—with her sister, Hannah.

Hannah knocked on the bedroom door. No answer.

"Anuya? We have to talk."

The doorbell rang.

Now what? Hannah hurried down the stairs and opened the door. Before her stood Jerry Dan, dressed in cycling clothes.

"Howdy! I was out training and decided to stop by. What's happening?"

Hannah thought again of the break-ins and the threatening message. If something dangerous was going on, Jerry Dan deserved to know.

"I got this call..."

"Last night I had the feeling somebody had been in my condo, too," Jerry Dan said when she had finished. He looked sheepish. "I'm not all that neat, so it was hard to tell."

"They're after the treasure map," Anuya said, emerging from the bedroom. Her eyes were puffy, but otherwise she looked composed.

"Man, you two are so alike," Jerry Dan said.

Hannah's eyes flew to Anuya, searching for the telltale that had revealed their secret, the indelible mark of their connection.

"You both do that thing with your eyebrows when you're thinking." He tapped a finger against his lip. "You know, Anuya might be right. The break-ins could be related to the map."

"That makes no sense," Hannah said. "No one even knows we have it."

"The spirits know," Anuya said. "We should give the map back to its owner."

Hannah recalled the room full of furniture at the auction. "It would be impossible to find out who the desk used to belong to. And the map is at the framers."

Jerry Dan gave a dismissive wave. "Aw, you're right. The map probably has nothing to do with this other stuff." His voice was confident, but from his widened eyes, Hannah could tell he was spooked.

She was, too.

Chapter Seventeen

Thursday, November 5

Dresden's call came midmorning.

"You were right."

"I'm sorry?" Hannah said.

"Garth Weller was shot. Small caliber in the back of his head. The ME missed it in the prelim because there was so much head trauma from the crash."

"*What?*"

"My question exactly. Ms. Dain, what is going on?"

"I'm not sure. Let me get back to you."

Hannah hung up and dialed the hospital.

"Nathalie Soule, please. She's a patient."

The operator put her on hold briefly. "There's no one registered by that name."

"I just visited her yesterday. She was upstairs, in a private room."

"I'll transfer you to the third-floor receptionist."

Thirty seconds of music grated against Hannah's already raw nerves, then another female voice came on the line. Hannah repeated her request.

"Are you family?"

Hannah didn't hesitate. "Sister. I just flew in."

"Ms. Soule signed herself out this morning." The woman's voice was disapproving. "Against doctor's orders."

Hannah thought quickly. "I better call her. Jeez, my PDA is dead and the charger is in my luggage. Let's see…her home number is…" Hannah recited the Pinnacle Peak prefix, then let her voice trail off, hoping the woman would supply the missing digits. She did, and Hannah tapped them into her phone.

Another female voice, this one Hispanic-accented, answered. "Señora Soule is at work."

"At the university?" Hannah said.

"*Sí.*"

"*Gracias.*" Hannah closed the phone.

She was looking up the geology department's number when Shelby appeared in the doorway. Her sister wore a soft pink top that was bright next to her pale skin.

"I don't really know why I did this, but I persuaded Franklin to postpone the settlement meeting until tomorrow," she said.

"Thank you. I'm leaving for ASU right now to check on the samples."

And to find Nathalie.

Neither Nathalie nor Glouster were in their offices. Hannah found the geology department's reception area.

"Nathalie Soule? She was in a car accident," said the woman behind the counter. "We don't expect her back until next week. And Dr. Glouster is teaching a class in the East Hall."

Hannah found Glouster outside the lecture hall, looking like a caricature of a professor—dressed in a worn tweed jacket, he was being peppered with questions by a group of twenty-somethings. The students dispersed, and he caught sight of her.

"Hannah! What brings you here?"

"Checking on the samples."

Glouster glanced at his watch. "Why don't we go to my office? The lab report should be ready."

The space was as overstuffed as Hannah had remembered. Glouster shut the door, then crossed the room to crack the window. He took a pack of Marlboros from a drawer.

"Hope you don't mind. Just a few puffs, and I'll put it out."

Hannah loathed cigarette smoke. "No problem," she said, discreetly edging away. Her glance fell on the desk, and an unfinished sketch of what looked like a dinosaur. *Either that, or a really scary bug. Anuya would know.*

She looked closely at the drawing, seeing its similarity to those on the walls.

"You drew these!" She indicated the framed pieces.

Glouster looked embarrassed. "A hobby of mine." He slid the sketch into a folder, then thumbed through the papers in his inbox, blue tendrils of smoke curling above him. "If the report came in, it would be here."

Hannah's gaze roved the room, catching a familiar face on a photo wedged between two fossils. She picked up the snapshot. Glouster and Jerry Dan sprawled on the dirt next to their mountain bikes, race numbers pinned to their shirts.

"Have you been doing orienteering for a long time?" Hannah asked.

"A few years. I happened across a race when I was on one of my geology trips. Started talking with one of the competitors. He convinced me that my mapping skills would make me a good course designer."

"He must have been right. Jerry Dan said you're designing the route for the state championship."

Glouster looked at her sharply. "Yes," he said after a moment.

There was another photo behind the first one. It showed Glouster and another man in the desert surrounded by college students. All wore shorts, t-shirts, and baseball hats. Behind the unknown man, her features half-hidden, was a dark-haired woman. Hannah recognized Nathalie.

She held up the photo.

"Is this Dr. Weller?"

Glouster glanced at the photo, then nodded. "Our last field trip together."

"Isn't that Nathalie Soule behind him?"

"Yes. Lab techs don't usually go into the field. But Garth told me she wanted to see the petroglyphs."

"Professor Weller and Nathalie..." Unable to think of a diplomatic approach, Hannah opted for straightforward. "They had a pretty close relationship, didn't they?"

"I guess so," Glouster said, still skimming the documents from the inbox.

"Exactly how close?"

Glouster stopped reading. He stubbed out his cigarette on a flat piece of rock on his desk. Dark smears showed it had been used as an ashtray before.

"Not that close, at least I don't think so." His eyes became slightly unfocused as he looked back in time. "I know she was helping him on your case."

"Really?" Hannah wondered why neither Nathalie nor anyone else had mentioned it.

Glouster rubbed a hand over his hair. Close-cropped, it was the color of iron dust. "I think that's what they were arguing about the day Garth..." He took a breath. "The day Garth died."

She considered telling Glouster that Weller's death was neither an accident nor suicide, then noticed the geologist was frowning.

"What is it?"

"I was just thinking about the van."

"Van?"

"The one that picked up Garth that day. It had a company logo on its side." Glouster rubbed his head again. "Thing is, the university has a real strict conflict-of-interest policy. Faculty can't take anything from a corporation, not even a ride."

Scorpion feet skittered down Hannah's spine. "Do you remember anything about the van?"

"Well, it was white, and just like mine, except ten years younger. My attention was on Garth."

"Why?"

"I can't explain it, but I had the impression that he didn't really want to get in the van." Glouster set down the stack of documents. "I don't see the lab report anywhere. Let me ring them."

He made a quick call.

"The report will be ready tomorrow morning," he said.

"That'll be cutting it close—there's a settlement conference Friday afternoon. I'll swing by and pick it up on my way back from the site."

"You're going out to the rez again?"

"The day the cars went into the lake, Shelby and I were on our way to videotape the site. Still needs to be done if we go to trial."

Her cell phone rang in her purse. She plucked it out and answered it.

"This is Detective Dresden," said the gravelly voice.

Hannah had a sudden premonition something bad had happened. *Nathalie?*

"Yes?" Her voice was a little shaky.

"I'm at the station. One of my deputies brought in a shoplifter, and she's asking for you."

The firm occasionally received collect calls from the prison and late-night messages from the county jail, drunks wasting their one phone call.

"We don't do that kind of legal work—"

"She says she's your sister."

Chapter Eighteen

The sheriff's deputy nodded at Hannah. "I'll get Detective Dresden."

There was something wrong in her life when law officers whom she had never met recognized her on sight, Hannah decided as she waited.

The air conditioner vent was rattling. A screw was missing from one of the corners, allowing the perforated metal to vibrate in the moving air. The sound made Hannah grit her teeth.

The deputy reappeared. "Come with me, please."

He ushered her into a windowless interview room. It wasn't her first time there, but at least on this occasion she wasn't a suspect. The air was rank with body odor and burned coffee.

Three people sat at a wooden rectangular table. One was Dresden. Facing him across the table was a thin man in a stylish suit. Anuya sat next to the detective with her eyes downcast, gripping the arms of the chair as though handcuffed to the wood. A suede bag with a stone clasp lay in the center of the table.

"Thank you for joining us," Dresden said. "Care to sit down?"

Hannah folded her arms and leaned against the wall. "I'm fine here."

"How much longer will this take?" the thin man said. "I have to get back to my store."

"We're almost finished, Mr. Spencer-Benton." Hannah heard the unsaid hyphen in Dresden's inflection.

The man continued to fuss. "I spoke to your officer and filled out the report. What more is there for me to do?" The whine in his voice had the unpleasant pitch of a leaf blower.

Dresden steepled his fingers. "We like to take a careful look at cases involving minors before charges are filed."

Spencer-Benton glanced at Hannah. "Who are you?"

"I'm—"

"Ms. Dain is a lawyer," Dresden interjected smoothly.

Anuya stole a glance at Hannah, then dropped her gaze to the scratched tabletop again.

"You're the public defender?" Spencer-Benton didn't wait for Hannah's answer. "Good luck. That *girl*"—he pointed a finger at Anuya, and Hannah saw the gleam of clear nail polish—"stole a six-hundred-dollar purse. Walked right out of the store with it. If I hadn't had my eye on her already, she would have gotten away with it."

Spencer-Benton's shop must have been in one of the boutique hotels cropping up along Saguaro Road, Hannah thought. Six-hundred-dollar purses were among the least expensive items. What had Anuya been doing there?

"Ms. Moore claims she took the purse outside so she could see it in better light," Dresden said.

"What else is someone like her going to say? Now may I go?"

"I wasn't going to steal your stupid purse!" Anuya said. A tiny pulse jumped at her temple. "Your dumb store is so dark, I took it outside to see if the fossil was real."

Fossil? One of Hannah's guilty pleasures was thumbing through beauty magazines when she got her hair cut. She vaguely remembered a recent article on a handbag line featuring "talismans of antiquity."

Spencer-Benton smirked. "With an eye to buying it? And how were you going to do that? I read the deputy's report—sixty dollars and no credit cards in your purse." He gave a little snort. "Not that I expect your type to have any."

Your type. Hannah flinched at the words. Although it had become less overt in the last two decades, Arizona was still an epicenter for racism, both fostered and tempered by its proximity to the Mexican border and Indian reservations. While the white majority largely ignored the Indians, except for envying casino wealth, they were becoming cognizant of their reliance on predominately brown-skinned landscapers, housecleaners, restaurant workers, and day laborers. Chaos would result should everyone of Hispanic descent boycott work on the same day. But Pinnacle Peak was as Neapolitan as the rest of the state: vanilla, chocolate, and strawberry worked, studied, and lived side by side, rather than mixed together.

She studied Anuya's dusky cheeks and shiny black hair, darker versions of her own, and doubted this was the first racial slur her sister had endured. Hannah wondered whether, had she grown up under her birth father's roof, she, too, would have been subjected to suspicious looks from storeowners, service delays in restaurants, and just-rented-to-someone-else apartments.

"You say you were watching Ms. Moore when she was in your store." Dresden's voice was as flat as the surrounding desert.

Spencer-Benton picked invisible lint off his sleeve. "We notice all the customers who come in."

"Was there a moment when you focused on Ms. Moore exclusively?"

"As soon as she picked up the Balencegna. I knew she couldn't afford it."

Dresden's expression was bland. "Because teenagers don't buy six-hundred-dollar handbags?"

"Of course not. This is an affluent community."

"Was it because you had not seen her in the store before?"

"No, we get quite a bit of trade from the hotel." Spencer-Benton made a show of looking at his watch, a thin disk of gold draped across his pale wrist. "If there's nothing else—"

Dresden ignored the hint. "Did Ms. Moore's clothes attract your attention?"

Spencer-Benton rolled his eyes. "She looks like every other teenager, for God's sake. I knew she was going to take the bag because—" Looking suddenly uncomfortable, he lapsed into silence.

"Because why? If teenagers dressed like Ms. Moore purchase handbags like this one"—Dresden held up the suede bag—"then why did you think Ms. Moore was planning to steal the bag?"

"I don't appreciate what you are insinuating!" Spencer-Benton said, his voice rising along with the color in his cheeks.

"I'm not sure a jury wouldn't insinuate the same thing. And the *Express*, too, for that matter. Doubt that sort of thing is good for business."

Spencer-Benton unfastened then fastened the clasp on his watch. "That's defamation," he said, his voice lacking conviction.

"Not if the paper just reports the facts, and lets its readers draw their own conclusions. Especially if those facts include the investigating officer's report on why he believes Ms. Moore was singled out for scrutiny."

Spencer-Benton fidgeted in his chair. "I don't have time for this."

Dresden spread his hands. "It's your choice whether to file charges, Mr. Spencer-Benton."

"Then I won't." He got to his feet and drilled Anuya with a look that made Hannah seethe. "Just make sure she doesn't come back to my store."

"I don't think that will be a problem," Dresden said. "The deputy will show you out."

Spencer-Benton snatched up the bag and, stiff-spined, followed the deputy through the door.

Dresden looked at Anuya and said nothing. She returned his gaze. The silent duel lasted nearly a minute before the teen caved and looked away.

"No more taking merchandise out of a store without permission, Ms. Moore," Dresden said.

Her lower lip caught in her teeth, Anuya nodded.

"No going back to Mr. Spencer-Benton's store."

Anuya lifted her chin. "That guy's a racist! I was just window-shopping, like everyone else. And his stupid purse—"

Dresden held up a hand. Anuya fell silent.

"Are we agreed?" he asked.

"Yes," she said sullenly.

"I'm releasing you to your"—Dresden hesitated—"lawyer."

"Anuya, please wait for me in the lobby," Hannah said. "I have to talk to Detective Dresden for a moment."

Still not looking at Hannah, Anuya pushed herself out of her chair. Pant cuffs sweeping the floor, she stomped out of the room, shutting the door with more force than necessary.

"Thank you for calling me," Hannah said.

"It didn't sound like a usual shoplifting case. And when Ms. Moore said she was your—"

"I'd like that to remain confidential," Hannah quickly said.

Dresden inclined his head. "No charges were filed, so there's no record."

"But the information…you'll keep it to yourself?" She twisted a piece of hair around her finger, then realized what she was doing and stopped. "Please?"

Dresden regarded her. "I don't see a reason to discuss it with anyone."

"Thank you." Hannah cleared her throat. "Did you find out anything more about Garth Weller's death?"

"I'll know more after the autopsy."

Hannah arched her eyebrows. "The bullet wound convince you something else is going on?"

Dresden looked grim. "That, and the missing-persons report on Nathalie Soule that her husband filed this morning."

Anuya stared out the window on the drive to the firm, her face reflected in the glass. Her expression was unreadable.

Hannah was preoccupied with thoughts of Nathalie Soule. In her mind's eye, she saw the SUV hurtle into the lake. Had Nathalie disappeared in order to try suicide again? Or had the person who shot Garth Weller made her the next victim?

"It wasn't even real," Anuya said.

"What?"

"The fossil. It was just a hunk of carved rock."

Hannah shook her head. "No wonder Mr. Hyphen didn't want you looking too closely."

"Who's Mr. Hyphen?"

"It's just a—Never mind." Hannah glanced at Anuya. "I'm sorry you had to go through that."

Her sister jogged a shoulder. "No biggie. It's not like it hasn't happened before."

Hannah heard the hurt under the teen's apparent nonchalance. She steered the rental SUV into the law firm's parking lot and pulled up next to the front entrance.

"I have to shoot some video at the mine site. Want to come?"

Anuya smiled. "Sweet!"

"Wait here while I get the camcorder."

Leaving Anuya in the car with the engine idling, Hannah pushed through the wooden doors and walked down the corridor to her office.

Her secretary sat at her desk, head resting on her cradled arms.

"Clementine!"

Clementine blinked open her eyes, then sat up. "They told me this might happen at the blood bank."

Hannah eyed her secretary critically. "How late did you stay up last night?"

"I should be asking you that question. It's two o'clock—where have you been?"

"Spending some time with Anuya. We're going out to the rez to shoot some video for trial. I just stopped by to see if Shelby still had Jake's camcorder."

"It's in the file room. I'll get it." Clementine heaved herself out of her chair.

Hannah picked up the phone on Clementine's desk. "I better call her and ask if I can borrow it."

"I wouldn't. Jake came by twenty minutes ago. He and your sister are holed up in her office. He's doing the shouting, and she's doing the crying." Clementine scowled with annoyance. "I wish your father had gone with hollow-core doors when he built this place. It would make listening in a whole lot easier."

"Clementine! What did I tell you about eavesdropping?"

Her secretary waved a hand. "Workplace surveillance—everyone does it. I'll get that camcorder. Why don't you call Cooper while you're waiting?"

Hannah scowled at her secretary.

As soon as Clementine rounded the corner, the phone rang.

Hannah stared at it. *Could it be...?* She picked up the receiver.

"Ms. Dain? This is Arlee from the frame shop. I'm sorry, but the map won't be ready until tomorrow after three."

"That's fine. There's no rush," Hannah said.

"No? That isn't what your assistant said. He asked if it could be ready today—even authorized an extra charge for expedited service."

"I think you may have my order confused with someone else's."

The woman's tone turned frosty. "So you're saying you *didn't* authorize the rush charge?"

"No, no, that's fine," Hannah said. "Thank you."

Clementine reappeared with the camcorder. "In case you were wondering, Shelby's door is still closed."

"I wasn't." Hannah took the camcorder. "The frame shop called. Did you put a rush on the order?"

"No. I didn't think you were in a hurry to get it back."

"I'm not. See you tomorrow morning."

Despite her feigned lack of interest, Hannah felt worried as she walked back to her car. Were Jake and Shelby over? She hoped not. The EMT was one of Shelby's better choices, and there was no telling what effect a break-up would have on her sister's sobriety.

With Anuya riding shotgun, Hannah drove south. Snowbirds clogged the main streets, and the SUV swerved around the slower traffic with the grace of a cement mixer. Anuya kept one hand wrapped around the door handle and the other propped against the dash. She was grinning.

This was the time of year Hannah found Pinnacle Peak the

most tolerable. Rock, heat, cactus—those three words pretty much summed up the desert in Hannah's view. When one was lessened, she was the happier for it. With the monsoon season over, the land seemed newly washed. Even the sky looked clean, a soft blue dotted with heavenly puffs of white clouds.

Hannah's cell phone rang. She didn't answer. It kept ringing.

"Aren't you going to get that?" Anuya asked.

Only a few people had her mobile number. And although Hannah hoped one in particular was calling, now wasn't the time for them to talk. "I usually don't when I'm driving."

"I will, then."

Before Hannah could stop her, Anuya had flipped open the phone. "Hello?" She listened, then thrust the phone at Hannah.

"It's for you. Some guy."

Cooper? Hannah grasped the phone. "This is Hannah."

"*Stay away.*"

It was the same voice that she had heard last night. The line went dead. Hannah closef the phone. Anuya looked at her curiously.

"Call dropped," Hannah said. "Can't get good reception out here."

Or in my brain either. She had no idea what the caller wanted her to stay away from. The mine site? Garth's murder? The treasure?

Hannah glanced at Anuya, now hanging out of the SUV's window, scanning the desert with the camcorder. Whatever the caller meant, she had better figure it out soon.

Chapter Nineteen

They had passed the fry bread stand twenty minutes ago, and were deep into the rez. The Salvador Dali landscape stretched out all around them, barren sand dotted with stunted bushes and lumps of rock.

The SUV sped by a dilapidated single-wide with a faded awning and battered aluminum sides. Behind the trailer, clothes flapped on a line like a cheap effect in a B western. Hannah wondered if Espera and Nando lived in something similar.

"There's the turnoff," Anuya said, the camcorder pressed to her eye socket.

All Hannah saw was a wrinkle in the horizon line. As they got closer, the wrinkle became a dirt track branching off the main road. She steered onto it, the SUV bucking in the loose earth. The road had been driven hard. Axle-deep grooves crisscrossed the red dirt for hundreds of yards, testimony to epic struggles to maintain forward movement.

"Praise Krishna!" Anuya said as they dropped into a deep rut and bumped up the other side. Even with their seat belts fastened, Hannah and Anuya bounced on their seats like corn in a popper. Hannah miscalculated a turn, and the SUV dropped off a foot-high ledge. Feeling as though several of her vertebrae had been fused, she braked and got out to survey the damage.

"The front bumper is bent a little," she said when she slid back into the driver's seat.

"Good thing it's not your car," Anuya said.

Hoping she had checked the box for extra insurance on the rental car form, Hannah parked next to the pile of rocks that marked the mine's location. When the dust stirred up by their tires had settled, she and Anuya climbed out. The air was spiced with creosote. Hannah rolled her sore shoulder while her sister consulted the photocopy of the map.

"I'm going to look over there," Anuya said, pointing to a sandstone boulder shaped like a giant sphinx.

"Don't go sticking your hand into any rock piles."

"I won't." Anuya scampered away.

Hannah readied the camcorder. She shot several minutes of the mine entrance where Glouster had taken his samples. Spotting another pile of scree, she moved eastward, filming as she walked. In her peripheral vision, she glimpsed a red racer slip between two stones, out of sight before she could react. Cloven tracks in rain-smoothed sand pockets marked a javelina trail.

She found another mine entrance, and then another. All looked as though they had been used for dump sites. Engrossed in her task, Hannah lost track of time. It wasn't until the distant cliffs glowed smoky rose, gathering in the afternoon shadows—and *Battery Low* appeared on the screen—that Hannah stopped filming.

She kneaded the base of her spine, trying to make the tightness go away, and gazed through the clear, darkening air. Despite three years in Arizona, she still found the wide reach of sky disorienting. In the west, a plane glinted briefly in the sun, so far away the whisper of its engines left the silence unbroken. Its remote presence made Hannah conscious of her solitude—she was alone among the cacti and rocks.

"Anuya?" All Hannah could hear was desert. She broke into a jog, backtracking toward the first dump site. "Anuya!"

"Hannah?" Her sister's voice sounded reedy and far away.

Slightly panicked, Hannah began to run. She sprinted around a house-sized boulder to find Anuya, dusty but grinning, standing under the spindly cover of a palo verde.

"Look! Ammonites!" Anuya opened a grubby hand to show

Hannah bits of tan rock imprinted with seashell whorls. "From when this was under the ocean, like Dr. Glouster said."

The pale sun had sunk down to an inch above the horizon, turning the sky the color of molten copper. Hannah narrowed her eyes against the metallic light. For a moment, ocotillos became seaweed, and cholla branched into coral. Barrel cacti bristled like sea urchins, while upthrusts of rock turned into schooners cutting through swells of sand. She blinked, and found herself back in arid desolation.

"We better get back," she said. She did not want to navigate the spine-shattering road in the dark. Already stars were switching on, and soon the shadows purpling the hills would be upon them.

"Wait. Let me show you something else." Anuya unfolded the copy of the map from Hannah's desk. "This is the lake, right?" She pointed to an amoeba shape with fish doodles in its interior.

Hannah looked at the paper. "Uh-huh."

Anuya traced a line drawn next to the lake, its peaks and valleys as sharp as an EKG printout. "And this looks like mountains, right?"

"Uh-huh."

Anuya swept a hand toward the water, now hammered pewter in the diminishing light. "But there aren't any mountains there, right?"

"Right. So either the map is wrong or we're not in the right place."

"No," Anuya said, excitement in her voice. "Look again. What if this line isn't supposed to be mountains? What if it's supposed to be *shadows* from the mountains?"

Hannah looked at the map, then to where the jagged rocks threw scapular shadows over the flatlands. Incredibly, the zigs and zags of the two matched.

"But why would someone draw the map this way?" she said.

"So if someone else found it, he wouldn't know where the treasure was!" Anuya's eyes sparkled. "I think the gold is over there." She extended a thin brown arm westward, where El Diablo stood like a bridesmaid beside El Piniculo's taller tiara and wider veil. Rocks lay on top of rocks at its base, the granite jumble spilling all the way down to the gray-green velour of the lake's shore.

"It's too late to do any more exploring tonight. Let's go back to the car." Hannah knew when the sun went down, the desert went dark—very dark. She shepherded a sulky Anuya back to the SUV.

Even in the twilight, Hannah could see something was amiss. The vehicle's hood tilted forward, as though it were trying to bury its grill in the sand. Closer inspection revealed two flat tires.

"Great," Anuya said, drawing out the word. "How long will it take for the tow truck to get out here?"

"Triple A doesn't cover the rez," Hannah said.

"Seriously? If we were in the city, all we'd have to do is push the car next to a hydrant. A tow truck would show up in five minutes."

Hannah looked at a rock-scarred tire. The small slit where the knife had gone in was almost imperceptible. She checked the other tire and found a similar cut. Was it from the same knife that had slashed her kayak? Forcing herself to stay calm for Anuya's sake, she popped the back window and reached for the crate of emergency supplies.

"There's no cell service out here and we're running out of light. We won't make it back before dark. Looks like we'll have to camp out."

Anuya regaled her with a look of horror. "Camping? I'm from New York. We don't do that."

Hannah handed her a sleeping bag. "What about all those homeless people? Like it or not, we're sleeping here tonight."

"Why can't we stay in the car? Don't the seats fold down?"

Because whoever flatted our tires might come back. Hannah stuffed some energy bars into her pocket. "Because we might run out of oxygen in the car," she lied.

"What? Cars aren't airtight."

Of all the sisters, I have to get the science geek. "We're not sleeping in the car because I said so."

Anuya started to protest, but Hannah silenced her with a look.

"Sleeping bags, food, bottled water, flashlight, insect repellent, matches, extra sweats, down parkas...I think that's everything." Hannah divided the gear into two piles, then loaded it into the nylon sacks that had held the sleeping bags. She gave a sleeping bag and a sack to Anuya.

"Drape the bag around your neck like a muffler, carry the sack like a backpack, and follow me."

Hannah switched on the flashlight and started walking at an angle toward the lake, planning for them to bed down out of sight but not hearing range of the car.

Anuya took the sack and hung the sleeping bag over her shoulders, but didn't budge. "Krishna says that if you're patient, something will always happen, and that even if you get stuck, it will never be for long."

"What does Krishna say to do if whatever happens makes things worse?" Hannah shifted her sack to a more comfortable position. "You can stay here if you want. Just remember what Clementine told you about javelinas."

The white around Anuya's eyes showed. "How do you know they're around?"

"There are tracks over by those rocks. Looks like a regular trail."

Hannah started walking again. She heard Anuya fall in behind, and bit back a smile.

They serpentined through the prickly pear and cholla, Hannah keeping an eye out for snakes. The trail went from white to tan to brown, then slipped into darkness with everything else. The surrounding chaparral was scraggly, like bundles of barbed wire. Hannah tried to avoid its branches. Moths swarmed the flashlight's beam, and their wings left powdery residue on the lens. A shadow flickered in the corner of Hannah's eye. *A bat.* Quiet death in motion—there were now three moths instead of four.

As she trod with care on the sun-hardened sand, Hannah thought about the events of the past few months. Moving back to Arizona had made her more aware of the precariousness of life. Had it also made her more tolerant of violence? In the desert, circumstances were more uncertain and marginal, evil more readily visible. Had this bred in her a more accepting attitude when bad things happened, a lack of surprise when situations took a brutal turn?

Lost in thought, Hannah wandered too close to a cholla arm. Spines raked the back of her hand and she dropped the flashlight.

"Ow!"

"What's wrong?" Anuya said nervously.

Hannah retrieved the flashlight. "Just clumsy." She looked out over the bizarre moonscape of yellowish earth and hulking rocks, satisfied they were far enough from the SUV. She shone the flashlight onto a flood-polished ledge. "How about here?"

"No. The burru might get us."

Scorpions, snakes, and javelinas—wasn't there enough to worry about without adding evil spirits, too? "We're in the middle of nowhere. The burru won't be able to find us."

"Yes, it will. This is the kind of place it likes. As soon as we're asleep, it will swallow us whole like a python. My grandmother told me their dung heaps turn into hills, with animal and people skeletons inside."

"Anuya, that's silly. The burru—"

"I want to go back to the car!"

Hysteria frayed her sister's voice, making Hannah even more certain that she shouldn't mention the slashed tires. A panicked Anuya would be harder to deal with than a petulant one.

"Is there a place where the burru won't see us?" she asked.

"In a tent, or under a rock, maybe."

Hannah stifled a sigh. "There aren't any—"

"A cave!" Paper rustled. "The cave on the treasure map—we can stay there. Give me the flashlight."

Hannah handed it over, sure they were in for a long night.

The dark would make finding the cave nearly impossible, assuming it even existed.

"Are you sure you can find it?"

"The ghosts will help me," Anuya said. Head tipped back, she stared skyward. "There's the Big Dipper, so the North Star must be..."

Hannah looked up, too. The star field spread across the broken cliff line to the north, arched overhead, then descended toward the lake, now more densely black than the sky. In the west, far out in the darkness, was a pale glow from the lights of the town.

Hannah remembered Anuya's comment to Glouster. "So ghosts are good?"

"Yeah." Anuya paused. "Our dad's a ghost. He watches out for me. You, too." She consulted the compass Jerry Dan had given her. "Follow me," she said.

Little eyes, caught in the flashlight's sweep, sparkled yellow and green. Something moved through the chaparral and Hannah hoped it wasn't people, or something big and carnivorous. She was about to tell Anuya that enough was enough, that they needed to find a spot to bed down, when her sister abruptly halted.

"We're here."

Here, according to Anuya, was the cave marked on the map. To Hannah it was just an overhang formed by two teepeed rocks. But as long as her sister thought it adequate to protect them from any passing burru, it was fine with her. A breeze whiffled softly through the branches of a creosote bush near the entrance.

"Did you hear that?" Anuya said. "The burru went by without noticing us."

They poked around with sticks to scare off any other inhabitants. Hannah rolled out the sleeping bags while Anuya played with the camcorder.

"Everything looks green, like we're on Mars," she said, her eye pressed to the viewfinder.

A would-be scientist who believed in Martians and ghosts and Hindu curses. "It's got night vision," she said.

"Hey! It just shut off!" Anuya pressed the power button, then shook the camcorder.

"I used up most of the battery. Here—put everything on, and wrap the extra sweatshirt around your head. It'll feel colder now that we've stopped moving."

"Why don't we make a fire?"

"Fires attract animals." *And people.* "I'll zip the sleeping bags together so we keep each other warm."

Hannah put on the extra sweatshirt and the down jacket, the latter a tight fit. Hopping from one foot to the other, she pulled on the sweatpants, hoping the extra layer would protect her from itinerant scorpions.

"I feel fat," Anuya said. She stood with her arms slightly extended from her sides, a sweatshirt twined around her head like a turban.

"As long as you stay warm." Hannah handed her an energy bar. "Make sure you eat it all. We don't want to attract mice."

Or the snakes that eat the mice. Of all desert fauna, Hannah's biggest aversion was to any that slithered. When they had finished the bars, she stowed the wrappers far from their sleeping area.

"Look!" Anuya was shining the flashlight toward the back of the cave. Highlighted in the yellow beam were figures etched into the rough wall. Mythical beings, long and narrow, alongside spectral figures with geometric-shaped, antlered animals.

"Pictographs!" Hannah said.

"Petroglyphs," Anuya corrected. "They're chipped into the rock, not painted."

One image caught Hannah's attention—a large creature with a humped back and long neck, holding a spear. The way it was drawn, it appeared to be looking right at them. The etching made her nervous.

"Climb in. And turn off the flashlight. We need to save the batteries."

Anuya crawled between the two sleeping bags, accompanied by the tinkling of the tiny hammered bells around her ankle. Hannah scooted in next to her, then pulled the zipper closed and her jacket sleeves over her hands. Despite the layers of clothing, her head swathed in a sweatshirt, and Anuya snugged up next to her, she was still cold. Was there a chance they could freeze? Hannah had no idea. As a matter of course, desert residents became familiar with the symptoms of heat stroke and heat exhaustion. No one worried much about frostbite—temperatures barely dipped below freezing during winter nights.

Nearby, a coyote yipped, and received a mournful answer from farther north. At the lake's edge, frogs croaked in dissonant counterpoint. Hannah listened as five minutes became ten, then fifteen. Did frogs really have that much to talk about?

Already bone-chilled on one side, she flexed her fingers and wiggled her toes, enviously noticing that Anuya was already asleep. Resigned to staying awake all night, she was surprised to feel herself drifting off.

Sleep brought visions of a large monster, remarkably like the creature etched into the cave wall, chasing her through the desert. Try as she might, Hannah couldn't elude it. No matter how well she hid, the beast always found her, forcing her to run again.

"Hannah! HANNAH!" Anuya's voice jarred her awake.

"Huh?" Hannah said. Her body felt stiff, and there was grit in her mouth.

"I had a nightmare." Anuya squirmed closer, setting her bracelets a-chatter.

"Want to tell me about it?"

"A big monster with an arched back and spines around its neck was coming after me."

Hannah felt the hairs along her arm prickle. "What else do you remember?"

"Only that I hid in a cave but it found me. It was horrible, like one of those gross video games." Anuya shuddered, her knees knocking against Hannah's. "Did you dream about anything?"

"No," Hannah lied. She felt Anuya's body go tense beside her.

"Listen! Did you hear that?"

Near-blindness made Hannah's hearing more acute. The frogs had shut up. The coyotes and owls had, too. All she could hear was the ruffle of water. A little stretch of imagination, and it became hushed voices.

"It's just the lake," she said.

Anuya's eyes gleamed in the new moon's light. "No. It's the djinn."

"Djinn?"

"Bad spirits."

Hannah massaged her aching neck. "Just how many gods and spirits and whatever do we have to worry about?"

"Thousands. Hinduism lets you choose what beliefs are best for you." Anuya started to worm out of the sleeping bag. "We're not supposed to be here."

Hannah's common sense told her to disagree, scoff even. A religion—a life—tailored by internal forces rather than external standards?

"Okay. Where to?" she said with as much enthusiasm as she could muster.

With Hannah lighting the way with the flashlight, Anuya walked to a spot about twenty feet deeper into the cave. She stood very still, her shadow large against the rock wall. Silence folded around them. Even the whispering from the lake was silent.

"This is the right place," Anuya said.

They bedded down again. The earth was more hard-packed, and Hannah could feel a draft blowing from between the rocks behind them. The air smelled brown, like dust and old bones.

Caves existed near the lake because of the limestone in the area—softer stone gave way under weather, leaving the harder granite. Hannah had never been tempted to do any exploring. She considered caves to be private places in the earth, doorways into its oldest parts. It seemed almost voyeuristic to intrude.

Despite the inability to see and the slight stuffiness, Hannah had to admit she felt safer. Their rear and flanks were protected, and there were enough throwing-size rocks within reach to repel a frontal attack. *As long as knives and guns aren't involved*, she mentally added, mindful of the slashed tires. She threw a comforting arm over Anuya.

"Doing okay?"

"You know how I told you I don't like small places?" Anuya's voice was muffled. She had burrowed deep into the bag. "I don't like the dark, either."

Hannah's reply was cut off by a rumble deeper than a chorus of bullfrogs. *Thunder?* A little late in the season. The sound grew louder, and Hannah recognized the roar of a truck's engine.

"Someone's coming!" Anuya said. She started to kick free of the sleeping bags.

"No!" Hannah tightened her grip around her sister, keeping her on the ground. She could feel Anuya's heart beating fast through the layers of clothing, and her eyelashes licked Hannah's cheek.

"Let me go!" Anuya twisted around and managed to scrabble to her knees. Surprised at her strength, Hannah wrestled her back down. Anuya's nails scraped against her neck, but Hannah didn't let go.

The truck blasted by the cave opening, vibration from its tires setting off a trickle of dirt from the earthen ceiling. When the noise had receded, Hannah loosened her grip on Anuya. The teen shoved her away.

"What's your problem? They could have given us a ride!"

Hannah decided it was time to stop babying her sister—a little bit. "Think about it. It's the middle of the night, in the part of the rez where no one is supposed to be. What do you think that truck was carrying? Illegal aliens? Drugs?" *People looking for us?*

Anuya was silent. After a moment, Hannah felt the touch of a tentative hand. She clasped it in her own and gave it a squeeze.

"I'm sorry," Anuya said.

"Let's try and go back to sleep."

"Can we turn on the light?" Her sister's voice was small.

"Better not, in case they come back." Hannah pulled Anuya close, and her sister's sweatshirt turban bumped her in the nose. "It's not really dark, you know," Hannah said. "You can still see the moon and the stars." A strip of Milky Way and a sliver of pale moon were visible through the craggy opening.

Anuya giggled. "That sounds like something Dad would say." Hannah felt her sister go rigid. "I'm sorry. I—"

Hannah realized they had run out of uncomplicated things to talk about. *Time to acknowledge the elephant in the room.*

"Do I look like him?" she asked.

The stiffness went out of Anuya's shoulders. "A little."

"I wish I could have met him. It would have been nice to know..." She didn't finish. Know what? The reasons for Elizabeth's betrayal? Why he had never contacted her? Maybe Cooper was right—some history was better left buried.

"You look more like your mom."

"What?" Hannah started to sit up, and a waft of cold air wedged itself between them.

"Hey!" Anuya tugged on the top sleeping bag, forcing Hannah to lie down again.

"How do you know what my mother looked like?" Hannah's whisper was harsh.

"I was a snoopy kid. One day at my grandmother's I was playing with my dad's old things. There was a photo of my dad and a lady. They had their arms around each other."

Grandmother? Hannah had a sudden picture of herself standing in a Baptist church, the sole occupant of a reception line greeting a parade of unknown ancestors, the line of people running out the carved red doors.

"When I was old enough to know what the empty chair at Diwali meant, I asked Dad if it was for the lady in the photo," Anuya said. "I thought maybe they used to be married and she had died. That's when I found out the chair was for you."

"How did your mother feel about...them?" Hannah didn't want to say *their affair.*

"She met my dad after he and your mom broke up. I used to think it was no big deal to her. But now I'm not so sure."

Having lived—uneasily—with Elizabeth's ghost, Hannah thought she understood. When someone died at the height of her beauty and accomplishments, no one else could ever measure up. Anuya's mom aged, the bloom of her and Tel's initial love faded, and individual quirks became annoying instead of delightful. Meanwhile, Elizabeth's apparent perfection was frozen in time.

"Did it bother you?" Hannah asked, and felt Anuya shrug.

"Nah. My grandmother said Americans worry too much. 'A *Harijan* doesn't ask why he is an Untouchable. He makes the best of it so his life is better when he is reincarnated.' My dad said almost the same thing."

"What's that?"

Anuya deepened her voice. "Go with the flow, baby."

Go with the flow? Was that the secret to Anuya's comfort with the fruit salad of her genes and upbringing? Hannah envied her sister's equanimity when it came to family matters.

Anuya's sweatshirt turban had been knocked askew and an escaped tendril of hair—slightly oily and smelling of jasmine—tickled Hannah's chin. Anuya squirmed, poking Hannah with her elbow.

"I was so pumped to find out I had a sister, even if we didn't ever know each other. And then we met! How cool is that?"

Not very when Shelby finds out. Hannah lay on her back and closed her eyes, then opened them again. The darkness, thick and silent, didn't change. She craned her neck for a reassuring glimpse of the slim band of stars visible through the cave's entrance. Was Tel Moore's ghost in the sky, too, looking down at them?

Anuya stirred beside her, then yawned. "It's so quiet out here, it hurts my ears."

Hannah exhaled a quiet laugh. "G'night."

Pillowing her head on one arm, she breathed in the freezing air and willed herself to be vigilant. But fatigue soon overcame her resolve, and she fell asleep, accompanied by the croak of a persistent frog.

Chapter Twenty

Friday, November 6

The cold woke her. Hannah rolled over, seeking a warmer spot in the bed. She found only hardness and more cold—and a set of arms and legs belonging to someone else.

She sat up with a start, confused. Then rock walls came into focus, and she saw Anuya sprawled next to her, loose-limbed, hair entangled in a sweatshirt.

Hannah pulled the sleeping bag closer. Anuya stirred, then stretched her arms overhead, opening and closing her fists, rotating her wrists, first one way, then another—exactly as Hannah did most mornings.

Her sister's eyes blinked open. "Is it time to get up?"

The sun had found its way into the cave opening as the day started to unfold. Purple shadows gave way to deep red that would become more and more orange. She glanced back into the cave. There was the petroglyph again, still staring at her.

"Let's go." Hannah started packing up their things.

Outside, she instructed Anuya on the finer points of bush bathrooms. They split an energy bar and the last bottle of water for breakfast. Anuya wolfed down her share, then ran her tongue over her teeth.

"Ugh. My mouth feels furry." She plucked a section of her t-shirt free from her pants.

"Why do you do that?" Hannah asked.

"The shirt thing? It's a habit. You tuck a sari a certain way so the gods can whisk away evil. My mom taught me to do it with my American clothes, too."

"Does she wear saris?"

"Most of the time. I only have to on special occasions, like weddings and stuff. They're not too bad, as long as you don't have to pee."

The sunlight sharpened and heat returned, gently baking the chill out of their bodies and making their walk back to the SUV faster and less treacherous than the previous night's journey. A hawk floated overhead, wings luffing, looking for something to eat on the desert floor.

Hannah had almost convinced herself that an encounter with sharp rocks had stranded them until she saw her tires, the clean-edged gashes unmistakable in the daylight. She saw something else, too—fresh tire tracks, close enough that even in the pitch of the night, the driver would have seen the SUV.

Anuya sprawled on the shady side of the car, her back against the door panel, and plucked seeds from her socks.

"Holy cow, do I want a shower. How long are we gonna have to wait until someone comes?"

"I told Clementine where we were going, so it shouldn't be more than a day or two. But if she's forgotten, might be as long as a week."

Anuya sat up. "A week? That's nuts!"

"That's the rez."

Hannah ran a hand along the kayak's bow, pleased to find no damage. Apparently the vandals' attack had been limited to the SUV.

"You know, there may be a way we could get out of here faster than walking or waiting for someone to look for us."

"Bring it on," Anuya said.

Hannah undid one of the straps holding the kayak. "We can paddle toward the fry bread stand. It'd be a lot faster than walking—less than an hour to cell tower range."

"In case you haven't noticed, your boat has room for only one person."

The second strap undone, Hannah hoisted the kayak off the roof. She missed her shorter Subaru. "We'll use one of these straps as a tow line. I'll paddle, and you swim behind."

"Me swim? Nunh-uh!" Anuya traced a *Z* in the air in front of her with a raised index finger, echoing the movement with her head and shoulders. "The closest I've gotten to water that wasn't from a faucet is driving over the Brooklyn Bridge. Oh yeah, and dipping my toe into the Ganges when my mom made me go on the pilgrimage to dump my middle uncle's ashes."

Hannah unlocked the SUV and took out her paddle. "I thought you were supposed to immerse yourself."

Anuya wrinkled her nose. "Do you know how gross that river is? Makes the Hudson look like it's filled with Evian."

"Then I guess we're walking." Hannah wedged the sleeping bags and carry sack into the kayak's seat compartment, using a roof rack strap to secure it. "Grab an end."

Anuya looked at her, goggle-eyed. "You want us to carry the boat, too?"

"It's not that heavy."

"Do you know how far it is to that bread place? We can come back for it later."

Hannah folded the sweatshirts into squares and handed one to Anuya. She wasn't in the mood to explain her possessiveness toward the plastic craft.

"We can turn it upside down and balance it on our heads. The sweatshirts will make good padding." She picked up the kayak's bow and looked at her sister.

Wearing an aggrieved expression, Anuya lifted the stern.

With a minimum of direction by Hannah—"turn it clockwise...a little higher"—they maneuvered the kayak until its deck rested on their cushioned heads. Hannah in the lead, the paddle tucked under her arm, they started walking.

"You know, this is how African tribeswomen carry water," Hannah said, concentrating on keeping her stride short so Anuya could stay in step.

"We look like a freakin' turtle," her sister muttered.

"Pretend it's one of those two-piece horse costumes."

"With me in the rear? No way!"

They followed the winding dirt track through the chaparral. Post-monsoon season, the earth sported a fuzz of green, but Hannah was unappreciative. In her view, the spindly grass wasn't even in the same phylum as the lawns back East.

Lizards genuflected as they passed, the mottle of their skins blending with the rock. Hannah noticed a trail of fresh cloven-hoof tracks—more javelina. Apparently quite a crowd of the wooly pigs had passed by last night.

Another eternal half-hour went by. Hannah squinted at the foothills south of town from under the plastic canopy, trying to gauge the distance. Heat waves diffused her focus, and the hills looked as though they were floating.

"You and Shelby aren't very much alike," Anuya said.

Hannah thought about her blond, fair-skinned sister. To Shelby, an Italian pump was a shoe, not a device for inflating bike tires, and "Sunset" was the name of a favorite lip gloss, not a hiking trail.

"No, we're not," she agreed.

"Is that why you don't like her?"

Hannah stumbled over a rut. The kayak jerked as she tottered a few steps, and Anuya nearly went down.

"Watch it!" Anuya said.

"Sorry." Hannah moved to the center of the road where it was smoother. The going was treacherous even without a kayak—or family dynamics—on her shoulders. One misstep could mean miles of painful limping.

"I'd say it was more a problem of distance," Hannah fibbed. "Shelby and I don't know each other very well. I went to school back East while she stayed here."

"You and I just met. Does that mean we'll never be like real sisters either?"

"That's different," Hannah said. How to explain she already

felt closer to Anuya than to the sister she had grown up with? A rabbit crouched beside the road, immobile in nervous attention. Hannah felt just as tense.

"It's bad karma not to be close to your family," Anuya said.

Then I'm never making it to nirvana.

Instinct finally broke through the rabbit's paralysis and sent it scampering into the brush. Hannah watched it go, half-wishing she could follow.

Heat and dust rose together, making further talking difficult. Hannah squinted against the brightening light—Why had she left her sunglasses in the car?—and guessed they were a mile, maybe a mile and a half, from the rez border. Even so close to civilization, the desert still was daunting and unpredictable. Death was always a possibility out here, usually from ignorance or bad luck. Or both, Hannah thought.

The road dipped close to the lake. The bright cyan surface sparkled, and the air was heavy with the smell of the vegetation that fringed the shoreline. An insect chorus played the same note over and over, while the sun shone mercilessly.

Hannah was about to suggest again that she paddle into cell phone range, then return to wait with Anuya for their ride, when the sound of an engine cut through the stillness like a menacing bee. They halted.

The tire vandals coming back to check on their handiwork—or do more harm?

"Put down the kayak and stand next to me," Hannah said.

Her bad shoulder popped as she lowered the boat. Trying to appear relaxed, Hannah adjusted her grip on the paddle, ready to swing it like a bat if necessary. Anuya slipped her hand into Hannah's as they watched the white SUV speed toward them, dust billowing from its tires. The road jinked, exposing the Pinnacle Peak city seal and the word SHERIFF on the vehicle's side door.

Anuya disengaged her grip. "For once I'm glad to see the cops."

"Behave," Hannah said, hoping it wasn't Dresden.

The SUV braked beside them. The driver lowered his window and Hannah was only partially relieved.

"Hey there, Ms. Dain. I've been looking for you and your friend."

"Need more brown people to arrest?" Anuya muttered.

"Morning, Deputy Frampton." They had met once before—when Hannah was questioned as a murder suspect. "We had some car trouble."

"I'll give you a lift home." Frampton nodded at the kayak. "Your boat can fit in the back."

Minutes later she and Anuya were in the front seat. The deputy drove, attempting to steer around potholes while he passed out water bottles and candy bars. Hannah took a deep swig of water, then bit into a Snickers, wanting to laugh with relief. Chocolate had never tasted so good.

"I don't remember this road being so tore up," Frampton said as a tire jounced through what felt like a refrigerator-sized crater.

"How did you know to look for us?" Hannah asked through barely parted lips so as not to bite her tongue.

"Your secretary called Detective Dresden this morning. She told him you hadn't come in to work and weren't answering your phone, and that no one had heard from you since you headed out to the old mines on the rez yesterday afternoon." He glanced at her. "You shouldn't have left your car."

"I know. But we decided to walk out." Hannah didn't want to mention the tire slashing in front of Anuya. "Sorry if you had trouble finding us."

Frampton leaked a small smile. "The green boat on your head made you hard to miss."

"It's a kayak," Hannah said stiffly.

"Told you we looked stupid," Anuya said.

The radio in the dashboard sputtered police jargon. Frampton picked up the handset, replied briefly in the same language, then hung up.

"I have to take this call," he said as the SUV hit the pavement and the sign marking the rez border flashed by. "I'll drop you at the edge of town, and another deputy will take you the rest of the way home."

"No need," Hannah said. With her luck, Dresden would be the one to show up. "Just leave us where there's cell coverage and I'll call a friend."

Hannah pulled out her phone as they approached the first strip shopping center. The screen displayed three bars out of four. Deputy Frampton helped them unload the kayak in the parking lot and handed Hannah a business card.

"If you can't find a ride, call this number."

"Thanks," Hannah said.

The white SUV sped off, overhead lights flashing but siren silent. Pinnacle Peak was the sort of town where people pulled over without an audible demand.

A sag in the low roof made the building look as though it had been beaten down by the heat. The tenants included a laundromat, a locksmith, and—incredibly—a South Indian restaurant. A *Closed* sign was propped in the restaurant window, but Hannah could see people moving about inside.

Anuya ran over to investigate food and drink availability while Hannah stayed with the kayak under a cluster of arthritic palm trees and called Jerry Dan's cell. There were no other cars in the parking lot, and passing traffic was sparse.

Her call went straight to voicemail. Hannah waited impatiently for the beep, noticing her knuckles were red with sunburn where they had wrapped around the deck of the boat.

"Jerry Dan, this is Hannah Dain. It's about ten o'clock. If you get this message in the next half hour, call me."

Hannah scrolled through her phone's contacts list, looking for someone who wouldn't require an explanation or deliver a lecture. And who has a car big enough to carry the kayak, she reminded herself, ruling out Clementine and Shelby. She paused on a name, scrolled past it, then hit the *Up* arrow to backtrack.

No explanation, no lecture, and owns a pickup truck. Hannah hit the green phone button on the keypad.

He answered on the first ring.

"Hey, it's Hannah. Can you come pick me up?" She gave directions and explained she had the kayak and a friend with her.

"See you in ten," he said.

"Thanks."

She closed the phone just as Anuya crossed the parking lot holding a white bag striped with grease and a six-pack of soda. There was a shiny smear on her chin.

"Paratha and nauvatan korma," Anuya said, opening the bag. "Smells way better than what my grandmother used to make." Anuya tore off a piece from the disk of dough and folded it into her mouth. "Grandmother was a really bad cook."

Hannah popped the tab on one of the cans and poured the cold drink down her throat, feeling the chill slide all the way down to her stomach. She drank until the can was empty, then helped herself to a slice of warm bread. "Our ride's on the way," she said between chews.

The scent of curry and red peppers jazzed the air. Anuya handed her a plastic fork. "You're supposed to eat spicy food when it's hot outside. Makes you perspire."

Hannah's shirt already hung sodden on her shoulders. But hunger made her dig in. The first bite made her mouth feel as if it were wrapped around a hot branding iron. She spit out the food and groped for a soda. It took two cans to extinguish the fire that had engulfed her taste buds. Hannah cautiously probed her gums with her tongue, expecting to encounter charred flesh.

Anuya scooped up another forkful. "Next time I'll ask for medium-spicy."

Hannah was finishing her fourth soft drink when the pickup pulled into the parking lot. The driver parked and got out.

"Hey," Jake said.

Chapter Twenty-one

Anuya's head lolled on Hannah's shoulder. After calling dibs on the first shower, she had climbed into the truck cab and fallen asleep between Jake and Hannah, who spoke in whispers so as not to wake her.

"If this turns into a regular thing, I'm going to get one of those magnetic signs made for my truck—*Kayak Taxi*." The crisp white shirt of Jake's EMT uniform was unbuttoned at the collar, revealing sunburned skin.

"Thanks for coming," Hannah said. "I don't know all that many people who drive pickups." *Who I can call*, she mentally added, thinking of Cooper's big Ford.

"Good to know that I'm on your list," Jake said cheerfully.

They were driving through the center of town, past Pueblo and Territorial architecture, which shunned the monumental for the more valuable quality of minimizing heat. Stucco walls dripped with bougainvillea that would turn blood red in another month.

Hannah clapped the top of her thighs, raising a puff of dust that was scattered by the draft from the air conditioner. "I can hardly wait to get cleaned up."

"You should call Shelby. She's always up for a trip to the spa," Jake said.

Hannah pushed a straggle of hair out of her face. "That bad, huh?"

Jake grinned. "I know better than to answer that."

Though her sister was the one who thought facials and massages were as necessary as teeth-brushing, right now Hannah could go for a pedicure, a manicure, and whatever other *cures* a salon offered. But the clock was ticking down to the settlement conference. Glouster's test results should be waiting for her at the firm.

The mention of her sister reminded Hannah of another concern.

"Does Shelby seem stressed to you lately?" she asked.

"A little. This trial is a big deal."

"Are things still good between you guys?"

A muscle jumped in Jake's cheek. "What are you getting at?"

"I'm worried about her health." Hannah decided there was no other way to say it. "And if she's relapsed."

"You think Shelby is drinking again? No way!" Jake had a stranglehold on the steering wheel even though they were cruising at the speed limit. "We're fine. Shelby's fine."

"Glad to hear it. I was concerned, that's all."

"Don't be." Jake let the words hang, as heavy and pointed as daggers.

They drove in uncomfortable silence.

"At least this time I recognized you—I mean, with your EMT uniform on," Hannah said in a chipper voice. As breacher of the peace, she felt obligated to smooth things over. "How's that going?"

"Fine."

"Heard you got transferred to days." Shelby had explained that EMTs worked three twelve-hour shifts, followed by the same number of days off, with an extra shift and day off every two weeks. Hannah thought trial and business practice would be a lot more streamlined if lawyers kept the same hours.

"Yep."

Hannah gave up. If Jake wanted to be mad at her for asking if Shelby were drinking again, so be it.

They were in the heart of the town's tourist section. A cinema-tainted version of the Old West rolled past their windows—store signs in circus-style fonts mounted on false-fronted wooden buildings, shoppes—spelled with two *P*s and an *E* at the end—selling western wear and cactus candy, a crowd gathering for the noon shoot-em-up. There were as many sedans ferrying white-thighed tourists as there were pickups driven by men in Stetsons and trucker caps. The neighborhood verged on tacky. It wouldn't take too many more saloons or pastel-painted coyotes with bandanas around their necks to push homage into caricature.

Jake yanked the wheel and the truck lurched onto the rental car company's lot. Wordlessly he unloaded the kayak while Hannah roused Anuya.

"Thanks again," she said when the craft and her paddle were safely on the ground.

"Shelby's just tense because of this stupid trial," Jake said. He slammed the door and gunned the engine, strewing pebbles as he sped off the lot.

Dis his girlfriend and pay for it. Or was Jake mad because she was right? And if she was right, about what—trouble in paradise or Shelby's slide back into the bottle? Feeling the beginning of a headache, Hannah guided a sleepy Anuya into the rental company's office.

Less than an hour later, arrangements had been made to recover the other car and Hannah was in a replacement blue SUV on her way to the law firm, with the kayak stowed in the condo garage and Anuya tucked in upstairs.

After a twenty-minute sojourn in the bathroom, her sister had declared herself clean and adequately revived to accompany Hannah. But by the time Hannah had finished her own shower, Anuya was asleep on the sofa, her oiled and braided hair coiled like a glossy ebony snake beside her.

Hannah drove with the window down, raking her fingers through her hair for an impromptu blow-dry. Patio homes flashed by, their small lawns hugging front walks—postage stamps of defiance against the surrounding desert.

The SUV's tires crunched across the firm's gravel lot. Hannah parked in front of the entrance, and headed for her office.

Clementine was leaning back in her chair with her eyes closed and her chin resting on her generous chest. Two éclairs were on a paper plate next to her keyboard. Cream oozed out of the ends, and the chocolate coating was sweating.

"Clementine, wake up! Are Glouster's test results here?" Hannah flipped impatiently through the papers in her inbox.

Her secretary raised her head and said, "In Jesus' name, Amen." She reached for an éclair. "In case you were wondering, I was saying grace."

"Sure you were," Hannah said. "Test results?"

"What, no 'Thank you for calling the police to rescue me and the kid so we wouldn't die in the desert, leaving our flesh to picked from our bones by buzzards?" Clementine took another bite of pastry.

"Thank you." Hannah walked into her office. "Even though there aren't any buzzards in Arizona. Are the results in here?"

"Blue folder, middle of your desk."

Hannah picked up the folder, pausing to admire its cover. Glouster had done a fanciful sketch of a mine site. A roadrunner perched on a tailings pile, boulders were decorated with petroglyphs, and, Hannah noted with amusement, the faintest of mushroom clouds hovered on the horizon. She turned to the first page and started reading.

All the samples had tested positive, with readings of up to eighty-five percent of the ore's original radioactivity. Glouster had done a chart, comparing the findings with what were deemed acceptable levels of exposure for children and adults. There was enough of a difference between the numbers to make Hannah queasy with images of babies born without bones or the correct number of chromosomes.

Glouster had also noted the composition of the radioactive waste. In addition to uranium, other minerals included sodium-24, iodine-131, cobalt-60, radium-226. Hannah didn't know what the numbers signified—references to atomic weight? There were chemicals, too—benzene, ethylene glycol, perchloroethylene.

More illustrations and charts fleshed out the data. Hannah couldn't wait to show the report to Shelby and Franklin. Glouster's findings more than justified calling off the settlement conference.

She was already thinking about what she'd say to Franklin when she turned to the summary section on the last page. The words hit her like a blow. *All samples tested showed trace amounts of material inconsistent with disposal within the purported time frame.*

"Clementine! Get Dr. Glouster on the phone!"

When the intercom buzzed, Hannah snatched up the receiver.

"I've been expecting your call." Glouster's voice was steady.

"Inconsistent with disposal within the purported time frame? What does that mean?" Hannah asked, imagining the prick of a shiv in her gut.

"It means that the radioactive material detected by the tests hasn't been in the soil for fifty years."

"That's impossible! The government admitted dumping nuclear waste into the mines."

"That may be true. But the soil samples I collected contained chemicals that are typically byproducts of computer chip manufacture."

"Couldn't they also have been from the A-bomb project?"

"Highly unlikely—they aren't used in uranium mining. And there's still the problem of the radioisotopes."

"What problem?" Hannah said, feeling the shiv go deeper.

"A radioisotope is the radioactive form of an element. The ones that were in the samples I collected are commonly used in cancer treatments."

"So? The government doesn't disclose what it puts into an atomic bomb."

"But it couldn't have used these elements, not fifty years ago. Their half-lives are too short."

Hannah knew from the case file that *half-life* referred to the time it took for one-half the atoms in radioactive material to disintegrate. "I thought depleted uranium didn't go away for billions of years."

"True. But not everything that is radioactive has such a long decay rate. The chemicals I found have half-lives that are considerably shorter: Sodium-24 is fifteen hours, iodine-131 is a little over a week. After that, they would be virtually undetectable."

The shiv nicked a vital organ. The samples Glouster had collected contained radioactive material with half-lives so short they wouldn't have shown up in the test results within fifty days, let alone fifty years, of being dumped into the mine.

"I'm sorry, Hannah," Glouster said. "Looks like the feds have bought some time."

Once it was revealed the mines had been contaminated from other sources, the government would demand to litigate liability. Espera's day in court, if it came at all, would be years away. What had simply been a difficult situation had now turned into a catastrophe. Unless…

"Ed, who else knows about this?"

"No one. Samples are sent to the lab under code names, to avoid claims of bias. I was the only one to see the results, and I typed the report myself."

"Keep it that way. Do you still have the samples you collected from deeper in the mines, where the original contamination occurred?"

"Yes."

"Have them tested."

"Okay, but isn't that—"

"Let me know the results as soon as you get them. I gotta go."

Hannah hung up. She had a settlement conference to postpone, without tipping defense counsel as to why—or losing her bar license, either.

Chapter Twenty-two

"She's at the OTA in a meeting," Shelby's secretary said in response to Hannah's call. "With Phyllis Juan and Mr. Rowley."

Hannah tried Shelby's cell, but her call went to voicemail. Hanging up without leaving a message, she called Franklin Rowley's office. She didn't expect to reach him, but hoped to find out the number for his mobile. His secretary wouldn't give it up.

Hannah rang the OTA. Phyllis' secretary was at lunch, and Hannah was transferred to the receptionist.

"I'm sorry, Ms. Juan is in a meeting and can't be disturbed."

"I know—I'm supposed to be there, too. Would you please tell her Hannah Dain is on the line?"

There was a click, and Hannah heard atonal flutes accompanied by bad drumming. *So Indians have Muzak, too.*

"I'm sorry, but Ms. Juan and her guests have gone to lunch."

She had to ask. "May I have her cell number?"

"I'm sorry, but—"

Hannah controlled the urge to shriek. The clock on her computer read ten after twelve. Managing a *thank you* before disconnecting, she found a large envelope in her desk, slid Glouster's report into it, and picked up her purse.

"I'll be at the OTA," she said as she passed Clementine's desk. "If Anuya calls, tell her I'll see her later."

"I could take her shopping after work, check out some of those new places on Saguaro Road."

Hannah stopped and looked at her secretary. Clementine's wardrobe reflected a fondness for plastic jewelry, neon colors, and anything with sequins—not the stuff usually sold on Saguaro Road. Was she trying to say she knew about the "stolen" handbag?

"Why there?" she asked.

"Because the salespeople are incredibly rude." Clementine batted blue-mascaraed lashes. "Figured the kid might be homesick for New York."

Hannah was the only visitor in the lobby of the Office of Tribal Affairs. The French doors behind the receptionists were open, and ceiling fans noiselessly whirred warm air pungent with sage through the room. In the garden beyond, hummingbirds engaged in aerial acrobatics among the Indian Birds of Paradise.

Two months ago Hannah had contracted to work on a real estate transaction for the tribe. Her office had been in the building where she now sat—down the corridor, first door on the left. Things had gone horribly wrong with the deal, with money missing and people killed...one of them Tony. An image of flashing dark eyes and a wide smile filled her mind, and she stuffed it away. Two months was too soon to go there.

She checked her watch. One of the receptionists noticed, and smiled apologetically.

"Ms. Juan should be back from lunch any moment."

"Thanks," Hannah said.

The other receptionist said something that Hannah didn't catch. In her twenties, she wore a white shirt with unfastened French cuffs that covered her knuckles. A silver pendant floated in the hollow of her throat.

"Pardon?" Hannah said.

The first receptionist scowled at her officemate. "Trina! Silencio!"

Trina swept a dark mane of hair from her face. "You know Ms. Juan should have testified. Maybe then the workers wouldn't have lost their case against the tribe."

"Are you talking about the sovereign immunity litigation?" Hannah asked. Trina gave a curt nod. "Why would Ms. Juan's testimony have helped?"

"She used to work for one of the men the workers wanted to sue. He's a pig—pulling down the front of the dealer's blouses to show more cleavage, asking the waitresses if they want to entertain special guests." Her air quotation marks around the word *entertain* left no doubt about the nature of the activity. "Ms. Juan could have told the court how he is. She's an executive—the judge would have believed her."

"I'm not sure it would have made a difference," Hannah said cautiously. "The issue was whether the casino is covered by the tribe's immunity."

"*The issue*"—Trina laid on the sarcasm—"was how to protect the pig. He's in charge of the casino initiative, and the tribe is afraid of being embarrassed."

Hannah was suddenly hollowed out by shock, empty save for the reverberation of memories within. On the ballot in next week's election was a proposal to allow the casino to increase the number of slots and poker tables, as well as add craps, roulette, and other big-money games. In return, the state would collect corporate income tax on casino profits. It had been Tony's project. Hannah took a few deep breaths, hazily aware that Trina was still talking.

"That's how Ms. Juan got all those promotions—going along with whatever the men in charge say." Trina's tone became vinegary. "Women may be second-class citizens elsewhere. On the rez, it's more like fourth."

"Hasn't the money from the casino made things better?" Hannah asked.

"Worse! The tribe controls jobs, housing, schools, the tribal courts. And men control the tribe."

"You shouldn't blame Ms. Juan for not trying to change things, Trina. You know she has to keep this job," said the other receptionist.

"Why couldn't she work somewhere else?" Hannah said.

"Ms. Juan's family—her husband, her mother, her little boy—were all hurt very bad in an accident," the receptionist said. "The little boy is still in the hospital, and her husband cannot walk. Tribal council members get good health insurance."

"What about a lawsuit?"

"The truck that hit them—*pfft!*—disappeared." The woman flicked her wrist.

A new job would mean a new health plan. And the exemption for pre-existing conditions would mean Phyllis would have to cover her family's medical expenses for as long as three years.

The receptionist arranged the collar of her sweater. "What's the big deal anyway? A man looks at you if you're pretty, sometimes gives a little pinch. If you work in a casino, these things will happen."

Trina's mouth twisted in disgust. "Only when women let them. Being pretty doesn't mean you have to put up with being harassed. Ms. Juan could have helped make people see the problem. But she sold out."

Hannah's cell phone rang.

"Excuse me," she said, and walked toward the front of the lobby to take the call.

"Hannah Dain?" said a woman's voice.

"Yes. Who is this?"

"Nathalie."

Nathalie Soule. "Where are you?"

Sniffling sounds. "I can't say."

Hannah cupped her hand around the receiver even though no one was near. "Look, I know the uranium in the mines wasn't from the government bomb project. Tell me what's going on, Nathalie, or I'm calling the police." Hannah hated being a bully, but she was running out of options.

Nathalie was sobbing. "It's my fault Garth's dead! When the test results came back, I talked him into covering them up."

"Garth tested the soil he collected? What happened to the samples and the lab report?"

"I gave everything to them." Nathalie moaned. "It was so much money, enough for us to go away. But then Garth changed his mind, and they murdered him!"

And that's why you decided to kill yourself, Hannah thought. *I should have died.* "Where are you?"

"Hiding. I know they want to kill me, too."

"*Who*, Nathalie? Who paid you off? Who killed Garth?"

"If I tell you, you'll go to the police. I'll be arrested, and then they'll get me for sure."

Was Nathalie being paranoid? Or did the murderers have a deputy on their payroll?

"Meet me, and we'll go to the police station together. I know the detective. You can trust him. He'll make sure you're safe."

Nathalie was silent. Hannah waited.

"My sister owns a condo," she finally said. "It's off Prickly Pear—"

Hannah fumbled for a pen and wrote the address on the palm of her hand. "Stay there. I'm on my way."

"Hurry," Nathalie said, and broke the connection.

Hannah strode back to the lobby counter. "May I have a piece of paper?" she asked Trina.

The message she penned to her sister was brief. *Got lab results—some confusion. Glouster doing more tests. DON'T SETTLE CASE!*

Hannah put the note into the envelope with the test results, sealed it, wrote Shelby's name on the outside, and gave the envelope to Trina.

"One of the lawyers with my firm is having lunch with Ms. Juan. Her name is Shelby Dain. Would you please give this to her as soon as they get back?"

"No problem." Trina dropped the envelope next to a stack of brochures. A swirl of blue above the fold caught Hannah's attention.

"May I see one of those, please?"

She unfolded the glossy flyer. *Eagle Environmental Services* was printed in blue across the top, next to a circular logo, the same design that she had seen on the trucks using the road to the mines. She skimmed the few paragraphs of information.

Specialists in hazardous and radioactive waste removal and disposal...including waste from computer chip manufacturing, hospital procedures, mining operations, chemical production...safe, convenient, cost-effective...

Cost-effective? Perhaps because the tribe's sovereign immunity protected it from federal regulation on hazardous waste disposal?

"Is this Eagle company owned by the tribe?" Hannah asked.

Trina shook her head. "It's Benny's latest project." Seeing Hannah's quizzical look, she added, "Benito Juan, Phyllis' little brother. Ever since he got kicked out of casino operations, he's been trying to come up with an idea that will make him millions." She rolled her eyes. "First, it was real estate development. Then he wanted to be a stockbroker. For the last couple of years, it's been the garbage company. Now he's talking about uranium mining."

Hannah looked at the back of the brochure. There was a photo of a group of employees, posed by the photographer to give the idea that Eagle Environmental Services was one big happy family. Like someone would really believe the maintenance crew in their grease-stained jumpsuits lunched with the shirt-and-tie executives, she thought, skimming the faces. It was easy to pick out Benny—despite the orange polo shirt and lightly tinted glasses, Hannah could see the resemblance to his sister. Her glance fell on a taller man in the back row, and she caught her breath.

Tilting the glossy paper to minimize the glare, she studied the image. Rangy build, blond hair sticking out from under a hat pulled low, broad shoulders—it was hard for her to be certain, but the man sure looked a lot like Jake.

Chapter Twenty-three

An Explorer with the city seal on its doors was parked at an angle to the curb, next to an ambulance, in front of a row of townhouses. A small crowd of neighbors huddled on the sidewalk. Hannah sidled up to join them.

"Did you hear anything?" asked an old man to nobody in particular. His white knees and shins looked like spindly chair legs poking out of his plaid shorts.

"Two loud cracks," said a brunette in yoga pants and a shrunken t-shirt with a Sanskrit squiggle on the front. "Totally screwed up my Ashtanga routine."

A sheriff's car pulled up. A deputy got out and dashed into the unit at the end of the row, talking into the radio attached to his collar.

"That's Larry and Michelle's place," said the old man.

"I didn't think they were back in town," said the yoga lady.

Hannah checked the unit number against the address Nathalie had given her. They were the same. "What happened?" she asked.

"Someone got shot at the Kruegers," said the yoga lady.

Two EMTs appeared in the doorway of the condo, guiding a gurney between them. Following closely behind was a tallish man in a suit. Hannah immediately recognized the boot-camp haircut and Superman jaw—Dresden.

She ducked her head and backpedaled away from the gaggle of onlookers. Once clear of the group, she turned and walked quickly down the sidewalk toward her car. The detective wasn't stupid—he would want to know why Hannah was there. But she couldn't explain about Nathalie and Weller and the samples without violating attorney-client privilege. She had to figure out what was going on before talking to him.

The ambulance passed her, lights pulsing. It slowed for the intersection, whooped its siren twice, then sped up again.

They wouldn't be in a hurry if Nathalie weren't alive. Hannah climbed into her SUV, not feeling very consoled.

Her cell phone rang almost as soon as she sat down in front of her computer. Afraid it might be Dresden, Hannah checked the Caller ID. Her own name appeared on the screen. She flipped open the phone and clamped it between her chin and shoulder.

"Hey, Anuya," she said.

"Where are you?" Her sister sounded tired and a little cranky.

"At work." Hannah typed in the URL for the Tohono O'odham website.

"Are you going out to the mines again? I want to look for the treasure some more."

Hannah briefly closed her eyes. In her haste, she had neglected to make arrangements to meet Glouster for the additional testing. "Not right away, but soon, sweetie."

"Wanna go to the dinosaur museum?"

"How about tomorrow? I've got some things to do here." Hannah scrolled through the tribe's website, hoping to find a link to Tohono O'odham-owned businesses. She wanted to find out more about Eagle Environmental Services.

"I'm b-o-r-e-d!" Anuya stretched out the word.

Hannah felt a twinge of guilt. Granted, her sister had shown up unannounced. But since then, Hannah hadn't been much of a host, dragging her from one law-related thing to another. And they hadn't yet talked about Anuya's acceptance to Bioscience

High—and her claim that she was living with Hannah.

"Can you entertain yourself for a few hours? Then we'll get together, do whatever you want."

Clementine appeared in the doorway. She wore a fruit-lover's dress—kiwis, mangoes, pineapple, and papayas tumbled across the fabric.

"Just delivered." She handed over the map from Hannah's desk drawer, now framed.

Hannah surveyed the little deer and miniature mountains, deciding they looked good surrounded by rustic wood. A nice memento of the case for Shelby...assuming they could resolve it successfully. Right now, Hannah wasn't too sure.

"I know—I'll cook!" Anuya said into her ear, sounding cheery again. "My mom says I'm really good at starters."

"What?" Hannah propped up the map on the credenza behind her while Anuya rattled off South Asian appetizers.

"Vada—do you like it better with dhai or sambar?—pakoras, chaat papri...samosas are boring, don't you think?"

Hannah had eaten in Indian restaurants, but she had no idea what Anuya was talking about. "I don't have any spices." *And unless cheddar bunny crackers are a basic of Indian cuisine, no ingredients either.*

Clementine hovered, openly eavesdropping.

"Thank you," Hannah mouthed at her and looked pointedly at the door. Her secretary settled into a guest chair.

"That's okay. I can take a cab to the store," Anuya said.

"But—"

"This'll be great. See ya!" Anuya hung up.

Hannah closed her cell phone, then typed *Eagle Environmental Services* into the search engine on her computer. Maybe her dearth of cooking implements would dampen Anuya's enthusiasm. Somehow she doubted it.

"You look familiar, but I gotta be sure. Can I see some ID?" Clementine said.

"Have you finished organizing the trial exhibits yet?" Hannah said, keeping her eyes on the screen.

"Of course. You know, you're gonna make a good mother."

Hannah stopped typing and looked at her secretary. "Do you really think so? Because—"

"But to have kids, you need to hook up with a man first." Clementine heaved herself to her feet, then folded her arms across the tropical cornucopia of her chest. "Did you call—"

"Out," Hannah said.

Clementine shook her head. "Why do you keep taking care of everybody's business instead of minding your own?"

"I do not—"

"Whatever, boss."

The globes of orange, yellow, and green disappeared through the door. Hannah went back to her computer.

The information on Eagle Environmental Services was sparse. According to the Secretary of State's website, the company had been incorporated last year. Benito Juan was president, and held every corporate office save one—Phyllis Juan was listed as treasurer. One way to keep an eye on an errant little brother, Hannah thought.

The mailing address was a post office box. Cross-referencing a satellite-map site with property records, she found the company's physical location. Tucked away on the southeastern corner of the rez, it was within a few miles of Lake Lagunita.

Were the EES trucks using the road near the mines as a shortcut? Or were they dumping waste where it was forbidden?

Hannah thought about the trucks that wouldn't stop when flagged, her SUV's vandalized tires. She wanted to call Dresden. But other than what Nathalie had told her and Glouster's test results—which were privileged work product—all she had at this point was conjecture.

And there was another complication—Jake. The jacket with the blue swirl in his truck wasn't from any baseball team. Were EMTs allowed to moonlight? If Hannah called in the cops without finding out the extent of his involvement first, Shelby would never forgive her. She needed more information.

Hannah printed out the map, planning to drive by EES and

see what the operation looked like. She picked up her cell phone and her purse, then hesitated.

Clementine's question wasn't a bad one. Why *did* she keep getting involved in these things?

Growing up, Hannah had not been close to Richard or Shelby. Consequently self-reliant, she had gotten used to the distance. But her decision to attend law school unexpectedly sparked a sense of obligation to fulfill her mother's dream of a family firm. *Dharma*, as Anuya would say. So after graduation, Hannah had left the East Coast for Arizona and a job with Dain & Dain.

There was another reason for the move, now clear to Hannah through the lens of hindsight. Tempering the ferocity of her independence was the hope that admission to the Dain clan would bring security and identity, protection in a kryptonite kind of way.

But birthrights can be booby-trapped, and what was handed down from the materfamilias turned out to be burden instead of boon. Despite Sisyphean efforts, Hannah did not find the sought-for acceptance. Worse, she uncovered terrible acts by Elizabeth as a wife and mother, misdeeds woven like miscolored threads through the fabric of her family's lives.

Worse...and better. The discovery of Tel Moore—and Anuya—had largely sated Hannah's curiosity, and brought her a sense of identity. And letting go of the power with which she had endowed her mother's legacy had freed Hannah to move forward.

But move forward to what? Over the past few months, something had changed inside Hannah. The life she had come back to wasn't the life she wanted to lead. The clamor in her head that told her to be alone had gone from a shout to a whisper. Hannah wasn't fine with being on her own anymore. For the first time, she was lonely.

Was the antidote immersing herself in the problems of strangers? Or, having left the limbo of waiting for others to change, was it to create what she had wanted all along—her own family? The foundations were in place—Anuya, Clementine, Cooper...

Cooper. The man she had walked away from twice—first back East, then again a few months later, all in the name of family obligations. In truth, Hannah had been driven away by fear. Easier to chase ghosts than to live with real people.

She suddenly craved the smell of hay on his clothes, the sound of the espresso machine in the morning, the feel of his stubble when they kissed. Buoyed by hope and longing, Hannah hit the first number on her cell's speed dial.

For once, she was disappointed when the voicemail came on.

"Hey, it's me." She gathered herself. "Miss you—a lot. Call when you can, okay?" She closed the phone with a snap, slung her purse over her shoulder, and grabbed a legal pad.

"I'll be on the rez—more field research for the case," she said as she passed Clementine's desk.

Her secretary didn't stop typing. "So that means you'll be out of cell range if a certain someone calls you back."

Hannah shook her head. "How come you never hear me when I ask you to bring me tea?"

Clementine's eyes twinkled. "Sorry, boss—did you say something?"

Hannah wove through downtown traffic with the window down, the satellite radio tuned to the *Hits of the 90s* channel. Her fingers drummed out the song's beat on the steering wheel. Stopped by the light on Prickly Pear and Brittlebush roads, the last one before the long stretch of road to the lake, she glanced at the cross street. Vehicles were parked nose-in, a red pickup in the closest end spot. She noticed the dent in the left quarter panel and her breath caught under her ribs. Her second time behind the wheel of the rig had put the crease in the metal. The truck belonged to Cooper.

The light changed. Hannah swiveled her eyes forward again. There was no oncoming traffic. On impulse, she turned left and pulled to the curb. Keeping the SUV's engine running, she stared at the truck. Should she leave a note? Wait for him to come back?

She hadn't yet decided when a thin redhead in low-rise jeans that exposed the top of her thong stepped off the curb and headed for the truck. The woman had a chest that made her look like a bureau with the top drawer out and a walk that a cat would envy.

The driver's side window lowered, and the redhead leaned in to kiss the man behind the wheel. It was Cooper.

Hannah felt herself go mentally off-line. She stared at the couple as though she were a voyeur. The redhead couldn't keep her hands off Cooper. First she caressed his arm, then twined their fingers together, then reached into his shirt pocket. Hannah couldn't look away. Her control thinned, and she unconsciously grasped the door handle.

Just then the redhead stepped away from the pickup and Cooper started up the truck. The pickup's taillights flashed white and Cooper glanced back into the street. His gaze met Hannah's, and for a second they both stared at each other. He shook his head, very slightly, and looked away.

Hannah felt as if she had been run through with a knife. Snapping out of her fugue state, she groped for the gear shift and pulled into traffic, oblivious of the complaining horns. Her foot punched the accelerator, and the SUV zoomed around the block and onto Prickly Pear.

The town dissolved into desert in the rearview mirror as Hannah sped down the pavement. She barreled by the fry bread stand and onto the rez, going so fast that she nearly missed the turnoff. At the penultimate moment, she wrenched the wheel. The SUV's tires spun, kicking up a spray of golden dirt. Then the tread bit into the earth and hauled the big car through the turn.

The road undulated and twisted through empty landscape broken here and there by corrugated-metal industrial buildings and adobe houses of varied vintage and states of repair. Tears burned down Hannah's face as she drove without care, grating the SUV's skidplate against the rocks and once nearly high-centering. Only when a particularly deep rut sent her head glancing against the roof did she ease back on the gas pedal.

Hannah swiped at her face with her shirt cuff and swallowed a sob. She had no one to blame but herself. She was the one who had left—twice. Forget the purgatory of *some day*—Hannah had descended into the hell of *what if?* What if she hadn't left Cooper after the accident back East? What if she hadn't thrown herself into the Indian real estate deal and finding her birth father?

A white sign marked with the now-familiar blue swirl materialized on the right. *Eagle Environmental Services. No Trespassing. Private Property.* The road ended a hundred yards beyond, at a small industrial complex.

With a screech of brakes, Hannah stopped in front of a door marked *Office*. She inhaled a few times, regaining some measure of steadiness, then got out. A lone flowering bush was in a pot beside the cracked concrete steps, shedding its white blossoms onto the dusty ground.

The receptionist's russet-colored ponytail bobbed with every movement of her head. Hannah decided she hated red hair.

"May I speak with the site manager? I'm the lawyer working on the uranium case for the tribe, and I was told your drivers may have information." Hannah had decided hiding the lie in as much truth as possible was the best course.

"Just a moment." The receptionist swiveled her chair to speak into a radio behind her, and Hannah fantasized about cutting off her red tresses. She was imagining the satisfying *snip* when a man pushed through the door.

"Ivan Marcovich, plant manager." He wore a snap-front cowboy shirt, a cap with the ever-present blue swirl, and a frown that deepened after Hannah introduced herself as a lawyer for the tribe.

"No one called to tell me you were coming, but that's no surprise. Benny's sister send you out here?"

"She's the tribal litigation liaison," Hannah said. Not telling the truth in this context could put her bar license in jeopardy. As for omissions, she was willing to chance it.

"I'm in the middle of scheduling. If we have to do this now, it's gonna have to be over at Dispatch."

Hannah followed Marcovich across the graded dirt space that served as parking lot and staging area. Large metal industrial buildings, doors shut, lined the north end. White trucks and vans bearing the blue logo and tractor trailers attached to flatbeds loaded with earth-moving equipment were behind chain link to the south. In between was what looked to Hannah like a mini-industrial plant—machines that mixed cement, cut metal, crushed rock, and undoubtedly did other things that involved grease, men sweating, and loud noise.

The foreman stopped in front of a construction trailer. He pulled a key attached to a retractable cord from the holder on his belt and unlocked the door. "So who's suing the tribe now?"

"Actually, the tribe is bringing the lawsuit, against the government," Hannah said. "For damages from improper uranium disposal."

Marcovich made a sound in the back of his throat. "You talkin' about when they dumped the stuff into the old mines? Makin' mini-Chernobyls is what they were doing."

He flipped on a light switch inside the door, then held open the door to the trailer for Hannah. It was a narrow, dusty space with no windows. A built-in counter ran along the wall to the right. In front of it were two stools upholstered in sparkly red vinyl. On top of the counter were a computer, a printer, a fax machine, and a plastic caddy for office supplies. There was a stack of documents next to the computer and a large laminated map of the western United States tacked to the wall, its glossy surfaced smudged with fingerprint whorls. The air smelled like bug spray.

A divider made out of chain link and metal pipes ran the width of the room, splitting it in half. A metal door secured with two locks was in its center. On the door was an orange sign with the word *EXPLOSIVES* and a drawing of a boulder being blown to bits. Through the wire Hannah saw shelves stacked with boxes marked DANGER! DYNAMITE. On the lower levels were bins labeled CAPS and FUSES.

Marcovich parked himself on one of the stools and gestured

for Hannah to take the other. The vinyl cushion-top sighed when she sat.

"Uranium stays around forever," Marcovich said. "You can't just leave it lying around. On all our hot jobs, the waste is sealed in special barrels—that aren't cheap, by the way—then taken out to burial sites in the middle of nowhere."

"What's a hot job?" Hannah said.

"Anything involving waste that is radioactive—mining, medical, high-tech."

"How do you bury it?"

"Dig a hole, using dynamite to make it deep. Drop in a barrel, then bury it in concrete." He moved the computer's mouse and typed in a password. "What does this have to do with the tribe's lawsuit?" he said, opening a calendar program.

Hannah knew this was where she had to be careful. "There's a chance the dump sites may have tampered with. I was wondering if any of your drivers going through the rez might have seen something."

Marcovich pulled a document from the stack on the counter. "We're talking about the mines east of the lake?"

"Yes," Hannah said.

"That area of the rez is closed. None of our trucks go there." Consulting the document, Marcovich began entering data into the calendar.

"What about someone taking a shortcut?"

Marcovich regarded her with chlorine-blue eyes. "A shortcut to where? The road around the lake dead-ends before El Diablo. Besides, since 9/11, hazmat routes and transport schedules are regulated by the DOT. Drivers have to follow a preset course and timetable. So none of our drivers would have seen anything."

"Thanks for your time." Hannah got down from the stool, accompanied by another sigh from the cushion. She felt like sighing herself.

No doubt about it—those had been EES trucks that she had seen on the rez. That raised a host of questions. Was it a company-wide scheme or a few rogue drivers? Could even be an outsider hijacking the fleet. And if the road around the lake didn't go anywhere, were the trucks out there to dump radioactive waste into the mines? Or to pick up or drop off something else?

Hannah massaged her forehead. She had no idea what the answers were, or how to find them before tomorrow's settlement conference.

Her discouragement must have shown on her face. Marcovich rummaged around in the plastic caddy. "Here, have a souvenir. You can tell Benny's sister I didn't send you away empty-handed, even if it isn't one of the gold ones they save for the VIPs." He dropped a keychain decorated with the blue swirl into Hannah's palm.

"Thanks," she said.

Marcovich typed in another name, and Hannah realized she had one more question to ask. Two, in fact.

"Do you do all the hazmat scheduling?"

He nodded, still looking at the screen. "Had to get cleared by the Department of Homeland Security. Not the easiest thing to do. That's how come I got the job instead of a Tohono O'odham."

Hannah understood what he meant. Most Indian-owned companies preferred to hire tribe members when they could.

"Jake Lyman drives a lot of hours for you, doesn't he?" she said.

Marcovich's frown reappeared. "I can't talk about a specific employee's schedule."

So it *was* Jake in the employee photo. "Oh, he's my sister's boyfriend," Hannah said. "She's always saying that between his EMT job and driving for Eagle, they never see each other."

"Jake's putting in the hours, all right. Told me to book him for every night he's not on paramedic duty."

Hannah quickly did the math in her head. Nathalie's car went into the lake on Monday, right after Jake went off shift. That meant he was back on duty as of today—so he could have driven for EES last night.

She closed her hand around the keychain, thinking about the SUV's slashed tires.

Chapter Twenty-four

Even before turning on the lights, when Hannah walked into her condo she could tell she was alone. The air was too quiet, the rooms, too empty. Silence usually gave her sanctuary, but now it just made her feel solitary. Thoughts of a red pickup and a red-haired woman swam into her mind, but she pushed them away.

The faint aroma of Indian spices hung in the air. So Anuya had cooked after all. The last thing Hannah had eaten was a veggie wrap at her desk before noon, but she wasn't hungry. Shedding her jacket, she glanced at the kitchen, expecting to see a mess. But there wasn't a dish or utensil in sight. Only a piece of paper on the clean counter.

Made dinner. Taking taxi to dinosaur museum.

The clock on the microwave read 6:35. What time did the museum close? Reflexively, Hannah opened her cell phone, then realized she had no number to call. The envelope icon flashed in the upper corner of the phone screen. She checked her voicemail.

"What do you mean, a problem with the test results? They agreed to postpone the settlement meeting until tomorrow, but I need to know what's going on. Call me!"

The strain in Shelby's voice was obvious, not that Hannah blamed her. This was all her fault. If she hadn't spoken up at the hearing, the judge would never have set the case for trial. Glouster would never have tested the soil and found evidence of more recent contamination. Shelby and the firm wouldn't be facing the loss of the case, nor Espera and the other plaintiffs the denial of compensation.

Maybe the second tests had different results. She dialed Glouster's office, but there was no answer. She scrolled through her mobile's phonebook looking for his cell number without success.

Hannah dropped her phone into its cradle. She didn't want to call Shelby until the new results were back. Opening the refrigerator, she hopefully scanned its contents. If there were ever a night she needed a glass of wine, this was it. But the only bottles she found held Pellegrino.

Plastic containers that she used to carry her lunch to work were stacked on the fridge's shelves. She opened one. From what she could tell, it was filled with chargrilled eggplant mashed with tomatoes and onions.

Hannah found a spoon and took a taste, immediately spitting the mouthful into the sink. *Anuya must have a flame-proof esophagus.* She hurriedly cracked a Pellegrino to wash away the burn of red chilies.

The next container held plump fried doughnuts smothered in a white gravy spiked with bits of green. Hannah took a cautious nibble, relieved to find the lentil mush only mildly piquant. The sauce was yogurt, thick and sour, and the green was crunchy leaves. She popped the rest of the doughnut into her mouth and ate another.

Headlights swept across the kitchen window as Hannah finished off a fourth doughnut. She rearranged the remaining ones in attempt to make the contents look undisturbed, shoved the container back into the refrigerator, and peeked through the blinds to see Anuya getting out of a dusty white van.

No bubble light on top, no company name on the doors—the van wasn't a taxi. Even in Pinnacle Peak, catching a ride with a stranger wasn't a good idea. Hannah headed for the stairs, preparing to greet—and lecture—her sister.

Anuya cruised through the front door. On top of her head was a pair of sunglasses that Hannah had bought on impulse several years ago. Deciding they were too celebrity, Hannah had never gotten around to returning them. But they seemed to suit her sister.

Seeing Hannah, Anuya broke into a grin. "The dino museum was way cool! Ed knows one of the tour guides, and he took us into the—"

"Wait a minute! Who's Ed?"

"Dr. Glouster, the guy who's working for your law firm? His first name is Ed?" Anuya spoke in teenage sing-song, the annoying turn-every-statement-into-a-question cadence that implied the listener was slow-witted. "He was at the museum when I was there, too. Anyway, he got this guy to let us into the closed area where all the really rad fossils are, and then he gave me his notes on—"

Tires crunched on asphalt.

"What happened to taking a cab?" Hannah asked.

Anuya gave her an exasperated look. "I'm trying to tell you! Ed drove me home. After we—"

"Dr. Glouster is here right now?" *The new test results.* Hannah dashed out the door.

"Hey, Ed!" she called while waving her arms. "Stop!"

The white van continued to sputter down the street.

Discouraged, Hannah kicked at a rock, then walked back inside.

"Hungry?" Anuya asked as they climbed the stairs.

"Not really," Hannah said, then remembered the refrigerator full of food. "I mean, not *really* hungry. But I could eat, that is, I'd like to eat—"

"Look, if you're mad I went to the museum, I'm sorry. But I was bored, and thought it would be no big deal."

The disadvantage of having two sisters, Hannah realized, was that it doubled the number of people who could be mad at her. She gave Anuya a quick hug.

"I'm the one who should apologize. I've spent too much time on work stuff instead of with you. And I *am* hungry—starved, actually."

Anuya beamed and began unloading plastic containers from the refrigerator.

"How did you make all this?" Hannah asked. "I don't have any pots or utensils. Or food, for that matter."

"I took a taxi to the grocery store, and I borrowed the cooking stuff from your neighbor—you know, the guy with the cat."

"My neighbor?" Even though Hannah had lived in the condo for three years, her contact with the people who lived on either side of her had been limited to an exchange of waves when they wheeled out their trash cans on Monday mornings. She had never seen any cat.

Anuya opened a container filled with pale dough. "Do you like chipatis?"

Hannah had no idea what a *chipati* was, but she wasn't going to make any more mistakes. "As long as they're not too spicy." Her tongue still tingled from the eggplant.

Anuya rolled the dough into balls, then flattened them with a rapid hand-to-hand movement. She took a large terra cotta disk from the pantry and slapped the circles of dough onto it.

"What's that?" Hannah asked.

"Pizza stone," Anuya said. "Your neighbors across the street make their own."

How many houses had she hit? Hannah wondered as Anuya reached for the oven dial.

"Wait!" Hannah said. She opened the oven door and looked in. "All clear." Seeing Anuya's expression, she added, "I sometimes put my paddling gloves in there to dry."

"Thank Krishna my mother is not here." Anuya slid the pizza stone into the oven with an air of authority that Hannah found endearing.

"Have you ever made the other kind of Indian food?" Anuya asked.

"You mean Native American? No, but when I worked at the OTA—"

Hannah broke off in mid-sentence. She had an idea how to find out more about EES without implicating Jake. While Anuya opened another plastic container, Hannah headed for the living room and her laptop bag.

"You ate some of the vada!"

"Told you I was hungry," Hannah said. "Back in a sec—I have to look up something on the computer."

She carried her laptop to her new desk and logged on to the Tohono O'odham website. The tribe kept its financial information private, but her work on the real estate deal had required accessing the tribe's internal database. Hannah was hoping that in the aftermath of the events that had aborted the offering, no one had thought to delete her password.

Her hands hovered over the keyboard. Hannah knew she was risking disbarment, even criminal charges. Then she thought about Shelby and her fragile sobriety and started typing.

The home page of the tribe's private website appeared. Across the top of the page, in big letters, streamed the warning*: For Use by Council Members and OTA Level A Staff Only.*

Hannah mentally inserted *former* before *OTA* and started scrolling through the site's directory. She found the link to the registry of Indian-owned companies that had requested financial assistance from the tribe and clicked on it. Eagle Environmental Services was the first entry under *E.* Hannah wasn't surprised. She had seen a lot of expensive equipment during her visit.

Companies that borrowed money from the tribe were required to submit semiannual balance sheets, income statements, and cash flow summaries. According to the figures from EES, the company had never been out of the red from the time it opened for business three years ago—until last March, when its six-figure loan was abruptly paid off. No longer a debtor of the tribe, EES had not had to file any financials since. Hannah poked around on the tribe's web site and then the web generally, but didn't come across anything else on EES that she didn't already know.

She closed the laptop. According to the financials, there had been no infusion of capital from other sources and no increase in the number or size of contracts. So how did EES manage to pay off its loan, especially all at once?

Hannah could come up with only one answer. Instead of

using proper disposal techniques, EES dumped raw radioactive waste into the reservation's mines and pocketed the cost savings off-books. Now that the loan from the tribe had been paid off, the extra money could go straight to the owner—Benny Juan, recurrent failed businessman.

"Dinner!" Anuya called.

Hannah returned to the kitchen to find laden plates arrayed on the counter. Anuya had turned off the fluorescents and lit her Diwali candle. The aroma of curry, cumin, and turmeric hung in the air, rousing Hannah's dormant hunger.

Hannah avoided the incendiary eggplant but gorged on everything else—spicy combinations of potatoes, onions, tomatoes, and spinach, along with chewy bread so stuffed with garlic that she pitied everyone she'd come into contact with tomorrow. She ate as though it were the Last Supper, beyond sating her appetite. Whenever a picture of a certain pickup truck with a redhead at its window came to mind, Hannah pushed it aside and helped herself to another scoop of mango chutney.

Dessert was rice pudding. When her bowl was scraped empty, Hannah sat back, feeling the uncomfortable snugness of her waistband. *I'll do intervals during tomorrow's paddle*. Her sigh of satisfaction turned into a burp.

"Sorry."

"Don't be. Burping is a sign of appreciation," Anuya said.

"Then that was a four-burp meal. Everything was delicious. I can't believe you made it."

Anuya shrugged but looked pleased. "Just followed my mom's recipes. It's like doing a chemistry experiment."

No wonder all her culinary attempts blew up, Hannah thought as she stacked the empty plates. On the counter were the papers that Anuya had brought back from the museum. She glanced at them.

"What are these?"

"Ed gave me directions to some fossils for the next time we go to the rez. See?" Anuya's elegant finger traced the dotted line that ran from the *X* marked *Mine* to a jagged line of mountains decorated with miniature sketches of primitive scorpion-like creatures and swirled shells.

Thinking of the rez brought Hannah back to EES. Should she call Dresden? Better yet, Zel Kassif? Clementine's reporter boyfriend would jump on the story, find out what Hannah couldn't. But if she did, Jake would undoubtedly get in trouble, maybe even lose his EMT job.

The red pickup invaded her thoughts again, and Hannah knew she wasn't going to call either the press or the cops. One Dain sister's heartbreak was enough for today. She wasn't going to wreck Shelby's newfound happiness.

Anuya scooped leftovers into the plastic containers.

"Hey, let me clean up," Hannah said.

"I got it." Anuya wrapped the chipatis in foil. "You know, Jake's pretty hot. How did Shelby meet him?"

Hannah was pretty sure Shelby wouldn't be pleased with any answer that had *rehab* in it. "I think they met when Jake was doing a fire inspection."

"Ooo—love at first sight." Anuya sighed. "How romantic. That's what I want to happen when I meet my husband."

"That would be at the altar, right?" Hannah said. All this romance talk was getting on her nerves.

"An arranged marriage doesn't mean you don't know the guy beforehand. And you can say no if you want to." Anuya had a dreamy expression. "My husband is going to be cute like Jake." She closed the lid on a container with an emphatic snap. "And own a software company, too."

Why not go to Jake for more information on EES? Hannah thought. In the best case, he wouldn't know anything, and Hannah could go to the press and the authorities without jeopardizing his job or his relationship with Shelby.

"I'm taking back these pots and stuff." Anuya headed for the stairs with a box of cooking paraphernalia. "Want to come?"

"You go ahead. I have to make a call." Hannah plucked her phone from its recharger.

Jake answered on the second ring.

"Need another ride?" he said in a clipped voice after Hannah identified herself.

"No. But thanks again for the rescue. I wanted to ask—"

"If you're looking for Shelby, she's not here. But she wants to talk to you."

"I'm going to call her," Hannah said. "Besides working for—"

"You should call her now. She's on her cell—"

"Jake!" Hannah cut in. "Do you have another job besides being an EMT?"

"The department allows only limited moonlighting," he said flatly.

"I'm talking about—" she searched for the word—"*casual* work."

"What exactly are you getting at, Hannah?"

She took the plunge. "Do you drive for Eagle Environmental Services?"

Jake said nothing. Hannah chewed on her bottom lip and waited.

"I did some driving for several companies before I went full-time at the department," he finally said. "*Eagle* rings a bell, but I'm not sure—"

"Do you work for Eagle *now*?"

"I work for the Pinnacle Peak Fire Department. In fact, I'm in the middle of a shift, and shouldn't be taking personal calls."

"Jake! Wait!"

But he had hung up.

The front door opened.

"It's me!" Anuya said. She appeared at the top of the stairs carrying the camcorder. "You shouldn't leave this in your car, especially if it's not locked."

Hannah looked at the camcorder. If Jake was on duty, that meant he wouldn't be driving for EES tonight. She could collect evidence of the dumping without incriminating him.

Hannah went into the bedroom to change her clothes, then paused. Her recent solo forays into the desert had been anything but uneventful—she had been chased and shot at, witnessed both kidnapping and murder. Even though her plan for that evening had little downside, Hannah didn't want to go it alone anymore.

Who could she bring with her? Neither Shelby nor Clementine did desert. Anuya was too young. Cooper was—Hannah inhaled—unavailable.

She opened her phone and scrolled through the entries. *No…No…Yes.* Hannah hit the speed-dial shortcut, pleased to get a person and not voicemail.

"It's Hannah. Saddle up—we're going prospecting."

Chapter Twenty-five

Jerry Dan threw his daypack into the footwell and climbed in beside Hannah. He wore a turtleneck and jeans. A pull-on knit hat made his head look rounder than usual.

"This is gonna be so cool!" he said, settling into his seat. "Much better than trying to score orchestra seats to *Othello*."

Hannah started at hearing her birth father's first name. "You like opera?"

"Not really. But this woman I'm seeing does, so I'm putting together a romantic weekend in LA."

"You do know that *Othello* is the one where the guy kills his wife?"

"Yeah, but it's in Italian. I'm hoping she misses that part." Jerry Dan looked Hannah up and down, taking in her dark long-sleeved sport jersey and pull-on mountain climbing tights. "Man, you look like a spy."

"This coming from a man dressed all in black, wearing a watch cap...and cowboy boots?"

"I always wear cowboy boots."

"Wouldn't running shoes have been better for walking in the desert?"

"Probably. But they don't make me feel like I do when I wear cowboy boots."

Hannah steered down the gravel driveway and onto Pima Road. "My sister said something like that when I asked her why she wore stilettos. I didn't understand it then, either."

Jerry Dan lived north of town, where cattle operations had not yet given way to houses on twenty-thousand-square-foot lots. The sparse traffic at that time of night meant the fry bread stand was only forty minutes away.

They passed by the turn-off to Cooper's ranch, and Hannah felt a hotness behind her eyes. "What did you bring?" she said to divert her thoughts.

Jerry Dan rummaged through the day pack. "Flashlight... food...water...camo paint...camcorder with night vision, even though you said you had one..."

"Camo paint?"

He uncapped a small tube of what look like black lipstick. "Camouflage. You put it on your cheeks and forehead so your skin doesn't reflect light."

"I'm not much of a makeup person." Hannah nodded at a curved, orange-colored plastic bottle. "What's that? Looks like it got bent in the dishwasher."

Jerry Dan cleared his throat. "You said we might be on stake-out for a while..." He cleared his throat again. "If I drink a lot of water, I have to..."

Hannah suddenly understood what the bottle was for. "Got it." After an awkward silence, she added, "You know, there are bushes where we're going."

"Yeah." Jerry Dan stuffed the orange bottle back into the day pack.

Hannah reached over and touched his arm. "I appreciate your coming with me. Although it's not too late to back out."

"And miss a chance to uncover corporate skullduggery and make America a better place? No way!"

Hannah couldn't help but laugh. "Has anybody ever told you that you eat way too many Sugar Smacks?"

"Actually, I'm a grits man. Just don't tell my momma I've switched to instant."

They had reached the nicer neighborhoods south of town. Soft lights shone beneath copper canopies, and clerestory windows glowed like Japanese lanterns. Even though there were hardly any other cars, Hannah kept to the speed limit.

"Where's Anuya?" Jerry Dan asked.

"At my condo. We got stranded last night at the lake and had to camp out. I thought she'd had enough of the desert at night."

Hannah didn't mention that Anuya had vociferously disagreed, and had begged to come along. Their argument ended with Anuya holed up in the bathroom and Hannah loading the car. Her good-bye knock at the door had gone unanswered.

Though sorry about the disagreement, Hannah didn't regret her decision. After what had happened to Shelby last summer, she wasn't going to put another sister into danger. From now on, windmill-tilting would be limited to one member of the family.

The SUV turned onto Prickly Pear Road. Fewer than ten miles to go until the fry bread stand. The Milky Way stretched across the tops of the mountains. Every constellation in the velvety sky was crystal clear.

"You think the tribe knows what's going on?" Jerry Dan said. Without mentioning Jake, Hannah had filled him in on her suspicions over the phone.

"I don't think so. Thanks to the casino, they don't need the money. And why would they poison their own land?"

Hannah was less sure about Phyllis Juan's innocence. Was she covering for her wayward brother? Or maybe turning a blind eye in subconscious payback for her denied promotion and sexual harassment on the job?

They sped by the fry bread stand, its parking lot empty. Hannah noticed the guard rail had yet to be repaired.

The SUV shuddered as its tires bumped off the pavement onto the dirt. Illuminated in the headlights, bats swooped down after moths, looking like flying gargoyles and reminding Hannah that the darkness beyond the twin beams was alive with creatures—lizards, mice, scorpions, rattlesnakes, deer, coyotes, ring-tailed cats, javelina…

Distracted by critter thoughts, she didn't see the rut. The SUV dipped, then jounced.

"Hold on!" Hannah said as she grappled the truck back onto the road.

"Yikes!" Jerry Dan exclaimed as his head grazed the roof.

"Ow!" said another voice.

Jerry Dan glanced at her. "Did you say something?"

"No," Hannah said. *She should have known...*

Clear of the rut, she hit the brakes, jumped from the car, and opened the rear door.

"What are you doing here?" she said.

Anuya's face appeared from under the sleeping bags. "I wanted to come."

"Get into the back seat."

Wordlessly, Anuya climbed over the seat back. Hannah slammed the rear hatch and got back behind the wheel.

"I'm sorry, Jerry Dan, but I've got to take Anuya home. We can try again tomorrow night."

"What about the settlement conference?" Jerry Dan said. "Don't you need this video before then?"

"It's too dangerous for Anuya to be here," Hannah said, even though she knew that Jerry Dan was right. She considered taking Anuya home, then returning. But given when the truck had driven by the cave last night, there was a good chance she would miss it. Hannah let the car idle while she stared at the soft moonlight moving down the cliffs.

"Please don't take me back," Anuya said.

*Espera and Nando, Shelby and Jake...*Hannah turned to face her sister.

"If I let you stay, you *cannot* leave the car. Agreed?"

Anuya nodded her head vigorously.

"And if things look bad, we turn around. No arguments."

Anuya's dark eyes met Hannah's. "Okay."

Hannah steered the big car back onto the road, trying to still the thudding of her heart and convince herself that she had made the right choice. Neither attempt was very successful.

Ten minutes later the SUV's headlights picked up a pile of tailings. Hannah kept going.

Jerry Dan squinted through the windshield. "Wasn't that the mine where Ed got the samples?"

"Yes. It's also where my car was parked when Anuya and I were stranded last night."

"You think they'll avoid where you're doing work."

Hannah nodded. "It's what I would do."

She shifted into first gear and turned the wheel. The SUV left the track and began inching down the rocky slope. Blue moonlight filled the horizon with the suggestion of shapes and bright angles, but deep darkness still enshrouded where the mountains began. The lake remained the darkest of all.

Hannah parked behind a stand of desert willow, just short of the drop-off to the water's edge. She lowered her window and turned off the engine, then stared out at the lake as if there were something to see there, listening to the water slap against the rocky beach.

Go back. Call Dresden. Hannah knew it was the right thing, the safe thing to do. She got out of the car.

"Is your camcorder ready, Jerry Dan?" Her throat muscles contracted in the cold, making her voice raspy.

Jerry Dan flicked on the dome light, pointed the camcorder at the darkness, and held down a button for a few seconds. He then lowered the camcorder, pressed another button, and stared at the small screen.

"Dang, but this night vision is cool. There's a rabbit hiding under that bush over there. Shows up better than if it were daytime."

"Sit up here, Anuya," Hannah said, holding open the driver's door. Her sister silently complied. Since Hannah's scolding, she hadn't said a word. When Anuya was behind the wheel, Hannah handed her Jake's camcorder.

"I want you to use this like binoculars to keep an eye on me and Jerry Dan. The keys are in the ignition. If something happens, drive back to town. Here's my cell phone. Once you're in range, pull over and hit number ten on the speed dial. It's the number for the police. Ask for Detective Dresden."

Anuya's voice was a tight as a drum skin. "Drive? I'm from New York. We don't do that!"

Hannah restrained the urge to laugh at her sister's remark. Anuya was too close to hysteria as it was. "We'll go to Plan B, then," she said, at the same time wondering when her life had started requiring lettered escape strategies. "If you see somebody other than Jerry Dan or me coming toward the car, climb out the window and hide behind that rock over there. I'll turn off the dome light. And whatever you do, be sure not to slam the door."

Anuya clutched the camcorder. "Okay," she said.

Hannah reached through the open window and gripped Anuya's shoulder.

"Don't worry. I'm sure things will be fine. I'm just being super-careful." She turned away from the car. "Ready, Jerry Dan?"

He was still looking through the camcorder lens. "There's a cluster of mines near where the road ends, and I think I see fairly recent tire tracks. But we're going to have to be closer to get good pictures."

"Let's go," Hannah said.

Jerry Dan picked his way through the uneven rocks. Hannah followed a few steps behind. She couldn't quite match his pace, and the night's thick blackness moved over him, soon swallowing him completely. Hannah strained her eyes, but couldn't see anything.

"Jerry Dan?" she said softly. Even though they were alone, she felt compelled to tiptoe and whisper.

There was no answer.

Slightly panicked, Hannah switched on her flashlight. Ahead and to the right, something crashed into a bush. She swung the beam toward the sound. Jerry Dan's pale round face shone back at her.

"Turn that off!" he said. "Out here, you can spot a light from a mile away."

"Then don't get so far ahead of me." Shielding the beam with her fingers, she caught up to him, then doused it.

"Hold on to me," he said. "If I walk too fast, let go, and I'll stop."

Hannah hooked a finger through one of his rear belt loops and they moved ahead again. After a few minutes, Jerry Dan halted.

"The mines are just ahead, in that flat space," he said. "Should be able to get a good look from here."

"I'll take your word for it." Even though the moon was fully risen, it was new, and Hannah could barely see ten feet in front of her. She sensed rather than saw the rocks that surrounded them, huge sandstone slabs that had calved off the cliff and now lay about like a scattered Stonehenge. Leaning against one of the boulders, she felt the pitted stone grate against her pants.

"Assuming they choose these mines," Jerry Dan said.

"Assuming they come at all," Hannah said.

The words were barely out of her mouth when a guttural rumble broke the quiet. In the direction from which they had come, two shafts of light pierced the darkness. The beams caught the lake water, making it gleam.

"That sounds like a truck." Hannah felt the hairs on the nape of her neck stand up.

Jerry Dan raised his camcorder. "Let me get the zoom going…" He thumbed a dial. "Got it. Definitively a truck, on the same road we drove in on."

"What's it look like?"

"Light-colored—think it's white—with a design on the door."

"Something that looks like a whirlpool swirl?"

"Uh-huh." Jerry Dan pivoted on his heel, keeping his camcorder trained on the truck. "I'm filming."

The headlights flickered as the truck passed behind some chaparral. Moments later, Hannah heard a break in the engine's throaty hum, and the headlights stopped moving.

Her mouth went dry. The truck had stopped next to where she'd parked the SUV.

Chapter Twenty-six

The engine noise resumed, now the whine of a higher gear. Hannah felt her muscles slacken with relief as the truck passed by the SUV's hiding place.

"Almost at the mines," Jerry Dan reported, his eye glued to the viewfinder.

Hannah chewed on the inside of her cheek.

"It's stopping!" Jerry Dan said. "Somebody is getting out."

The truck's back-up bell started dinging as it shifted into reverse.

Jerry Dan kept up a whispered commentary. "Looks like two guys...Now they're taking barrels out of the back...Can't tell if they're dropping them into the mine as is or pouring out what's in them...Gotta get closer..." He took a few steps into the open from behind the rock.

"Don't!" Hannah whispered, grabbing for his shirt. "They might see you!"

Her hand closed on air. She pressed against the boulder, straining to hear, but a breeze had picked up, rattling the dry creosote and drowning out all other sound.

She peered around the rock's edge. The thick, pitch-black night enveloped her, and she was blind. The wind gusted and she leaned into it, hand cupped behind her ear.

"Han..."

Jerry Dan? Hannah debated whether to answer.

"Han..."

The voice was closer, and definitely Jerry Dan's. "Jer… where…" The wind tore the words from her mouth.

Something broke through the chaparral to her left.

"Han…car…Anu…"

Even though she caught only fragments of his sentences before they were snatched up into the air and carried away, Hannah got his message. *They were in trouble.*

She whirled and sprinted in the direction of the SUV. Her sleeve snagged on the desiccated arm of a dead ocotillo, but she jerked it free and kept running. Behind her, gears ground through a Y-turn. *The truck.* Hannah ran harder, tripping over stones, oblivious to the cactus needles.

Headlights flashed in front of her twice, replaced by the jack-o'-lantern glow of the SUV's parking lights. Hannah wrenched open the driver's door and saw Anuya cowering in the back.

Her sister sat up. Her words came out at a gallop. "I saw they were after you and I know you told me to get out of the car but I was afraid you would get lost so I turned on the light and then—"

"You did fine," she said as Jerry Dan threw himself into the passenger seat.

A crack split the night and Hannah flinched, recognizing the sound.

"Get down on the floor and stay there!" she screamed at Anuya, starting the engine.

Jerry Dan pounded on the dashboard. "Let's go, let's go!"

Another crack, closer this time.

Hannah floored it. The tires sprayed sand for heart-stopping seconds before finding traction. The SUV leaped forward and Hannah stiff-armed the vehicle back onto the road. She veered around the bigger potholes, driving like a bail jumper with bounty hunters on her tail. It was last summer all over again—the chase through the desert, the gleam of the rifle that had almost killed her and Shelby. She jammed down the memory.

Anuya peeped over the seat back. "They're shooting at us, aren't they?"

"Nah," Jerry Dan said. "Those are just rocks hitting the undercarriage." He gripped the dashboard and door handle, bracing himself against the curves. The camcorder swung from a strap around his neck.

"I know what guns sound like!" Anuya said.

"Get down and keep quiet!" Hannah said.

Jerry Dan glanced back, then did a double take.

"They're not following us," he said.

"What?" Hannah eased off the gas and looked over her shoulder. The twin beams were immobile, and getting smaller. Hannah slowed some more. "Why not?"

"Because they called for reinforcements." Jerry Dan's voice was grim. "Cell phones may not work out here, but two-way radios do."

Hannah squinted through the windshield. Two pairs of lights edged the lake. Like the headlights behind them, they were immobile.

"What are they doing?" she said.

"Waiting for us," Jerry Dan said.

"Anuya, give me your camcorder." Hannah looked through the viewfinder. She saw men standing beside two trucks parked perpendicular to the road.

"Should we turn around again?" Jerry Dan said. "There's only one truck behind us—maybe we can get by."

Hannah remembered what the EES plant manager had said. *What shortcut? That road dead ends.* "The road stops at the base of El Diablo."

"So we have no place to go?" Anuya said. The teenager drawl had vanished, leaving a little girl's contralto.

The men in the truck that had chased them had at least one gun. Were the four ahead armed as well? Hannah pressed her fingertips to her temples, trying to think. Through her open window, the lake murmured to itself. A wet, mineral smell permeated the night air.

The lake.

"I have an idea." She opened her door. "Get out of the car."

The others obeyed.

"Jerry Dan, untie the kayak and carry it down to the beach." Hannah lifted the SUV's rear door. "Anuya, come help me."

She began to pull items from the crate of emergency supplies. First out was a life vest. Even though required by law, she never wore it. Instead, she left the vest in her car in the hope it would help her dodge a ticket should the water police ever stop her while paddling.

"Put this on." She handed the vest to Anuya, then grabbed several bottles of water and energy bars and put them into a wet bag. The cold stiffening her fingers, she tied a jacket around her waist, then did the same for Anuya.

"Kayak's ready," Jerry Dan said. His face looked ghostly in the penumbra of the car's overhead light.

"Look around for anything that will float," she told him. "A scrap of lumber, a dead tree branch, anything."

"Got it." He disappeared into the darkness.

"Put this on, too." She handed Anuya a thick sweatshirt.

"But you just—"

"The one around your waist is for Jerry Dan. He's going to get wet, so we have to bring a change of clothes."

Hannah looked north, then south. The headlights were still keeping their distance. They reminded her of circled wolves waiting out wounded prey. *Crossing the lake is our only hope.* She threw a few more items into the wet bag, grabbed her paddle, and slammed the rear door just as Jerry Dan clambered back toward her.

"Find anything?" Hannah asked.

"Nothing but cactus."

"Sorry. Means a wetter trip for you." *And a greater risk of hypothermia.* She hoped they had enough extra clothing.

Jerry Dan's voice was wry. "I hated swimming class almost as much as rope climbing. What now?"

"Drive the car back up the road. If they decide to come after us, I don't want them looking in the lake first thing."

"Because we'll be sitting ducks," he murmured, too softly for

Anuya to hear. Hannah couldn't disagree.

Jerry Dan got into the SUV while Hannah lashed the wet bag to the kayak's deck. The webbing was snarled, and she yanked on it. "Dammit!"

"We can't all fit in there," Anuya said, looking at the seatwell.

"Of course not!" Hannah said with false heartiness. "Jerry Dan will swim and I'll paddle. You're chief navigator, and get the seat of honor on the bow. I'll be watching you the whole time, so you won't fall in. But just to be safe, you'll have the life vest."

"I'm afraid," Anuya said.

Hannah stopped pulling on the webbing. She was sending three people across a freezing lake in the middle of the night with only a single kayak among them? Maybe it was better to face down the truck drivers. Maybe they had shot to scare, not hurt them…

She dismissed the thought as wishful thinking. Just as she was certain it would be futile to storm the roadblock, she knew how things would end if they were caught. Abandoned mine shafts were perfect places to make bodies disappear, especially if buried under toxic waste. With the rifle cracks sharp in her mind, Hannah gave another tug on the webbing and the snarl disappeared.

"I'm a little afraid, too. But we can do this," she told Anuya. She picked up the kayak and snugged its rounded hull on top of her hip.

"C'mon. Once this is floating, I want you to step into the seatwell. Don't worry—I'll have hold of both you and the boat."

After she eased the kayak into the water, Hannah helped Anuya crawl onto the bow. Despite the layers of clothing, she could feel her sister's heart beating like a hummingbird's.

Hannah lowered herself into the seatwell and balanced her paddle across her knees. The kayak rode low under the unaccustomed weight. She checked that the wet bag was secured next to the sleeping bag under the webbing across the stern deck.

A low whistle came from the beach, followed by a sound of a branch snapping and a muffled exclamation.

"It's me," Jerry Dan said unnecessarily as he emerged from

behind a stand of willows. "The car is about a quarter mile away. I scattered some stuff on the road, made it look like we dropped it running into the desert."

Hannah unfurled another wet bag. "Hope you're into skinny-dipping. Hand me your clothes."

Jerry Dan put a hand on his salad-plate-sized belt buckle, then hesitated.

"Oh, for Pete's sake!" Impatience chafed Hannah's whisper. The headlights hadn't moved, but there was no telling when the men behind them would tire of waiting. "Clothes will drag you down and won't keep you any warmer. And you won't have anything dry to put on when we get to the other side."

"After Monday, I swore I was never going back into this lake." Jerry Dan kicked off his cowboy boots, then shucked his shirt and pants, revealing a pair of striped boxers.

"Leave your socks on. The rocks won't hurt as much," Hannah said.

Jerry Dan waded into the water with a yelp. "It's freezing!"

"It'll feel better once you get all the way in." Hannah stuffed his clothes into the extra wet bag and secured it beside the other one.

With a stifled cry, Jerry Dan ducked under the surface. He reappeared a moment later. "Can we start moving? My toes are already going numb."

"Try to stay horizontal. The water is warmer on top," Hannah said.

"Five degrees isn't going to make much of a difference. Ice is ice," he said through chattering teeth.

Hannah pushed off the rocky beach with her paddle blade.

"Grab this line." She tossed Jerry Dan a rope that she had tied to the rear cleat.

Jerry Dan splashed about for a moment. "Got it."

"Frog kick, don't flutter. And breathe to the side. It'll be easier on your neck."

Waves lapped at the side of the boat. The moon appeared from behind a cloud, and the rocks along the shore cast black shadows on the even blacker water. Hannah dipped her paddle and took a tentative pull. The lake felt different—deeper, darker, unfamiliar.

Following the shifting moon and Anuya's whispered directions, Hannah headed north. The air was light and sharp, swelling her lungs. She concentrated on her form, feeling the long muscles in her arms begin to work as the boat moved through the inky water.

Ten minutes, fifteen. The splashes from Jerry Dan's heels began to slow. Hannah's palms burned, and cramps seized the muscles in her back and thighs, payback for no warm-up. *Twenty minutes.* Hannah could feel the heat being drawn from her body and the strength from her arms.

"Jerry Dan, you okay?" she said in a low voice.

"Friggin' c-c-cold."

"Did you know water is the doorway to another life?" The fear in Anuya's voice tugged on Hannah's heart. "The gods make whirlpools to suck you in."

"I can paddle out of any whirlpool, Sis." The word slipped out before Hannah could catch it.

Anuya didn't respond. Instead, she sat perfectly rigid, unflinching at the paddle spray save for a slight trembling in her shoulders. Behind them, Jerry Dan sucked in a noisy breath.

They're relying on me. Hannah redoubled her efforts. She found a sustainable cadence, and the rhythm of her paddle became nearly hypnotic, as fluid as the water itself. Shadows barely kept up with them as the shoreline rushed by.

The breeze quickened, turning the glassine surface into small chop. The kayak rose and fell, and Hannah dug deeper. Her muscles tightened as she sucked in raw, cold air, the irony of being surrounded by water intensifying her thirst.

The kayak shot forward without warning. Hannah immediately jabbed her paddle into the lake, dragging the boat to a stop. The letup in resistance meant Jerry Dan had let go of the tow line. Hannah knew it was easy to lose the power to move or even think in water so cold. She gathered up the floating line and was about to toss it to Jerry Dan when he reached up and grabbed the stern.

"Tired," he panted. "Rest just a second."

The boat listed, the starboard rail dipping under. Lake water poured into the seatwell and the kayak made an eerie creaking noise.

"Jerry Dan, you're swamping us!" Hannah said.

She shifted her weight to compensate, burying the port rail. The kayak rolled, threatening to capsize. Anuya whimpered in fear.

He's too tired to understand what he's doing. Water cascaded over the back of the kayak. Hannah leaned forward and dug in with her paddle, driving the boat out from under Jerry Dan's grip. Once they were beyond his reach and had regained an even keel, Hannah pulled up. She twisted around in her seat and spoke in a low voice.

"Say something so I know where to throw the rope."

"I'm over here," Jerry Dan croaked. "Sorry."

"No worries." Hannah wasn't sure that she wouldn't have done the same thing.

She tossed the line and felt the boat jerk backward when Jerry Dan grabbed it. She began paddling and soon got into a rhythm again. *Five minutes until shore, five minutes until shore.* Hannah had just decided they were going to make it when Anuya spoke.

"Look over there…lights!"

Hannah glanced toward land. One of the trucks was on the move, accompanied by a white light that scanned the desert like a lighthouse beam.

"Do you think it's the police?" Anuya said.

"I think it's a spotlight." Hannah rested the paddle on her knees and watched the moving arc. "Looks like the truckers got tired of waiting."

Jerry Dan tread water on the port side. "What's happening?"

"We're going in," Hannah said.

The truck would have to follow the road's turns, while she

could head straight for the shore. Her blade cut through the water, and she prayed that Jerry Dan's grip on the tow rope was secure. *Left, right, left, right.* Her gloveless hands had been rubbed raw by the friction of the paddle shaft. Meanwhile, three sets of headlights now bobbed along the shore.

How long had they been in the water? *Minutes? Hours?* Hannah had lost all sense of time. She kept paddling, feeling as if she were an astronaut trying to spacewalk back to the capsule before her air ran out.

Polished fluted walls of granite loomed up, silvery in the moonlight. Hannah slowed her stroke, taking care not to slice the kayak's bow on the sharp rocks that hid below the surface. The boat rounded an outcropping and scraped against sand. Hannah wanted to shout in relief.

She unfastened their gear, then stood and held the boat while Anuya climbed off its deck. Together they waded through the chilled, calf-deep water. Anuya balanced the sleeping bag on her head like an African princess while Hannah's arms quivered under the load of the wet bags.

Jerry Dan followed them ashore. He stood on the rocky beach, overcome with shudders. His sodden boxers clung to his waxy legs, and small puddles formed in the sand beneath him.

"Lap swimming at the Y is never gonna feel the same again," he said through quivering lips.

"Put these on." Hannah handed him his shirt and pants, then turned her back to give him privacy.

"Hannah, can you—"

He had managed to fumble on his pants, but zippers and buttons were beyond his stiff fingers. Hannah helped him finish dressing, keeping her eyes on the lake. While the headlights had stopped moving, now powerful beams from commercial flashlights raked the water.

"We have to hide the kayak." Hannah grabbed the bow line and dragged the hull farther out of the water. Jerry Dan finished pulling on his boots, then lifted the stern. They duck-walked the craft to a nearby stand of creosote and set it on the ground, then pushed it into the brush until the leafy branches hid it from view.

Hannah noticed that one of the trucks was on the move again, coming toward them.

"Now where do we go?" Anuya's voice shook.

One hand massaging her bad shoulder, Hannah scanned the cliff line, the absence of stars plotting its shape. Her pulse quickened as she recognized where they were.

"To a place where the burru and the bad guys can't find us. Jerry Dan, get the sleeping bag."

"The cave!" Anuya said.

Hannah slung the two wet bags over her shoulder, then grabbed Anuya's hand. "C'mon."

The desert was silvery in the moonlight. Hannah waded through knee-deep shadows, hoping it was either too early or too late for the rattlers and javelinas to be out. A stray bat wheeled overhead, and she ducked. Anuya struggled to keep up, softly grunting as she stumbled over the rocks. Jerry Dan's heaving breath cut through the still air.

A shout went up from the beach where they had landed. Hannah looked back to see a pair of headlights trained on a spot near the waterline. Jerry Dan groaned.

"My boxers—I left them on the beach."

Now that the men knew where they had come ashore, it wouldn't take them very long to find their footprints, Hannah thought. Sure enough, the truck engine revved and the vehicle lurched forward.

She searched for the overhang. Clouds swirled over the moon, transforming the rock formation into something unfamiliar. Hannah hesitated. The rational part of her brain knew they were near the cave, while some other part of her simultaneously believed otherwise.

Anuya yanked on her arm. "It's over here!"

Chaparral thorns tore at their pants like kitten's claws, and left long scratches on their bare arms. By the time they reached the opening in the rock, Hannah's thighs were screaming. Behind them, the maleficent truck drew closer.

"Go!" Hannah whispered.

Her sister disappeared through the fissure in the rock, and Hannah gestured for a stunned Jerry Dan to follow. She was about to join them when she thought about their footprints, pointing the way to their hiding place as effectively as a neon arrow.

Voices ricocheted off the boulders. Fear shrank Hannah's chest muscles and chopped her breath. She swallowed twice, forcing her lungs—and mind—to slow. Was this how the Indians had felt when Coronado's troops marched through almost five centuries ago?

Cowboys and Indians. A stupid movie trick, but it was the best she could come up with.

Hannah darted to a brittlebush, broke off a stem, and broomed away the telltale marks leading into the cave. She then laid down a new trail through the sand to the south, where the mountains' knees poked through the desert's skirt. Anyone following would think they were on the run through the boulder-strewn canyon. Satisfied the pockmarks left by her shoes would be hard to miss, Hannah crouched low and backtracked toward the cave, walking on the granite where practicable and brushing away her footprints where it wasn't.

She had almost made it to the entrance when the headlights of the truck swept over the rock wall behind her, just clearing the top of her head. Hannah squatted and stayed still. The lights disappeared as the truck went around a boulder.

"Hold up!" one of the men said. "I think I saw something."

The back-up bell began to chime. Hannah dashed through the cave opening, sweeping the branch over her footprints as best she could. Once inside, she stood still and blinked, willing her eyes to adjust to the darkness. In the trickle of light from the entrance, she made out two shapes at the rear of the chamber. Hands outstretched Frankenstein-style, Hannah groped her way to where Jerry Dan and Anuya stood. A draft blew over her face, carrying the whiff of something foul. At least the moving air meant they wouldn't suffocate.

"God, I'd give anything for a thermos of hot chocolate. Hot

anything," Jerry Dan said as he shivered uncontrollably.

Was he becoming hypothermic? "Everyone huddle together so we stay warm," Hannah said.

"Did they see you?" Anuya whispered.

"Don't think so," Hannah whispered back in a way that meant *Hope not.*

Running into the cave had seemed like a good idea, but now Hannah saw how dumb it was. In the desert, they could have scattered, with the odds that at least one of them would escape. Instead she had led them into a trap, the only way out taking them into the arms of their pursuers.

The truck growled closer. The ground started to vibrate, sending dirt sprinkles onto their heads.

"Move next to the wall," Hannah said. "Squat down, like you're a rock. Tuck your face between your knees so it won't reflect light."

Anuya knelt beside the wall. Hannah crouched over her in an upright fetal position. Was there a Hindi god of invisibility?

"Don't move, no matter what," she whispered. With luck, the truckers wouldn't venture far into the cave, and maybe their flashlights wouldn't reach the chamber's far wall.

Hannah could hear Anuya's breath—*huh huh huh.*

"Breathe through your mouth," she said as insects trilled and frogs croaked. Unlike last night, Hannah wished they were louder. "Pretend you're a rock."

Then, as though someone had pulled the plug, the desert chorus went quiet. Hannah tightened her hold around Anuya. She heard footsteps outside the cave, then voices.

Don't move.

"They're in there," a man said.

Breathe through your mouth. Hannah let a shallow exhalation escape through barely parted lips.

A light flickered at the entrance. More talking, followed by a low laugh. The squeak of a hinge, then a thud of something being dropped.

Minutes that felt like weeks went by. Hannah felt Anuya

gather herself, ready to run, and she tightened her grip, willing her sister to melt into the earth.

You're a rock.

There was a shout, followed by the scuffle of footsteps. Hannah listened in disbelief. Were they leaving?

She started to straighten up just as the blast hit.

Chapter Twenty-seven

Saturday, November 7

Hannah came to lying on her stomach. She'd been flung against the rock wall. Rubble covered her legs and dust was everywhere—her hair, eyes, nose, even between her fingers. There was a ringing in her ears.

The cave was black. Was it still nighttime? How many minutes had she been unconscious? And where were Anuya and Jerry Dan? Hannah tried to call out, but her voice wouldn't work. The muscles in her throat had closed up and she could barely swallow.

"Hannah?" Anuya's voice penetrated the buzzing in her head.

Jerry Dan coughed. "I guess that answers the question of whether they saw you."

"What happened?" Anuya said.

"There was an explosion." Jerry Dan's baritone again. "The front of the cave collapsed."

Hannah got to her hands and knees, now remembering a boom followed by a storm surge of air rolling through the cave, the feeling that she was flotsam. Last summer she had been in the vicinity when a car bomb detonated. That blast had dissipated into the open air. This time, the concussion had been contained within rock walls. No wonder she could barely hear.

"Everyone okay?" she said. The drivers must have set off the dynamite they carried for sealing dump sites.

Anuya and Jerry Dan responded with tentative assurances. Hannah felt a trickle of blood on her elbow. She probed the wound with her fingers, but it wasn't deep. Otherwise, she seemed to be in one piece.

The earth began to vibrate again, and Hannah tensed, waiting for another blast. But after twenty seconds, the trembling stopped.

"That was the truck driving away," Jerry Dan said.

"They left us stuck in here?" Anuya's voice was approaching hysterical, and Hannah remembered her sister's fear of the dark and small places.

"Pretty smart," Jerry Dan said. "A landslide makes it look like we died of natural causes. That is, assuming anyone finds our bodies."

Anuya's wail echoed off the chamber's walls.

"That's enough, Jerry Dan!" Even though he couldn't see it, Hannah sent a glare in his direction, then crawled toward the sound of her sister's voice.

"I think they wanted to scare us and things got out of hand," she said, cradling Anuya. "Probably they'll make an anonymous call to the police when they get back to town."

Jerry Dan snorted, and Hannah knew it was prompted by disbelief, not dust. But her words had the intended effect on Anuya. Her sister's sobs subsided to sniffles.

"We walked out of the desert yesterday. We can do it again," Hannah said.

"But how are we going to get out of here?"

Good question. So good, Hannah decided to sidestep it.

"Let's get organized. Anuya, are you still wearing your backpack? Where's the sleeping bag?"

After more crawling around, Hannah found the wet bags. Unbelievably, Jerry Dan's camcorder still hung from the strap around his neck. Even more astounding, it worked.

"This waterproof case rocks." Jerry Dan looked through the viewfinder. "Man, you guys are a mess. But you'll be stars on that video website. I'll call it *Buried Ali—*"

"Jerry Dan, does the flashlight work?" Hannah interrupted. The idea of live entombment was sure to send Anuya into a panic again. The idea didn't sit all that well with her either.

He slid the switch. Nothing happened. He shook the flashlight and the bulb glowed just barely.

"I've got a candle," Anuya said. "Shine the light on my pack so I can find it."

"Why did you bring a candle?" Jerry Dan asked.

Warmth suffused Hannah. "For Diwali." Maybe Hindu gods also worked in mysterious ways.

Anuya produced the waxy cylinder, but kept poking through the bag. "I forgot matches."

"I have my lighter," Jerry Dan said, pulling it from his pocket.

"I thought you gave up smoking," Hannah said.

"I did." Jerry Dan lit the small candle. "Except when I'm nervous."

Light from the meager flame played along the shallow rock dome and across their faces. Bits of chaparral were caught in Anuya's hair, and dirt darkened Jerry Dan's pale complexion. Hannah knew she looked as bad as they did.

Jerry Dan started, then backed away from the rear wall. "Jeez, look at those!"

Hannah had forgotten about the petroglyphs. Her gaze found the hump-backed creature with the spear. The image quivered in the flickering light, as if it were trying to peel itself off the wall. She looked away.

They emptied the other wet bag—two watch hats, energy bars, two gallons of water, and a flashlight with a cracked lens and a suspicious rattle. Hannah divided every stitch of clothing among them, insisting that the others wear the hats. She was worried that Jerry Dan was still chilled after his lake swim, and Anuya's shivering had become constant.

"Okay," she said. "Let's see about getting out of here."

While Hannah held the flashlight, Jerry Dan examined the confusion of rocks and debris that clogged the entrance. Anuya waited in the rear of the cave. Hannah had forbidden her to come closer. She didn't want her sister caught in a secondary cave-in.

Jerry Dan managed to pry a rock free. "Hard to tell how much we have to get through—could be as little as a foot or as much as a yard or more." He kept his voice low so only Hannah could hear. "Everything is wedged pretty tight—I can't even find a crack where air is coming through. Not sure we can move it without tools."

"Even then, if we dig the wrong way, the whole thing could come down on top of on us," Hannah whispered back.

Jerry Dan regarded her with bloodshot eyes.

"We're all beat. Why don't we crash for a few hours? Who knows—maybe one of those guys will turn out to have a conscience and send someone after us."

His tone rang hollow, and Hannah could tell he thought the chance of that happening was as remote as she did. Still, a nap sounded good. Delicious, actually. The adrenaline that had carried her through the pursuit was gone, and her muscles were depleted from the long paddle. According to the luminous dial on her watch, it was a quarter past one in the morning. Maybe a few hours of sleep would give her a fresh perspective on the situation.

"Fine by me," she said.

Hannah and Anuya split an energy bar and half a bottle of water. Before drinking, her sister dribbled a little water onto the ground.

"For the gods."

"I'll take all the help we can get," Jerry Dan said. He drank some water but declined the offer of an energy bar. "I prefer cowboy grub." He pulled a strip of jerky wrapped in plastic from his pocket.

Anuya wrinkled her nose. "Ew."

Jerry Dan tore away the wrapper with his teeth. Growling, he bit off a piece and chewed vigorously. Anuya giggled.

Hannah spread out the sleeping bag on the relatively flat place under petroglyph man. Anuya punched her daypack into a cradle for her head and crawled under the layer of down. Within minutes her breathing slowed. She was asleep.

"You take the bag with Anuya. I'll be fine over here," Jerry Dan said. He pulled off a cowboy boot. "Pillow?"

Hannah scrunched against Anuya for warmth, her tired muscles aching on the rocky ground. Staring up at the blackness, too cold to sleep, she felt the puff of her sister's breath on her cheek, the in-and-out of her ribcage. The cave stank of sweat and dirty bodies and dust, and the peculiar odor that she had noticed earlier seemed stronger. Hannah rolled onto her side, missing the sound of the frogs.

At least the burru won't find us, she thought, and closed her eyes.

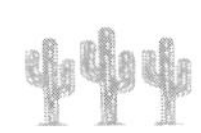

"Yuck! What's that smell?"

Hannah opened her eyes to see Anuya looking down at her, lit candle in hand. Tentatively, she stretched stiff muscles, then sniffed the dank air. The stench from last night was worse.

"I don't know." She looked at her watch—five thirty. In the morning, she assumed.

"Whatever it is, it's nasty," Jerry Dan said. He sat propped against the wall, legs extended, one boot on.

Hannah got to her feet. "Thanks for the pillow." She handed over the boot's mate.

Breakfast was another shared energy bar and some water, the candle balanced on a stone beside them.

"Tell me again why dining by candlelight is considered romantic," Jerry Dan said.

"It's better if you can't smell the other person," Hannah said.

Anuya rubbed a finger over her teeth. "Holy cow, I'd give my second-favorite purse for some toothpaste."

As she ate, Hannah considered their predicament. By now, it was pretty certain the truck drivers weren't going to send help, anonymously or otherwise. How long would it take them to dig out? Her rock-climbing instructor had taught her humans could last three minutes without air, three days without water, and three weeks without food. Theoretically, that meant they had enough water to survive until the beginning of next week.

Did the same rule apply to stick-thin teenagers? Hannah pushed her hair back and her shirt chafed under her arms, stiff with salt. Sweat meant more loss of water. Did that drop the limit to two days?

She stared at the guttering flame. The candle had a few hours left, and the flashlight was questionable, too. That meant digging in the dark—without tools. Then, if they managed to get out, a half-day walk back to the fry bread stand. She fought back tears. *Don't waste water.*

Hannah focused on the rocks blocking the entrance. The chunks of granite were big—hard enough to move with tools, nearly impossible by hand. Her eyes roved the chamber. Was there another way out?

The candle danced in the acrid breeze. Hannah stared at the flame, unable to shake the sense that something was there, obvious but also hidden from her, like a word on the tip of her tongue. There was another gust of acrid air. Hannah wrinkled her nose and moved out of the draft.

The draft. Air had to be getting in from somewhere. With the front entrance blocked, that left the rear of the space. Holding the candle aloft, Hannah examined the shadowed depths of the back wall.

"What are you doing?" Anuya said as Hannah dropped to all fours.

"Found it!" Hannah pulled aside a wad of dried brush to reveal a hole in the rock. The smell became worse, making her eyes water.

Anuya clapped her hand over her nose. "Found what?"

"Another way out. Feel that draft? It's coming from the outside." Loose rocks clogged the opening. Hannah began clearing them out of the way.

"Let me help." Jerry Dan joined Hannah in pitching the stones out of the way. "Whew! You've found the bat cave, girl—grade A guano."

"Bat poop?" Anuya made a noise in her throat.

Jerry Dan tossed aside a stone and looked at the enlarged opening. "Think you can fit?'

"I'll try. Pull me out if I get stuck." *Or attacked by bats,* Hannah wanted to add, but she didn't want to scare Anuya.

Dropping onto her stomach, she started to wiggle through the opening, lighting her way with the flashlight and concentrating on breathing through her mouth. The stench from the guano was awful.

Her head and shoulders cleared the hole. Hannah kept her gaze focused on the ground, eyes averted from the ceiling and what might be hanging there. She knew her fear was unreasonable, the monster-under-the-bed variety—bats didn't fly into humans' hair or bite their necks and turn them into vampires. But she couldn't help it.

Once she was all the way through the makeshift tunnel, Hannah rested on her knees and used the flashlight to look around. She was in a cave about twelve feet square, with a ceiling that felt twice as tall, as though she were in the bottom of a cereal box. A sliver of pale light shone through a fissure in the rock wall. Hannah scrambled to her feet and pressed her face against the crack. Before her stretched wide-open desert, startlingly quiet. A few stars winked in the receding violet sky, white-bright at the horizon where the sun prepared to fire up.

Hannah opened her mouth to shout for help, then thought better of it. Any rescuers would be on the other side of the hill where the cave-in was, out of earshot. Because they were in the closed area of the rez, there were no hikers, no mountain bikers, no one to hear her except for maybe an O'odham shepherd—or a truck driver posted to make sure they didn't escape. She reluctantly turned from the opening.

After the few breaths of outside air, the bad smell seemed worse than ever. Steeling herself, Hannah turned the flashlight upward. Dozens of bats hung from the ceiling. Disturbed by the unaccustomed illumination, they rustled and squeaked, their eyes demonic in the reflected light.

"Great," Hannah muttered, and quickly doused the beam.

"You okay?" Jerry Dan called.

Hannah took a few sips of air though her mouth and swallowed the sourness that had risen in the back of her throat. "Yeah. Come on through. There's a hole in here that goes to the outside. Be quiet, though, so you don't bother the, um, residents."

Jerry Dan pushed their supplies through the opening, then his belt with its rodeo buckle. "I'm gonna need all the room I can get." He squirmed partway through, then stopped. "I'm stuck like a boot in a muddy pasture!"

"Grab on and I'll pull," Hannah said. They grasped wrists and Hannah sat back on her heels.

"Oof," Jerry Dan said as he squeezed through the tunnel. "That was harder than zipping up my line-dancing jeans."

Anuya poked her head through the hole, saw the bats, and quickly retreated.

"Nunh-uh, no way," she said from the other side.

"It's the only way out," Hannah said. "If you don't bother the bats, they won't bother you."

Coaxed by Jerry Dan, Anuya reluctantly crawled through.

"When Buddha said life was suffering, he wasn't kidding. Let's hurry up and get out of here," she said once she was in the smaller chamber.

The three of them attacked the crevasse, pulling rocks from its edges and scraping away earth. Jerry Dan talked to the bats—"I think you'll like the larger entrance"—while Anuya kept her gaze averted from the ceiling and mumbled mantras.

Before long, Hannah's eyes were so crusted with dirt, she could barely keep them open. The muscles in her bad shoulder felt like road bike tires with two thousand miles on them. Water would alleviate the cramping, but she was worried about conserving their supply. Instead, she pounded a fist against the complaining muscle and continued working.

After a half hour, they paused for a breather.

"We aren't getting very far," Jerry Dan said. He rubbed dried blood from his knuckles. "If we just had a tool—"

"Will this help?" Anuya held up a long whitish stick, slight bowed in the middle.

"What's that?" Hannah said.

"An old bone, I think, or maybe petrified wood," Anuya said. "I pulled it out of the wall over here."

Jerry Dan crouched down to get a better look.

"It's bone, all right—a whole skeleton." His hands brushed away the dirt to reveal an assemblage of pale curves and knobs protruding from the rock wall.

"A deer maybe?" he said. "They don't usually come down this far. It's not the right shape for a cow. Maybe it's a mule?"

"What's a mule doing out here?" Anuya asked.

"It could have belonged to one of the O'odham," Hannah said. "A mountain lion might have killed it, then dragged it to the cave to eat later."

"Or it could have been a miner's mule from a long time ago." Excitement quickened Jerry Dan's voice. "They say the Lost Dutchman's gold came from a pack train that was scattered during an Indian raid. Maybe this mule escaped from a pack string. Maybe its pack is—"

"Full of gold!" Anuya said.

She and Jerry Dan grasped the bone that was most exposed and pulled. It popped out of the wall and hurtled across the small space.

When Hannah came to, Jerry Dan was kneeling beside her.

"Hannah? Can you hear me?"

"Sweet Krishna, are you okay?" Anuya peered over his shoulder.

Hannah blinked, trying to focus her vision. There was a soft throbbing near her temple.

"What happened?" She started to push herself onto her elbows, then quickly lay back down. Her stomach was doing somersaults and she felt dizzy.

"Take it easy," Jerry Dan said. "The bone hit you and knocked you out. You were gone for nearly a minute."

"Bone? What are you talking about?" Hannah sat up, managing to remain vertical despite the spinning. "God, do I have a headache."

Anuya and Jerry Dan exchanged worried glances.

"The bone that Anuya found in the wall," Jerry Dan said.

"From the mule carrying the treasure," Anuya added.

Hannah stared at them. "Are you sure *I'm* the one who was hit on the head? There's no miner's mule, no gold. That skeleton is from a deer or a lost cow. Now help me up so we can finish making that hole big enough to get out of here."

"You should rest a little longer. Anuya and I will dig," Jerry Dan said.

Hannah protested, but not very much. Her head really did hurt. After Jerry Dan helped her lie down, Anuya folded one of the sweatshirts into a pillow. "Better than a cowboy boot."

Jerry Dan and Anuya worked as though they were on an assembly line. After Anuya dug away any loose earth around a rock, Jerry Dan used the bone as a lever to pry it from the wall. Thirty minutes later, the opening was wide enough for a person to fit through.

The rest had done Hannah good. With Jerry Dan's help, she pulled herself up over the lip of rock and onto the desert floor. The air was a cool violet, and Hannah took a deep breath. The oxygen cleared her head and confidence flowed through her. *We're going to make it.* She got up to help her sister.

Under the dawn's first streaks of color, Anuya emerged. A piece of bone stuck out of her daypack.

"Even if there's no gold, I still want to show it to my friends," she said, pulling a twig from her hair. "You know, the desert really isn't all that different from New York."

"How's that?" Hannah said.

"At home, it's the people who got attitude. Out here, nature does. Every plant, every animal is in your face, all the time."

"Hey, can somebody grab these?" Jerry Dan said.

The sleeping bag and wet sacks appeared in the opening.

Anuya collected the gear as Hannah helped Jerry Dan through the hole.

"Man, it's good to be out of there. Talk about skanky! At least the smell will keep everyone else away," he said.

"Everyone else?" Hannah gestured at the empty desert. "Who exactly are you worried about?"

Jerry Dan didn't answer. He was busy untangling dead branches from a stand of chaparral and piling them in front of the opening.

"That hides it pretty well, don't you think?" He took his camcorder from one of the wet sacks. "Let's give it up for long-life batteries."

Hannah stared at him. "What are you doing? I want to get on the lake before it gets too hot." They had agreed that Hannah would paddle to the fry bread stand and call for help, while Jerry Dan and Anuya waited in a safe place.

"Just give me a minute to record some landmarks. I want to be sure we can find this place again."

"There's a big hole from a dynamite blast on the other side! Isn't that enough of a landmark?"

"We're talking about what could be a major gold find. Can't be too careful." Jerry Dan began filming.

"That is *not* a miner's mule in that cave! Even if it were, I told you—any gold belongs to the tribe."

"I know that. This is for the glory of discovery." Jerry Dan lowered the camcorder to look at her. "Do you think the tribe would pay a finder's fee?"

Hannah blew out a breath. "Anuya and I are going to pack up the gear. Then we're leaving, with or without you."

"No problem." Camcorder still going, Jerry Dan disappeared around a large boulder.

"You might be wrong, you know," Anuya said as she stuffed a sweatshirt into a wet sack.

A small lizard moved speculatively out from under a bush. Hannah watched as it, pausing for many push-ups, climbed the rock beside her, closed its eyes, and basked. The sun was just over the horizon, its appearance heralded by the whine and whir of unseen insects. Something bit Hannah's arm, and she slapped at her skin.

"Anuya, the only way there's a treasure in that cave is if you and Jerry Dan shoveled out all that bat shi— guano and sold it as fertilizer."

Her sister scowled.

"I have a slogan you guys can use," Hannah said. "*Bury this treasure in your garden.*"

Anuya pressed her lips together, but Hannah caught the twitch at the corner of her mouth.

"Maybe you'd prefer *Grade A guano—mined fresh from the source*?"

Anuya gave in. "*Bat scat dat's phat,*" she said, and laughed.

Hannah joined in, her guffaws making the lizard scurry for cover. Then something shifted inside her, and her laughter nearly changed to tears.

If the idea of sisterhood was like some eternal spring, Hannah now saw that she had been wading into it to tantalize only herself when it came to Shelby. Her older sister would never be a person with whom she would share a special connection. Distinct law practices, different interests, separate lives—and there was nothing Hannah could do about it.

Not that she wanted to so much anymore. Hannah realized that she had started to move on. What had been compelling enough to bring her back to Arizona and join the family firm no longer had such a tight grip. Hannah still felt its hold, but it was slipping.

"Anuya?"

Her sister was adjusting her iPod. "Yeah?"

"Everything that's happened—involving you in the case, getting stuck in the desert, being shot at..." Hannah paused. "I'm sorry. This can't be what you expected."

"For sure." Anuya looked at Hannah from under her lashes. "It's *way* better."

A high whistle pierced the quiet. Squinting against the sun,

Hannah spotted Jerry Dan partially hidden under a palo verde tree about fifty feet away. He held his finger to his lips, then pointed at Hannah and gestured for her to join him.

"I'll be right back," she said as her anxiety meter clicked on.

Anuya crossed her legs into the lotus position and rested her hands on her knees. "Cool. I'm going to catch some *Oms*."

As Hannah approached the palo verde, Jerry Dan motioned for her to keep low. The psychological beeps became faster. *Now what?*

"Check out the road," he whispered once she was behind the shelter of green. He handed her the camcorder.

Hannah peered through the viewfinder and found the dirt track. She adjusted the focus, then panned south, past chaparral, cacti, boulders…

The sight struck her with the force of a blow. Parked in the middle of the road, about a half-mile away, was a white van with a blue swirl on its door. Lashed to its roof was Hannah's kayak.

Chapter Twenty-eight

Hannah zoomed in on the driver's side of the van. A man sat behind the wheel, the shadow from his cap obscuring his features.

Jerry Dan took back the camcorder. "Next time you ask me to go prospecting, remind me to say no."

The taste of old pennies filled Hannah's mouth. She had bitten the side of her cheek.

"We have to go the other way." She spat bloody saliva onto the dusty ground. "West around the lake until we're past El Diablo, then north to the casino. You ever been there?"

"Nope. It's all rez, off-limits without a permit."

Hannah pushed a strand of hair behind her ear. "I looked at the topos when I worked at OTA. The hard part will be figuring out where to go after we cut away from the lake."

Jerry Dan nodded. "Got that right. It'll be easy to get turned around out there."

Hannah knew by *turned around*, he meant *lost*. Every year the *Express* published accounts of hikers found less than a mile from town, without water or a clue as to where they were. They were the lucky ones—the paper ran stories on deaths from exposure, too.

"How much water do we have?" she asked.

The lake might as well be a mirage. Used by the Indians to water their sheep, it was contaminated with giardia. The parasite gave unwary drinkers the runs, which only worsened dehydration.

"A little over a gallon. We'll be thirsty. Presuming not too many wrong turns, we should end up at the casino before dark."

A six-hour hike after two nights of barely sleeping. "I don't want to tell Anuya about the van, at least not right away," Hannah said.

Using the chaparral as a screen, they made their way back to Anuya. Hannah's sister still sat cross-legged, eyes closed and headphones on.

Jerry Dan tapped her on the shoulder. "Do you still have that orienteering compass?"

Anuya switched off the player and took the chromed disk from her daypack. "Indian giver."

"Seeing that you're Indian, true. Also Indian borrower—I'll return it. Do you have paper and a pen, too?"

Anuya handed him a notebook and a ballpoint.

"Why do you need all this? Don't we just follow the road?" She threw Hannah a dark look. "This time, I'm not carrying any boat."

"Shortcut," Jerry Dan said.

"No boat," Hannah said.

"Whatever. Just get me to food that isn't rectangular and doesn't taste like plastic."

"Speaking of which, here's breakfast." Hannah gave her half an energy bar.

Anuya chewed while Jerry Dan sketched on the paper.

"Is that a map?" she asked.

"Sort of. I'm doing some calculations. We don't want to miss the turn-off from the lake."

Anuya stared at Jerry Dan's squiggly lines and triangles.

"That looks like…" She rummaged in her daypack and produced a square of folded paper. She smoothed it open and placed it beside the diagram Jerry Dan had drawn. "Holy Krishna!"

Hannah recognized the copy of the map from her desk. The two drawings were startlingly similar—the curve of the lake, the location of the mountains. Anuya jabbed the *X* on the treasure map with her finger. "That means the treasure—"

"—is somewhere near here!" Jerry Dan finished.

Anuya looked at Hannah with wide eyes. "Laxmi saw my candle. She was the draft you felt!"

"That's ridicu—" Hannah began.

"It's in the cave," Jerry Dan said, looking from the map to the surrounding desert, then back to the map again. "See that curve? It's the entrance."

"Before it was *blown up*." Hannah emphasized the last two words, hoping to remind him of the van. But Jerry Dan was in the throes of gold fever.

"These figures? They gotta be the petroglyphs," he said.

"There's the scary one!" Anuya said.

Hannah took a look. The largest stick figure did appear to be holding a spear. But it could also be a mark on the glass of the photocopier.

Anuya stood. "Let's go back in and look for it!"

"No!" Hannah's voice was as sharp as barbed wire. She locked eyes with Jerry Dan. "We *have* to get out of here."

He flushed and dropped his gaze. "She's right. Besides, we need tools, lights, a way to take back whatever we find...I'll come back in my truck."

"And bring me, too?" Anuya said.

"Absolutely," Jerry Dan said.

"We'll see," Hannah said.

Anuya folded her arms. "I'm not leaving unless you promise I get to come back."

Hannah thought about the van. "Fine—you can come back with Jerry Dan. But only if we leave *right now*."

Anuya slung her day pack over her shoulder. "Let's go," she said.

Hannah draped her sweatshirt over her head in a makeshift visor, tying the sleeves under her chin so her ears would be covered. Already the sun had slid liquidly down the mountains to the desert floor, and she could feel the prickle of its heat.

"Ooo—bad turban day," Anuya said.

"Remember, javelina like to pick off stragglers," Jerry Dan said.

He started off compass in hand, the two wet sacks criss-crossed on his chest Pancho Villa-style. Anuya fell in behind, her spindly legs in step with his thicker, freckled ones. Hannah brought up the rear.

Jerry Dan picked a circuitous route to the lake, and Hannah realized he was trying to keep out of view of the road. Anuya was too busy chattering about treasure and gold and Indian curses to notice.

They made their way through rocky geometry, past precariously balanced piles of sandstone boulders decorated with prickly pear and brittlebush. The sun was at their backs, and the shadows made it hard to walk without stumbling. Hannah kept looking over her shoulder against the glare, but no one was following. At least no one she could see.

Fifteen minutes into the hike, Hannah regretted downing her water ration all at once. Bladder full, she ducked behind a bush. She was pulling up her pants when she heard a dry rattle.

Snake. Hannah lunged forward and sprinted clear of what she thought was the strike zone, then turned to see Jerry Dan and Anuya looking at her with puzzled expressions. Jerry Dan held a handful of round red objects.

"I'm showing Anuya what prickly pear fruit look like. Too bad these are dried out. They're not bad eating." He shook the fruit in his hand like they were dice, producing the rattling sound Hannah had heard.

"Yeah, too bad." Hannah straightened her pants with as much dignity as she could muster. "Can we get going again?"

An hour had passed under the hard blue sky when Jerry Dan abruptly pulled up. He spread his arms to stop Anuya from going past him.

"Got a live roadblock. Careful." He backed up, and the snake did, too, undulating across the sand.

"Not as big as a viper," Anuya sniffed. But she still gave the bush where the snake had disappeared a wide berth.

A second hour came and went. Hannah felt overheated and thirsty, and they weren't even halfway. The sweatshirt had become too hot, and rubbed the sore spot where the bone had hit, so she had taken it off. The sun blazed down on her bare head, making her wish for the kayak's circumference of shade. Hannah imagined her skin roasting under a solar broiler, turning brown and bubbly like a cooked chicken at the supermarket deli.

Hearing their approach, a chuckwalla had wedged itself into a crack between two boulders.

"Snake!" Anuya said, seeing the protruding striped tail.

"Nah," Jerry Dan said. "Just an ol' lizard with his lungs filled with air. Makes his belly big, so you can't pull him out of there."

As they hiked, Jerry Dan alternately teased and told stories to Anuya, making her giggle. But to Hannah, his good cheer was somber, his jokes hollow. She watched him check his hand-drawn map and compass, then frown.

The third hour found them between the lake and El Diablo, the big mountain casting zigzags of malachite and lapis lazuli shadows on the water. Hannah kept shaking her water bottle to make sure it wasn't empty.

"You have to admit the view is great," Jerry Dan said.

"Not really in the mood for sightseeing," Hannah muttered. God, but she was tired of the sun. If it were July, it would be forty degrees hotter, she told herself. It didn't make her feel better. Hot was hot, as far as Hannah was concerned.

After four hours of walking, they were on the western side of El Diablo. Jerry Dan stopped to consult his map and compass as the early afternoon sun washed over them, warm and soporific.

Although Hannah's legs had stopped moving, her stomach hadn't. Afraid she was going to heave, she crouched in the thin shade of a palo verde and worked her fingers into the sand, vainly seeking coolness.

"You doing okay?" Jerry Dan said.

"Just tired."

Hannah sucked in a mouthful of warm air, then blew it out. Her tongue felt thick and cottony. She uncapped her water and took a sip, rolling the wetness around her mouth before swallowing. She considered taking another drink, but instead dampened her shirt cuff and laid it against the nape of her hot neck. Hannah imagined she could feel its moisture turn to steam.

"This is where we turn," Jerry Dan said.

Hannah saw a faint path meandering north. "Is that a trail?"

"Animal path. But it might lead to those artificial ponds behind the casino. The location looks right."

The tribe had dug a series of ponds to store the water used to keep the two-soon-to-be-three golf courses green. They had been designed to look natural, and local fauna often drank from them.

"Are you sure this way is shorter? My ankle hurts," Anuya said. She had twisted it about a half hour back. Jerry Dan had cut her an agave stalk to use as a cane.

"We're almost there," Jerry Dan said. "See that mountain over there, the one with the notch at the top? That's where we're going."

His gaze met Hannah's over the top of Anuya's head. She understood his unspoken question—backtrack and hope the van was gone, or keep going and hope to end up at the casino?

"Mountain, here we come," she said.

They headed north through copper-hued rocks that bounced the sunlight at them from all angles. The path narrowed and occasionally disappeared, requiring head-down concentration as they negotiated their way through the treacherous ground studded with cacti of the vicious variety.

Jerry Dan circumvented a cat's cradle of fallen saguaro, then skidded to a halt, nearly tripping up Anuya.

"Hey, what's with the..." Anuya's voice trailed away.

Hannah stared as a dozen javelinas minced toward them on tiny hooves that made her think of high heels. They farsightedly bumped against one other as they snuffled the ground with long tusked snouts.

"Oh Shiva," Anuya whispered.

Hannah quickly stepped between her sister and the spiky-haired pigs.

"Move off the trail to the left. *Slowly,*" she whispered.

With Anuya shadowing her, Hannah shuffled sideways, putting a dozen feet between them and the lead porker by the time he teetered by. Jerry Dan watched from the other side of the trail. He had climbed a boulder and clutched a rock in each hand.

The caravan trotted past without giving Hannah or Anuya a glance—until the last pig. He dug his cloven feet into the sand and swiveled his head like a radar dish in their direction. Hannah willed herself to be invisible as the prehensile-like nostrils twitched in the breeze. She hoped she smelled more like bat than human. The big head swung around again and its owner wobbled off to catch up with his mates.

"Holy cow! My friends are never going to believe I almost got mugged by a gang of pigs." Anuya fanned herself with her hand, her bangle bracelets jangling.

Hannah puffed her cheeks, then blew out a breath. "Like you said, nature with attitude. At least they weren't armed."

Jerry Dan jumped off the boulder. "Let's get out of here."

They resumed their rugged walk. Anuya, still worried about the risk of a porcine pulping, stayed close to Jerry Dan. A stabbing pain had begun to shoot through Hannah's right leg with each step. Her water bottle was empty, and she was certain her lips had started to crack.

Where were the immigration vigilantes? *La migra*? Hannah was certain they were the only people walking through the Arizona desert who hoped the Border Patrol would show up.

Six months ago, Hannah would have said that bad things happen to other people—people who didn't know what they're doing, people who were unlucky. Up until then, her life had been ordinary, nice even. But beginning in July, through a chain of events she was still struggling to understand, Hannah had become one of those *other people*. It was as though she had been caught up in a tornado, unable to control its direction, much less its repercussions. At this point all she could do was hope to ride it out.

A desiccated skull of a small animal sat trailside, a grim

reminder of what could happen if things went wrong. Hannah thought of the bone remnant in Anuya's day pack and briefly imagined their femurs and tibias becoming trophies for other hikers. She looked in vain for signs, even unpleasant ones, of civilization—white plastic grocery bags, beer cans, fast food wrappers. But the landscape was pristine.

She checked her cell phone—no signal. The time on the screen read a little after five o'clock. Hannah could hardly believe they had spent a whole day doing nothing but walking. A volcanic sunset was erupting at the skyline, but she barely noticed it.

Think positive. Someone would come looking, or they would make it to the casino. And when they did, she was hanging up her hero's cape. No more jumping into lakes or digging out of cave-ins. From now on, Hannah would let other people's problems stay that way.

As though on cue, Jerry Dan let loose a happy whoop. "We have pavement, ladies!"

They had reached Ocotillo, the road that ran from town to the casino, continuing beyond into the rez. Anuya did a little dance, her hands and hips moving with serpentine grace. Dizzy and trail-weary, Hannah did her best to sway a little. She thought the celebration premature. They were on the section of road that had been extended past the casino in anticipation of future development. Building wasn't to commence for several years, and the area was deserted. Hannah figured they were seven, maybe ten miles from the casino. She checked her cell phone. Still no signal.

They resumed walking as twilight settled around them. Shadows hung from the trees like curtains. A quarter hour passed, their moods darkening along with the sky.

"How much longer?" Anuya said, drawing out the words.

Hannah couldn't bring herself to reply. It took all her energy to put one foot in front of the other.

Sound carried in the empty air, and they heard the car before they saw it. A silver orb materialized out of the evening haze and moved tantalizingly toward them. Jerry Dan stuck out his thumb, while Anuya and Hannah stood beside him. But instead of slowing, the car sped up, the driver looking past them with a blind-man's stare.

They decided that a teenage girl had a better chance of flagging a ride alone than accompanied by two ratty-looking adults. When they heard the next car, Hannah and Jerry Dan hid behind a mesquite tree while Anuya stood roadside. The plan worked—the car stopped.

It was an older sedan. The blue on the trunk and rear fender didn't quite match the blue of the rest of the car, and a cardboard pine tree dangled from the rearview mirror. The Hispanic driver didn't look too surprised when Hannah and Jerry Dan materialized from their hiding place. But when Jerry Dan said "*Policia*" through the open window, he shook his head emphatically. Before Jerry Dan could explain, he drove away.

A third car appeared ten minutes later. Anuya stuck out her thumb, but the car edged left, making the driver's intention clear.

"I can't take this anymore," Jerry Dan said. When the car was nearly past them, he dashed in front of it, shouting "Help!" and waving his arms.

Brakes screeched and the car rocked to a stop. The gray-haired woman behind the wheel looked nervously at them.

"Can you take us to the police station?" Jerry Dan said.

Anuya limped forward on her agave stick. "Please?"

The elderly woman's face softened when she saw Anuya. She lowered the front passenger window. "Sweetie, what happened?"

"We've been walking for *hours*," Anuya said.

"Got lost hiking," Jerry Dan added.

Hannah nodded mutely. Her dizziness was getting worse.

The woman made a clucking noise. "You poor things! Come on, get in."

After settling them in the back seat, the woman got out and popped the trunk. "Have to be prepared when you live in the desert," she said, and produced three tall bottles of water.

Another soul of preparation. Hannah took one of the bottles, too overwhelmed to speak.

"Thank you, ma'am," Jerry Dan said.

The water tasted as sweet as sugar. When her bottle was empty, Hannah leaned back against the cushy upholstery, vaguely worried about her body-and-bat odor permeating the fabric but too tired to do anything about it. She was so exhausted, she barely had enough energy to breathe. She closed her eyes.

It seemed only seconds later that the car glided to a stop.

"Here's the police station," the woman said.

Hannah heard Jerry Dan thank the woman and get her contact information. Tomorrow she would send their Good Samaritan a case of water. And a case of cardboard pine trees, too.

Chapter Twenty-nine

"The EMTs will be here any minute," Dresden said. "That bump on your head should be looked at."

"Nothing a long shower won't fix," Hannah said. In truth, her head was killing her, but she wasn't going to admit it to the detective.

They sat across from each other in the interview room. Hannah didn't blame Dresden for not bringing her to his office. Being back among people of ordinary hygiene made her realize just how fabulously dirty she was. If the grimaces of the deputies and office staff were any indication, air-conditioning made guano stench more pungent.

"A day-long hike through the desert without enough water—"

"Is something many Arizonans have done, except they start at the border and go longer," Hannah said. "I'm fine. Unless you're worried about the after-effects of those stale cookies from your lunchroom."

"I thought the cookies were good," Anuya said.

Dresden passed a hand over his face. "Hannah, you are so like my sister, sometimes I think she sent you to haunt me."

Hannah did an aural double take. *Hannah?* When did they get onto a first-name basis? And what did he mean by *haunt*?

She puzzled over his remark while Anuya sucked noisily on her straw, draining the last of the soda. She then took the lid off the cup and swallowed a mouthful of ice, the cubes making squeaky noises when she crunched down on them. When the ice was gone, Anuya wiped her hand on the back of her mouth and burped.

"Where's Jerry Dan?" Hannah said. After they had been fed and watered, Hannah and Jerry Dan had been separated.

"Still talking to a deputy. Does this mean you have something to add to your story?"

Hannah bristled. Twice already she had told the detective what had happened since the cars had gone into the lake—the sabotaged kayak, the telephone threats, the break-ins at her condo and the law firm, her visit to EES, her plan to film the dumping on the rez, and the resulting chase, explosion, and escape. She had even told him about Nathalie's note, and what she had said during the lake rescue and in their later conversations.

Hannah hadn't mentioned the treasure map. During their trek through the desert, the three of them had agreed to keep the location of the cave secret until Jerry Dan and Anuya could return to look for the gold. At least Jerry Dan and Anuya had agreed. Hannah had been so woozy, she'd barely known they were speaking English.

She also hadn't told Dresden about Jake's apparent connection with EES. She owed it to Shelby to find out just how much her boyfriend knew about the dumping scheme before giving his name to the cops.

A deputy stuck his head into the room. "EMTs are here, sir."

"Send them in," Dresden said. "Where are we on executing the warrant?"

"Unit One is en route to the waste disposal company, and I'm coordinating with the tribe on accessing the blast site."

Anuya sucked in her lower lip and Hannah knew she was thinking about the treasure.

"When you get onto the rez, you should also see Ms. Dain's dark blue SUV parked next to the lake. She tells me the men who chased her may have come into contact with it. Have the vehicle towed and processed."

The truck drivers had probably trashed the SUV, Hannah thought, glad—for the second time—she had signed up for the extra insurance.

A paramedic entered with his kit. While he examined Anuya, Hannah took out her cell phone and made a call.

"Clementine?"

Her secretary shrieked. "Where have you been? I called everybody, and no one knew where you were."

There was a funny sensation in Hannah's chest. "Sorry. Didn't think anybody would notice."

"You have no idea how many people worry about you, girl. Now what idiot thing did you do this time?"

Hannah told her a sanitized version of events, downplaying the danger. Still, Clementine was upset.

"Next time you feel the urge to get into other people's business, why don't you instead take up bullfighting or wing-walking? It'll be a lot less nerve-racking for the rest of us."

"I gotta go. The EMT is waiting. Tell Shelby I'll talk to her about the case later." Until she knew the extent of Jake's involvement, Hannah wanted to avoid talking to her older sister.

"I can't believe you're worrying about work. So much for that hit on the head knocking some sense into you." Clementine hung up.

Hannah closed her phone and scowled at the EMT, a brunette with a cheerful face. "I'm not going to the hospital."

"Why don't I check you out? Then we'll decide."

The EMT went through a list of questions that Hannah could nearly recite from memory. Did she hurt anywhere? Was there ringing in her ears? Did she have nausea or double vision? The tech wrapped a blood pressure cuff around her arm. Hannah stared at the snowy front of the woman's crisp white shirt and wished she had a fresh change of clothes.

"Now for your eyes." The EMT took out a penlight. "Follow my finger."

When the physical exam was finished, Hannah said, "I do hurt, actually." She eased off her shoe and sock to reveal a fairly impressive blister where the second toe had rubbed against her big one.

"You'll want to watch that doesn't become infected," the

EMT said. "More importantly, you should come to the hospital for a CT."

Hannah shook her head, the motion making her dizzy. "I've been banged up enough to know when I need a doctor. This isn't one of those times."

"You may have a concussion."

"Wouldn't be the first time."

"All the more reason to go to the hospital. Every time you take a blow to the head, there's a greater risk of permanent injury."

Hannah was tempted to say that given all the stupid things she had done lately, it was probably too late for her. But she curbed her tongue. Another EMT appeared in the doorway.

"Mr. Kovacs is fine," he said.

"Jake!" Hannah got to her feet, swaying slightly. She would have to get some more food. "We need to talk."

Disregarding his weak protests, Hannah herded him into the empty office next door. When they were alone, she said, "What's the deal with you and EES?"

"I don't—"

"Jake! I saw you in the company photo and you have one of their uniform shirts. How long do you think it will be before the police know, too?"

He rubbed the stubble on his jaw, looking tired. "There's a limit on how many hours an EMT can moonlight. I was ten, sometimes fifteen hours over every week." He looked at her with troubled eyes. "I need the extra money."

Was the extra cash for Shelby? Hannah felt uneasy. An engagement ring...or another rehab stay?

"Did you know EES was dumping toxic waste on the rez?"

"No! They have a lot of drivers. I heard rumors about extra pay for special night runs, but they never asked me to do any."

Hannah's next question was interrupted by Anuya's raised voice.

"But it's mine!"

Hannah hurried back to the interview room to find her sister and a deputy faced off across the table.

"You have to give it to me, Miss. It's part of a crime scene," the deputy said.

"No it's not!" Anuya hugged what Hannah recognized as the bone fragment from the bat cave. "It's a dinosaur bone. And it's mine—I found it."

Hannah understood her sister wanted to keep the mule-with-pack-filled-with-gold story quiet. But the rules of evidence meant this was a battle the police would win.

"Anuya, you know that bone is from a mule or a deer. When the police are finished, they'll give it back—"

"It's not!" Her thin frame vibrated with emotion as she held up the bleached shaft. "Look how heavy it is. And see these ridges? They're just like the ones on the bones in the dinosaur museum."

The certainty in Anuya's voice struck a chord in Hannah. If her sister was telling the truth...She bent down until she was eye level with Anuya.

"Did you tell anybody other than Jerry Dan about the treasure map from my desk?"

Looking miserable, Anuya nodded. "Mr. Glouster."

Hannah didn't know if it was what Anuya had said or the head rush from getting up too fast, but she had to grab a chair to keep from toppling over. She waited for her balance to return, her mind going over what she knew about Jerry Dan and Glouster—the orienteering championship, the drawings in the geologist's office and on his report, smokers and reformed smokers...How could she have missed it?

"Where's Jerry Dan?" she said.

"With Detective Dresden," the deputy said. He advanced on Anuya. "Please, miss, give me the bone."

"No!" Anuya darted behind Hannah.

"Where is she? Let me through!"

Shelby burst into the room, a worried-looking Jake in tow. She was wearing a man's t-shirt over sweatpants and no make-up, the latter a sight Hannah had never expected to see. Her signature perfume was absent, too.

"You shouldn't be back here." Jake tried to steer Shelby out of the room. "Let's wait for Hannah in the lobby."

Shelby ignored him. She stared at Hannah. "How could you not call me? I had to hear what happened from Cooper."

Hannah's breath got caught under her ribs. *Cooper?* Clementine's words ran through her head. *You have no idea how many people worry about you.*

The deputy grabbed Anuya's arm. "Miss, I need that bone."

"No-o-o!" A sobbing Anuya clung to Hannah's waist.

"Let go of her!" Hannah said.

The deputy shot her a look. "Who are you, her lawyer?"

"No," Hannah said. "I'm her sister."

A hush fell over the room. Hannah curled a protective arm around Anuya's shoulders and knew that the last twelve hours weren't nearly as awful as what was about to happen.

Shelby's eyes were shiny. "When were you going to tell me?"

For an instant, anger and self-righteousness coursed through Hannah. *Tell her?* After all those years her sisterly overtures had been rebuffed? Then the shine in Shelby's eyes melted and tears trickled down her cheeks, taking Hannah's indignation with it.

"Shel—"

"I'm pregnant."

Hannah gaped at her sister. "You're going to have a baby?"

Shelby's bout of "flu," shapeless clothes, questions about parenting—and Jake's need for extra funds and the tension between him and Shelby—all made sense now.

Shelby didn't answer. Instead, she pivoted and walked out of the room, the only sound the slap of her bare heels against her sandals. Jake hurried after her.

"Wait!" Hannah said. She got as far as the door before the room began to spin. "Shelby!"

She staggered into the hallway, nearly colliding with a man standing there. Hannah glimpsed eyes as green as the lake, caught a whiff of fresh hay, and collapsed.

Chapter Thirty

Sunday, November 8

Hannah walked onto her small balcony and looked over her neighbors' gardens. The units were so close together that the squares of color melded into a brilliant collage. The accompanying riot of scents reminded her of Shelby's perfume. She went back inside.

After a doctor had confirmed Hannah's collapse was from a lack of sleep, food, and water—and not a concussion—Clementine had collected her from the hospital, dropped her at the condo with a pan of non-Italian lasagna ("If you make me use tofu instead of cheese, I'm not putting my people's name on it"), then taken Anuya home with her for a sleepover.

After finishing off half the lasagna, Hannah had gone to bed and slept for twelve hours. Her muscles were still sore from lying down.

Her cell phone trilled. She checked the Caller ID and flipped it open.

"Hi, Clementine."

"I ate bacon in your honor for breakfast this morning," her secretary said.

"What?"

"Revenge. Anuya told me about the javelinas. How are you feeling?"

"I have a new appreciation for sleeping in a bed. And thanks for taking care of Anuya. How is she?"

"A little post-dramatic stress last night, but she'll be okay."

"Don't you mean *traumatic*?"

"You obviously don't know teenagers."

"Can I talk to her?"

"No. She and Jerry Dan went out to the rez."

The gold. No wonder Jerry Dan hadn't answered when she'd called that morning.

"By the way, that girl can cook," Clementine said. "Dinner last night tasted just like takeout."

Hannah was struck by a thought—a bad one. "Your gun—"

"Relax, all firearms are at my brother's. What do you think I am?"

Firearms, plural? "I hope a good example."

"More like a horrible warning." Clementine paused. "She's a good kid, Hannah. Makes you one for two in the sister sweepstakes."

Hannah didn't say anything. She had rung Shelby last night and again this morning, but her calls had gone straight to voicemail. She hadn't been able to reach Jake, either. According to the EMT dispatcher, it was his day off.

"I hate telling you this," Clementine said, "but Franklin Rowley pitched a fit when you didn't show for that settlement conference. I've told him what happened, and he wants you to call him at the office today."

"On Sunday?"

"He said he'd be there. Zel would love five minutes with you, too. He wants a quote for tomorrow's story."

"I'll call him after I speak with Franklin. Maybe by then my head won't feel like someone used it for T-ball practice."

Even though she'd been exhausted, Hannah hadn't gotten much rest last night. Dreams, mostly involving Cooper, interrupted her sleep. *Nightmares*, Hannah mentally corrected. A curvy redhead had been in them, too.

"You shouldn't have called Cooper," she told Clementine.

"*Mea non culpa*. Being in love isn't easy, Boss, but it's simple. Choose. Act. That's all there is to it." Her secretary hung up.

Hannah dialed Jerry Dan's number again.

"This is Hannah. Call me," she said after the beep. If her suspicion was correct, it would explain a lot of loose ends.

She thought about going for paddle until she remembered the truckers had stolen her kayak. Car in the lake, boat stolen, nearly buried alive—not a good week.

Hannah emptied the dishwasher and checked the laundry. The clothes she had worn in the desert were still stained brown, even after a trip through the *Sanitize* cycle, so she added more soap and started the washer again. She considered taking out the vacuum, then realized what she was doing.

She sat down and called Franklin's number. He answered on the first ring, and Hannah briefed him on the events at the lake.

"We need to discuss what this means for the lawsuit," he said. "I know it's the weekend, but can we meet today? Then we can go in front of the judge tomorrow morning."

Hannah thought about it. She was tired and under doctor's orders not to drive, not that she had an available car And she really should track down Shelby for a long-overdue conversation.

"Okay," she said.

The taxi dropped her in front of a single story brick complex. The neighborhood was shabby, a few blocks shy of the area dubbed *up-and-coming* by local Realtors. Four pairs of undistinguished rectangular buildings connected by breezeways faced one other across a courtyard. In the middle was a dry fountain filled with bougainvillea leaves. Chipped tiles decorated its rim.

There were three offices per building. Each suite's metal door opened directly to the outside, and was painted a red that had faded to varying hues, depending on exposure to the sun.

Hannah consulted the directory posted next to the fountain. Franklin's suite was in one of the buildings closest to the road. A fleece of old cobwebs arched in the corner where the passageway roof met the wall above his red door. She knocked.

"Thank you so much for coming," Franklin said as he ushered her in.

The older lawyer looked as though he could have used a few more days in the hospital. His eyes were sunken under bushy brows and his collar gaped away from his neck. There was a sprinkling of dandruff on the shoulders of his navy short-sleeved shirt.

Hannah lightly touched the bruise on her temple. She probably didn't look much better.

The room's decor was consistent with the building's tired exterior. Plastic-wood furniture, more fake than *faux*, sat on carpeting of an unfortunate orange color, and the spray-on ceiling had sparkles in it. The swamp-cooled air was musty and smelled of fried chicken.

"I'm finishing a letter for another client. Can I get you something to drink?" he said.

"No, thank you. But may I use your restroom?" Following the doctor's rehydration orders meant frequent pit stops.

"Outside and to the left, between the third and fourth building." Franklin handed her a key. "You'll need this to unlock the door."

Hannah followed the breezeway past a dentist's office, a one-man accounting practice, and a title company, all closed. Turning down the alley between the last two buildings, she stopped in front of the door with the lady-in-a-triangle-skirt pictogram. She raised the key to the lock. And froze.

A blue swirl dangled from the key, its yellow-metal edges glinting in the sunlight. Hannah had been given its plastic double by the EES plant manager. *Gold ones for the VIPs.*

The harsh trill of her cell phone made her jump. She fumbled to answer it. "Yes?"

"Howdy! Jerry Dan here. Where are you?"

"Franklin's office," Hannah said, her mind still on the implications of the keychain. No wonder the older lawyer had been so eager to settle the case.

"Big news!" Jerry Dan said. "The—"

Hannah interrupted. "Jerry Dan, did you take something that didn't belong to you?"

His voice became subdued. "Sort of. I mean, I didn't know what it was when I took it. I thought—"

Someone wrested the phone from Hannah's grasp, pulling her hair.

"Ouch! Hey!"

Hannah whirled to see Franklin standing in the alley. He held her phone in one hand, and in the other, a small shiny gun pointed straight at her.

Chapter Thirty-one

A shudder ran up Hannah's spine. Not from fear, although she was afraid. More, it was a signal that her body had gone on high alert—neurons firing, muscles poised for action. Coolness from prior experience? This wasn't the first time she had stared down a gun barrel. For a split second this struck her as both amusing and terrifying before her mind shifted back to the moment.

Hannah's phone rang. Franklin let the call go to voicemail.

"Give me the key," he said.

Hannah closed her fist around the blue swirl.

"I know EES is dumping waste on the rez. So how much were they supposed to pay you to settle the case and keep quiet?"

Franklin's mouth stretched into a grin that was almost a smirk. "I don't know what you're talking about. Benny Juan's a long-time client. When he told me his new business had cash-flow problems, all I did was advise him to look for less expensive waste-disposal sites. Any payment I received was for legal services."

Hannah thought of Nando, and outrage burned through her. "You knew what EES was doing! Didn't you care about people getting cancer? Kids with birth defects?"

Franklin was unruffled. "The government poisoned those mines. If there were a little extra contamination—not that I know anything about that—would it make a difference? Besides, I negotiated a fair settlement."

"That settlement wasn't fair, and you know it. Don't pretend to care about the plaintiffs. You only took the case to make sure no one found out about the dumping. Why the tribe ever picked you as lead counsel—" Hannah stopped talking and shook her head. "Phyllis Juan."

Franklin spread his hands. "I understand Benny's sister may have had some input into my selection. As for my clients, their claims would already be resolved if—"

"If Weller hadn't collected soil samples and figured out that the toxic waste had been dumped last week, and not sixty years ago," Hannah said.

Franklin's expression turned sour. "His assistant saw the value in keeping quiet and collecting a bonus. Unfortunately, she couldn't persuade the good professor. EPA, BIA, bar association—Dr. Weller was going to tell them all. Kept blathering about 'poisoning the land,' as if that part of the desert were worth anything."

"So you killed him." As she spoke, Hannah took a step back. Franklin didn't seem to notice.

"Of course not." He looked aggrieved. Hannah moved a little further toward the alley exit. "I did inform my client about his expert witness' anticipated testimony. What Benny did after that…" Franklin shrugged. "The suicide setup was impressive. Phyllis Juan must care for her brother very much. Or very little for her people."

A bitter taste rose in Hannah's mouth. So Phyllis was the one behind Weller's death. No wonder she wanted to settle the case as much as Franklin did.

"I don't suppose you know who shot Nathalie," Hannah said, easing back another step.

"No," Franklin agreed. His detachment was frightening.

Hannah tensed, ready to run for it. Maybe Franklin's misguided belief in his blamelessness would stop him from pulling the trigger. Or at least from aiming to kill.

As though hearing her thoughts, Franklin aimed the gun at her chest. "Give me the key."

Hannah didn't. Instead, she shifted her weight onto the balls of her feet.

Franklin pulled the trigger. A bullet skidded along the brick wall, spattering Hannah with slivers of clay. *So much for his restraint.*

"Next time I won't miss," he said.

Hannah believed him. She tried a different tack. "What happened to the lawyer who was only giving advice to his client?"

"He's also a lawyer looking for a long-overdue payday."

Hannah gave a little shoulder roll, trying for nonchalance. "So let's settle the case. I won't say anything about the test results."

Franklin's mouth curled into something ugly. "If Richard Dain weren't your father, I'd consider it. But his ethics were a pain in the ass when we were at the firm, and from what I've seen, yours are the same. So I don't think so."

If Richard Dain weren't her father... Hysteria rose in Hannah's throat. If only he knew.

Still pointing the gun at her, Franklin punched a number into her cell phone.

"Benny? Send one of the trucks out the rez, to the mine farthest from the road. I'll explain later." He snapped the phone shut, then gestured with the gun.

"Turn around. We're going to my car."

So you can drive me to the rez and kill me. Hannah imagined an "accidental" fall into one of the mines, a grave in a remote spot, a drowning in the lake. There were many ways to die in the desert.

Her eyes raked the alley for an escape option, roving from the chipped concrete walkway to the brick walls to the slice of blue sky, then down to Franklin again—and Jerry Dan standing behind him.

Hannah sucked in her breath. Jerry Dan put a finger to his lips, then began a careful, heel-toe walk toward them. He held a white stick in his hand. Hannah wished it were a gun.

"Get moving." Franklin's voice was sharp.

Jerry Dan inched closer, and Hannah glimpsed a pointed toe under his jeans hem. *Cowboy boots.* She tightened her hold on the keychain until the metal edge of the blue swirl dug into her skin. Franklin surely would hear the grind of grit under Jerry Dan's leather soles. She had to create a distraction. Preferably, one that wouldn't get her shot.

"Don't you want this? Catch!" Hannah tossed the keychain.

She had intentionally thrown short, and the piece of metal landed at Franklin's feet.

With his gun hand propped on his knee, the older lawyer bent over to pick up the keychain. As he did, Jerry Dan sprinted forward with the stick raised. Hannah threw herself to the ground, expecting to feel the searing pain of a bullet any second.

But it never came. Instead, she heard two sickening thuds, followed by the sound of something heavy hitting the ground.

Hannah raised her head. Franklin was sprawled on the concrete. Jerry Dan stood over him, still holding the stick. There was a smear of red on one end.

"Howdy," she said weakly.

"Howdy yourself," Jerry Dan said. The southern in his accent was thicker than usual.

Hannah let him help her up. After one glance at the bloody place at the base of Franklin's skull, she turned away from the inert body, seized with a bout of shivering.

"Is he—?"

"Unconscious." Jerry Dan stripped his belt from his pants, then did the same to Franklin's. He fastened one belt around Franklin's wrists and the other around his ankles. "In case he wakes up."

He used his shirttail to pick up the gun by the barrel, then guided Hannah out of the alley to a seat on the rim of the empty fountain. He set the gun and stick beside him, then took Hannah's hands and began to rub them.

"What are you doing here?" she said when her teeth were no longer chattering.

"I thought something was weird when you hung up. When you didn't answer after I called back, I decided I better come over."

"Good thing I mentioned where I was. Did you find the

treasure?"

"Sort of. I promised Anuya I would let her tell you."

A siren whooped close by, making Hannah jump. "The police! Did someone hear the shot?"

Jerry Dan shook his head. "I walked into the courtyard in time to hear the stuff about killing Weller. I ran back to my car and called 911, then grabbed this just in case." He studied the white stick unhappily. "Talk about bad déjà vu."

Relief was flushing the adrenaline in her system, and Hannah felt almost giddy. "Are you referring to insane lawyers or hitting someone over the head?"

Jerry Dan smiled without mirth. "Believe it or not, both. A buddy of mine…" His voice trailed off, and Hannah could tell he was somewhere else. "It's another story," he finally said, and Hannah realized he wasn't going to tell it.

She put an arm around his shoulders and squeezed.

"Thanks."

Jerry Dan stood. "I better go head off the cavalry before they come in with guns blazing. You okay here?"

"Sure."

After he'd left, Hannah pulled her knees to her chest, rested her chin on top of them, and let her eyelids droop. She wasn't tired so much as depleted. Her fingers twiddled with a sneaker shoelace, then started to scratch off a splotch of brown-red on the material before she realized what it was. Hannah frantically wiped her hand on her pants, then grabbed the tiled edge, leaned over, and began to retch.

She was still being sick when Jake found her.

Chapter Thirty-two

Tuesday, November 10

Jerry Dan sat in Hannah's guest chair. His straw Stetson was upside down beneath his seat.

"You know how much trouble you caused stealing that map from Glouster's office?" Hannah said.

"I thought it was the map for the orienteering championship." Jerry Dan looked pained. "My one chance to be a star jock."

"But why did you hide it in *my* desk?"

"When Ed showed up after the auction, there wasn't any other place to put it. I knew right away he thought we'd taken it. All that hugging—like going through a pat-down at the airport."

"So that's why he went through my condo and office."

Jerry Dan ran a hand over the top of his head. "Uh, that was me. I left Anuya playing video games for a half hour. And your secretary was napping when I snuck into your office."

"*You broke into my house?*"

"It wasn't technically *breaking*. You really should lock your doors, by the way."

"I cannot believe—"

"Look, I know it was stupid. I just wanted to find the damn map and put it back in Ed's office." Jerry Dan held up his hands in surrender. "You have no idea how much grief this has caused me. I even started smoking again because of the stress. Five thousand bucks on hypnosis, down the drain."

Hannah drummed her fingers on the desk.

"Five thousand dollars?" she said after a moment.

"Yeah. Plus Miss Opera-Lover dumped me. She can't stand the smell."

Jerry Dan looked so miserable, Hannah nearly felt sorry for him. "You really didn't know it was Glouster's map to the dinosaur."

"No! Ed never told me anything about it."

"Because he found the skeleton when he was trespassing on the rez. What a bunch of criminals," Hannah said. She shook her head. "If only I'd believed Anuya when she said that bone was too old to be from a mule."

"She's an amazing kid. But who expects to discover a new species of dinosaur?"

"Speaking of which, what happens now?"

"The tribe is coordinating with the dinosaur museum's paleontologists to dig up the big guy. The science guys think it's a fairly humungous plant eater, from A.D. who-the-heck-knows." Jerry Dan frowned. "I don't know what they're going to do about that bone the police confiscated. If Franklin doesn't plead out, it's going to be stuck in an evidence locker for a couple of years."

"The archeologists are probably furious, but I'm sure glad you had it with you."

Jerry Dan had told her how he and Anuya had gone to the cave to find the treasure before the police arrived to investigate the explosion. When their digging unearthed not miner's gold but the skeleton of a creature three times the size of a mule, they had taken one of the bones for the museum to analyze. Still in Jerry Dan's truck when he went looking for Hannah, it had been his only available weapon.

"Sorry you didn't find any gold," Hannah said.

"This is *way* cooler. The tribe said Anuya and I get to name it. I like Sonorasaurus Barni or Sonorasaurus Anuyai."

"What about Sonorasaurus Jerrydani?"

"*Not.* By the way, did you know Arizona doesn't have an official state dinosaur? I'm already planning the campaign. Could be tough—there's a big anti-vegan block in the legislature." He sobered. "Do you know if the tribe is going to prosecute Ed?"

"For trespassing? I doubt it. Publicity about the case will only encourage more people to fossil-hunt on the rez." Hannah thought about her frantic paddle across the lake in the sinking boat. "I can't prove it, but I'm pretty sure he slit my kayak."

"He must have been paranoid about someone else finding Sonorasaurus. He's up for tenure, so being credited with the discovery would have made his academic career. No wonder he wanted to be your expert witness."

Hannah nodded. "And why he kept bugging me for his own rez permit. With a legitimate reason to be there, he could 'find' the dinosaur and get the glory. Amazing what people will do to get an edge."

She looked pointedly at Jerry Dan. He dodged her gaze, leaning over to retrieve his cowboy hat.

"I heard they picked up Benny Juan this morning." Jerry Dan twirled the Stetson in his hands. "What do you think Franklin's arrest will do to your case?"

Hannah wondered if the two defendants would plead out. She secretly dreaded testifying at trial. Other than seeing his photo in the EES brochure, Hannah had never laid eyes on Benny Juan—and she didn't want to. She'd had enough of staring evil in the face. The nightmares had started again, and Hannah was beginning to worry that no matter where she went, the memory of the past four months wouldn't be far enough behind.

"Do you think the judge will dismiss?" Jerry Dan said.

"I hope not. She scheduled a pretrial conference for later this morning to sort everything out. Defense counsel says the government is still willing to settle, even though we can't prove radiation from DOD projects caused plaintiffs' damages."

"God bless national security. The feds would rather keep their secrets than contest liability." Jerry Dan settled his hat on his head, then stood. "Where's Anuya? I wanted to say goodbye before she left for the airport."

"In the lunchroom," Clementine said as she bustled into the

office carrying a large envelope. Today she wore a voluminous dress the color of cut pineapple with sequins edging the neck. "Now shoo—I got business with my boss."

"Yes, ma'am."

"Thanks again for the GPS." Hannah extended her arm, admiring the watch—heart rate monitor—navigation system strapped on her wrist. The device did other things, too, but she was only partway through the owner's manual.

"Least I could do after causing that mess with the map." Jerry Dan tipped his hat. "*Shalom*, y'all."

Clementine handed the envelope to Hannah. "Since you've been so busy trying to get yourself killed, I made the arrangements with the insurance company for your new car. Had to—the car agency won't rent to you anymore, and no way am I driving Miss Hannah."

"Another Subaru, right?" Hannah said with some apprehension.

"Of course! They got the highest crash-test rating, perfect for you. But I got you the SUV instead of the wagon. Figured you could use the room for all that sports junk. Same color as before. But the thing looked so plain, I had a friend of mine pimp it up a bit."

"Pimp?" Hannah said, imagining chrome spinners and painted flames.

"I signed your name on all the paperwork. The keys are in the envelope and the car is in the parking lot." Clementine propped her hands on her hips. "I almost got hit driving it here. Totally the other guy's fault. I was programming your satellite radio and drifted just a little bit into his lane. Fool didn't honk his horn fast enough." Her secretary frowned. "Some people shouldn't be allowed on the road."

"Thank you. I think."

"Keep that thought, at least until you write the check for my Christmas bonus next month. Let me see that watch."

Hannah held up her wrist so Clementine could examine the plastic rectangle.

"What does this button do?" she asked, then pressed it.

The watch began emitting a high-pitched beep. Hannah stabbed at various buttons, but the beeping continued. She looked at her secretary in exasperation.

"Don't give me that attitude. You shouldn't wear things that you don't know how to operate. It's like sneakers—don't move up from Velcro until you know what to do with laces."

Hannah yanked on the end of the watch strap, trying to unfasten the buckle.

"I'm out of here. That noise is driving me crazy." Clementine paused at the door. "Oh yeah—that detective called. Wants to ask you something about what the woman who drove into the lake told you."

Another jerk, and the watch was off her wrist. Hannah slid off the plastic cover on the back, popped out the battery, and the beeping blessedly stopped.

"Nathalie? Did he say how she was doing?"

"Well, she's not dead. And they won't be able to charge her with felony-murder—the bribe she took from the lawyer isn't a predicate offense. Where I come from, that's a win-win."

Hannah was impressed. "You weren't kidding about acing Crim Law."

Clementine's chest puffed out with pride. "I'll tell you something else—Nathalie didn't do it for the money. That professor was married, right?"

"Weller? I think so."

"She was in love with him. So either the bribe was enough money for them to go away together, or she took it for the partners-in-crime-bringing-us-closer-together thing."

"Partners-in-crime-closer-what?"

"Extortion may not qualify as a hobby in an eMate profile, but it would get you a lot of dates in my family. Crime can be a real bonding experience."

Hannah pinched the bridge of her nose. "Was I a bad boss in a former life? Is this karma at work?"

Clementine gave her a pitying glance. "You need me. You

just don't like to admit how much." She disappeared in a shimmer of yellow.

Hannah opened the envelope and slid out the keys. She ran a finger over the indentations in the metal shaft, pressed the buttons on the remote. There'd been a lot of newness in eight days. *Car, sister, dinosaur...*

Girlfriend for Cooper. Hannah put the keys back in the envelope, her heart feeling as though it had been doused with ice water.

"Do you have a moment?"

Hannah got up and came around from behind her desk. "Yeah, um, come in. Do you prefer the chair or the sofa? Are you thirsty?"

Shelby wore a green dress oddly similar in style to Clementine's and carried a small white paper bag. She sat in one of the guest chairs. "I'm pregnant, not sick."

Hannah pulled up the chair next to her. Before Shelby could say anything else, Hannah launched into the speech she had been rehearsing since Friday.

"I apologize for what happened at the police station. I never meant for you to find out about Anuya that way." Hannah sucked in a quick breath. "There are some things you need to know. When Mom—"

"I talked with Richard. He told me everything."

Hearing the brittleness in her sister's tone, Hannah fell silent. And when had *Daddy* become *Richard*?

"Why didn't you tell me?" Shelby said.

Unable to keep her fingers still, Hannah picked up the watch pieces. The battery slid into place with a percussive snap.

"I didn't want you to be hurt," she said, trying to work the black cover into place.

"To be *hurt*? Don't you mean *relapse*?"

Hannah didn't answer. Blindly, she moved the piece of plastic one way, then another.

"How many months did I have to be sober before you were going to tell me you had another sister? Three? Six? Just how little faith do you have in me?"

The rawness in her voice stilled Hannah's hands. "I'm sorry."

Shelby rested a hand on her belly. "I shouldn't be mad." The ire was gone from her voice. "You weren't the only one keeping secrets."

The intercom buzzed, and Clementine's voice crackled through the speaker.

"Car service is here."

The judge had scheduled a pretrial conference in the dumping case for that morning, at the same time Anuya's flight was to depart. Not only had she denied Hannah's request for a postponement, she ordered her to attend.

After declining her secretary's offer to serve as chauffeur, Hannah had booked a car service to take Anuya to the airport. Bumped as a driver, Clementine was going along as escort.

"Why don't I meet you in the lobby," Hannah said, hoping to avoid a sisterly run-in. She didn't think Anuya and Shelby had seen each other since the police station.

Shelby stood and handed Hannah the white bag.

"I brought you something."

Hannah reached inside and took out a nearly full bottle of perfume. A familiar scent filled the air.

"It's more you than me," Shelby said.

Hannah thought of the redhead leaning against Cooper's truck. "I don't think so. But thanks."

Shelby walked to the door, then turned. "If you give my kid a drum set, I'll never talk to you again."

Hannah bit her lip. "I was thinking more along the lines of a pony, maybe a motorcycle."

"I'm not going to the pretrial conference."

Hannah raised her eyebrows. "But it's your case."

"Doctor's appointment."

Something flitted across Shelby's face, and Hannah thought she was going to say something else. She waited.

"Well…good luck," Shelby said after a moment.

Hannah nodded. "You, too." Shelby left.

When she was alone again, Hannah was hit with the most

peculiar sensation. It was a sort of a psychic jolt, as jarring as a kayak running aground. *She and Shelby would never be close.* Their lives would continue on different tracks—her sister would marry Jake, maybe have another baby, work part-time at the firm. Hannah would do she wasn't sure what, except that it wouldn't be that. If Hannah left the firm again, she and Shelby would go stretches without seeing each other and their sporadic reunions would end awkwardly. And if she heard that Shelby was seriously sick or dead, Hannah would at last cry for what they had never had.

Her thoughts were interrupted by Anuya, who clattered into her office, Clementine huffing behind. Her secretary met Hannah's eyes and nodded. So one sister's arrival had been choreographed to another's departure. Hannah mouthed the words *thank you*, then turned her attention to Anuya.

Headphones draped around her neck, her sister wore jeans and a t-shirt—one corner untucked—that billowed from her waistband. Even though it was too big for her small frame, Hannah could still read what the letters spelled out—*Bioscience High*.

Yesterday Hannah had confronted Anuya about her acceptance letter. Faced with Hannah's threat to make the call herself, Anuya capitulated and rang her mother.

Initially furious with her daughter's duplicity, then awed by the dinosaur find—Anuya gave her an abridged version of events, leaving out the dangerous parts—Mrs. Moore had talked with Hannah and Anuya for over an hour. The resulting decision made Anuya ecstatic. Hannah was pretty happy, too. Starting with the new semester next month, Anuya would live with Hannah and attend Bioscience.

Mrs. Moore's private conversation with Hannah had been brief.

"I'd like you and Anuya to get to know each other. She already cares very much for you."

"I feel the same way about her. She's a great"—Hannah stumbled, not sure whether the word *sister* would sting—"person.

But before she comes back next month, you and I need to talk about Hinduism."

"Is there something specific you're interested in?"

"The rules for all the gods. Sometimes I'm not sure if..."

Mrs. Moore had a musical laugh. "Anuya embellishes them a bit? We will talk."

"I'd also like to ask you..." Hannah's throat tightened, and she couldn't finish.

"About your father? Of course."

At that point, Anuya had picked up the extension again, and the conversation moved on to what well-dressed teens wore in Arizona.

Anuya spied Jerry Dan's gift. "Ooo, one of the new models." She grinned. "With that GPS, you'll never get lost in the desert again."

Hannah grinned back. "We didn't do too badly."

Anuya inspected the watch, then set it on the desk. "Where's the battery cover?"

Hannah fingered the piece of plastic. "Right here."

"Clementine told me you can buy baby cactus at the airport. I'm gonna get one for Christy and Tanika and—" Anuya started to cry.

"Hey," Hannah said, getting up to envelop her in a hug. "You'll be back before you know it."

Anuya gripped her tightly. "I'm glad we're sisters," she said into Hannah's shirtfront.

Hannah stroked her hair. "Me, too."

"We better go, sweetie," Clementine said.

She herded Anuya toward the door, as the teen rattled off final instructions to Hannah.

"Text me every day. Don't eat in Indian restaurants—I'll cook when I get back. Buy some pots and pans. And furniture!"

She was gone.

Hannah sat down in the guest chair. She felt a little lightheaded, as though the air had thinned in the room.

Shelby's bottle of perfume was still on her desk. Hannah

picked it up, spritzed some scent into the air, then tipped back her head and inhaled. A kaleidoscope of images tumbled through her mind, most involving a redhead and the occupant of a certain pickup truck.

Stop. She picked up the watch from Jerry Dan and tried to insert the battery cover. First, she used gentle pressure, then more force. The piece wouldn't move into place.

Giving up, she leaned back and closed her eyes, still fingering the square of plastic. *So this was what heartbreak felt like.*

There were no sounds of footsteps, no smell other than perfume. But Hannah suddenly knew that she was not alone. There was a presence that she could feel. Her eyes opened.

"Hey," Cooper said from the doorway.

Hannah's fist closed, and the battery cover snapped in two. She stared at him.

Almost six weeks had passed since they had been together. Six weeks in which she had found one sister and lost another. Six weeks to run into trouble—again—and discover she didn't want to live without the man now in front of her.

People didn't usually change much in a month and a half. Outwardly, Cooper looked the same, but she sensed an extra layer of reserve, a coolness that hadn't been there before. She could see some extra miles on him, then realized she had accumulated more of her own, too.

"Can I come in?"

"Of course." She dropped the pieces of battery cover onto the desk, then pressed her hands together, feeling the wetness on her palms.

Hannah wanted Cooper to know how thrilled she was that he was there. She wanted to tell him about the joy she felt, way deep inside, at seeing him again, at remembering what he was like and how he made her feel and how close to him she wanted to be. But she kept quiet. He was the one who had come to her.

Cooper walked into the office—athletic shoulders, white oxford shirt rolled up at the wrists, and a hitch apparent in his stride.

"You're limping," Hannah said, then realized how that had

sounded. "I mean, Shelby said you were getting better, that the physical therapy was working."

"It wasn't the physical therapy."

Hannah sensed there was more to his answer and kept quiet.

Cooper looked out the window as though to find the words he wanted there. His eyes really were the color of the lake. Mostly green, with hidden depths.

"I have always loved you," he said.

Have loved. The breath went out of her.

"But something's happened." His voice was thick.

Hannah's heart plummeted. *The redhead.* He was here to tell her that he had found someone new, that he had moved on, that—

"—so I've got to go away for a while."

Hannah suddenly realized that he had continued talking, but she hadn't heard him over the roaring in her ears. *A while*? That wasn't usually part of breaking-up speeches.

"What?" she said, confused.

Cooper's smile was forced. "Maybe I'll get Shelby's old room."

Shelby's old room? Why would he be moving into Richard's house?

"What are you talking about?"

"My ankle. Now you know why I stopped limping. But the cure ended up being worse than the problem."

All of a sudden, Hannah got it.

"Pain," she said.

Light from above washed over Cooper's cheekbones, creating angles on his face. "The pills made it go away. But it didn't take too long before I needed more of them, more than the doctor wanted to give me."

"That woman I saw you with…"

The green in his eyes went flat, like the lake's surface on a cloudy day. "She knew where to get them."

"She was your dealer." The words felt wooden in Hannah's mouth.

Cooper closed a hand over hers. "I can't be with someone who has doubts, Hannah, no matter how small they are."

Could she give him all her heart, not just part of it? Hannah thought of Shelby...Anuya...Remorse burned through her like one of Anuya's Indian dishes. She turned her hand over and interlaced her fingers with his.

"I want to be with you as much as you want to be with me." She leaned in and kissed him.

He kissed her back, and Hannah felt something unfurl between them as his arm circled around her and pulled her close. She smelled hay and sweat and sun.

"When are you supposed to check into rehab?" she asked when they pulled apart for a moment.

"This morning."

Hannah looked at her new watch. She had an hour until the settlement conference.

"Want a ride?" she said. "I got a car."

Cooper examined the two pieces of broken plastic. "This can be glued."

"I know," she said. "I'll fix it."

The back of his hand brushed her earlobe. "You smell nice."

Sometimes, Hannah realized, despite their best efforts, people managed to collide anyway.

"Thanks. It's my new perfume."

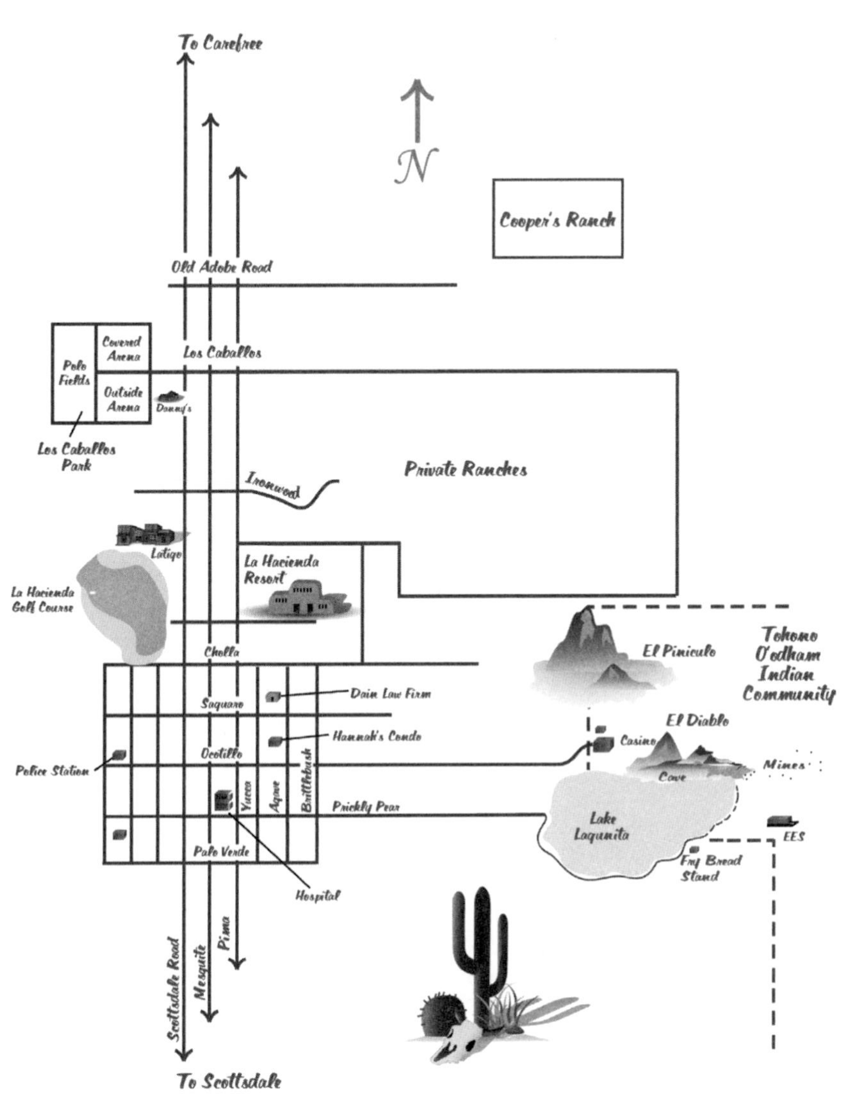

The Town of Pinnacle Peak

To receive a free catalog of Poisoned Pen Press titles, please contact us in one of the following ways:

Phone: 1-800-421-3976
Facsimile: 1-480-949-1707
Email: info@poisonedpenpress.com
Website: www.poisonedpenpress.com

Poisoned Pen Press
6962 E. First Ave. Ste. 103
Scottsdale, AZ 85251